The Iron Chalice

Book Four of the Iron Soul Series

J.M. Briggs

Contents

For all the puppies who have graced my life: Cleopatra, Molly Brown, and Sophia.

1

Hope in Magic

Magic. It had started all of this. Nicki regretted it now: regretted being a mage and finding herself in the sort of magical adventure that she'd read about growing up. At first, it had been wonderful, and Aiden had been there with her. They'd both been born to be mages, and the years of friendship seemed to have led to some glorious story that they'd help write. There had been monsters to fight, new friends to make, and even Merlin and Morgana le Fey there to teach them. She'd gained power over water and ice and had even learned how to heal wounds with magic. Even in the terrifying moments against Sídhe Riders and Hounds, it had been exciting and a dream come true. Her dull life in Ravenslake had become important and special.

Last year it had been much simpler; maybe not easy, but she'd thought she'd known who the bad guys and good guys were. There had been a plan, well maybe not a plan, but at least a pattern. She and the other mages had used fantasy books and movies to give them ideas for using magic and had gradually been getting stronger and more confident. She'd made friends with Alex and found herself enjoying the first real female friendship of her life. Yet now Nicki couldn't think about Alex without an odd, sharp pang of anger and guilt in her chest. The story had taken a nasty turn. Arthur, the pinnacle of the all-American boy; the quarterback with his tall, muscular figure, blond hair, and blue eyes, wasn't the hero. He wasn't the Iron Soul, despite everything seeming to point to him. No, instead, the real Iron Soul was Alex, the tall blonde girl with the gray eyes who'd fallen head over heels for Arthur and nearly been killed by him in return.

They'd all been stupid. They'd all been so confident that they were genre-savvy, that they knew who was who and what was going on. Nicki had felt like part of a team that was unbeatable even when things were dangerous. Now Aiden, her best friend, was lying helpless in a coma, and Arthur had left Ravenslake to meet up with the Evil Queen of the Sídhe, who was so confident that she'd called to gloat.

Nicki shook her head and tried to banish the dark thoughts from her mind as she marched into the hospital and headed straight for the ICU. The smell of the intensive care unit made Nicki wrinkle her nose. She could see movement through the small windows as the nurses moved around for shift change. Looking at the sign that forbid access until the shift change was over, Nicki sighed and barely reigned in the desire to kick the door.

As she waited, the anger faded away as a sad fog began to roll over her mind; a spinning sense of being trapped in a growing storm and knowing that far too soon it would overwhelm her. The air felt too dry against her skin, and the lights were too bright, adding to the sense of displacement. Nicki's eyes itched as she looked towards the doors and tried to catch a glimpse of Aiden's room, but she held back the tears. If she started crying, then all of this would become real: it would mean that Aiden was dying and that their best chance to save him was some kind of ancient cup. Bran's vision hadn't given them much to go on. All he'd seen was an old chalice and a skull, probably underground. All Morgana had to offer was that it might be in Wales somewhere. It was next to useless, and yet their best chance.

She'd never believed in any deity; her grandmother had been a lapsed Protestant of some kind as long as she could remember and had never tried to instill any beliefs in her. In her high school days, she'd been interested in paganism and had entertained a passing curiosity in Buddhism, but nothing ever took. Still, there was a sudden desire to pray, though to who or what she didn't know. If there really was a God, or if Earth was somehow sentient in the form of Gaia or an Old One was listening and could help, then maybe it could achieve something. Maybe they could help Aiden, or at least give them more to go on than Wales.

But she didn't pray. Instead, Nicki pushed herself away from the wall and glanced towards the clock before stepping into the small waiting room. She sat down, ignoring the soft weeping of a couple on the far side of the room. Movement in the hallway made her look up, and she caught sight of Morgana looking through the ICU windows. There was a slightly helpless expression on her face, and her eyes were pensive. Nicki wondered how much hope Morgana had in them actually returning with the Iron Chalice. Was this whole quest just for Alex's benefit, so she could look back and know that she'd tried?

Nicki's stomach twisted at the terrible thought, and she focused her attention on Morgana. The older mage understood the reality of things, Nicki reminded herself. She wasn't praying, screaming, or trying to bargain with anyone, or even crying for the loss of Aiden. Morgana understood that they were all just flickers of life in a huge universe, all except for her and Merlin. She wondered if Morgana even mourned for those who died around her. It was a nasty thought, but it was Aiden: her brother in all but blood, her best friend, and someone who always had and was supposed to always be there. He couldn't be in danger of dying.

Tears were prickling again, and this time Nicki wasn't able to hold them back. A short sob escaped her, and tears slid out of the corners of her eyes, running down her cheeks. Someone set a hand on her shoulder and squeezed it gently. There was a soft, warm pulse of heat down her arm that settled in her chest. With a sniff, Nicki looked up and blinked in surprise to see Morgana watching her with a sad and gentle expression. She'd never seen the professor look at her like that.

"They're opening the doors," Morgana said gently. "Say what you need to say; I suspect you'll be leaving soon."

"We'll be back, won't we?" Nicki shivered, her voice was weak and childlike. "We'll save him, right?" She asked before she lost her nerve.

"I hope so." Morgana squeezed her shoulder again, sadness flashing in her eyes.

It wasn't an answer. There was no reassurance in the statement; there was no promise to it, but somehow knowing that Morgana did care made her feel a little better. Nicki swallowed and pushed the sorrow away. It would be back; she knew that, but for now, she sniffed and stood up. Outside the doors were opened by one of the nurses, and Nicki forced herself to walk into the ICU behind the weeping couple.

Everything was clean, and the packrat and messy artist in her hated it. The floors were too shiny, the walls too white, and the glass separators and doors that divided the patients were too clean. Nicki nodded to the nurse at the station by Aiden's room and forced herself to step in. It was wrong to see him lying there so still. There was a small tube in his nose and four different IVs leading into his arm. Somehow, he already looked pale and frail against the stark white sheets. Aiden was breathing slowly, and the rise and fall of his chest helped her step all the way into the room as the nurse gave her a soft, knowing look. His dark brown hair was messier than usual and made him look smaller and more childlike.

"Hey Aiden, it's me." Nicki chuckled nervously. "I'm back. Your Mom and Dad are taking care of a couple of things, but they'll be in soon." She glanced around the dim room before she sank down into the uncomfortable chair that his mother had been using the night before. "Things are pretty nuts right now. Alex is safe: you saved her. I'm not sure if you knew it at the time, but Alex is the real Iron Soul." She exhaled and reached over to take his hand. "We have a plan, Aiden: we're going after the Iron Chalice. You did a lot of damage to yourself when you healed Alex, but the Chalice can fix it. Apparently, it's the prototype for all those Celtic myths that inspired the Holy Grail story."

He didn't react; she hadn't expected him to but hadn't been able to quiet the hope that he'd respond to her voice. She looked over at the counter where a large cardstock board with pictures of his parents and sister Aisling had been put up. A well-worn copy of *Harry Potter and the Philosopher's Stone* was sitting next to it with a bookmark about halfway through.

"I remember when your gramps gave you that book," Nicki chuckled. "It was weird reading all the British words. It's only sort-of the same language now. Is your mom reading it to you?" Nicki paused and sighed softly. "I'm sorry: I don't know how to do this. It's always just been Gran and me, and thankfully she's never been sick. Never had to visit anyone in the hospital like this before; not that I had to do this, of course I mean I love you, you're my best friend and my brother, so I had to come and see you, but no one made me. I'm rambling now."

Nicki shook her head and used her free hand to pull off her coat, letting it fall back in the chair. In the corner of her eye, out the window, she thought she saw Morgana glance in and then move away. With a soft sigh, Nicki forced herself to look back at Aiden. She didn't know what to say and wondered if he could hear her at all. Squeezing his hand, Nicki pulled on the spark of magic beneath her heart and felt it warm her hand. She closed her eyes and willed a little more power through her hand and into Aiden, aware that Morgana would yell at her if she was caught.

"I can't save you with my magic," Nicki admitted in a low voice. It hurt just to say the words. "You hurt yourself pretty bad saving Alex. I guess it was a good thing; otherwise, we would have lost the Iron Soul, but I wish you could have just... I don't know, stabilized her, and called an ambulance. But we're going to find the Chalice; it can heal anything." Nicki let the flow of magic fade. "Bran's interested in it too, I can tell. With you injured, he doesn't want to bring it up, but I know he'd love to get his leg healed."

She was going to say more. She wanted to keep talking to Aiden like he could hear her and might respond at any moment, but the sound of someone moving outside made her pause. Her back was to the doorway, and Nicki glanced over her shoulder quickly.

"Nicki," Alex called softly from the doorway.

She hadn't been back to her dorm room since finals were over. She hadn't seen Alex since yesterday morning, and a lot had changed. Alex was pale with dark bags under her eyes. Her long blonde hair was back in a ponytail but looked dull and dirty. Her gray eyes were locked on Aiden's prone form, and she looked ready to be sick. Nicki began to release Aiden's hand in preparation for grabbing the trash can, but Alex swallowed thickly and bit her bottom lip. Nicki remained silent as Alex stepped into the room a little further.

"We've got to get going," Alex said.

"You've arranged tickets?" Nicki stood up from her chair. "Already?"

"Yeah, Jenny took care of it: guess having daddy's credit card is a good thing." Alex's eyes darted between Nicki and Aiden. "I, uh, went ahead and packed you a bag and grabbed your passport."

"Okay, just a second." Nicki turned back to Aiden, wondering if she should encourage Alex to come in and see him. Turning back to look at Aiden, she stood up and leaned forward to kiss his forehead. "I love you," Nicki whispered. "Don't you dare slip away while I'm gone. We're going to find the Chalice and save you."

Alex walked over beside her, and Nicki almost felt like she could hear the other girl's internal conflict. Nicki considered leaving the room to give Alex a moment, but couldn't bring herself to do it. A small spark of anger flashed in her chest that she did her best to quickly smother. She stepped back from the bed just enough to pull on her coat as Alex glanced between her and Aiden. Nicki didn't meet her eyes and just waited as Alex walked around the hospital bed to stand next to Aiden.

"I'm sorry," she heard Alex whisper. "Thank you for saving me. Now I'm going to save you."

Nicki bit her lip to keep from saying anything in response. Emotions were churning painfully in her gut, and her blunt nails were digging into her hands. After a moment, Alex stepped back from Aiden and glanced towards her before they stepped out into the hall. A few Christmas decorations were already hanging above the nurses' station despite it only being December 14th, but winter break had officially started in the small college town, which meant it was Christmas time. Morgana was nowhere to be seen, and Nicki decided not to mention her.

Nicki walked a little slower than normal and forced herself to stay a step behind Alex so the other girl could lead her out. She made a mental note to tell her grandmother to come and get her car, or maybe Morgana would take care of it. Rather than taking the elevator, Alex led Nicki into the stairwell, and they both shivered at the sudden temperature drop. A few turns took them to the main floor, and they stepped out into the rear parking lot next to a snowdrift.

Lance was leaning against the side of his large truck and looking down at his cellphone. Even at a distance, Nicki could see Bran and Jenny inside the cab. The emotions in her stomach jolted at the reminder that the former Lancelot and Guinevere or whatever their names had been were coming along. She glanced towards Alex and wondered how the real Iron Soul was taking that part of the big reveal. She'd lived with Jenny for a year and even walked in on them once. It had to be a mess.

"We'll all fit," Alex told her softly. "It'll be tight, but less to worry about."

"What's our route?"

"We have to drive to Portland: the first leg is to Minneapolis and then to Amsterdam,"

"Amsterdam?" Nicki brushed a stray strand of red hair out of her face and frowned.

"Cardiff isn't a major American flight destination." Alex shrugged as they arrived at the truck. "There weren't many choices."

"At least the layovers are short." Lance offered her a small smile as he pulled open the back door.

"Do we have return tickets?" Nicki asked, eying Jenny on the far side of the back. Bran turned around and looked at her.

"No." Jenny straightened up and gave Nicki what seemed to be a warning look. "We'll handle getting back once we have the Chalice, and we can save your friend."

Nicki slowly nodded. It didn't feel like the right answer, but she supposed it was the best they could offer. She grabbed the seat and hoisted herself into the rear of the pickup. Alex followed her a moment later and closed the door with a heavy metallic thud.

2

Dark Flight

Nicki was asleep with her head against a pillow tucked into the window niche. Across the aisle from her, Bran was slouched in his chair and absentmindedly playing some kind of game on the personal screen in front of him with headphones on. Thanks to the assignment of their seats, Alex had found herself in the middle seat of the center aisle between Lance and Jenny, with stiff legs and sore shoulders. Jenny was soundly asleep with her head resting on Alex's shoulder at an awkward angle as she cradled the pillow she'd been given in her lap. Lance was snoring softly on the other side of her with his head tilted back and his face completely relaxed.

She wasn't even sure what time it was anymore. Her phone was stowed in her bag beneath her seat, and she didn't dare move. The airplane was dark and almost completely silent. Behind them, she could hear some low voices and the sounds of someone moving around, but the earlier noise and bustle was gone. Alex wished that she could move over by Bran and at least talk with him about what they were going to do. In Minneapolis, they'd managed to locate a book on the British Isles, but it was in Nicki's bag and out of her reach.

Alex knew she should be asleep; she really should be asleep. They'd be in Amsterdam soon, and then it would be just a quick flight to Cardiff, and Alex had no idea of what would happen then. Nicki had mentioned heading for Glastonbury, where there was a lot of Arthurian myth, but Alex doubted they'd find the Iron Chalice there. Bran had slept from Oregon to Minneapolis like the dead and had been asleep the first few hours of this flight, but she had yet to sleep. Even Nicki, who was so stressed about Aiden's condition and not being there for him, was asleep.

Closing her eyes, Alex tried to meditate. She was tempted to reach for her magic but held back. Alex didn't dwell on her hesitation. She hadn't connected with her magic since she'd found out that she was the Iron Soul, the so-called protector of the Iron Realm that had been made by the Iron Realm itself thousands of years ago. Yeah: she wasn't ready to go there just yet. Giving up, Alex opened her eyes again, glancing around for any signs of other people awake and moving. Everyone she could see other than Bran was asleep.

The knowledge that far below them was the open ocean only added to the sense of silence and isolation. Alex swallowed and shivered as the small voice of doubt in her head became louder. What the hell were they doing? They were flying from freaking Oregon to Wales to find an ancient Celtic artifact that apparently a former incarnation of her had made so they could save Aiden. It was completely insane. It was the plot of some kind of lame adventure movie or video game. Then again, if it was, then she and the others would have been older and had weapons rather than having to leave their iron daggers in Lance's truck back in Portland.

Alex's hands were gripping the armrest so tightly that her fingers were beginning to ache. Some hero she was. She'd been tricked by her own boyfriend, stabbed and left for dead, and gotten one of their ancient allies, the Lady of the Lake, killed. Morgana seemed to have faith in her, but in the rush to leave, Alex hadn't even spoken with Merlin in private. Was he disappointed in her? Did he think she could do this?

She was in trouble, Alex reflected with a sigh; if she needed to hear it from the old mage that she could do it. Aiden's life was in the balance, and she was feeling sorry for herself, but she couldn't help it. Alex was a modern girl. Life had prepared her for school and probably a desk job with the careers available to Literature majors. Karate lessons instead of ballet and piano lessons would have been a better idea, but she'd been a kid and certainly hadn't known the insane destiny that she had. This was much more entertaining in books and movies when it happened to other people.

A phone rang, distracting Alex from her thoughts. She'd heard a few during the long flight, but this sounded very close, even if it was muted. It was a soft jangle that was very familiar, and Alex tried to look around without rousing Jenny. A moment later, however, the girl asleep against her jolted awake and reached down towards her feet. Alex suddenly realized with a soft sting of embarrassment why the ring tone sounded familiar. She'd only lived with Jenny for most of freshman year, minus those last couple of weeks where she'd lived with Nicki after Jenny's affair with Lance had been exposed.

Alex stayed still as she watched Jenny. The Hispanic girl retrieved her purse from underneath the seat in front of them and pulled out her cellphone. Jenny looked down at the phone nervously and brushed a black curl from her face. She muted the ringer but did not answer the call. Then the phone began to ring again, and Jenny sighed softly as if defeated. Alex remained still as Jenny raised the phone to her ear, both in a desire to give Jenny some sense of privacy and in curiosity.

"Hi, Daddy." Jenny's voice was barely louder than a whisper. "No, I'm not on my way home."

The tone of Jenny's voice was careful, nervous, and guilty all at once, and Alex felt bad for her just hearing the defeat in her voice. There was a long pause, and Jenny flinched slightly with a sad and resigned expression crossing her face. Jenny toyed with her necklace for a moment and then tugged on her turquoise shirt absentmindedly.

"Yes, I did, Daddy. Please believe me that it is important." Another pause and Jenny closed her eyes tightly. "No, I can't explain: it's not my situation to explain, but please try to understand that I have to help, however I can."

Jenny's expression softened a little, and Alex could see a few tears gathering. She closed her own eyes tightly and willed herself to stop hearing Jenny's words. They twisted uncomfortably in her gut and made her heart hurt.

"Thank you, Daddy," Jenny whispered a few moments later. "I don't know when I'll be back. I'm sorry about getting the tickets without asking, but I really do have to do this." She stopped talking again. "Yes, I'll try to be home for Christmas, and maybe then I'll be able to explain."

Jenny lingered on the phone for a few more minutes. She didn't say anything more but made small sounds of agreement. Finally, Alex opened her eyes to check on Jenny's expression. She still looked guilty, and there were faint tear tracks on her cheeks, but she was holding the phone gently with a sad, little smile on her face.

"I love you too. I'll be careful, I promise." The call ended, and Jenny sighed deeply, falling back into her seat. "That sucked."

Alex was at a loss of what to do. Part of her knew it would probably be smartest to pretend to be asleep and spare Jenny anyone overhearing the conversation. Bran had only glanced up when the phone had rung, but with the headphones, she doubted that he'd heard anything. But then Jenny leaned her head against Alex's shoulder, and she could feel the moisture of a tear through her shirt.

"You okay?" Alex asked.

Jenny didn't look up at her and instead kept her face turned down. "Not really," Jenny replied after a long uncomfortable pause. "He's wonderful, as usual, which just makes me feel worse." She laughed sadly. "He seems to think that some friends and I are going to help a friend from Wales. At least that's a plus of college; the international students help explain buying five tickets."

"I'm sorry," Alex apologized, feeling a rush of guilt. "It wasn't fair to saddle you with that."

"I'm the rich girl," Jenny muttered. "Your mother may be a doctor, but Daddy is a senior partner in a multi-million-dollar law firm."

"Rub it in," Alex teased.

Jenny laughed softly for a moment before she sighed, still not moving her head. "I was almost over it," she told her in a low voice. "I was actually feeling okay about being the reincarnation of Guinevere, with Lance being the reincarnation of Lancelot, or whatever their names were in the Bronze Age. I was actually starting to think about going out with him," Jenny admitted, so softly that Alex almost didn't hear her. "I mean, the guilt was nasty, but at least Arthur was okay, and he had you there to pick up the pieces. I was the one who had cheated, so I deserved the guilt and doubt as I worked my way through things, but now I have no clue how to feel. Things were getting better, getting easier. Lance still wanted me, Arthur wanted us to be happy, and you and I were patching up our friendship. Now the rug has been pulled out from under me, and I just... I haven't got a clue."

"I know," Alex admitted. "I'm trying not to think about all of it. It's just too much."

"But we've got to, don't we? In another life, we were married to each other, which is weird to think about because I love you, Alex, but not like that."

"Right back at you," Alex told her. She grabbed onto the more familiar banter quickly.

Jenny chuckled and sniffed loudly, clearing her throat. "But Arthur, the guy we all thought was the real reincarnation of the... Iron Soul was just using all of us. I keep thinking back to high school when we started dating and wondering...." She shook her head and pulled away from Alex's shoulder to rest her head against the back of her seat. "It was all just an act for him, a means to an end. I trusted you when you told me that: I believe you when you say that he tried to kill you and that it's his fault that your friend Aiden is in the hospital, but I can't reconcile it. I just can't."

"I can't either. That's why I'm trying not to think about it." Alex turned slightly in her seat so she could better face Jenny. "When I met Arthur, I had a vision, I was the only one, and I guess I convinced myself that it meant we had a special connection. I liked him from the first time I met him, and when I thought I found out who he was, I was so sure that there was something important between us. Now, I just wonder if that was a leftover from us being cousins in that life, or if Arthur caused it to get me to trust him."

Jenny said nothing, and they lapsed into silence. Then in a low voice, Jenny asked, "You were cousins?"

"Yeah, I asked Morgana about it. The original Iron Soul and Arthur's previous life were cousins, and apparently Medraut, that was his name, not Mordred, killed him out of jealousy for his position."

"I just can't imagine the guy I dated for years doing that."

"Me neither. I keep waiting to wake up from this nightmare. I keep hoping that it is some trick of Chernobog's, but in my gut, I know that isn't true. He lied to all of us, and he did it so perfectly that there were never any hints."

"Maybe there were," Jenny told her. "Your friend Aiden said he was a little too perfect once, and there were moments here and there when he seemed to be watching us just a little too closely."

"Yeah, I guess he was a little too perfect." Alex looked up towards the ceiling of the airplane cabin. She didn't say anything about Jenny's other point but silently agreed with it. "But where does that leave us now?"

"I don't know. We're probably starting with the only thing we can: saving Aiden. Once that's done, then... I don't know; maybe I'll just finish sophomore year and transfer. I only came to Ravenslake University because of Arthur."

"You're going to leave?" Alex looked back at Jenny sharply. "I know that things are a bit weird but-"

"What is Guinevere's role if she isn't the king's wife? Who is she if she isn't betraying him with his best friend and best knight?" Jenny asked her in a small voice. "That's her role in the story, isn't it?"

Alex couldn't think or speak for a moment. There was a part of her that was angry at Jenny for the question, but she understood it. Guinevere and Lancelot. They were such a huge part of the western consciousness. She couldn't remember ever learning about them. Instead, it felt like she had always known about them and their affair. What did that mean, and what did it leave for Jenny?

"Yeah, but I'm starting to learn that sometimes you have to go away from the traditional story," Alex managed to say around her dry mouth.

"Look at me: I'm a female King Arthur, or close to. There aren't any stories that I've ever heard of about that."

"True," Jenny agreed with a small smile that reached her dark eyes. "That's a good point," she conceded before lowering her eyes for a moment. When she looked back up at Alex, she asked, "Does that mean you want me to stay?"

"You're my friend in this life. Not my wife, not someone who cheated on me. You were there for me and supported me when all this magical stuff started, and I was freaking out. You made me feel happy, and like I wasn't alone. I know that I hurt you with everything that happened with Arthur, and I'm sorry for that. More so now than ever. So yeah, I'd like my friend to stay, but only if she wants to."

"I'll think about it," Jenny promised.

The other girl shifted in her seat so she could reach her purse. Alex watched silently as Jenny turned off the phone and dropped it in. As Jenny leaned back in her seat and put the pillow beneath her head, Alex felt a little better. Reaching down, she retrieved her own pillow and carefully put her seat back a little more. She turned off the overhead light and closed her eyes with a sigh.

3

Badb

⟶ ☙ ⟵

721 B.C.E. North Pembrokeshire Coast

Dark clouds hung over the cold, rocky landscape. The last chill of winter was hanging in the air even as the small trees showed the first signs of budding, and green was beginning to return to the dull brown of the ground. His staff thudded against the earth with each of his rapid steps as Merlin scaled up the steep slope towards the top of the cliffs. The roar of the waves against them was almost deafening, and his lungs were beginning to burn, but he pressed on. Up ahead, he could see a figure with a blue cloak billowing in the wind and long dark hair flying around her. He sighed in relief but did not slow down.

There was something heavy in the air, and even with the wind howling along the cliffs, he thought that he could feel some kind of stillness in the world around him. Like it was holding its breath in anticipation of what would happen next. His staff struck the small rocks in a steady rhythm, and he only slowed down when the figure turned and regarded him for a moment. She was shivering slightly in the wind but made no move to tighten her cloak and turned to look back at the sea.

"Morgana." Merlin wheezed as he leaned forward to support himself on his staff.

"Merlin," she answered in a voice that was almost lost to the wind.

She turned to look back over her shoulder at him once more. For a moment, her green eyes met his brown ones, and he was struck by how old she was beginning to look. It was only her eyes. Morgana, like himself, had aged very slowly over the last hundred winters. There were thin lines around her eyes and mouth, but her hair was still a vivid dark brown, and she moved with natural grace.

"You are distressed about something, Morgana," Merlin said. It was an empty question as they both knew what was bothering her. "Please speak with me."

"Why are we still here, Merlin?"

He stepped up next to her, debating the wisdom of touching her shoulder. Even a century after losing Arto to the Sídhe, he was so often at a loss of how to interact with Morgana. She both enjoyed and loathed being touched, depending on her mood, and as of late, her mood had been dark and stormy.

"We are half Sídhe, me by birth and you by fusion with your Changeling," Merlin said. "We are not human, and our lifespans... simply reflect that."

"Is there nothing else? How long are we to endure like this?"

"There are still Sídhe to fight. The descendants of those who invaded us still linger in the dark caverns and tunnels. I hear that on the west island, they are even calling them the mound people now."

She did not chuckle at his remark, and Merlin felt his worry intensify. Normally Morgana took pleasure in the humiliation and mocking of the once terrifying Sídhe. Her childhood as a slave to them had not prepared her to grant compassion to them.

"Arto and Mother died in the last battle," Morgana sighed softly, tilting her face up towards the sun. "And Airril has been gone for so long. I feel like a memory lingering in the Iron Realm. We are half Sídhe, Merlin; perhaps we are not as welcome in the Iron Realm as we would wish."

"Morgana-"

"We fought for this realm, we helped create the Iron Gates, and we protected the Iron Soul," Morgana said. She stepped back from the edge and moved to sit on a large smooth boulder. "I don't know what to do now, Merlin," Morgana admitted. "Hunting the surviving Sídhe lost its appeal over thirty years ago."

"I understand," Merlin assured her. "I keep waiting for Cyrridven to come and tell me what to do now, to reveal my purpose."

Morgana looked at him with a hint of surprise shining in her eyes, and Merlin felt regret and guilt for not sharing this with her before. He owed Arto's sister better than that. She'd proven herself loyal to the Iron Realm a hundred times over, and now she was drifting. Merlin shifted and swung the large bag strapped across his back down and opened it. A Sword with a golden hilt that was just over two feet long was secured in an old, but well-cared-for leather sheath.

"We still have to protect Cathanáil." Merlin shifted to touch the Sword's hilt. "This is Arto's legacy, and must not be allowed to fall into the hands of the Sídhe or others who mean harm to the Iron Realm."

"Nothing has sought the Sword since Medraut's death," Morgana scoffed, spitting the name of Arto's dead cousin.

"Morgana, there is still magic in this world. We cannot let our guard down."

"The magic has been fading for a century." Morgana tightened her cloak around her shoulders.

"Yes, but it is not gone. Please put these dark thoughts out of your mind." He nodded towards the cliff. "There is no guarantee of anything."

Morgana did not move for a long moment before she looked back towards the cliff. A soft sigh escaped her and drifted on the wind, but she turned and stepped towards him. She reached for him, but her hand settled on the heavy bag slung around his back, and he knew that she was feeling the shape of Cathanáil. They began to slowly walk away from the cliff, saying nothing of Morgana's darker thoughts or Arto. It was a familiar heavy silence that often haunted their time together, and Merlin had to bite back the urge to sigh himself.

Away from the cliffs, more trees grew along an old, worn path that long before had been part of the road down to the shore. So much had changed since Arto's death. The old trading network was all but gone, and the religion of old was falling away as the priests of the earth and the ancestors were replaced by followers of the Old Ones. Even Cyrridven was known across the isles as a goddess, despite that he knew she did not seek such a title.

The small ships that once were constantly along the shores transporting tin, copper, or finished bronze goods to the southern land were almost gone. Iron had been scarce for a long time after Arto's death, but it was appearing more and more in the hands of regional chiefs who now ruled as kings rather than simply being leaders. Merlin wasn't sure what to think of it. Worse still, this was what Medraut had predicted would happen. It all made him feel so very old, and while he would never consider taking his own life, he understood Morgana's doubts all too well.

"Merlin." Morgana reached out and grabbed his arm, shaking him from his thoughts. "I think we are being watched," she told him in a low voice.

Her green eyes were sharp even as she tried to appear unconcerned, and Merlin was able to instantly banish the thought that Morgana might still be upset. Glancing around carefully, Merlin tried to appear calm and unconcerned. They passed under a budding tree, and Merlin spotted a gray and black bird. Looking up at it, Merlin almost smiled at the sight of the small crow with its black head and wings and silvery body. Yet, there was a sense that something was wrong as he examined it. It seemed to be watching them. From his position, it looked like an ordinary hooded crow except that there was a slight red tint to its black feathers that he wasn't sure he'd ever seen before.

"Morgana," Merlin said in a deliberate voice. "I think we've lingered here long enough. We should seek shelter for the night in the next village."

She nodded in agreement, and they sped up their pace. As they passed the tree, the crow cawed and ruffled its feathers. Merlin felt a sharp desire to swing his staff at it, but the crow swooped out of the tree with a loud cry, and Merlin shivered at a sudden chill working its way up his spine. With a smooth turn in the air, the crow flew down in front of them and flapped its wings to stay suspended in the air directly ahead. Red sparks danced over the bird's feathers, creating a dark-red glow around the creature that lasted only a moment before the shape of the crow began to grow larger and shift in midair.

Feathers shimmered and rippled in the wind as they shrank into the growing form. It took only a moment, but Merlin felt his stomach turning at the small cracking sounds that reached his ears. In a swirl of a gray cloak, a figure emerged from the rush of magic. The figure adjusted their long gray cloak, exposing one bare shoulder and a hand with long, talon-like fingernails.

She appeared female, but Merlin was not going to take anything about this creature at face value. Towering over both Morgana and himself by more than a foot, she had wild-looking dark eyes that glinted in the light of the sun and were lined with blood red. Her skin was grayer than that of a human, and long black lines were painted across her face. Black hair hung around it, making her features appear shadowed and gaunt even in the daylight. A mantle made of long black feathers surrounded her neck, and while he had never met this being before, Merlin was very confident in its identity.

"Good day," Merlin greeted. "One who takes the form of a crow? You are Badb, I believe? Worshiped by some humans as a goddess and an exile of the realm of Avalye."

"I am," Badb replied. Her cold voice seemed to echo in the still air around them. There was a hint of irritation at his introduction in her tone. "Give me the Iron Sword."

"That is not possible," Merlin replied with a kind smile. He gestured for Morgana to stay behind him. A moment later, he felt her smaller hands pull the bag that concealed Cathanáil off his back. "The Sword is an artifact of the Iron Soul that we are charged with protecting."

"You will give me the Sword, mages, or I will destroy you and take it by force," Badb informed him imperiously with a dangerous flash in her eyes.

"What is your interest in the Sword?" Morgana demanded. "Its power is limited when not in the hand of the Iron Soul, and he is long gone."

"That Sword touches other worlds," Badb said in a greedy voice as she took a step towards them. "It has potential in the right hands."

"Those hands are not yours!" Morgana drew back with the bag in her hands and fire in her eyes.

Badb's dark eyes narrowed on the bag, and a slow smile spread over her face. Merlin placed his staff in front of his body and studied the Old One for a moment as she tore her gaze from Morgana and returned it to him. None of them moved for a time until a gust of wind howled along the nearby cliffs and tore through the trees. Badb raised a hand, and before either of them had a chance to react, sent a swirling mass of dark-red magic at them.

Air was pulled from his lungs roughly as the sparks of magic wafted around him. Merlin raised his eyes to glare at Badb. She was watching them calmly, her head tilted as she waited for his reaction. Merlin felt something familiar and yet almost forgotten thrumming in his chest. Without thinking about it, Merlin pulled sharply on the sensation and felt a rush of magic up his throat and down his arms. Green magic flashed off his right palm and pushed Badb's magic away from them.

"It would seem that I have not been as diligent as I had thought," Merlin groaned. "There is more magic in the world than I realized."

"Give me the Sword, old abomination," Badb ordered.

"Abomination." Morgana laughed behind him. "It's been a long time since anyone called us that." There was a giddy note to her tone, and Merlin was almost afraid to look at her, but he did. Morgana's green eyes were blazing, and she had raised her right hand. Cathanáil's bag was slung over her shoulder now, and her own silver magic was beginning to coil around her palm. "A long time indeed, but I think I remember how to be that woman."

Merlin summoned his magic and smiled despite the danger at the warmth that spread through his entire body. It was suddenly easier to breathe than it had been for longer than he cared to remember. His magic surged into his fingers, and the world looked a little sharper and clearer. Green sparks of magic blended with the brilliant silver magic of Morgana as she released a charged wave of power. The swirl of magic spun through the air and struck Badb in the chest.

A strange cry, half-scream half-caw, tore from her throat only to turn into a vicious snarl. Her dark eyes flashed red as she regained her balance and raised one hand towards them. More dark-red magic sparked over her palm and around the vicious-looking nails. Morgana did not give her a chance to attack again as a whip of shimmering silver slashed through the air and struck Badb's hand. A cry of raw rage sang across the hills, and dark-red magic flared around the Old One.

Morgana pulled him sharply to the right just in time to avoid a blazing ball of fire. The rush of heat at his side spurred Merlin into action, bringing years of combat experience flaring back to life. Quickly he shifted away from Morgana to create two targets and two points of attack against Badb as blood began to pound in his ears. Adjusting his staff, Merlin pushed his magic into the old wood. It pulsed in his hand, and he flexed his fingers against the wood experimentally. It would do.

As his magic flowed into his hands, Merlin gently pushed it into the staff. There was resistance only for a moment before the wood, and his magic remembered the long-ago connection. He moved once more to avoid another blast from Badb. He almost smiled as the magic began building up in the wood, and the Old One snarled with anger. Gritting his teeth, Merlin raised his staff into the air and sent one last jolt of magic into it. In his hands, the wood shivered and glowed with a soft green light just before he brought it down sharply against the earth.

The old wooden staff creaked and shuddered as his magic surged through it and into the ground. Flashes of green light illuminated Merlin's hands and face as the ground glistened beneath his feet. Around

Badb, the earth trembled. Chunks of rock and turf violently shot up around her in flashes of green light. Badb merely chuckled and blasted a stream of dark-red sparks at a slab of stone sliding up next to her, causing it to explode in a shower of rock and dust.

Merlin was beginning to feel faint as the constant pull of magic through his body sucked all the air from his lungs. In the corner of his eye, he could see Morgana still attacking Badb with quick, low-powered attacks to keep the Old One distracted. His chest burned, and the staff was glowing the same spring leaf green as his magic now. The staff began to crack beneath his hands with a large fragment pushing painfully into his palm, but Merlin poured more magic into the stressed wood. His connection to the Iron Realm was thrumming painfully, even as he demanded more and more magic. Earth was pulled up by flashes of green faster than Badb could destroy the slabs. Around her feet, the ground was beginning to cake over her legs and threaten to trap her. A whip of silver magic flashed through the air, striking Badb's arm. She shrieked again, and her eyes flashed a bloody red as she turned her full attention to Morgana.

Her distraction gave Merlin the moment he needed, and with a final shove of magic, the ground around Badb's feet swelled up violently around her. Earth molded around her feet, locking her in place. That strange scream and caw sound escaped her, and her arms flailed wildly as Badb sought to balance herself. All around her legs, the earth crept up like a living creature seeking to swallow her whole. A triumphant laugh from Morgana was followed by a slash of silvery magic striking Badb in the chest.

Badb screamed in rage, a mixture of a yell and a caw, as a cloud of dark-red magic loomed and swirled above her. With one last murderous look at them both, she brought her hands down and sent her magic crashing into the earthen trap holding her. The rocks cracked, and the turf was thrown all around her, releasing her feet. Morgana sent two more silvery orbs crashing into Badb, causing the Old One to flinch and scream. Golden blood shown brilliantly against her gray skin as Badb's magic swirled up around her. The shape of her body changed rapidly, and as Merlin took a step forward, a hooded crow appeared in her place. It opened its wings and took to the sky, dodging another wave of crumbling rocks.

Morgana wasn't done, and the crow barely avoided the final swirl of silver magic. Merlin turned to Morgana and almost chuckled as she angrily stomped her foot. There was a look of rage, but also a glimmer of excitement on her features. He shifted and felt the staff finish crumbling in his hand, leaving scattered chips of wood in front of him and a layer of dust on his palm. Turning his eyes away from it, Merlin watched the bird fly far off toward the horizon and sighed loudly. The warmth of his magic was quickly being overtaken by a sense of loss and sorrow that he could not deny, even as he felt foolish for it. As the last glimmer of black wings vanished, Merlin turned his attention to his shattered staff.

"Merlin," Morgana called hesitantly. He examined the fractured pieces of wood. "Are- are you alright?"

Merlin smiled sadly as he turned to look at her. Morgana was clutching the bag with Cathanáil tightly in her hands and watching him with a pitying and worried expression. Shaking his head, Merlin selected one of the smaller pieces with an intact symbol carved on it and slipped it into the small pouch on his side. The rest of the shattered pieces of wood he let fall to the ground.

"My mother made me that staff," he said softly to answer Morgana's question. "Carved with symbols of protection, and covered with a bit of her own blood. She always wanted me safe, despite what I was." Shaking his head, he stepped back from the fragments. "I suppose I should be grateful that it lasted as long as it did." He gestured towards the hills. "We should resume our journey."

"Badb will be back," Morgana reminded him. She stepped up next to him, and they began to walk. "I doubt that an Old One with plans for the Sword will give up easily."

"I agree, and I called on far more magic than I thought still existed in the world."

"That might be a bad sign." Morgana glanced around at the trees with clear tension in her shoulders. "Something is happening."

"Well then, I suppose we have a new mission," Merlin replied with a falsely cheerful smile. "A new purpose."

Morgana smacked him on the arm and sighed, but in the corner of his eye, Merlin saw a very small, pleased smile appear on her face. Inwardly he sighed in relief and sent a wish to the ancestors that they could meet this new challenge without the Iron Soul.

4

Choosing a Direction

Nicki wasn't sure what she had been expecting when they'd gotten off the plane in Wales. Despite the nap she'd managed to take during the longest leg of their journey, she still felt exhausted, and the sense of confusion she was suffering didn't help matters. Cardiff was a strange thing to her. In her youth, she'd traveled across the country with her parents, never staying long anywhere and spending more than one night in the backseat. Over the years, the memories of elegant brick buildings, dingy side streets, and tall skyscrapers had faded into a dull blur. Yet this city was something quite different, she realized as she watched it sweep past through the train window.

The buildings were small and compact, with older and classic looking buildings pressed up against modern structures of glass and metal. For a moment, the realization of just how old the city was hit her, and Nicki grinned as she eagerly looked around. But she turned on instinct to say something to Aiden and froze as everything rushed back to her. Swallowing, Nicki did her best to stay calm and looked across the aisle to where Alex and Bran were leaning over a small pamphlet they'd gotten at the airport. She couldn't hear what they were saying and glanced towards

Jenny and Lance, who were sitting across from her and clearly trying not to notice that they were right next to each other.

"Are you sure we should head to Glastonbury?" Bran asked. "I mean, it is associated with the King Arthur myth, but it's in Devon, not Wales."

"I know." Nicki's stomach threatened to turn at her own uncertainty. "But the Glastonbury Tor is one of the possible places where Arthur is buried, and a lot of grail stories link to Glastonbury. I know Morgana suggested Wales, but maybe the person who had it took the Chalice out of Wales. Unless your visions can give us more, then we're a bit stuck."

"She has a point," Jenny said carefully, giving her a look like she expected to be bitten or something. "We don't have much to go on, and if nothing else, going to Glastonbury will give us some time to research and try to find other possibilities."

Bran shook his head and glanced towards Lance and Jenny. "But wasn't it catholic monks who encouraged the connection to the King Arthur myth?"

"Sure, but they probably built on local legends," Nicki agreed. "The area has been connected with Avalon for a long time, so maybe there is something there."

"I think that Morgana and Merlin have mentioned it before," Bran said. "But they don't tell us much. I hate the idea that we spend time searching in an area that is just a medieval tourist trap."

"There are a ton of Arthurian myths," Alex protested. She looked a bit ill as she said the words. "Hell, we even took a whole semester class about them, but most of the stories are combinations of different myths from all across the British Isles and even other parts of Europe. Then they were rewritten and romanticized by the French. I don't think we'll find much guidance there."

"All the more reason to start with something obvious," Lance said. He reached over to touch Alex's shoulder. "Maybe we need to take a step back and start where anyone else would start. Stop thinking about all the different myths and what Merlin and Morgana have told you."

Nicki felt a flare of irritation, but Bran regarded Lance with a small and thoughtful smile. "You think what we know is distracting us?"

"Sort of, yeah, sure Merlin and Morgana didn't tell you about it, but there were probably other mages running around with the different Iron Souls. They didn't hide the Chalice, so they might not know all the events surrounding it. Hell, maybe some storyteller mistook one of those mages for Merlin or Morgana at some point in time."

"By that logic, then Glastonbury is as good a place to start as any," Alex agreed. Nicki caught Alex glancing her way. "But according to the information we got, getting there isn't as easy as we hoped."

"I thought you could get anywhere by train in England?" Jenny asked with a curious frown and a tilt of her head.

"Not to Glastonbury. We can get train tickets to Bristol, but we'll have to take a bus to Glastonbury itself," Bran informed her with an apologetic look. "It isn't a very large town and is apparently really dependent on tourism."

"Okay, so here's a plan," Alex said. "We get tickets to Bristol as soon as we reach the central station. If there is a delay, then we get some real food, and if it is soon, then we just grab some snacks to go. When we get to Bristol, we get to a bookstore and get some research material and a place to sleep for the night."

"You don't want to get to Glastonbury today?" Jenny asked with a nervous glance her way that made Nicki frown.

"If a train doesn't go to Glastonbury, then it must be a small town," Alex explained, sounding unsure of herself but trying anyway. "We're all exhausted and jet-lagged. Let's get some sleep while we can, and see about getting ourselves some internet access. Now that we're over here, it might be safe to try and get some more information out of Merlin and Morgana. Not to mention finding a place to stay in Glastonbury. I doubt we're going to find the Chalice in only a day."

"Agreed," Bran said. He nodded and adjusted his backpack. "We need to really focus on potential underground locations in the area. The Chalice is underground somewhere."

Nicki frowned and nibbled at her lip as her fingers toyed with the tips of her braid. There was churning anger in her gut as she watched Alex fumble with her words and try to take the lead. It was almost funny in a sad, stupid way. Nicki shivered and turned to look out the window in order to distract herself. She knew she wasn't really angry at Alex or Bran. She wasn't even angry at Jenny and Lance. Hell, she now found herself wishing that their betrayal had actually led to Arthur's death. No, she was angry at Arthur, and the Sídhe and whoever this Queen was that frightened even Morgana, but they weren't here.

"You're probably right," Jenny sighed, "I just wish we had more to go on."

"Me too," Bran agreed. "Unfortunately, we don't have much, Glastonbury is known for mythical connections to King Arthur, and one legend I found suggests that the Holy Grail was hidden in the Chalice Well. Obviously, that well is probably a lot newer, but the use of the word Chalice rather than grail could mean something."

"What if we find nothing there?" Lance asked. "What's the Plan B here?"

"Come back to Wales and start searching the old tunnels, I guess," Alex muttered, sounding a bit ill. "I don't like it either, guys, but we need a starting point, and Glastonbury isn't that far away."

The train began to slow down, and Nicki let out a small sigh of relief. Standing, even if only for a few minutes, sounded really good to her. Outside the window, it was easier to get a clear view of the buildings, cars, and people. As the train pulled into the station, she could see signs in English and what she guessed was Welsh. She almost smiled at the notion that it was probably the existing language closest to what Merlin and Morgana spoke growing up here three thousand years ago.

They came to a full stop with a gentle shudder, and all around them, people stood up and collected their bags. There were a few people without bags who rushed out the doors ahead of everyone else. Lance stood up and helped Bran with his bag after making sure that Jenny had her suitcase. Alex glanced Nicki's way as she hoisted her backpack over her shoulder and tugged her small rolling suitcase towards the door. Nicki lingered at the back and allowed the others to step off the train ahead of her. She took a deep breath and followed the others out onto the platform and looked around.

Everything was a lot bigger than she was used to, and the press of people around her was completely foreign. Bran seemed to become smaller as he stepped closer to Lance and tried to keep his cane close to his body in the initial crunch. Thankfully the crowd spread out as they walked into the main terminal. A soft gasp of surprise escaped Nicki as she looked down the long massive structure. It was one long room with a high ceiling filled with skylights that allowed the sun to shine down on their faces as they walked underneath.

"There isn't much here," Jenny remarked with a frown as the group walked down the station.

"No, but there's a ticket counter." Bran gestured towards it. "Come on. We need to find out about how to get to..."

Bran trailed off and swayed in front of them. Nicki took a step towards him as she noticed his eyes turning glassy, but Lance was already holding his shoulder steady. To her surprise, the football player dropped to a knee next to Bran and let the other boy lean on his shoulder. A small grimace crossed Lance's face as Bran all but collapsed against him, but it passed, and Lance said nothing.

"Bran?" Alex called nervously. She began to reach for him only to think better of it and pull back her hand.

Nicki glanced around: they were attracting attention. Jenny was smiling at a few of the people looking on and giving quick reassurances. Finally, Bran blinked his eyes and shook his head.

"I'm okay," he muttered. Bran shook his head again, and his eyes cleared a little.

"Did you see something?" Alex asked as she moved her hands nervously.

"Yeah, I did. I didn't see the Chalice or the skull, instead this place ... I don't know, faded away? There were trees along the river and some people. It was like I was seeing how it used to be."

"Maybe this is the right place then," Lance said. He stood up after Bran regained his balance.

"No," Bran clutched at his head and groaned. "I don't think so. I didn't get the sense that the Chalice was close. Hell, I didn't even see it this time."

"We're attracting attention," Alex said carefully. "Come on; let's get some tickets to Bristol and go from there."

If Jenny was irritated at her job as a piggy bank, she made no sign of it as she went up to the ticket counters while the rest of them took Bran off to the side and waited. She returned only a short time later with a stack of tickets and a wide grin.

"Hey, guys, the trains are very frequent. I got us tickets for one leaving in about an hour, so we have some time to eat. The trip won't take too long, but there isn't any foodservice onboard or Wi-Fi, so we'll have to take care of stuff on this end."

"Great." Lance gave Jenny a shy smile. "We should see about finding someplace with Wi-Fi so we can try and book some rooms in Bristol."

"Good plan," Alex agreed. She nodded towards the main doorway. "There's probably stuff just outside the station, so we don't have to go too far." She reached over and snagged Jenny's hand to give it a quick squeeze. "Thanks for taking care of that, Jenny."

"Of course," Jenny replied, trying to sound nonchalant, but she beamed at the praise and recognition.

Nicki stomped down an odd twinge of jealousy blended with fear, but as they headed for the large doorway, she couldn't help but wonder if Jenny and Lance might find themselves betraying Alex. Sure, their original story was all about the love triangle, and Lance seemed completely enthralled by Jenny, for whatever reason, and Jenny and Alex both seemed straight. Bran touched her arm just before she almost ran into a doorway. She shook her head and gave him a grateful look.

Alex hadn't been wrong about finding something outside the station. Stepping outside brought them into the main core of the city itself. Just beyond some nearby rooftops, Nicki could see the huge roof of a stadium and tall buildings standing alone amongst shorter brick and metal structures. They were next to some sort of pedestrian area with no cars on the street and a series of buildings that included shops and restaurants surrounding it. In front of them was a large square facing a bus depot that made Nicki feel lost, just looking at it. Thankfully, the smell of food helped them all focus on the mission at hand. Nicki swayed on her feet for a moment as they walked through a cloud of cigarette smoke on their way across the square. Alex grabbed her arm and kept her steady as they all stumbled into a fast-food restaurant.

Forty-five minutes later, with some food in their stomachs and after a quick face washing in the bathroom, they stumbled back into the train station, but this time with reservations at a hostel in Bristol that they could check into as soon as they arrived. Platform 2 was bustling with people as everyone spilled into the different cars. Some had luggage, and others looked like they were just heading off for the day. Nicki briefly wondered what it was like to really live in a country where trains were such a backbone of daily life.

The interior of the train reminded her of an airplane rather than the trains she'd seen in movies. There were rows of padded seats, but they faced each other with a table between them. It was a feature that surprised her, but as Lance grabbed her bags and lifted them up to the large shelf over their heads, she decided it would be nice to have some workspace. She pulled out the book on Britain from her bag and set it on the table as she climbed into the far seat. But as she sat down and leaned her head back, Nicki felt her eyes trying to slide closed. The seat wasn't very comfortable, but she had some real legroom, and exhaustion was beginning to catch up with her.

"Take a nap, Nicki," Alex told her gently as she sat down next to her. "It'll be about an hour to get there. Jenny says the train makes a couple stops."

There were only four seats around the table and five of them. Bran sat down across from Alex leaving Jenny and Lance glancing at each other uncomfortably. In the corner of her eye, she saw Alex give Lance what looked like an encouraging smile as he and Jenny sat down at the table across the aisle from them. They were all quiet as the rest of the passengers climbed into the train and began to settle down. As the train gave a small lurch and began to pull away from the station, Nicki saw Alex flip open the guide book and begin talking with Bran. She tried to listen, but the smooth rhythm of the train on the tracks was strangely relaxing. Her eyes felt heavier, and not even thoughts about Aiden could keep them from sliding shut.

5

On Top of the Tor

There was something very strange about this place, Alex reflected as they climbed up the long path towards the square stone tower at the very top of the tor. The massive conical hill made for a pleasant and easy little hike. St. Michael's tower stood several stories high in front of them, looking over the small town below and the terraces of the hill. She didn't like the tower, but couldn't put her finger on why. With each step as they got closer to it, Alex felt herself frowning at it and the concrete path that led their way up. Dark gray clouds filled the sky above them, blocking out the sun and adding to the lingering jet lag she knew they were all still feeling.

She glanced towards Nicki; the redhead had her hood over her head and her hands in her pockets. Her shoulders were tense, and Alex knew that Nicki was still angry. She wasn't sure if Nicki was angry at her for failing so fantastically against Arthur and Aiden having to save her or if she was angry about more than that. Maybe Jenny and Lance being with them bothered her, but Alex felt stronger with them here. She didn't want to think about that too closely and hoped it was simply a case of them being more removed from the trauma that had happened recently. Last night at the hostel, when she'd woken up from a nightmare, Jenny had simply reached over between their beds to hold her hand for a bit while Nicki just lay there staring at the ceiling.

"I'm not sure about this climate," Lance muttered. He looked up at the sky with a frown. "Winter without snow is just odd."

"They get snow some places here," Bran replied. "We're just pretty far south, and the Gulf Stream helps keep the west coast of Britain a bit warmer than it would be otherwise."

Bran looked towards Nicki and waited for her to add in her usual tidbit of information, but she said nothing, and Bran gave Alex a helpless look. Alex wondered just how she was supposed to fix something like this. She'd sworn to be worth the sacrifice, and she was doing her damnedest with what they had so far. A flash of anger in her chest reminded Alex to calm down. Nicki's best friend, pretty much her brother, was lying in a coma with the clock ticking down on how long he'd be stable, and she needed to just suck up and deal with this. The desire to let out a string of curses was really strong, though, and she promised herself that she'd let it all out when they finished up here.

They reached the top of the tor without any more conversation, and Alex looked up at the tall tower. It was far too recent to have anything to do with the Chalice. Bran was standing calmly next to Lance, who seemed to have decided it was his job to keep an eye on Bran and was looking out over the village. Alex watched him for a moment, hoping that maybe he'd have a vision, or that something would happen to give them even a little guidance.

Then Alex shivered at a cold burst of wind and tightened her coat around herself. It wasn't as cold as she had been expecting, and there was no snow on the ground, but the dark clouds overhead threatened rain. She couldn't see the morning sun and felt a chill working its way up her spine only to be banished by an odd brush of warmth against her cheek. Glancing around in surprise, Alex couldn't see anything, but the odd feeling lingered. She wasn't sure what she was feeling. It was like a soft whisper in her ear and then like the brush of fingers over the palm of her hand the next. Alex inhaled deeply as they paused to take a break and tried to isolate the sensation. Toying with her fingers, Alex tried to determine if she felt threatened by the feeling or if it might be something else.

"What is it?" Bran asked. His voice seemed muffled in the cold winter air. "You look confused."

"I'm... well, actually, I'm not sure." Alex looked out across the fields and houses below. "It feels like, I don't know, I'm being brushed, maybe poked at is a better way to describe it."

"Poked..." Bran repeated slowly with a raised eyebrow. "Uh..."

"Don't worry about it." Alex laughed rather forcefully. "Probably just, well, everything."

"Possibly." Bran nodded but looked around carefully.

It was odd being the only group up on the tor as they circled the tower. Alex wasn't sure what they were supposed to be looking for. At that moment, she felt downright silly as she waited for anything special to happen. She'd felt Cathanáil the moment it touched her hand: was it possible that she'd sense the Chalice? Alex grumbled at herself; she was hoping for clichés now. They were that lost and desperate, but then again, they'd known that when poor Jenny's father had paid for plane tickets from Oregon to Wales.

Alex shifted as something moved in the corner of her eye, and the odd tingling sensation on her skin intensified. Alex rubbed her hands together, wondering if she was having some kind of allergic reaction or something. Then she began to hear something. It was an odd little chattering noise that was very faint as the soft breeze carried the sound around her. Turning around, Alex searched the hill for any sign of the source of the noise as it grew louder and louder. Thanks to the wintery British weather, they were alone up on the tor, and she could see nothing that explained the noise. She noted that the others were looking around in confusion now too and shared a quick look with Jenny. Alex shrugged in confusion and noted a worried expression appearing on Jenny's face.

Whatever she'd been expecting didn't prepare her for the sudden appearance of several small creatures around the base of the tower. They looked as if they had sprung out of the ground and were unlike anything Alex had ever seen before as she examined one in stunned silence. It was a small humanoid creature with dark gray skin that was wrinkled all over its face, but it had large violet eyes that made Alex hiss in recognition.

Her hand went to her bag, and she fumbled as she tried to find her iron dagger before the memory of leaving it behind in Portland caught up with her. In her chest, her heart was beating faster even as she eyed the group; she could see ten of the little things. They were all dressed a little differently in what looked like old rags. One had what looked like an old knitted hat on that barely covered its pointed ears that jutted out awkwardly. These were the freaking fairies that she'd grown up hearing about, just more ragged.

"We're the only ones up here!" Nicki shouted. "Lance, Jenny, you'd better stay back. We'll take care of them!"

"Wait!" Bran said. "Try talking first."

He had a point, and Alex forced her magic to stay contained in her hand. She eyed one of the creatures and tried to keep calm even as the violet eyes narrowed on her. They shared that little trait with the Sídhe, and if Morgana and Merlin's stories were right, they shared a weakness to iron, but she wondered what else they shared.

"What do you want?" Nicki demanded. She stalked forward and took a position next to Alex and protectively in front of Bran.

"Mages stink of iron magic," the nearest creature hissed in a thin, scratchy voice. It sniffed loudly at the air. "Queen wants you dead." Its violet eyes flashed brightly.

For another moment, no one moved, and the creatures shifted as if they were in pain, but it passed as one of them leapt forward with a snarl. Tugging on her magic, Alex let her instincts take over. Lightning jumped from her fingers to strike the nearest creature in the chest, knocking it back against the tower. More of them were appearing, squeezing out of tiny holes around the tower's base that Alex would have sworn weren't there before.

Lance glared at the small creatures as a couple rushed towards him and Jenny. Standing protectively in front of her, Lance, in one graceful movement, dropped his backpack and stepped forward to kick the creature squarely in the chest. There was a dull thump sound blended with a crack just before the creature went flying through the air. It landed down the hill and released a sharp, pained scream as it rolled down the tor.

They were fast critters, Alex grumbled as one of them dove away from the dark silver blast of her magic. Ice washed over the grassy top of the tor catching three of the small creatures. They tugged at their feet as the layer of ice crept up their legs, and Alex couldn't help but smile, impressed. But as she was focusing on those, one of the little stinkers darted forward and slashed at her leg with long sharp claws. Alex danced out of the way only to stumble over another of the creatures behind her. Falling backward, Alex released a blast of magic around her just before her back collided with the cold ground.

Cringing, she rolled to the side and flinched as her ribs hit a rock. One of the tiny things lashed at her, and Alex felt a sting in her forehead as she twisted her hands and released a blast of magic right into its chest. It released an ugly cry and began to dissolve in a flood of grayish gold sparks, a much duller color than that of a dying Síd. She could feel a light stream of blood dripping down her forehead and started to adjust her body. Another creature was approaching her only to be flung across the ground in a small swirl of yellow sparks. Smirking, Alex rolled onto her knees and began to stand. A droplet of blood fell from her wound onto the ground as she planted her feet and stood up.

The world stilled. Everything around them seemed to stop: the wind calmed, and the distant sounds of the town below faded away. The tingling across Alex's skin intensified a hundredfold as a wave of magic crashed over her. It rose out of the ground around them and enveloped her, tugging at her magic. Blood ran down her face, and Alex tasted the bitter iron on her tongue.

Blood red waves of magic shimmered over the ground. A knot in Alex's chest eased, and the chill of winter faded away as power seeped into her bones. Looking around her, Alex could see the strange glow flowing over the tor from the spot where her blood had hit the soil. It illuminated the short dry blades of grass and began climbing over the tower and pouring into the strange holes made by the creatures.

The small creatures screamed, their bodies withering as the red magic rose up in small waves over their bodies. It rolled over them, and almost instantly, they began to fall apart into dust. Two of them reached towards each other, and Alex felt her stomach drop at the sight of the fear in their tiny violet eyes. Around her, the magic radiated outward across the glassy slope of the tor, and in only a few moments, all the creatures were gone in puffs of dull grayish gold dust. The glow began to fade, but the warm feeling didn't, and her connection to magic thrummed happily. The wind returned, blowing her blonde hair into her face. Letting out a shaky breath, Alex began to look around at her friends only to have Jenny wrap her arms around her in a tight hug.

"That was amazing," Jenny shouted. She was almost vibrating with excitement. "I mean, it was terrifying, but what you just did was incredible. Just like in the movies, Alex!" Jenny released her and reached for the small cut on her forehead. "Are you okay? Stupid question! You're bleeding."

"Easy, Jenny," Lance said as he came jogging over. "Head wounds bleed a lot." He put one of his hands on Jenny's shoulder. "Let me check her pupils."

Jenny stepped to the side, but her hands dropped and grabbed Alex's hand tightly. Alex twined their fingers gratefully and tried to hold off the exhausted shakes threatening to overwhelm her. Inside her chest, her connection to her magic felt strained, but all around her, she could feel it pulsing gently. Slowly it was seeping into the ground, receding, but still vibrantly there at the edge of her senses. She realized with a small start that she'd felt it earlier, only much weaker.

Lance hummed softly to himself and pulled out a tissue. Alex almost pulled away from him as he gently tilted her face and dabbed away the blood. She forced herself to still as Lance used the flashlight on his phone to check her eyes, but he nodded in satisfaction. Jenny pulled some more tissues from her purse and leaned up on her tiptoes to press them against Alex's forehead. Despite the closeness of Lance and Jenny and the little flutter of happiness that their attention brought her, Alex looked to the right for the others. Bran was standing by Nicki, watching the proceedings with a small knowing smile. Jenny licked her thumb and wiped some of the blood from her face.

"I think your blood caused a magical reaction." Bran came over and studied the trail of blood down her face.

"There was some kind of old magic in the ground," Alex explained. She glanced towards Nicki, who was glaring at the space where a few of the creatures had been. "I'm not sure where or rather when it was from, but that's what I was feeling earlier."

"You must have reactivated it," Bran suggested gently. "Maybe a previous Iron Soul laid the magic, and as magic declined, it lost power only for you to recharge it."

"Maybe," Alex said. There was an odd flutter in her chest at the idea. It was exciting and terrifying all at once. "Any idea what those things were?"

"Probably some creatures from the Sídhe branch: Morgana and Merlin did say that they enslaved a lot of races and that some of them escaped here," Bran said.

"Then why would they help the Queen?" Nicki asked in a tight voice. She stepped up to join them. Nicki pulled some more tissues out of her shoulder bag and passed them to Jenny. "It would make more sense for them to help us, so she doesn't enslave them again."

"I don't have any theories on that one," Bran admitted. "But we need to get down the tor and see about taking care of Alex."

"I'm okay," Alex said quickly. Jenny carefully pulled the tissues away. The wound had already stopped bleeding, and with a nervous flutter in her gut, Alex tried to push some magic towards the area. It warmed up a tiny bit, and Alex felt the pain ease slightly. "Really, we need to stay focused. If the Queen has alerted creatures to hunt us, then she knows that I'm alive and might have some idea of what we are looking for."

"Those things were fairies?" Jenny asked. She turned to look at Alex with wide eyes. "They looked more like goblins or something."

"Goblins share mythological roots with fairy stories," Bran explained. He looked out across the tor. "There's nothing visible up here," Bran sighed a moment later. "Come on. We need to look at Chalice Well."

"Do you think there'll be anything there?" Jenny asked as she stepped away from Alex and Lance to rush over to Bran as he started back down the tor.

"Not really to be honest, but the spring water is slightly red due to iron oxide in the water, and in Irish and Welsh mythology springs were seen as doorways to other worlds, so it might have become a hiding place."

"But you don't think so," Jenny clarified with a frown.

"No: my vision had the Chalice underground, but it seemed dry. There wasn't any water around it."

"Maybe a hidden cave up above the water."

"Chalice Well is just that, Jenny, a well," Bran explained patiently with a small smile. "And the others are springs. There aren't really any tunnels or caves connected to them." He shook his head. "Even with the local legends surrounding the tor, most stories point to Glastonbury Abbey as the site of the Chalice, and I don't think that's right."

"Any particular reason?" Lance asked as he fell into step with them.

"Morgana told us that the Iron Chalice was the creation of an Iron Soul in 682 B.C.E.," Bran replied. "That predates Christianity by a long time, so myths too strongly tied to Joseph of Arimathea or the establishment of the Abbey are from at least a thousand years later."

"Yikes," Jenny muttered. She nervously looked between the mages. "Then, we really are just searching for a needle in a haystack, aren't we?"

"Maybe yes, maybe no. It might not be in Glastonbury, but it's somewhere in Great Britain," he said firmly.

"But can we find it?" Nicki demanded with a dark expression. Taking a deep breath, Nicki shook her head and started walking again. "Come on. We've got to keep moving. You didn't have any visions up here."

"We should call Morgana tonight," Alex offered in a softer voice. "This magic that activated up here; maybe it had something to do with the Chalice and maybe not."

"Okay," Bran said. He looked between Nicki and Alex with a frown. "We'll check the old Abbey area, but if I don't have any visions and Morgana says that what happened here wasn't about the Chalice then we need to get back to Wales and try there. We've got things after us now, and it's only a matter of time before Arthur, and his mother figure out what we're doing over here; if they don't know already."

Alex nodded her agreement and swallowed down a rush of bile. She shoved the bloody tissues into the pocket of her coat with trembling fingers. As the others headed down the tor, she lingered for a moment, and with an angry huff, stamped her foot against the ground and released a long string of curse words. She felt a tiny bit better for about a minute.

6

The Smith

21 B.C.E. North Pembrokeshire Coast

Merlin inhaled the ragged scent of fires, food, and animals with a hint of nostalgia. That mixture of smells would seem the same everywhere to most, but he'd learned to pick out the distinct hints of the area over the years. Here he could catch the hint of the roots his mother had been fond of cooking in several houses. Smoke curled elegantly out of each of the twenty roundhouses that filled the small hill fort, and people were moving around rapidly to prepare for nightfall. Merlin eyed the wooden walls surrounding the village and nodded, pleased with the construction. They were buried deep in the ground, and he had a sense that they were much more solid than the walls of his childhood home.

Strange to think that in a time when the Sídhe could no longer ride, the villages were much stronger forts. Then again: attempts to fortify and protect themselves were not met with raiding parties, the sounds of screaming children and torches being thrown on anything that would burn. Around him, men were walking with iron axes strapped to their backs or belts, and women were carrying iron cooking vessels in addition to their clay pots. Houses looked much the same as ever, but there was a different sense of the community now.

It was a different time; he recognized as they walked inside. Those with weapons were not braced for a Sídhe attack; instead, it was the warring tribes that now covered the isles that were the cause of war. Merlin was uncertain how he felt about that: during his childhood, he'd heard of the wars in the far south, but such a thing had been distant from the world that he had known. Guards at the gate kept a close eye on the horizon and seemed to relax more and more as night approached, and darkness fell. It would have been the opposite when he was young; they had had reason to fear the night.

"We require shelter for the night," Merlin said calmly, with what he hoped was a disarming smile. He found it more difficult to play the old man without his staff to lean upon. "We've been traveling on the old road all day."

"Wait here." The man's eyes lingered on Morgana for a moment, but if she noticed, she said nothing. "I'll see if someone will take you in."

There was only silence from the other guards as one of them slipped into the village and vanished from sight. Around them, farmers came wandering into the village with their tools and small carts of produce, sending only curious looks their way. Merlin wondered how often they had visitors here. Ever since the rise of iron, there hadn't been as much need for trade, and the once important copper mines served little purpose now. Still, the looks of suspicion and curiosity were a touch annoying.

Thankfully the guard swiftly returned and gestured them down the well-beaten road with a few words about the man offering them shelter. Morgana thanked him calmly and pushed on Merlin's shoulder to get him moving. There was a lingering look from everyone in the village as they walked between the roundhouses and moved around those finishing their work for the night. Their suspicions made Merlin want to huff with irritation and give them all a stern lecture. A lifetime ago, he had been welcome wherever he went as a priest of the Iron Realm, but with the rising influence of Old Ones on the populations, the welcomes had become more and more awkward each year. He was still a great figure, a living legend to many, and an ancient man by all calculations of their time. His fingers itched and twitched by his side, already longing for the smooth and well-worn feel of his staff. One more part of his old world gone.

"Stop sighing," Morgana hissed, but her voice lacked any real bite. "Things will look better in the morning. We just need a good rest, and then we can start sorting things out."

"Optimism from you," Merlin teased. He was grateful for the distraction and familiar banter. "Will wonders never cease."

"We haven't used magic like that in a hundred years." Morgana sent a stern look his way. "We're both tired, Merlin, and in no condition for this discussion."

He couldn't argue with her point as he kept himself moving despite his knees strongly protesting. Merlin was relieved when they found a small balding man standing in front of his roundhouse waiting for them and wringing his hands nervously. Smiling at the man warmly, Merlin nodded deeply to him in greeting. Their host relaxed and smiled hesitantly at them both before stepping to the side and drawing back the animal skin covering his doorway.

The small roundhouse was warm with a fire burning away cheerfully in the hearth. A small shelf displayed only a few items, but there was a fine-looking iron axe clearly on display and shining in the firelight. One side of the roundhouse was well lived-in with a bed and plenty of possessions, but the other had an empty bed and two mats laying out for them. A dusty loom dominated the left side, and an unfinished basket made Merlin's smile turn sad. He said nothing of the man's loss and asked no questions; instead, he sat down next to the fire.

"Thank you for sheltering us," he said gratefully.

"You are welcome." Their host couldn't hide his nervousness but tried. "There is some stew in the pot," he told them with a gesture towards the fire.

They didn't say much as they each had a bowl of the stew. It was warm, the meat was tender, and the vegetables tasted fresh, and after days of much more simple rations, Merlin thought it tasted wonderful. In the corner of his eye, he could see that Morgana was enjoying it as well and smiled when she complimented their host, who beamed at the praise. The last of the nervous tension faded away, and Merlin hummed softly in contentment as he set aside his bowl.

Standing up, Merlin took a few steps away from the fire and felt his legs stretch out with a dull pain. He examined the items on display with mild interest, but his eyes were drawn almost magnetically to the axe. Merlin frowned as he picked up the axe and turned it carefully in his hand. A fine, slightly ornate iron axe head was fixed tightly to the wooden grip. It was far from the most impressive piece he had ever seen and looked as if it was actually used as a weapon rather than just being a showpiece. Yet, there was something about it that tickled at the back of his mind and the edges of his senses. With a glance towards their host, Merlin ran a finger over the metal curiously. Something sparked on the surface, and he leaned forward eagerly, earning a look from Morgana.

"Merlin?" she asked. "What is it?

"Morgana, look at this." Merlin cautiously ran his finger over the metal again. The iron seemed to shimmer with a soft light for a moment, and he felt a tug on his magic that made him look at her with excitement. "Try it." He quickly handed the axe to her.

Morgana frowned, but accepted the axe and carefully placed one index finger on the axe head. Her silver magic sparked briefly on the surface as her eyes widened comically. Merlin chuckled and rubbed his hands together in excitement.

"There is magic infused into the metal," he said in a low voice. "Magic in the iron itself, bound into the structure."

"So, there is a mage working iron." Morgana looked torn for a moment, and Merlin said nothing so she could collect herself. "Interesting."

"Interesting? That's all you can say? Magic is rising once more, and there is another mage."

"Yes, Merlin, this might be a good thing, but more magic means that there is a true threat, and that isn't something I wish to celebrate."

He didn't know how to respond to that as he watched Morgana trace a finger over the axe blade with a sad and distant expression. Instead, he nodded and gently took the axe from her hands, brushing his fingers against hers in a silent demonstration of understanding. The magic swirled beneath his fingers, drawn to the surface by his own power. It wasn't like Cathanáil, with every inch of the metal infused with magic. This carried only a few sparks, but it was there, deep within the metal like a faint pulse of life. Merlin doubted that the effort had even been intentional, a notion that filled him with giddy excitement.

"I don't suppose you know who made this axe?" Merlin asked conversationally. He turned back to their host with a slight smile. "Or which village it came from?"

"Oh, it's local, the smith lives in the village." Their host's nervousness was gone, now replaced by curiosity. "He's just at the edge of the village by the south gate. He's a nice lad, not the best smith in the world, but he does solid work, and he's young enough that he'll only get better."

"The person who made this lives here?" Morgana's green eyes flashed suspiciously, and she pulled the bag with Cathanáil closer. "You are certain?"

"Yes." Their host took a step back from her. "What do you want with him?"

"Only to speak with him," Merlin assured him quickly. "Hopefully, we will have the chance to."

"Well, he's probably still awake; he tends to work late. The banging keeps us all awake, but he does his best work at night."

Morgana shifted and moved towards the doorway before Merlin had even returned the axe to its proper place on the shelves. His hand grasped at the air for his staff, and an irritated grumble escaped him as he nodded to their host and followed Morgana out of the roundhouse with a quick promise to return before it was too late. The sun was setting, making the sky glow with brilliant oranges and darkening reds.

Merlin felt a hint of something in the air and wondered if this meeting would be for good or for woe. He was moving slower than he should have been, but a glance towards Morgana reassured him. She was moving slowly too, Cathanáil still held close in her arms. Protected and cherished, making Merlin wonder, for the first time in their long acquaintance, if Morgana might have made a good mother after all. He almost laughed at himself. He was trying to distract his own thoughts and keep the nervousness at bay.

It was a simple matter to find the right roundhouse. The small yard around the building was well stocked with stacks of wood and lumps of unprocessed iron ore. He paused for a moment to admire the slight reddish hint to the rocks in the light of the dying day, but Morgana coughed, and all he could manage was a sheepish smile. With excitement and nervousness churning in his gut, Merlin stepped towards the door, noting that the animal hide covering was pulled back and secured, allowing fresh air inside. Morgana pushed him forward, and Merlin almost stumbled over his own feet, wondering why he was so hesitant. Meeting another mage should be a grand moment, but all he could think about was how odd it would feel to train someone other than Arto. He wondered if this young man would be too old to properly learn magic; if he had any idea of what he was doing with the iron, or if the knowledge would spur him into taking foolish action.

Nonetheless, Merlin moved into the roundhouse and straightened his back. He stopped short just beyond the doorway to give his eyes a moment to adjust to the fiery light of the forge. The small furnace was radiating heat, and Merlin inhaled the hot air, letting it warm his entire body. There was a small bed, and a dresser set up next to it with a few items on display beyond the hearth like most roundhouses, but the layout was quite different otherwise. A furnace was set into the side of the roundhouse and filled the room with heat. A stack of wood stood at its side, ready to feed the glowing orange flames that surrounded the golden coals. He recognized the fire as almost hot enough to work iron with and marveled at the notion of someone working on such a thing at night. The smith's back was turned to them, and he hadn't noticed them yet as he laid out his tools next to his anvil. Even across the roundhouse in the terrible light, Merlin could see the thick muscles of the man's back from hours at the forge.

Merlin coughed and cleared his throat to draw the man's attention. "Excuse me; terribly sorry to disturb you, but my companion and I have some questions about your work."

"Bit late, isn't it?" a deep, but young sounding voice replied. They sounded more amused than irritated. "Be with you in a moment."

"Thank you." Merlin once again missed his staff as his fingers yearned to drum against something.

They didn't have to wait long as they watched the smith rearrange a few things and move some half-finished pieces to the side before he turned to face them. He was a young man with soft brown eyes that glinted almost red in the light of the forge and messy brown hair that had a natural curl to it. His skin was smudged with charcoal, and one long burn mark was visible on his left arm. He smiled at them in welcome even as his eyes darted between them in barely veiled confusion. Merlin stepped forward the rest of the way into the room and met the young man's eyes with a smile only for the world to fall away.

The sound of a hammer against iron rang all around him even as the smell of the salty sea air filled his nose and lungs. Merlin could see small hot flames licking at a long piece of metal that was glowing bright orange before him. An anvil hummed beside him with a hammer lying across its top. The hammer began to glow, and the sounds of the ringing of metal on metal intensified as small bronze-colored sparks exploded from the glowing hammer.

A loud gasp brought Merlin back to reality, but the sound had not come from him or Morgana, who was panting softly and clutching at his shoulder for support. Shaking his head, Merlin raised his eyes to look back at the young man. The smith had taken several steps back and was staring at them both with frightened-looking eyes. One hand moved to grab his hammer, which he held protectively at his side even as he swayed. Behind him, the fire crackled dangerously in his forge, and Merlin thought for a split second that he saw a flash of fiery orange magic along the boy's fingers.

"We mean you no harm," Merlin said. "You have magic, young man. The visions you just saw were the result of our meeting, but it will not happen again. We found you because you have been using magic in your work." Gesturing towards the stack of iron axe heads near the forge, Merlin offered the young man a smile. "Even if you don't realize it."

"Who are you?" The young man glanced between them as confusion and excitement warred in his eyes.

"I am Merlin, and this is my comrade Morgana."

"Uh, hello, then." He gave them a nervous little smile, but Merlin could see the tension in his shoulders. "I'm Gofiben."

"Gofiben," Merlin repeated with a smile. "It is very nice to meet you, my boy."

Video Conference

It was storming when they found their way back to the small hostel near Bristol's train station. The locals were rushing about with their umbrellas on the streets, completely content in the rain and the dark night sky.

"We'll go and get something," Lance offered. "Any requests?"

"Just something edible," Bran muttered. He adjusted himself on the bed and stretched out his leg with a pained hiss. "Shit, this was a long day."

"Yeah," Jenny agreed in an exhausted voice, but she straightened up and forced a smile. "Food will help, though; Lance and I will be back."

"The hostel has a kitchen," Lance pointed out to her with a small smile. "We could hit a grocery store and make something. Might be tastier than take-out."

"Good idea, we'll ask at the front desk," Jenny replied with one last look at the others. "We'll be back soon."

Alex nodded absentmindedly as she pulled out her tablet and set it up on the small table. Her fingers seemed to move a little slower as she entered the Wi-Fi password and brought up her email. There were a couple of messages from her parents that she didn't have the energy for, but after a moment of scrolling, she found what she was looking for.

"You've really got Morgana's skype information?" Bran asked curiously. "Seriously?"

"Better than paying for a long-distance call." Alex's voice wavered nervously. "She sent it to me last year just after school let out."

"You two have always been close." There was a soft expression on his face that Alex couldn't read. "Maybe that should have been a hint right there."

"I doubt she's gotten along with every lifetime," Alex said. That odd, sickly feeling that seemed to consume her every time the Iron Soul came up returned. "I doubt they've always been nice people."

Bran gave her a searching look but shrugged in perhaps some kind of agreement. He eased himself off the bed and reached down to grab his shaving kit. "I feel like a bloody mess if you'll excuse my British," Bran teased with a small smile. "I'm going to get cleaned up."

"Someone should keep an eye on the door, too," Nicki said. She was already standing up and rolled her shoulders, grimacing slightly. "So, none of the tourists walk in on you talking about magic and fairies."

Alex didn't say anything about how unlikely they were to have a roommate: just before Christmas wasn't a big tourism season, but she nodded anyway. She looked down at her tablet and quietly got herself set up as they both vanished out the door. With Bran gone to shower and Nicki outside the door, the barracks-style room with its four bunk beds suddenly felt very large. As she typed in Morgana's username, Alex could swear that the sound of her fingers on the screen echoed. As the call was trying to connect, Alex wasn't sure if she wanted Morgana to answer or not. It was either really early there or really late, thanks to the time difference. Then the call connected, and the webcam clicked on as Alex licked her lips nervously.

The video connection wasn't that good with Morgana's image flickering every few moments, but Alex couldn't help but feel a profound sense of relief washing through her at the sight of the older mage. It surprised her, really, but Alex pushed it aside to mull over later. A small smile tugged at her lips, and she noted that Morgana was smiling softly at her in return.

"Alex," Morgana greeted gently. "How are you doing?"

"Not so good," Alex admitted with a sigh as she dispensed with the pleasantries. "I don't know how long we'll have privacy here," she told Morgana quickly. "But first things first; how is Aiden?"

"No real change. Merlin is staying close by in case Arthur tries something. He is very cross about you leaving Ravenslake. He's very worried that something will happen to you without us nearby to keep you safe," Morgana said. Alex couldn't help but smile a little, recognizing that Morgana was worried too. "But to other matters, tell me everything, and I'll give you what assistance I can."

"Well..." Alex struggled to put her thoughts in order. Outside the door, she could hear some laughter and figured that the alcohol was already coming out in the main hostel. The small table she was sitting at suddenly felt tiny and confined. "We went to Glastonbury earlier today, but didn't find anything."

"Glastonbury? I told you to try Wales," Morgana said. There was a hint of reproach in her voice that made Alex feel like she'd gotten her hand caught in the cookie jar.

"I know, but we didn't know where to start, and there is a lot of grail mythology associated with King Arthur there! We were hoping that Bran would see something or that we'd learn something or get some ideas from the local sites."

"That's valid, I suppose, but Glastonbury's Arthurian links come from when I lived there." For a moment, there was a wistful expression on Morgana's face. "Local legends have a way of holding onto grains of truth."

"It was your home?" Alex repeated softly. "You and Arto's?"

"Mine, but it wasn't Arto's home. As the mythology suggests, Arto and I were born in modern-day Cornwall; it's actually why I use that as my current surname. I moved to Glastonbury after my marriage to Airril, and years later, Arto used a powerful spell on the area which lingered for a very long time."

"A blood spell, right?" Alex straightened up, ignoring the flutter in her stomach at hearing about Arto's life.

"Indeed." A suspicious expression took over Morgana's face. "But I believe you were telling me about what happened today."

"Yeah, okay. We went up to the tor, you know, to see if it triggered any visions for Bran, but I kept feeling something weird up there. Like something was poking at me or brushing against me. Then we were attacked by these little... I don't know, pixie creatures or Brownies or something."

"Pixie? Oh, yes, I think I know what you are talking about." Morgana frowned, making her lines stand out sharply. "But why would they attack you?"

"They said the Queen ordered them to attack mages."

"That doesn't make sense, though, Alex," Morgana argued with wide eyes. "The Sídhe and other creatures from their branch of the Tree of Reality aren't human and don't operate or think the exact same way as us, but I can't understand why they would help her. The creatures that live and hide in our world are descendants of escaped slaves. I remember the sight of them fleeing through the weak tunnels during the last battle when the Sídhe were throwing everything they had at us and took the guards off of them. Why would their descendants simply fall in line with the Queen?"

Alex didn't like the question and didn't have an answer. Morgana was frowning thoughtfully, her eyes slightly glazed over as she stared off into space. Then a moment later, she shook her head.

"Any ideas?" Alex asked, hopefully.

"Nothing comes to mind. It's obviously some kind of magic, but the exact nature is unknown to me. Perhaps some kind of Sídhe magic that I was never introduced to, that she didn't trust me with," Morgana suggested with a hint of bitterness. "It would be like Queen Scáthbás to have some secret weapons at her disposal before making a move against us."

"But she knows that I'm alive: she sent them after us!"

"Did they say mages or the Iron Soul?" Morgana asked.

"Uh, they said mages, and then that the Queen wanted us dead; they did say that we or maybe I stunk of iron. It really wasn't specific. We didn't have much of a chance to chat."

Morgana hummed thoughtfully but nodded her understanding. "It's possible that Queen Scáthbás made a standing order of some kind to kill all mages."

"But aren't we all the mages there are?"

"Perhaps, my instinct is to say that yes, the four of you and Merlin and myself are probably the only living mages in the world. You four were all born in the area that would be the epicenter of the rising levels of magic and were drawn to Ravenslake. That said, it is possible that there could be others, or that the Queen isn't aware of how unlikely it is that there are more mages and is just being sure, or even whatever magic she used only allowed for one broad order across the whole of the Iron Realm."

Alex nibbled at her bottom lip, unsure of what to say in response to that. The idea that there may be other mages was both exciting and worrying. Arthur was some kind of mage, and yet he'd been able to use his powers against her. They still didn't have a good answer for how the hell that was supposed to work. She trusted the others, but another mage would be a whole new set of questions.

"If there are other mages... would these things be able to find them? What about those other people who use magic through rituals?"

"Maybe," Morgana answered cautiously. "But if there are other mages, and that is a big if, then it is unlikely that they've been using their magic. Hopefully, the ritual users won't attract the attention of any of the Sídhe creatures." Morgana shook her head and cleared her throat. "But as to your search for the Iron Chalice, I've been trying to remember more about those days," Morgana informed her with a sad look. "Unfortunately, everything went south all at once, and Merlin and I were left trying to keep things from getting really bad. Your... previous life, Gofiben-"

"Gofiben?" Alex couldn't help but laugh, almost tripping over the name as she repeated it. Her own laughter sounded sharp and almost hysterical to her as she brought herself back under control. "Sorry, I'm really tired," Alex explained as she wiped at her eyes.

"Gofiben and that was a valid name at the time, Alexandra," Morgana said calmly. "His name actually changed over the years and became associated with the Celtic smith god of the region."

"Really?" Her eyes were wide, and Alex couldn't help the stupid grin that took over her face. Clearly, she needed to get some rest.

"Yes, you inspired a god myth in another life; it wasn't the only time. We'll talk about your life as Thor at some point when we have time."

"Thor? Seriously, as in the hammer and lightning Thor?"

"Alex…" Morgana shook her head, but there was a small indulgent smile on her face. "Yes, as in Thor, the Norse God of lightning, thunder, oak trees, war, and protection. Don't ask about the oak trees, but the hammer that you made and used in that life became famous. It was one of the most powerful magical items ever created; at the time, Merlin thought that it might actually rival Cathanáil."

"And Merlin is the basis of Odin? The old wise wanderer?"

"Don't be silly: Odin is one of the Old Ones as was Thor's wife Sif. Some deities are really Old Ones, some are inspired by mages, and some are outright made up, but let's focus on the Iron Chalice for now. As I was trying to tell you before, Gofiben lived near the Pembrokeshire Coast, so that area may yield something for you."

"Pembrokeshire Coast," Alex repeated dutifully as she opened a note on her tablet and typed that as best she could. "Anything else?"

"Not really; the area has changed, so I can't give you details, but Gofiben lived in a small village in the area, though he made the Iron Chalice further north. Going to that area may help you."

"Maybe Bran will have a vision," Alex said optimistically. "He had one in Cardiff; said it was like time got turned back, and he was seeing the area as it used to be."

"Really?" Morgana asked curiously, bringing a long finger up to tap thoughtfully at the corner of her mouth. "That's interesting," she said carefully, and Alex was instantly curious.

"What are you thinking?"

"I'm honestly not sure, but that is a very odd way to see things. Sometimes I've picked up flashes of the past with my mirror, but dreams of the future or symbolism are far more common."

"Well, maybe he didn't see the past and was instead seeing something else, someplace far away."

"That's possible, I suppose," Morgana agreed with a tilt of her head. "In any case, I know it isn't much to go on, but it may help. Around trying to help Aiden and keeping Merlin from dragging you back here, I'll see if I can find anything that may help."

"You're doing grail research?"

"Yes, and feeling rather foolish about it, to be frank," Morgana admitted with a dismissive wave of her hand. "I'm afraid that I'm not really sure what to look at. There are so many legends that could be connected with the Chalice, but even more that were probably the creation of monks in search of pilgrim traffic." She rubbed the right side of her head, and Alex smiled softly in sympathy. "I'm not sure how much help Merlin and I can be, Alex."

"Okay: we'll head back to Wales and keep trying," Alex promised with a forced smile. She wanted to sound confident and brave for Morgana but felt like she was falling a bit short. Nonetheless, Morgana nodded in agreement. "Besides, Lance has pointed out that maybe it is our assumptions based on what we think we know that is distracting us... or something like that."

There was an odd flurry of emotions over Morgana's face that made her look ill for a moment before she settled on a tired and tight smile. Alex almost sighed in irritation. Morgana's continued discomfort with Lance and Jenny was annoying at best, and at worst, made fear and doubt pool at the bottom of Alex's gut. She had to wonder if Morgana would ever be capable of forgiving the two of them for the crimes of their previous lives, or if there was something more that she was clinging too. But Alex wasn't brave enough to approach the subject today. She probably would never be.

The door creaked open as Alex tried to find something to say, and Nicki poked her head in. "Some people are on their way up here," she warned, and Alex nodded right before the door closed.

"Well…" Alex sighed, toying with a strand of her hair. "Anything else?"

"How is Nicki?"

"Distant," Alex muttered with downcast eyes. "She won't really talk to me right now. She could forgive her parents for abandoning her, but she's mad about Aiden."

"Give her time," Morgana said kindly. "I doubt she's really angry with you, Alex. You're just something she can project her frustration on. There is nothing worse than feeling helpless when someone you love is in danger."

Raising her eyes back to the screen, Alex's gray ones met Morgana's green gaze for a moment. A sense of falling overtook Alex as if the chair had been pulled out from under her, but thankfully it faded into other emotions. There was something like guilt, understanding, and a sense of shared pain suddenly clutching at her throat. Alex managed a cough and a weak nod. Something felt rubbed raw in her chest, and she could see the feeling reflected in Morgana's eyes.

The door banged open a moment later with two loud boys hauling bags over their shoulders coming into the room. One of them was tall with blonde hair and bright blue eyes. He grinned at her, and Alex tensed: he reminded her far too much of Arthur. She managed a shaky smile in return as they tossed their bags onto their bunks. Glancing towards the doorway, Alex saw Nicki watching them carefully. A soft sigh escaped Alex, and she looked back down at her screen. Forcing a smile, she waved at Morgana.

"Bye, Morgana, talk to you soon."

"Good luck." Morgana nodded and gave her a warm smile. "Take care of each other."

"We will," Alex promised as the video feed was cut, and she was left wondering if Morgana had even heard her.

8

Break a Few Eggs

Warm sunlight poured into the decently-sized kitchen through a small window, illuminating the pale-yellow walls and white cabinets. A slight chill was seeping inside around the pane of glass as the winter cold persisted outside. In the middle of the kitchen was a long white island with yellow trim to match the walls, and mismatched black and red stools. Lingering in the kitchen doorway, Nicki watched a few specs of dust float gently through the sunbeam. Everything was very still in the hostel. At the front desk was a sleeping man a bit older than her with his head pillowed on his arms.

The main sitting room behind her was a mess with odds and ends from guests scattered about, along with a few half-crushed water bottles that didn't smell like water. Last night there had been a rowdy crowd of boys who came in late, but this morning it was quiet. Nicki thought that she just might hate it as she shook her head and walked into the kitchen with a bag of groceries clutched in her right hand.

Nicki thought she heard someone moving around upstairs as she dried off a large skillet pan and dug out some matches for the stove. There was the sound of a shower being turned on, and Nicki sighed softly at the intrusion but kept working. She found a splash of oil in the cupboard by an opened box of white rice and half-a-box of crackers. Pulling the eggs out of her grocery bag, she delicately cracked four of them into the pan and began to wait.

Taking a deep breath, Nicki held it for a long moment as she watched the eggs beginning to cook. The pan's handle wobbled in her grip, but she was still grateful for the decently stocked kitchen and the small store down the block. The shower overhead turned off after a few minutes as she flipped the eggs. Digging around in another cupboard, Nicki found a few small paper packets of salt and pepper. There were a couple of colorful plastic plates stashed in a drawer by the sink, along with some flatware that had seen better days.

"Oh... morning," Alex greeted in a weak little voice that broke into Nicki's concentration.

Straightening up, Nicki turned towards the doorway only to falter when she saw Alex. The other girl was lingering in the doorway with uncertainty written all over her face. The dark bags that had dominated Alex's features for the last few days were still clearly visible. Her long, wet, blonde hair was in a tight braid over one shoulder, making Alex look more like a wet, little kitten that was afraid it was about to be kicked than some supernatural savior. Nicki felt like a bitch; the sort that she'd hated all through school who punished with little whispers behind your back and battled with cold silence.

"Morning," Nicki said, forcing herself to meet Alex's eyes. She couldn't quite manage a smile, but she knew Alex deserved better than she'd been getting. "Take a seat, I've got some eggs ready."

"I don't want to take your breakfast," Alex said quickly.

"It's fine," Nicki insisted. She grabbed a bright blue plate and one of the slightly bent forks and dished up a couple of the eggs. "I've got two dozen eggs, so there'll be plenty for everyone." She slid the plate over in front of an empty seat at the island. Tossing some of the salt and pepper packets up next to the plate, Nicki turned back to the stove and cracked a few more eggs into the pan. "How did you sleep?"

"Okay." Alex slid into the seat in front of the plate of eggs. "It was nice talking to Morgana," she admitted with a small smile in her eyes. "That seemed to help."

"Good, uh, did you have any luck with Pem... wherever she suggested that we go?"

"There isn't much there," Alex admitted with a small grimace. "I really hate it, but we are really relying on Bran's visions to guide us."

"Yeah...." Nicki flipped one of the fried eggs. Overhead she heard a shower turn on again, signaling that someone else in the hostel was awake and moving. "It's not like in films or books, is it?"

"Huh?"

"Well, you know, in the books and movies, the people who hid something left clues so that it could be found," Nicki explained as she waved the spatula around. "And the clues always survive even if it's been hundreds of years."

"This isn't a book or a movie," Alex pointed out with a strange, little smile and a shake of her head. "Though god knows it seems like it sometimes. But sadly, we haven't got any clues to follow, and even if there had been clues, they would have been long gone after two thousand years. Between wars, building, and people just living their lives, it would all be gone."

"I am the grass; I cover all," Nicki intoned as she turned back to the pan.

"I'm not sure that's the best quote for this conversation, but true," Alex agreed as she looked around the kitchen. "Is there any coffee?"

"There's a coffee maker over there." Nicki gestured towards the old brown, and black machine shoved back in a corner on the counter. She managed a small smile for Alex this time and pointed to the small plastic bag on the counter. "And I picked up some at the shop this morning. Figured if we're going to be doing this hostel thing, then we should stock up on some stuff."

"I bow to your superior wisdom," Alex replied seriously with a deep nod as she dug out the small package of coffee.

They both worked on their small tasks for a few minutes in silence. The smell of the simple black coffee made Nicki's nose curl, but Alex emerged from the large fridge a moment later with a victorious grin.

"Found some milk," Alex said as she opened the top and sniffed at it. "Still good too."

"Does it have a name on it?"

"Nope, better: it has a sticky note saying help yourself."

"I'm not so sure about this hostel thing," Nicki muttered with a shake of her head. "But I suppose we'll risk it."

"I doubt the fairies snuck in and poisoned it on the off chance that we'd drink it." Alex rolled her eyes, but Nicki saw her sniff at the milk again and swirl the small jug.

"I don't know; you remember all those stories about them making milk go bad," Nicki said with a small smirk. "But yeah, it's probably fine. The girl at the desk this morning did say that lots of people leave the perishable stuff here when they leave. Most of it gets eaten, and the rest they throw away."

"A weird solution, but I think I might just like it," Alex agreed.

Alex set the milk near the coffee and poured herself a small mug of the dark liquid. Nicki turned her attention back to the eggs in the pan as Alex returned to the island and began nibbling at her serving. Movement overhead made them both look up, and Nicki noticed Alex shifting her left hand very deliberately, so it was on the counter next to her. Around her fork, the fingers of her right hand twitched. For a moment, Nicki was torn between smiling at the fact that Alex was developing fighting instincts and regretting that she'd had to. Perhaps the biggest hint that Alex was the real Iron Soul was that it was Alex who had been in the biggest confrontations so far. While she'd been the last of them to develop her magic, it had been Alex who was taken into the Sídhe tunnels and fought her way out, and it had been Alex who had seemingly protected Arthur when Lance and Jenny's cheating came to light.

The footsteps overhead moved down the hall above them, and Nicki looked towards the main entrance and eyed the bottom of the stairs. It was the rhythm of the footfalls that made Nicki relax and smile. She could just hear the slightly metallic sound of Bran's brace that accompanied his steps and could make out the soft thump of his cane against the stairs. Alex seemed to have noticed the same thing and set down her fork so she could turn to look at the stairs. Grimacing as Bran came into view, Nicki took in his tired appearance and noted that he was leaning on his cane a bit more than usual. His wet hair hadn't been combed and, to her surprise, revealed that it had a natural curl.

"Morning," Alex called to him as she shifted uncertainly in her chair.

Bran gave them both a tired smile and waved them off as he moved to the kitchen island. Propping his cane up against the wooden side of the island, he leveraged himself into one of the chairs. Nicki stepped back after a moment and turned to check on the eggs quickly before looking back at Bran only to find him looking right at her.

"Do I smell coffee?" he asked her with wide green eyes, looking at her imploringly. He reminded her a little bit of a puppy, and it wouldn't have surprised her if he'd started whimpering. "Please tell me I smell coffee."

"Coming right up," Alex said kindly, jumping away from the counter and moving to retrieve another mug from the cabinets. "Nicki is making eggs," Alex added quickly as she pulled down another plate.

Nicki took the plate from Alex and began dishing up a couple of fried eggs for Bran as Alex poured a cup of coffee. Alex took the plate from her as she walked back to the island and handed both to Bran. A soft, happy sigh escaped him, and Nicki smiled as she dished up a couple of the cooked eggs for herself before cracking a few more into the pan along with another dash of oil. She turned back to the others with her plate in hand and cut a small bite of her own eggs. Bran's eyes darted between her and Alex as he quickly consumed one of his eggs before setting down his fork with a determined expression.

"I had a dream...," Bran confessed carefully before he took a long sip of his coffee. "It was underground again, and I saw the Chalice and the skull, but..." He shivered and looked down into his coffee. "The eyes started glowing, the skull's eyes I mean and then... I don't know; it was like I was being pushed back or something. I didn't really move or anything, but I felt and saw this tunnel shift around me."

"Well, that hints that it could be in a large cave somewhere," Alex offered with a forced smile. She was twisting her fingers together nervously. "There's that, at least."

"How does that help?" Bran rubbed his eyes, frustration obvious on his face.

"It means that we probably aren't looking at a mining network," Alex pointed out gently as she gripped her own cup of coffee. "Just one tunnel, so it's probably more isolated. That will hopefully make it easier to find."

Bran smiled a little at Alex's words, and Nicki conceded that she did have a point. It wasn't much to go on, but it at least ruled out a couple of things. At least it seemed to. For a few moments, everyone was silent, and Alex nudged Bran's shoulder slightly and nodded towards his eggs. Then there was only the sound of the three mages eating and the subtle hiss of the eggs cooking on the stove.

"I figured we'd find the Iron Chalice stashed under a church some-where," Nicki offered with a small chuckle. "In some kind of old carved out chamber with the remains of a saint or something. Guess we can rule that out."

"I'm not sure that an iron cup would have been what they were look-ing for," Alex pointed out with a hesitant smile in her direction. "Holy Grail mythology usually has a golden chalice with jewels or something. They probably would have scoffed at a hunk of iron as far too common."

"Indiana Jones didn't," Bran reminded her, glancing between Nicki and Alex with a small growing smile. "That was the trick at the end of the movie, remember? The right cup was the wooden one. The golden ones caused your body to turn to dust."

"I remember, but it was more like it caused the body to age and decay at a fast rate rather than it just turning to dust," Nicki pointed out as she turned back to the pan of eggs to flip them over quickly before looking back at Bran. "But they were also looking in the Middle East for the actual Holy Grail of Christian mythology, not the apparent Celtic chalice that inspired the later European myth."

"True, but take a moment and enjoy the fact that we're on a grail quest," Bran told her with a grin now firmly in place as he gestured with his coffee cup towards Alex. "With the actual King Arthur, or you know, close to."

"I don't think Arthur did well in that myth actually," Alex said with a grimace and a pained expression. "It was Galahad who found the

Grail only to vanish with it, and only one knight survived; I don't even remember which one it was."

"Well serves you right for not bringing Galahad with us," Nicki huffed with a raised eyebrow only to get an odd look from Bran.

"Galahad?"

"It's the name of... my stuffed puppy," Alex replied with a red blush creeping up her cheeks.

Bran didn't laugh, but a fond expression took over his face before it turned thoughtful. "I wonder if that is significant? You being drawn to the name Galahad I mean. I'm not really clear on if he might have a historical counterpart. The name sounds sort of Welsh, but I don't think he fits into the life of the original Arto."

"Me neither," Alex agreed with a shrug and an obvious look of discomfort that she was fighting her way through. "Merlin and Morgana don't share much. I only just found out the name of the Iron Soul incarnation who made the Chalice after all."

"It's probably hard to talk about the past when you've got so much of it," Bran suggested, still looking thoughtful for a moment. "But anyway, is the plan still to head for Wales today?" he asked, shaking his head a bit and picking his fork back up.

"Yeah, we'll go and get tickets back to Cardiff once Jenny and Lance make an appearance," Alex agreed with a nod, pushing her empty plate away. "Then we need to look at options to go west."

"Are there tunnels and caves there?" Bran asked with a raised eyebrow. "Of the sort we're looking for, I mean."

"I don't know; I didn't see anything about mining or caves when I was googling last night, but Pembrokeshire Coast is the area that Morgana suggested," Alex explained as she leaned against the counter. "It's a modern national park in Wales, but it covers something like 240 square miles and runs along the coast. I wish Morgana had been able to give us a more exact area."

"She probably doesn't know herself anymore," Nicki said. Picking up Alex's plate, she gestured towards the eggs questioningly. Alex shook her head, and Nicki tossed the plastic plate into the sink. "The landmarks are probably different, the village is long gone, and whatever roads or paths they used are long buried under layers of dirt. Say what you like about Glastonbury, but that tor does at least provide one hell of a landmark."

"So, it's all on divination," Bran muttered thoughtfully. "How about you, Alex? Anything yet? You had the dreams about the Sídhe tunnels before you were captured."

"Yeah," Alex replied with a barely visible shudder. Her fingers tightened harshly around her coffee mug, and she didn't look at Bran. "But I haven't had any dreams like that."

There was a pained note to the way Alex said those words that made Nicki inwardly flinch. Alex was probably having nightmares of her ex-boyfriend, stabbing her and leaving her to die. Probably having nightmares about Aiden dying or something god awful happening to Earth since it was apparently her role in life to protect the Iron Realm. Yeah, Nicki decided as she turned away from the other two mages and dished up the next batch of fried eggs, she was a bitch.

9

Light in the Forge

—⁂—

21 B.C.E. North Pembrokeshire Coast

Gofiben was staring at them with wide brown eyes that made the young man look much younger. The awe on his face had melted away, leaving worry lines and tiny wrinkles forming at the corners of his eyes. For a moment, Merlin couldn't help but think of another pair of wide brown eyes that had looked at him in shock and awe so long ago, when Merlin told him that he could use magic. Despite the horror that had followed that young man's life, and the guilt that Merlin occasionally felt for how Arto's story had ended, he had always cherished that first memory.

The rush of emotion left him frozen in place. Merlin couldn't speak as the words lodged painfully in his throat. Morgana looked at him with concern, which dissolved into a soft, knowing look. She rested her hand on his arm and turned her attention back to Gofiben. As the young man turned to look at her instead, Merlin felt his throat loosen, and he could breathe again.

"As Merlin was saying, Gofiben, magic appears most strongly when it is needed. There are always traces of it in the world, but strong, powerful magic is a tool of mages to protect this world."

"But doesn't that mean that magic is needed now, then?" Gofiben's eyes darted between Morgana and Merlin. "If I'm a mage, I mean, that's how it works, right?"

He was a clever lad, better than Merlin had expected. The look of worry on the young man's face helped pull Merlin back to the present, and he coughed to clear his throat. Nodding in response to Gofiben's question, he gently patted Morgana's hand in silent thanks for her support. Forcing a small smile, he tried to relax as Morgana pulled her hand away, and his fingers clenched at the air in search of his staff.

"I'm afraid that you bring up an excellent point," Merlin admitted to Gofiben with a proud little smile that quickly turned into a frown. "It could have to do with that Old One we encountered on our way here, I'm afraid. She seemed interested in us, and wasn't surprised that we were able to fight back against her."

"An Old One," Morgana repeated doubtfully. "But they've been in the Iron Realm for centuries. Cyrridven, for example, and she's an ally of the Iron Realm."

"Indeed, she is." Merlin glanced her way before looking back to Gofiben, eager to see how the young man would respond. "But she is far from the only one. Many have been exiled into our world over the years, and some are even worshiped." He didn't hide his distasteful frown, and noticed that Gofiben shifted uncomfortably. The young man looked nervous, and a shadow of disappointment covered his face for a moment, but he raised his eyes to watch them again. Merlin sighed at the idea of a mage having been one of those apparent worshippers, but that was the result of the boy's upbringing, he reminded himself sternly. "Perhaps there are too many of them in our world now, or perhaps... one of them has become a true danger."

"Badb," Morgana announced sharply with a dark expression and stormy, green eyes. "She was bold enough to challenge us for...." she trailed off with a tentative look towards Gofiben. "You may be right, Merlin, perhaps she has something planned."

"But what? And is she alone?" Merlin questioned. His fists clenched and unclenched as he tried to think. "And why now?"

"We don't know enough about the greater scheme of the worlds to be aware of other matters." Morgana gave him a pointed look. "Perhaps events elsewhere are the cause of our troubles. We still suffer infestations of former Sídhe slaves thanks to their previous wars of conquest: it is not impossible that something similar is happening in another branch."

"Perhaps," Merlin agreed. Looking back to the boy, Merlin felt a twinge of guilt at Gofiben's obvious confusion. "Forgive us, please; two old mages trying to sort out things too quickly." He gestured towards the furnace with a fond look. "You had some work you wanted to do, please don't let us distract you."

"Well, the thing is.... What I mean to say," Gofiben started to explain nervously, tripping over his words. "There is something that I need to tell you, though I'm not sure how to start-"

The door flap behind them opened, bringing in a cool rush of night air that made Merlin and Morgana both spin around sharply. Behind them in the doorway was a young man about Gofiben's age who looked startled to see them there. Gofiben moved quickly around him and Morgana to stand at the young man's side, almost protectively.

"This is my friend Bran," Gofiben introduced with a hint of nervousness. His eyes moved between his friend and the mages before him. "He works with me here in the forge whenever he's not in the fields. Another set of hands is useful."

"I see," Merlin greeted. He forced himself to smile as he turned his attention fully to the newcomer.

Gofiben's reaction was a bit distressing, and Merlin wondered what it was that he was so concerned about. Bran was a strong-looking young man, though he was not as broad and strong looking as Gofiben. His build was slighter, and he stood a few inches shorter than his friend, with messy, long dark-brown hair only half contained in a braid, brown eyes bright with curiosity at their presence in the forge, and a scruffy little beard. Merlin glanced at him and nodded with a small smile before raising his gaze to meet Bran's eyes.

Wind howled along the coastline, bringing the smell of the sea straight to him. In the distance, he could hear the low rumble of thunder and taste the scent of the coming rain on the air. The soft cries of the animals made him smile as he turned to see a dog rushing about to herd the stray sheep. Thunder rolled once again, and he had a strange sense of foreboding.

Merlin shook his head as the vision cleared, and coughed as the smell of the smoke from the forge assaulted his nose. For a moment, he had trouble remembering just where he was, but the metallic taste in the air helped him gather his senses. A large hand was holding his arm, and Merlin turned to find Gofiben next to him with a sheepish smile on his face. The young man's eyes were soft and gentle as he guided Merlin back to the bed and let the old mage sink down onto it. He looked over at Bran and found the boy staring at Morgana, no doubt experiencing yet another Connection judging from how wide his eyes were.

"Sorry about that," Gofiben said. He stepped back from Merlin and looked towards Morgana. "I was about to tell you about him. Wanted to warn you that you might have a.... Connection you called it, with Bran."

"No harm done," Merlin assured the young smith before looking back at Bran. "Though I am surprised."

His heart was pounding in his chest almost painfully, and for a moment, he felt as if he'd been tossed out of a boat and left to paddle for his life. Merlin knew he needed to say something more, reassure the newcomer, and explain what was happening to him, but he was at a loss of where to begin. Two mages in one village: the thought both excited and worried him.

The young man, Bran, looked nervous, and his eyes were darting between them both with a look that was an uncomfortable blend of curiosity, confusion, and terror. Merlin could sympathize, it was one thing to experience a Connection with a trusted friend who was as confused as you were, but another thing entirely to walk into a room and experience two in rapid succession. Thankfully his fellow mage straightened her back and moved away from the door to give the young mage more space. She glanced his way with an odd expression on her face, a blend of excitement and resignation.

"Two mages," Morgana said as she slowly walked over to him. "Two in the same little village." She put a hand on his shoulder, but her fingers tightened almost painfully into his flesh. "This isn't just chance."

"Indeed." Merlin turned his attention to Gofiben. "You said you should have warned us; you two have experienced a Connection before then?"

"It was a few weeks ago," Bran said, speaking up from his place near the doorway. "We've known each other for years, but I went with my father on a trip to the north with some of the livestock. When I came back and saw Gofiben again, I had a vision."

"We didn't think much of it at the time," Gofiben explained quickly as if he feared they were in trouble. "Thought maybe I'd been in the forge too long, or we'd eaten something that disagreed with us. I mean... there wasn't anyone we could ask about it, and we didn't want to worry anyone. And nothing else happened, so we just sort of decided to forget about it."

"A Connection occurs as magic grows in the realm," Morgana explained. Her tone was softer than before, and she finally released his shoulder. "It is not a small thing; it doesn't just happen. I've only experienced it a few times myself, but it occurs when mages meet."

"Does it always happen?" Bran asked.

"In my experience," Morgana said. She moved away from him and towards the young men. "It is the magic of the two mages reacting to each other."

Bran looked towards Gofiben and met his friend's eyes. Merlin almost smiled as he watched some kind of silent conversation take place between the two of them. Gofiben had regained much of his color, though Bran still looked a bit pale. Shifting on the bed, Merlin considered standing up but decided that he probably appeared less threatening where he was. Morgana was still tense despite her attempt to appear friendly. Bran glanced her way once again and toyed with his hands.

"So why are we like this?" Bran asked, looking to Gofiben.

"You were just born with the potential," Morgana explained to him. "I suspect that there are a few in every generation with the potential, but magic comes only when it is needed."

"So, what are we supposed to do with it?"

"They said that we're mages because there is a threat to the world," Gofiben told his friend, reaching over and resting one of his large calloused hands on his friend's shoulder. Then he looked over at Morgana. "I'm sorry, but maybe you should start from the beginning for Bran. I should have told you about him earlier, but I was just so shocked myself."

Merlin watched Morgana bite back a sigh, but she nodded and explained everything to Bran. Gofiben remained next to his friend, offering his support, though Merlin saw his eyes glance towards the forge every so often. A smile tugged at his own lips as he considered the behavior. It struck him as odd that a young man who just learned he had magical powers would only want to return to his forge, but then again, hadn't he done the same? He'd run from Cyrridven when she'd told him of his heritage as the son of a Sídhe. He'd returned home and stubbornly polished his first bronze sword to give it a sharp edge despite anything his mother said.

"Wow." Bran stared at them with a stunned expression. "Just... wow."

"And now you know what's going on, or at least what we know for the time being," Morgana told Bran, and Merlin realized that she had finished her explanation.

"So, you think that something is going to happen? Do you know what?" Bran questioned.

"No, we've only become aware that there is even a potential problem today," Morgana replied, tightening her fingers into a fist.

"But what about-"

"Please," Merlin interrupted. "We won't find answers to what is happening so easily tonight." He gestured towards the forge with a small, fond smile, remembering the times he and Arto had worked iron together. "You had work to do, please don't let us keep you."

"Are you sure?" Gofiben asked in an almost timid voice. Merlin smiled at the young man and nodded. "Alright, then." Gofiben glanced towards Bran.

"If you don't mind, we would like to remain and watch for a little while," Morgana added in a gentle tone, mindful of startling the gentle young man.

"That's fine," Gofiben assured them. "Do you know much about smithing?"

"I understand the theory," Morgana informed him with a calm nod as she moved away from the two young men and back towards the bed.

Merlin couldn't help but chuckle as he nodded. "Yes," he answered wistfully. "I know a great deal about smithing. Please don't let us keep you any longer."

"Uh, alright..." Gofiben managed to say, still shifting nervously in place. "If you need anything-"

"We won't linger too long," Morgana promised. "As we told you, Gofiben, you seem to be already using your magic when you smith. Watching you and Bran's work will help us determine a starting point for teaching you."

"Then you're really going to teach us?" Bran stared at Morgana.

Merlin chuckled; the boy seemed to have recovered from his shock and fear. Morgana glanced back at him with a warning look, but he could see a spark of something in her green eyes and sat up a little straighter.

"Yes," Merlin answered with a wide smile. "We are going to teach you."

Bran nodded with a small smile starting to form on his face. Morgana walked over to the bed and sat down next to him without a word. Gofiben called Bran's name, and the two jumped into action. Bran put more fuel into the furnace and used the bellows to fan the low coals that had begun to cool since they came in. Gofiben selected a long rough piece of iron from a pile near the wall and thrust it into the fire. Bran pushed open the door flap and tied it open, letting a cool evening breeze into the roundhouse. Merlin became aware of the late hour with a look out at the darkness, but couldn't bring himself to move away.

Heat rolled across the roundhouse from the fiery furnace as smoke billowed up through the thatched roof. The flames and the moving bodies of the two young men cast strange and marvelous shadows on the far side of the small space. They didn't speak much to each other as they worked. Gofiben dominated the space with his broad shoulders and the swing of his arm as he brought the hammer down against the long strip of iron he was crafting into a sword.

Bran moved around his friend with graceful ease. He retrieved wood and fed the furnace each time that Gofiben took the metal from it, and kept the heat high with the use of the leather billows. Merlin couldn't help but smile as he watched the two work so smoothly. Gofiben may have been the smith at work, but he could see how Bran's steady presence helped him move so quickly.

Merlin watched Gofiben's hand very closely as he gripped his hammer. In the orange light spilling from the forge, he almost missed it, but when Gofiben's hand passed through his own shadow, Merlin could just see the faint outline of magic around his hammer. The soft bronze sparks around his fingers that were only visible in the shadow as they jumped from his hand and sank into the metal of his iron hammer made Merlin smile.

Glancing over at Morgana, Merlin saw her own eyes fixed on Gofiben's hammer and smiled to himself. She had noted the glow of magic as well. It was impressive that the young man was using magic without even realizing it. His connection to his magic was very strong, though teaching him to control it could be something of a challenge. Merlin shifted his gaze to Bran as the young man moved around his friend without hesitation. His every action and move supported Gofiben's. Merlin smiled wistfully once more as a soft sigh escaped him. Teaching these two was now a priority, along with finding out why magic was growing. Gofiben had been enough of a surprise, but Bran's own magic made it clear that something was changing in the world.

"It would seem that we have a purpose once more," Morgana said in a low voice that made Merlin's heart skip a beat. Her words were tired, but he could hear a slight undertone of hope in them. "Even if it is to be another war."

"So, it would seem," Merlin heard himself agree.

Morgana sank further back on the small bed, her shoulder brushing his own. They said nothing more, and Merlin lost all sense of time as he watched Gofiben and Bran work on the sword. His bones ached, but as he sat in the warmth of the forge listening to the familiar song of hammer against metal, Merlin felt something easing in his chest. It became a little easier to breathe, and even the lingering worries about the challenges the next days would bring were not enough to discourage him. Shifting his hand, he found Morgana's curled into the blankets next to his own. Without a word he slid his hand over hers and squeezed gently, saying nothing when she turned her palm and took his hand in return.

10

Scuffle in Cardiff

They were back in Cardiff with only a tiny bit more information and with fairies after them. Aiden was still lying in a coma and slowly dying in front of his parents, who'd almost lost his little sister Aisling to cancer years before. There was a painful ache at the bottom of Alex's spine that she couldn't shake, and the sick feeling in her stomach had settled in for the long haul. The entire situation made her feel helpless and lost. Even when she'd been leading those children out of the Sídhe tunnels, she hadn't felt helpless. There'd been a clear enemy to fight: she'd known who to stab and what to do. There was no such clarity here.

Cold air rushed over Alex's exposed face as she stepped out into the freezing Cardiff air from the warm grocery store. The light of the sign illuminated the dim street, and Alex glanced around at the few other shoppers still out and about. She couldn't help but shiver despite her winter coat. The combination of December chill, low elevation, and the ocean breeze meant that the cold was seeping into her bones. Behind her, Alex heard Jenny make a soft, distressed noise as the others joined her. Nicki breezed past them and walked to the edge of the sidewalk with a bag of food in hand. A moment later, Bran stepped up next to Alex with Lance right behind him carrying another bag.

"I think we're good for at least tonight and breakfast," Bran said as they began to walk up the street towards their hostel.

The Cardiff streets in this area were of a good size and pretty clean. New metal and glass buildings were right up against older and, in Alex's opinion, more attractive brick buildings. Shops, some large and some small, filled the bottom floors along their route to their home for the night. There were several obvious office buildings, and a few that Alex thought might have flats above the shops. It was a city that blended old and new, but Alex was in no mood to enjoy being there.

"Thanks for paying again, Jenny," Bran said, breaking the silence. "When we get back, we'll see about trying to get Morgana or Merlin to reimburse you."

"I'm not sure they like me that much." Jenny's voice didn't hide her nervousness. "But seriously, don't worry about it. If Daddy decides that he's really angry about this, then I'll suggest cutting off my allowance until things are paid back."

"You'd have to give up shopping," Alex said. She looked back at Jenny only to have the shorter woman meet her eyes straight on.

"I can live with that: this is more important."

Bran chuckled and looked down at his free hand, where he was still holding a few coins, one of which had a slightly rounded octagon shape. "The pound isn't so bad," Bran remarked casually. He slid the coins into his pocket. "I always thought that English money was weirder than that."

"It used to be," Nicki said from where she was leading the group lazily towards the hostel. "Sort of like the money in Harry Potter, but they went to a metric system like ours sometime in the 70s."

"What, no year?" Bran asked with a teasing smile. "No exact date?"

"I have no bloody idea," Nicki replied in a rather bad British accent, finally cracking a bit of a smile. "Years are difficult to keep track of, and I'm not British, so I don't care that much."

"Still, it's almost scary the amount of random stuff that's in your head." Alex smiled and sped up, so she was walking alongside Nicki.

"Are all your conversations like this?" Jenny asked. The question earned a muffled chuckle from Nicki and an outright laugh from Alex.

"Pretty much, yeah," Alex agreed. "You can't keep it too heavy all the time. We'd probably be crazy by now if we didn't allow ourselves some levity."

Alex grimaced at her own words as the pain in her back flashed rather brilliantly along with an answering pain in her head. She forced herself to keep smiling. Her pace slowed, allowing Nicki to move ahead of her once again. A moment later, Jenny darted up next to her and reached over with her hand to brush over Alex's own gloved hand. The touch was simple and muted thanks to their gloves, but to her surprise, Alex could feel the knot at the back of her spine ease a tiny bit. She smiled at Jenny and was rewarded with a warm look in return. Jenny gently knocked her shoulder against Alex's upper arm, and a soft laugh escaped her.

Looking over her shoulder, Alex caught Lance watching them with a fond smile as he walked at a slower pace to match Bran. Alex studied Lance for a moment, waiting to see if he'd react further. He didn't seem distressed by the action, despite Jenny and her apparently having been married several times in previous lives; instead, he seemed happy. A soft sigh of relief escaped her, both for Lance understanding that she needed her friend, and that she was a straight woman who had dodged the Guinevere and Lancelot bullet.

Whatever moment of calm she almost had ended abruptly when Alex felt an odd turn in her stomach. There was a sudden but brief smell of something rotting before she heard a strange giggling sound in the distance. She glanced at Bran and saw him shaking his head and looking a bit distressed. Nicki had stopped in front of them and was looking around with wide eyes. The giggling sound was getting louder, and the Cardiff natives were looking around in surprise, confusion, and some in fear. Many were moving into stores or speeding up their pace as if driven away by some distant memory of the danger.

"Into the alley," Alex ordered the others as she gestured into the dark side street to the right. "Come on!"

Nicki reacted last, turning and staring at Alex for a moment with an unreadable face, but then Nicki lowered her eyes and walked past Alex into the alley. The creepy little giggles were getting louder, and in the distance, Alex could hear sirens. That wouldn't do much good, and she had the urge to shout 'its fairies, evil little nasty fairies you bloody idiots' at them. Instead, she joined the others in the alley and looked around. The brick walls of the three-story buildings made her feel closed in, with the gray sky overhead offering no sense of freedom. She forced herself to focus and glanced around for any cameras in the alley. Thankfully there didn't seem to be any.

"Is it more fairies?" Jenny asked. Alex noted that Jenny wasn't trembling even as she looked around with worry.

"Do you think we can make it back to the hostel?" Lance moved closer to Jenny, his usual casual and relaxed stance shifting to alert and protective.

"I don't think we should lead them back to civilians." Bran looked around the alley with a frown, flexing his fingers in preparation. "They're after us."

"Lance, you and Jenny head back to the hostel. Hopefully, they'll only attack us," Alex ordered. Her eyes jumped to the alley entrance, bracing herself for whatever was coming.

"But-" Lance cut himself off and swallowed, glancing between Jenny and the three mages. "You sure?"

"Yes, now go!"

Lance grabbed Jenny's hand and tugged her towards the alley entrance. They only made it a few steps before a small creature dropped down in front of them. It laughed and reached out to scrape its claws on the old bricks of the alley wall. Lance cursed and pushed Jenny back as they retreated into the alley. The sound of more eerie giggling over their heads made Alex look up in alarm.

Small creatures crept into view off of the roof, moving down the brick walls like large spiders. Alex caught sight of small violet eyes underneath the piles of dirty rags that covered their small bodies. Her hands shook, and her heart beat harder and faster in her chest at the sight of those eyes. She distantly heard someone calling out to her, but it was the movement of the creature that helped Alex look away from those eyes. One of the creatures crashed down on top of a trashcan with a low hissing sound. White sharp teeth stained with red were flashed at them just before a swirl of yellow magic smashed through the air and knocked the creature against the bricks. Its small clawed hands slashed helplessly at the air as it was pinned.

Raising her hands, Alex inhaled deeply and closed her eyes. It was getting easier and easier to find the small warm spark below her lungs. Energy and adrenaline surged through her veins as the small spark burst to life, pulling on the soft flow of magic around them. Opening her eyes, Alex called the magic through her arms. Dark silvery sparks, the color of wrought iron, danced off her fingertips, and formed an orb in her right hand. Alex swung her arm forward and released the orb through the air. It collided with the pinned creature held by Bran's magic, and Alex watched with a hint of satisfaction as the creature dissolved with a low crying sound. The soft giggles from above turned into hisses, and more of the creatures dropped down into the alley.

These were smaller than the things that had attacked them in Glastonbury with gray wrinkled skin and smaller ears. As they spread out and moved into the better-lit parts of the alley, Alex could see more clearly that their little ragged hats were dark-red, and her stomach turned as a vague recollection of something from her book of fairies poked at her memory. One of them snarled and lunged at her. Alex dove to the side and looked over her shoulder to see the creature catching itself on the wall. It looked back towards her with flashing violet eyes and grinned at her, showing its red-stained teeth once more.

A spear of ice glowing a soft blue color shot past her, impaling the creature in the leg against the brick wall. Alex stayed still and began to form another orb of magic in her hand as another spear of ice blasted through the air, leaving a wave of cold air in its wake. Alex saw the creature dissolving into dull gold dust in the corner of her eye as she turned to find more creatures moving in on them. Bran had his back up against one of the walls and was throwing creatures away from him in waves of yellow sparks, but Alex could see that he was already panting.

Blue magic swirled around Nicki's hand and illuminated her angry features in a terrifying manner. Nicki waved her hand through the air in front of her sending blue sparks flying all around the creatures. They began to move towards her only for the wave of magic to solidify into spikes of ice that swept up to crush them. Three more came towards Alex, and she tightened her grip around the orb, pulling the magic back into her fingers. They jumped towards her, and Alex opened her hands and released the pent-up magic. It lashed through the air as small dark lightning bolts and struck the small fairy creatures with a hiss.

Alex lost track of how many there were as her gray magic swirled in the air alongside Nicki's blue sparks and Bran's yellow waves. Bran's telekinetic use of magic wasn't great for killing them, but Alex noted gratefully that he was keeping them away from Jenny and Lance. Nicki's ice shards hurtled through the air, sometimes striking the creatures fatally, sometimes injuring them and sometimes leaving dents in the trash bins. It was a rush of adrenaline: a release of anger as the fear dissipated, leaving a sense of certainty of victory that Alex tried to banish as soon as it began to emerge.

Alex could almost feel the hum of the light mounted over one of the heavy metal doors on the back of her neck. It was like an itch as the energy ran over her skin. Her fingers were beginning to ache as another blast of magic was released through them. There were fewer creatures now, and no more seemed to be coming. Around them were piles of little rags, and Alex kicked a few out of her way as she spun and blasted one of the creatures trying to sneak up on Nicki. Vaguely she wondered if the cloth remained since it came from this world, unlike the Sídhe's armor, but the sight of one last creature climbing along the wall towards Jenny and Lance made everything else vanish.

Claws slashed towards Jenny, gleaming in the low light of the lamp. In the corner of her eye, Alex saw Bran push his hand out towards the small creature. The claws snapped through the air even as the creature was tossed back, but they sliced into the sleeve of a letterman jacket. Yellow magic flared, and the small creature smacked against the side of the alley while Lance groaned in pain. Anger hit Alex in the chest as she saw red blood seeping out of Lance's wound before he slapped a hand over it. Alex thrust her arm out towards the creature and felt her magic rush forth into her fingertips. Lightning jolted off her fingers and struck the creature in a blast of flickering light and energy. It didn't even make a sound as it dissolved.

Bran was close enough that he reached Lance in two quick strides. The torn sleeve of Lance's letterman was already turning red, and Jenny was gripping Lance's other arm with a horrified expression. Alex stared at them both for a moment, painfully aware of her shaking limbs and the sudden difficulty she was having breathing. She was uncertain if it was from the combat or from the shock of fearing Jenny was going to die.

"The leather sleeve protected you some." Bran examined the injury. "Could have been worse."

"Good," Lance huffed around clenched teeth.

Lance bit back a groan and shifted his arm carefully to examine his wound. Alex grimaced at the sight of the sliced flesh just visible around the oozing blood. Forcing herself to move forward, Alex looked at Jenny, who was shrugging out of her coat. In one quick motion, Jenny pulled off her black outer shirt and tied it around the wound. Blood splashed onto her blue camisole, but she didn't lose focus until the shirt was secure.

Alex stepped forward and touched Jenny's arm gently. Her friend nodded and took her hand off the rough bandage long enough to pull her coat on. A hand on her shoulder tugged her back, and Jenny stepped right up next to Lance again, once more in her coat. There was a look of intense concentration on Jenny's face, and her hands were shaking the tiniest bit.

Looking up at Lance, Alex braced herself for a pained or maybe angry expression. Instead, he was watching Jenny with a slightly slack jaw and dazed eyes. Soft worried noises were escaping from Jenny while Lance almost smiled and looked ready to melt. Alex froze as she looked at the pair of them. For the moment, in light of his injury, Jenny seemed to have abandoned all her embarrassment and residual guilt, and Lance was soaking it up like a puppy in a sunbeam.

"This is deep; we need to deal with this." Jenny looked right at her with stern eyes and a determined, tight jaw. "There has to be a hospital in a city this size."

"There'll be questions about how he got injured," Bran said.

"Bran's right," Alex agreed.

Holding back a grimace, Alex turned to face Nicki, who was standing off to the side near the alley entrance watching them. Her expression was blank, and she looked like someone merely watching something on television or studying a painting. The distance in her eyes and the far-off expression made Alex uneasy. Then Nicki's eyes turned to her, and she could see a flash of realization in them.

"Nicki, we need you to heal him," Alex said as calmly as she could manage.

"He's not a mage!" Nicki protested sharply. Nicki's face went from strangely blank to a blend of different emotions. "It might not even work on him. I've only ever healed Alex and some minor shit, nothing major. That's Morgana's field."

"Nicki, he may not have any magic," Bran cut in smoothly, "But that will probably make it easier since he doesn't have any magic to fight against you with."

"It will drain me: healing is exhausting, and I'm already a bit tired." Nicki started to pant.

She was faking being exhausted when two seconds ago she'd been fine. The knowledge rattled Alex, and she clenched her fists. She didn't like the hot feeling churning in her stomach; it felt too similar to how she'd felt when she first found Lance and Jenny together; it felt like when she'd realized just what the Sídhe used children for and how she felt whenever she thought about Arthur. Stalking forward before she'd even fully processed how angry she was, Alex stopped in front of Nicki and stood up straight to use her extra four inches to look down at the other girl. Nicki's eyes flickered with regret and guilt, but then the stubbornness was back. Something inside Alex nagged at her that this wasn't the right way to go about this, but she couldn't stop herself.

"Look, Nicki," Alex said in a low voice that carried an edge to it. "I know you're angry at me right now, and I'm not going to argue about that." Alex's heart was beating almost painfully in her chest now, and her lungs felt constricted. "I'm sorry for my mistakes about Arthur, and I'm sorry that Aiden is the one who had to pay for it." Nicki's face was paler than usual, and the ice in her blue eyes was fading. "But right now, I need to know if you are willing to heal Lance or not. If you aren't, then we need to get him to a hospital and figure out a story to tell the cops. That wound is deep, and if we don't there will be permanent damage."

"I'll take care of it," Nicki promised, raising her chin and glaring at Alex. "But not here, we're too exposed. The hostel should be empty right now."

"Okay," Alex agreed with a nod, forcing her shaky legs to take a step back before she looked back at Lance. "Just a few blocks, Lance," she promised before returning to Jenny and him.

They gathered up the grocery bags quickly and in silence. Alex picked up the bag that Lance had been carrying. She looked back at Nicki, who was standing just outside the alley waiting for them. Her body was tense, and her eyes were fixed on something up the street to avoid looking at any of them. As they stepped back out into the street, Alex noted that there didn't seem to be many people around, though she caught sight of a police car parked on the next street. Sighing softly in relief that they hadn't been seen, she forced her cold legs to keep moving, barely noticing that she was moving so slowly that Bran was keeping up with her easily.

"Human blood didn't seem to affect them," Bran observed in a low voice. They turned a corner back onto their hostel street, and everyone sped up a bit more. "That's not good."

"Their weakness to iron might not be as strong." Alex grimaced at the tremor in her voice. "Their hats were red."

"Like red caps," Bran agreed in a softer voice. "Maybe like the legends… maybe interacting with blood over the centuries has let them build up some resistance. These would probably be descendants of the escaped slaves."

"Great," Alex grumbled darkly. "Let's hope that they're the only ones who figured out that trick; otherwise, we're in trouble."

"First things first: find the Chalice and save Aiden," Bran said. "Then we can work on finding out why they are taking orders from the Queen."

"Yeah," Alex agreed in a soft, tired voice. "That's not the only mystery we have to solve, though."

"What else is on our plates?"

"We still don't know what Arthur really is." Exhaling, Alex watched the mist of her breath twist in the air for a moment. "After all, he managed to have a Connection with me, but not with you lot. But he has magical powers. How was Med- Mordred brought back by the queen, and how does he have powers if he isn't loyal to the Iron Realm?"

"Maybe there are some other powerful objects like the Sword and Chalice."

"Maybe?" Alex repeated with a bitter laugh. "Oh, Bran, I think we can count on it."

11

Hostel Healing

Their hostel was a three-story brick building that Nicki had considered rather charming when they'd checked in earlier that day. It was on the street corner and only a short walk from the train station and the grocery store for their supply run. The dark brick was accented with off white corner bricks and frames around the windows. White Christmas lights surrounded the main lobby window, and the bright colors on the sign had made it seem very welcoming when they came in off the train.

Now, as she walked towards it, Nicki was fully aware of her heart beating too quickly in her chest. Jenny and Alex were huddled around Lance, keeping pressure on his wound and hiding it. Nicki knew that drawing attention to themselves would only cause trouble in one form or another, whether cops or more fairies followed them into a medical facility. The whole situation made Nicki's blood boil. Her anger itched beneath her skin like something she could claw at. She had vague memories of being angry like this when she realized that her parents weren't coming back for her. She remembered how outraged she'd been when Gran had made her start going to school. Over the years, that anger had gradually burned itself out as life saw fit to remind her that she had nothing to complain about in the grand scheme of things. Even when her parents had swanned back into her life and acted as if they belonged there, somehow, she hadn't been this angry.

Climbing up the stairs, Nicki rang the buzzer and waited for the door to click open. Looking back, she saw the others following her with Lance moving away from Alex and favoring Jenny to help him up the stairs as he began to sway. His brown eyes caught hers and flickered with worry before Nicki looked forward once again. She could count on one hand the conversations that she and Lance had shared in the past. Thankfully the door buzzed and clicked open, allowing them to enter.

The hostel was quiet as they entered the main hall, which opened into a larger reception room. A few bags were sitting by the front desk, and a tall Chinese girl was talking in broken English with the receptionist. He waved at them without ever looking their way. Nicki shifted slightly to make sure that she stayed between the desk and the stairs. The others passed her, quickly helping Lance up the stairs. Nicki glanced down at the wood stairs and thick rugs, noting with relief that there wasn't any blood. Satisfied, she followed the others up the stairs, moving slowly and reluctantly.

It took forever to reach their third-floor room. The large room was filled with seven bunk beds, some against the walls, and some turned sideways. There was a card table set up near the door in an awkward space where another bed wouldn't fit with one metal chair in front of it. Their bags and suitcases were locked up in the bins under the beds, and Nicki could see bags belonging to at least two other people at the side of the room. They weren't here: probably out starting a pub crawl or some other ridiculous use of time in Europe. She knew her thoughts weren't charitable, but Nicki couldn't help it as she shrugged out of her coat and tossed it onto her bed.

Behind her, the others scrambled with Jenny staying next to Lance and keeping pressure on her ruined shirt while Alex pulled the metal chair over by Nicki's bed and motioned for Lance to sit down. Bran vanished into the bathroom and returned a moment later with a moist, dark blue hand towel that they'd probably have to dispose of or use magic on later. Jenny dropped to her knees, seemingly unconcerned with the wooden floor to keep her hand on Lance's arm. He was looking at her with an expression that made Nicki want to roll her eyes and hit them both.

Despite the irritation, fear, and worry bubbling up in her chest, Nicki gave them a moment. She kicked off her shoes and curled her toes as she willed herself to relax. When she looked up, she caught Bran watching her with a worried and cautious expression even as he moved over towards the doorway. He glanced out the door and coughed lightly to get Alex's attention.

"Do you want us to stay?" Alex asked in a softer voice. Nicki wondered if the other mage wanted to apologize for her earlier 'command,' but Nicki shook her head.

"I think this will be easier that way, and someone needs to mind the door."

Alex stepped forward and touched Jenny's shoulder. For a moment, Nicki really didn't think the other girl was going to leave, but then she slowly stood up. She gave Nicki a sharp warning look with her dark brown eyes, and Nicki almost chuckled at the notion of being frightened by Jenny, who had a grand total of one inch on her.

"Come on," Alex urged Jenny. "Magic takes a lot of concentration, and healing magic is a little complicated." Alex looked back to Nicki. "Do you want Morgana on the phone?"

"No, I know what I'm doing," Nicki said. She reached out and carefully unwrapped the shirt from around Lance's arm. Bran handed her the moist towel, which she used to wet the places where the drying blood tried to stick. "And do you really want to risk letting Merlin know about this?"

"We'll be outside if you need anything," Alex added as she took a hesitant step back towards the doorway. "Just shout."

"Fine, Alex." Nicki looked at Lance, who appeared more distressed with Jenny gone. "Do you want to take your coat off first?"

"Will it help?" he asked in a strained voice.

"Probably not, but this could take a bit," Nicki said as she mopped up some of the blood around the wound. Her stomach was tightening up at the sight of the blood, and her mouth tingled uncomfortably. "And I need to see the wound."

"Alright," Lance agreed in a weaker voice.

Jenny was back across the room like a shot and gently helped him guide his arm through the sleeve with a pained and sick expression on her own face. A long, pained hiss escaped Lance, and Nicki felt a twinge of guilt even as he freed his arm, and the wound was fully revealed. Without the flaps of leather sleeve falling over the wound and trying to stick to his arm hairs, she could fully see the damage.

"Thanks." Nicki glanced towards Jenny. "I'll deal with this," she heard herself say in a slightly softer tone to the other girl.

"Okay," Alex answered from by the doorway. "Uh, good luck... and thanks, Nicki."

Nodding, Nicki watched Jenny move back to the doorway and linger there for a moment with her eyes fixed on Lance. As the door closed, Nicki reached out to take Lance's arm in her hands and extended it, so his palm rested on his knee. He bit back a hiss as the adjustment stretched out his arm muscles, and a little more blood oozed out of the wound. Exhaling slowly, Nicki tried to meditate while she studied the cut. Medicine had never been on her career list despite her having no trouble with dissection in biology class, and as she began to feel ill, she congratulated herself on that decision. The creature's claws had sliced through the skin and muscle cleanly, leaving the wound hanging open like a gaping hole. There weren't any jagged bits of skin, but the depth gave her pause. Nicki swallowed as her stomach churned and shivered as a chill swept through her body.

"You're shaking," Lance observed in a tight pained voice.

"I'm fine!"

Nicki closed her eyes and inhaled deeply. She did her best to ignore the sounds drifting up from downstairs and the streets outside. Nicki pushed away the urge to wonder about the creatures that had attacked them this time. She'd overheard a bit of Bran and Alex's talk and couldn't help but find it interesting. Instead, she focused on the spark she could feel low in her chest beneath her heart. Her magical connection opened, and Nicki sighed softly at the smooth, calming feeling that ran through her like cool water on a hot day. She allowed herself a moment to marvel over how much easier it was getting to call on her magic.

Yet when she opened her eyes and looked at the wound in Lance's arm, she couldn't help but wonder how bad Alex's wound had looked to spur Aiden on to heal her with such disregard. With that stray thought, the magic slipped away from her like water through open fingers. Whimpering at the sudden chill left where the magic had warmed her, Nicki couldn't help but grimace. She bit the inside of her mouth and tried calling on the magic again, but now could feel her stomach churning at the unpleasant memory of Aiden's still form in that hospital bed.

"I'm in a lot of pain," Lance groaned. A bead of sweat was rolling down the side of his face. With his good hand, he reached over and gripped her left arm. "Look, Nicki, if you don't want to do this, I can go to the hospital."

"I said I'm fine," Nicki said.

She gave Lance a glare that he didn't react to. Moving her hand over the wound, she pulled at her magic more insistently. The small spark flared to life, but the flow of magic up her chest and into her arms seemed sluggish. Nicki closed her hand into a fist, willing her cold and stiff fingers to work properly while remaining very aware of Lance's eyes on her.

"You're scared." Lance shifted off the chair and stood up. He grabbed the scraps of fabric and pressed them against the wound to mop up the blood. "Shit, I need to get to the hospital."

"I am not scared," Nicki protested. She jumped off the bed and grabbed Lance's right arm tightly. "Sit your ass down and let me do this."

"Nicki..." Lance hissed as she accidentally knocked into his injured arm in her attempt to force him to sit down. "You look ready to fall over, just let me go to the hospital. You're too freaked out over Aiden."

It was like an electric jolt through her body. The downside to her vivid imagination was that she couldn't turn it off even when she wanted to. Nicki hadn't been anywhere close to that lake after Arthur stabbed Alex. No, she'd been off with her Gran and had gotten a frantic call about something being wrong, but now she could see it in her mind's eye. Alex collapsed on the pebbled beach in the snow with her blood mixing with the mud beneath her body, and Aiden leaning over her with a frantic expression. His compassion and loyalty overriding all common sense, that damn promise he'd made when Aisling was sick that he wouldn't ever just stand by, and him pouring more magic and life-force than he had to give into Alex.

"I am sorry about Aiden," Lance told her, gently pulling Nicki from the terrible vision. "I don't know him, but based on what he did for Alex and how much you care, he's got to be one hell of a guy."

"He is," Nicki agreed. Swallowing, Nicki fought back the prickling of tears in her eyes. "He's my best friend, like my brother."

"How did you two get to be friends?"

"We punched each other," Nicki replied with a watery laugh.

"What?"

"I'm serious... I was mad about my parents; they left me with my grandmother, and Aiden had one hell of a temper back then. He said something, I don't even remember what it was, but I thought he was teasing me about my parents. We just went at it with each other despite the teacher standing right there. We punched each other, and I even bit him."

"And you became friends?"

"Yeah... we did. It was a weird friendship at first, but.... He mellowed when Aisling got sick and I- I tried to remember that while parts of my life sucked, I never had to live in fear of someone I loved dying right in front of me. It helped me be better." Nicki reached up and wiped the tears from her cheeks. "Aiden's important."

"Of course, he is." Lance's voice was soft, and he was looking at her with gentle, understanding brown eyes. "There are people who love him."

Nicki didn't respond: the words felt choked up in her throat. Instead, she reached out her hand and brought it over the wound. Inhaling, Nicki did her best to remember the sound of Merlin's voice as he walked them through meditation. Lance stayed completely still as she gradually pushed away the grief trying to bubble up once more in her chest. This time she kept her eyes open and focused on Lance's eyes instead of closing her own. His were filled with pain, despite his kind words and concern for her. They were a warm shade of brown with flecks of amber that caught the light like the cut axinite gemstones her grandmother was fond of.

Keeping eye contact, Nicki pulled, more gently this time, on her magic, trying to coax it forward despite the lingering fears and reservations. Lance was hurt and in pain, but he wasn't dying. This would tire her out, but it wouldn't truly hurt her unless she lost control. Grabbing onto her desire to heal him, Nicki allowed her magic to slowly stream up through her chest. She wasn't someone who lost control, she told herself stubbornly. She thought things through, embraced knowledge and the grand scheme of things. Nicki licked her dry lips as the first wisps of magic flowed into her hands.

Soft blue sparks illuminated her fingertips and swirled gently around her hand. Nicki relaxed as she felt the connection warm up, and the tension in her shoulders begin to ease. Lance was watching the raw magic dancing around her hand with an expression of awe and surprise. The look of pain was almost gone, replaced instead by childlike wonder. Smiling, Nicki gently touched her index finger to the abused flesh just to the side of Lance's injury and exhaled slowly.

The magic spun into a thin stream of blue that made the tip of her finger glow. Her hand and arm pulsed as magic began to sink into Lance's skin. Nicki tightened her hold on the flow of magic, forcing it to slow down. This felt very different from her first experience healing Alex when her magic had reached for Nicki's. Instead of another flow of magic wrapping around her own, pulling strength from it, she instead had the sense that she was pouring magic into something that was empty, like filling up a pitcher with water. It made her shiver, but Nicki kept control of the slight stream of magic.

Ending the eye contact, Nicki studied the wound with a frown; it wasn't closing yet. Nicki grimaced and closed her eyes, letting out a deep sigh before sucking in a breath of fresher air. The room was beginning to smell a touch like blood, and she thought she could taste iron on the tip of her tongue. Beneath her fingers, she could still feel her magic pulsing softly within Lance's skin. She gently brushed his arm, feeling the flickers of magic reaching for her and sparking up to meet her skin.

"Nicki," Lance called softly. "Look if you can't-"

"Lance." She focused on her goal and didn't even open her eyes. "Shut up."

Keeping her eyes closed, Nicki focused on one thought: heal. It wasn't as elegant as she probably could have managed, and probably wasn't the best way to do things, but she couldn't open her eyes. Pulling on every experience she'd ever had of envisioning an artistic project, whether with her grandmother or by herself, Nicki tried to guide her thoughts to what she wanted. She told herself it was like envisioning a vase or a painting before you even started. It was establishing the finished product in your head before you even started so that every action could lead towards that. 'Course she hadn't exactly spent much time studying or envisioning Lance's bare arm. The idea actually made her giggle, unknotting a bit of the tension around her lungs.

"Holy shit!"

Nicki opened her eyes and looked down at his arm. Slowly the flaps of skin on either of the side of the wound began tugging towards each other. The dark-red, cut muscles below the dark flesh began to glow a soft blue. Nicki forced herself to keep her eyes on the wound despite the urge to look away. The blood flow had mostly stopped, and a spark of blue magic shimmered deep within the wound. Slowly the deepest part of the slash began to close in tiny flashes of blue magic. An odd, pained sigh escaped Lance, and Nicki noticed that his arm was shaking.

"Hold on," Nicki told him in a soft voice. "Almost there, Lance."

The blue magic began to fade away as the flesh knitted itself together. A ticklish laugh escaped Lance, and Nicki had to tighten her grip on his arm to keep it from moving too much. A drop of sweat rolled down the side of her face, and Nicki felt her lungs beginning to constrict painfully as the last of the red skin irritation vanished. Releasing her grip on the magic, Nicki felt it quickly recede, like the tide going out, back deep into her chest. Lance gently reached over with his free hand and carefully opened her clenched fingers so she would release his hand. Nicki finally dropped her eyes away from him and closed them tightly to banish the dryness she hadn't even noticed taking over them.

Then Lance took her hand in both of his, giving it a gentle squeeze before he released it and set it down on her knee. Nicki opened her eyes to find Lance gently inspecting his arm with his free hand. His fingers brushed over a thin pale line in his skin, and Nicki hoped that he didn't mind the scar too much. It was a faint thing and would hopefully fade in time. Then he turned his arm and flexed it with a growing smile.

"Feels alright?" Nicki managed to ask as she slumped back on the bed with an exhausted but pleased smile.

"Feels good." Lance flexed his arm, letting the muscles shift and grinned. "Thanks, Nicki."

"You're welcome." She found that she meant the words and smiled. Nodding towards the door, she felt a wave of exhaustion. "Probably should let your girlfriend know that she doesn't need to kill me."

"Yeah, and I bet you're hungry." Lance stood up and pushed back the metal chair. "Do you want something else, or is pasta okay?"

"What, do you cook too?" Nicki asked with a raised eyebrow.

"My mother was of the mind that a man should be able to do everything a woman can except have babies."

"I think I'd like her," Nicki chuckled in response. "Pasta sounds good."

Lance looked uncertain even as he turned and headed for the doorway. He glanced back at her before he opened the door, nearly causing the others to fall into the room. Jenny reacted first by grabbing his arm and studying it with a worried expression that melted into a pleased smile. Then she jumped back and blushed while Bran grinned behind her. Alex smiled and nodded to Lance as he stepped out into the hallway before she looked in at Nicki.

She found herself in another slightly awkward lock of eyes as Alex considered her with that gray gaze. Then the current incarnation of the Iron Soul moved around the others and stepped into the room. She moved across the room with soft footsteps as Lance and the others headed downstairs to the kitchen. Alex stopped in front of Nicki, and the two just studied each other for a long moment. Then Alex sat down in the chair that Lance had vacated, kicking away the bloody towel as she lowered her eyes.

"Thank you, Nicki." Alex raised her eyes to meet Nicki's again. They were a darker shade of gray than normal. "I'm sorry I put you through that."

"You need to learn to heal." Nicki forced a pained smile before nodding towards the door. "But you know something... he's not half bad."

A weak chuckle escaped Alex which quickly turned into a pained, almost hysterical laugh, and a moment later Nicki felt herself join in.

12

Revelation of the Lady

21 B.C.E. North Pembrokeshire Coast

The early morning mist was still lingering in the air as Merlin reached the small lake. It was nothing impressive, and Merlin almost hesitated to think of the small body of water as a proper lake. Nonetheless, a small river ran into the water out of the nearby hills where it joined a few small streams, and a short way to the south of where he stood, it flowed out once more towards the ocean. Just up the slope, a small grove of trees was swaying in the wind, the leaves rustling gently behind the curtain of mist.

For a moment, Merlin stood still and silent with his hands hanging limply at his side. The twitch in his right hand to grasp his staff was still there, like a phantom at the edge of his awareness, but it was becoming easier. Instead, Merlin carefully loosened the tight leather strap over his chest, which released the long leather bag on his back. He caught it smoothly and reverently pulled Cathanáil from the bag. The Sword was snugly secured in its leather scabbard, and its hilt gleamed brilliantly in the low morning light. Merlin settled his hand on the hilt, allowing the peace of the early day to soothe his frayed nerves. Against his palm, he could feel a faint humming of magic within the Sword that brushed warmly against his skin.

Removing his hand from the hilt of Cathanáil made the world seem colder as he could no longer feel even a hint of Arto's magic that had been bound into the blade all those years ago. Despite the temptation to brood at the side of the lake, Merlin dug into his small side bag and pulled out a small sheathed blade. It was a simple old bronze dagger, and Merlin smiled at it fondly. The surface was dull and covered with small dents and marks from years of abuse. Nonetheless, Merlin knelt down and picked up one of the larger stones by the shore of the lake. Placing the dagger against another rock, Merlin harshly banged the stone down against the metal. It took several smashes, but the tip of the dagger broke off and clinked against the pebbles beneath him.

Bringing his arm back, Merlin whispered a name so softly that the wind carried it off without him hearing it himself. He brought his arm forward and sent the dagger flying through the air. It spun for only a few moments before hitting the surface of the lake with a thunk and instantly sinking out of sight. Merlin exhaled and licked his dry lips as he laid his hand back on Cathanáil's hilt. In the distance, he heard the call of a bird and something moving in the misty trees.

Time seemed to stretch by, but Merlin stayed where he was. He kept Cathanáil clutched tightly in his hands as he waited on the edge of the lake, trying not to wonder what was taking so long. He was aware of the rapid beat of his heart as he searched the surface for any sign of movement. A soft sigh escaped Merlin, and he stepped back from the shore, sweeping Cathanáil and his bag up over his shoulder as he prepared to leave.

But then he heard the soft lapping of the water against the shore becoming faster and louder. Turning on his heels, Merlin smiled as he saw ripples swirling in the middle of the lake. Small waves of water began to lash up into the air as if being splashed from below. The ripples grew larger and larger and then churned up above the lake in a spiral of water. More water was pulled from the surface, causing the water to recede from the shore. A tall form like a pillar appeared in the middle of the lake. Then, with a splash, the water fell away, leaving a feminine figure draped in a gown of glistening blue water rising out of the surface. All around her, the lake stilled, and she opened a pair of sea-green eyes. Smiling at Merlin, she drifted towards him, her face illuminated by a small circle of softly glowing droplets of water and her dark hair spilling over her shoulders.

"Merlin," Cyrridven greeted warmly. Smiling, she glided over the surface of the lake towards him. Water lapped at the shore as she approached, and Merlin gave a small bow. "It is good to see you."

"I am pleased to see you as well, milady," Merlin greeted with a small smile. "It has been some time. I hope you have been well."

"I am content, and I remain clean of madness," Cyrridven replied gently. "Sadly, more from my world have been banished to yours, and many will not heed my advice."

"Yes… Morgana and I had the displeasure of meeting one of your kind recently called Badb." Merlin carefully shifted Cathanáil into his arms. "She was after the Sword, I'm afraid."

"After the Sword… that is unexpected for one of my kind," Cyrridven said thoughtfully with a frown. She tilted her head and studied Cathanáil for a moment. "But perhaps under the right circumstances, another could force the magic within outward." Cyrridven moved her eyes up to meet Merlin's and smiled warmly once more. "But you have other news, my dear Merlin."

"We've found a new mage," Merlin announced with an uneasy smile. "Well, two of them: Gofiben and Bran, both living in a nearby village." He gestured over his shoulder the way he'd come to the lake. "They seem to be solid young men; Morgana is in the village now keeping an eye on them."

Gofiben," Cyrridven repeated with a small smile spreading over her face as her green-blue eyes lit up with interest. "So, that's his name."

"And Bran." Merlin frowned in confusion at her odd response. "There's two of them, Cyrridven."

"Merlin?" Cyrridven looked at him for a moment in stunned silence before she laughed. The sound echoed around them, and Merlin looked around with a slight blush. "Oh, my dear sweet Merlin, have you truly not realized?"

"Realized what, Cyrridven?" Merlin asked as patiently as he could manage. "Please be direct, Morgana and I are uncertain as to what the new threat is that is strengthening the flow of magic, and your amusement isn't helping to make things clear."

"Oh, forgive me, Merlin." Cyrridven stopped laughing, though a stray giggle did escape her. "I thought for certain that you and Morgana would feel it, but I suppose that submerged deep in the water as I was, I felt his magic more clearly. The water does seem to amplify my senses as well as let me keep them."

"Cyrridven!" Merlin called, sensing that his mentor was going off on a tangent.

"Merlin... the boy Gofiben... he has the Iron Soul. It has returned through him."

The words struck him like the blow of an iron axe, leaving Merlin shaking on the shore with wide eyes. He stared at Cyrridven, who was studying him with a blend of worry and pity, a tentative hand stretched towards him. She came a little closer to him with only the barest bit of water on the shore beneath her. Water swished over his feet as she called more towards her to keep her watery form stable, and a cool hand brushed his cheek.

"Merlin," she called gently. "Merlin, it's alright."

"He's... He's Arto?"

"No, Merlin, he isn't Arto. Not precisely." Cyrridven pulled back her hand and withdrew further into the lake with a sigh. "It is rather complicated to explain, but the spark, if you will, that gave Arto his strong link to the Iron Realm has been passed to Gofiben."

"B-but... when we die, our power and essence pass back into the Earth."

Cyrridven gave Merlin a soft and patient smile even as he stuttered on the shore. It was a bizarre feeling, being so uncertain of what was happening and what it meant. His chest felt tight, and his mind kept stumbling over Cyrridven's words.

"That is what you've been taught, Merlin," Cyrridven informed him gently. "And indeed, there is wisdom in it, but-"

"We never burned Arto's body!" Merlin looked at her with wide eyes. "We weren't sure if it would affect the Iron Gates, is that why this happened?"

"I do not know," Cyrridven told him gently. Holding her hands up, she tried to calm him. "Merlin, I do not have all the answers. All I know is that I felt the same power flow when Gofiben was born and heard his name whispered to me while I slept, just the same as it was with Arto." Her eyes narrowed on him, and she sternly said, "He is the Iron Soul, Merlin. In a new body and maybe with new talents, but it is him."

Merlin's hand tightened on Cathanáil's hilt as he swallowed thickly. The idea seemed so very incredible, and yet he'd been somehow reminded of Arto the moment they met. Had it merely been because he was meeting a new mage for the first time in years who shared a talent for smithing with Arto, or had there potentially been something more at play? A deep sigh escaped him, and he looked down at Cathanáil, drawing it a few inches out of its sheath. The blade gleamed in the low light as if it had just been polished, though it had been some time. Arto's magic had endured in the Sword and in the Iron Gates, despite all their fears. They'd buried Arto rather than burn him: a choice that had inspired the new fashion of burying people, due to their fear that if he fully rejoined the earth, his magic might slip away.

"What does it mean, Cyrridven?"

"The Iron Realm created the Iron Soul as a manifestation of magic and because of the need to protect itself. While mages serve as soldiers against invaders who mean harm, the Iron Soul has always been more than that." Cyrridven drifted towards him once more and tilted his face towards her. "Merlin, magic is growing once more. There is always a spark due to the many beings from other realms dwelling here like myself, the children of the Sídhe enslaved, and those Sídhe who still hide within this realm, but something new is coming. Something strong enough to trigger such a reaction. The Iron Soul needs your guidance once more. Will you help him?"

"I'll help him." Merlin dropped his eyes in resignation. "And then he will die like Arto before him, and Morgana and I will again be left to wander." He slid Cathanáil back into its sheath with shaking hands. "And then will he be born once more? Will this simply become a never-ending cycle?"

"Shhh." Cyrridven laid a hand upon his curls, dampening his hair. It was so similar to what he used to do with Arto that Merlin's heart ached. "Do not despair, Merlin. Please just train the boy. Think of him as someone, something else if it pleases you, but remember that he made no plans for this. He simply is what he is, just as you and poor Morgana were made what you are."

Merlin nodded and wiped at his eyes before raising his chin. "I apologize, Cyrridven; I thought myself stronger than that."

"Oh, Merlin, dear Myrddin," she sighed using his old name. "Take strength in your emotions: they are the human part of you. The best part of you." She brushed a hand down his face leaving small cool droplets on his cheek. "I will seek out and speak with the other exiles and see what I can learn from them. Perhaps Badb has sought information or allies amongst the others."

"Be careful." Merlin forced himself to smile for her. "Morgana and I still have great need of your guidance."

"Less with each passing year," she replied fondly. Her watery circlet glittered as the sun began to emerge from behind the clouds. "But I shall be cautious in who I approach," Cyrridven promised. "The newer exiles are more violently tempered than my own early companions were."

Merlin nodded, uncertain of what he could possibly say. Cyrridven gave him a gentle, understanding look before lifting her hands and causing the water to swirl around her. She vanished from sight as the pillar sunk into the lake, and the water gradually stilled. The rays of the sun had finished banishing the last of the mist, and up on the hill, he could see a deer walking amongst the trees. Birds were singing, and the soft breeze was gentle and cooling. Everything was at peace, yet his thoughts would not settle.

Stepping back from the lake, Merlin looked down at Cathanáil and ran his finger reverently over the golden hilt. He just stared at it, trying to make sense of the intense mess of emotions that were threatening to overwhelm him. Merlin realized he was crying softly only when a tear rolled off his chin. Chuckling, Merlin raised a hand to his face to wipe away the tears and took a few steps back from the water. He regretted Cyrridven leaving him with his thoughts so quickly. Their conversation had been a distraction from the strange truth that was suddenly echoing in his mind.

The Iron Soul had been reborn in Gofiben. Somehow, someway, the spirit that had linked Arto with the Iron Realm had found a new form. Merlin's hands shook as he gently wrapped Cathanáil back up and hoisted the Sword onto his back. It was difficult to tighten the leather strap that kept the Sword in place, as his whole body swayed uneasily. His first steps up the slight slope away from the lake were amongst the most difficult in his life. Around him, the world seemed dreamlike, with his teary eyes blurring the details. Merlin was torn between a desire to rush back to the village and fear of seeing Gofiben once more. The young man had reminded him of Arto in several small ways, but could he look at the young man and train him knowing that once he had been Arto?

Would he remember them in time? Could the knowledge of that life transcend his physical form and become a part of who he was now? Should he be told, or should it remain a secret? Should he even tell Morgana, who mourned her lost brother as fiercely as he mourned the loss of his foster son? These and more questions haunted Merlin with each step he took. At one moment, he felt confident in his ability to teach Gofiben whether he remembered or not, but in the next, the idea of keeping it a secret and leaving the training of him to Morgana was all too tempting.

He reached the village sooner than he wanted, looking up and suddenly realizing that he was at the gates. Thankfully the guards let him pass into the village with only curious and worried glances at his pale face. Around him, people moved about their daily lives with only a few looks his way. His pace slowed, and he carefully retraced his way to Gofiben's roundhouse. The structure looked so calm and peaceful, with only a faint swirl of smoke escaping the thick thatch roof. He wondered if the boy was still asleep after working for so much of the night. As he approached, he noticed Morgana out in front of the house in the small yard with an unfamiliar figure. Even from his distant vantage point, he could see that she was frustrated and in some kind of argument. Speeding up his pace, Merlin gripped the harness holding Cathanáil and hurried up the path.

"Morgana," he called in greeting as he joined the pair. He tried to force a smile, but couldn't manage it. His body felt heavy and tired, but his heart raced as Morgana looked at him. Merlin still didn't know what to tell her.

"Merlin." Morgana looked tense and irritated. "This is Galath," she said. She gestured to the tall young man with dark brown hair cut at his shoulders that she'd been speaking with. "Gofiben's brother."

Grateful for the temporary distraction from his problem, Merlin turned to study the young man with a smile. He had broad shoulders and the bearing of someone who'd handled an axe more than a few times. His clothing was rather plain, but he had a beautiful hand axe fastened to his belt and a small clasp on his cloak. It was clear that Galath was a few years older than Gofiben, and his dark brown eyes bore into Merlin's suspiciously. Had he been in a better mood, Merlin would have been pleased by the brotherly display of concern about the two mysterious people who were suddenly a part of his brother's life.

"Greetings." Merlin could only manage weak pleasantness.

Morgana glanced at him with open surprise at his brief greeting and clear exhaustion. Her green eyes flickered over towards the door of the roundhouse, where he guessed Gofiben was working.

"What is your interest with my brother?" Galath straightened up to his full height, putting him several inches over Merlin. He was reminded too much of Uthyrn and wondered if Morgana had gotten the same impression. "This morning, he informed me that you're going to teach him magic."

"And we are," Morgana said, drawing Galath's attention towards her. "I already showed you a demonstration. He has a gift and must learn to control it."

"There are stories about you," Galath said. Looking towards Merlin, his frown deepened. "Both of you. They say you're heroes who fought with Arto against the Sídhe, but this is my brother. What danger are you drawing him into?"

"We do not have that answer yet," Merlin told Galath honestly. It earned him an irritated look from Morgana. "An ally of ours is seeking answers, but we fear that Badb may have plans that are a danger to our way of life."

"Badb," Galath repeated with a frown. "That explains what he said this morning, I suppose, but I'll not have my little brother fighting a goddess."

"I'm afraid that he has no choice in that," Merlin told him bluntly. He stepped past Galath and patted his shoulder wearily. "Perhaps Bran can choose not to fight, but Gofiben must. It is why he is."

"Because he's a smith?" Confusion and irritation were apparent on Morgana's face. "What are you talking about Merlin, what did Cyrridven tell you?"

"He's a smith because our father was a smith," Galath cut in sharply. "I had the skill to wield weapons, and Gofiben had the skill to make them; that is all."

"No, I'm afraid it is not," Merlin said with a sad little smile as he turned his eyes to Morgana. "Gofiben has Arto's powers. He's the new bearer of the power of the Iron Realm."

Her eyes widened with shock, and her jaw went slack at his words. A strange sense of relief flooded through him at the assurance that he wasn't alone in his surprise. He had felt blindsided by Cyrridven's words, but at least he wasn't the only one.

"That's not.... He can't be."

"Cyrridven is certain of it." Merlin reached out and gently gripped her shoulder. "Morgana-"

"Don't!" Morgana stepped back from him, shaking her head. "Just... don't, it's not him, Merlin. Not really, even if he has the power. He didn't recognize us, didn't recognize me."

Merlin moved towards her, an arm outstretched to comfort her, but a wave of magic brushed over his senses just before he heard screams from the west side of the village. Then there was a thunderous crash and fire began to rain down around them.

13

Heart Ache

Her sides were aching, and her lungs felt constricted by the time Alex could stop giggling. The edge of hysteria made up of the numerous uncomfortable emotions she was currently stuck dealing with had been a bit of a surprise, but that terrible itch at the back of the mind didn't seem so bad now. Breathing deeply, Alex shut her eyes for a moment and felt her shoulders relax when her brain didn't automatically supply her with the sight of Aiden in that hospital bed.

"Whoa," Nicki gasped in a slightly pained voice. "Guess we needed that."

Forcing open her eyes, Alex looked down at Nicki, noticing that she was still pale despite the flush of red on her cheeks. Alex slumped in the chair, letting one arm drape over the back as she studied Nicki. For her part, Nicki had leaned down to retrieve a bottle of water, which she opened with a soft crackling sound. Alex stayed quiet as Nicki took a long drink, pleased when the water seemed to invigorate her a little bit.

"I'm sorry about earlier," Alex said in a rush before she could start overthinking things. "I didn't mean to go all 'I'm in charge' on you."

"Well, you are sort of in charge, aren't you?" Nicki still didn't look at her.

"Maybe, I suppose, though, that seems to be a bad way of determining leadership."

"You're the Iron Soul," Nicki said as she finally looked at Alex. "You're the one who's been doing this shit for three thousand years."

"And remembers none of it," Alex countered. "Not exactly an ideal method of protecting the world."

"You've noticed that too, huh?" Nicki chuckled before taking another sip of the water. "It is an odd way of doing things; I would have figured you having at least some memories would make things easier. It would make you less dependent on Merlin and Morgana finding you and explaining things."

"Maybe it isn't possible; apparently, souls or at least something like that is real, but they don't know how that actually works." Alex managed a weak shrug as she stubbornly denied the feeling of her stomach dropping violently. "They've never died after all, and only have their knowledge thanks to observation"

"Fair point," Nicki conceded with a nod. "Though... you are protective of Lance and Jenny; maybe that's something left over."

"I don't think so; they were my friends at college even before you guys," Alex reminded her with a thoughtful frown. "When the visions, the Connections between us started, and I was confused, Jenny was very kind. She made a point of including me and introducing me to new people," Alex recalled with a small, fond look. "And sure, Jenny is flawed, but she's a good person and Lance...well, he was always so polite and thoughtful. I think my affection is based solidly in this life; at least that's what I'd prefer to believe."

"What about you and Morgana?" Nicki questioned. She gave Alex a tentative searching look. "You've always been her favorite. I know you argue about that, but the two of you always just seemed to click more than the rest of us. I mean, she was your sister in another life, and apparently, she and Arto were close."

"Haven't thought about that much," Alex confessed with a tired chuckle. "I suppose we are pretty close. I'm comfortable with her and like her, but I'm not sure that our relationship is sibling-like, or maternal for that matter." Alex shrugged and looked towards the window, staring out at the gray sky beyond. "Probably closer than your usual student-teacher thing, though." A soft sigh escaped Alex as she watched a small bird fly past the window. "She doesn't talk about Arto much, but they were close, and she misses him. I think... I think she feels guilty about him and maybe some of the other Iron Soul lives." Alex sighed softly and looked back at Nicki. "And while I like Professor Yates, we aren't exactly super close."

"That'll probably change now that he won't be distracted by Arthur." Nicki shrugged only to grimace when Alex flinched. "Sorry," she apologized quickly.

"No, it's fine. I'm going to have to get used to it after all." Alex swallowed and shook her head. "He's still out there and working with the Sídhe Queen. We'll have to deal with them once Aiden is safe."

There, she'd said his name to Nicki. Alex looked tentatively at Nicki, waiting to see the tight anger and withdrawn look that had been dominating her face since he slipped into the coma. Instead, Nicki just looked tired and sad. She was looking down at the bottle of water in her hands and was silent. Alex wondered if she needed to get up and leave Nicki alone, but lingered for a few more moments. When the silence became too much, Alex started to get up, but then Nicki looked up at her.

"He's my best friend; really, the only family I've got other than Gran." Defeat washed over Nicki's features, and the other woman sniffed. "It kills me that I see him in that room with those IVs and the tubes every time I close my eyes, Alex. Every time I look at you... shit, I just think about how unfair it is that his parents are going through this again; that Aisling has to understand how Aiden felt when she was sick. And I'm angry: I'm that dark, bitter kind of angry that just seeps in and becomes a part of you."

Swallowing, Alex felt ready to be physically ill as Nicki choked on her words. If tears were gathering in Nicki's eyes, Alex pretended not to notice despite the fact that she couldn't force herself to look away. Her mouth felt tight, and her fingers clutched at the bottom of the metal chair for something to hold on to.

"But it wasn't your fault," Nicki finally said in a soft voice. "Not really, and I'm sorry for how I'm acting, I really am. I know that it was Arthur's fault: that bastard manipulated all of us even to the point that we stopped asking important questions, and he tried to kill you. Aiden wanted to do what was right; honestly, if he didn't hate hospitals so much because of Aisling's illness, he probably would be studying medicine. That's just who he is, and I shouldn't be angry with him over that." Nicki sighed and shook her head, running a hand through loose strands of hair. "I'm rambling again, sorry about that, but the point is I know I shouldn't be angry at you." Nicki looked at Alex with teary blue eyes that begged her to understand. "And I know that I've been more than a bit of a bitch about something I know you wouldn't have let happen if you could have changed it. I know that, but I can't promise that I can redirect my anger where it should be overnight. I'll try Alex, I will, but I'm not really that good."

"You forgave your parents," Alex said before she could slam her mouth shut.

A bitter laugh escaped Nicki that echoed in the room as the redhead shook her head. "That was actually pretty easy. The anger mattered, the resentment, but they really didn't, and by the time I was thirteen, I knew I was better off without them." Nicki sighed and looked back up at Alex. "Thing is, Alex, I tend much more towards vindictive bitch than compassionate hero. I could forgive them because it made me the better person because it let me put that shit in the past. It was better for me even though it was fucking hard to do. Selfishness won the day there because they just weren't worth it." She shrugged and gestured at Alex, "Like I said, I know this wasn't your fault, and I'll try to do better, but it won't be that easy for me."

"Okay." Alex could barely speak and couldn't bring herself to move away from Nicki just yet. The moment felt too fragile like she could break it with the wrong word. "It's almost a relief to know you're not perfect."

Nicki laughed; the sound was much more natural and honest this time. She gave Alex a small, tired smile, but a real smile and leaned back on the bed. "Oh, Alex, I am perfect." Nicki winked at her with a small smirk. "You know you want me."

"I thought I wasn't your type."

"You're not, but I'm a touch depressed and horny right now." Nicki's lips twitched into a smile, and she chuckled as she looked at the bottle of water. "I wonder if I could do water to wine?"

"Well, you've got the healing bit down, so maybe that's next," Alex said. "Though don't talk about that in front of Jenny. She's having enough trouble with magic being real as it is."

"Maybe you should learn healing next, so I'm not the only cleric in the party for this quest," Nicki said. There was only a small hint of bite in her voice this time. "That's never a good idea."

"Oh god, can't you go a day without a geek reference?" Alex asked in a more forceful voice than she meant to.

"You're supposed to be the most powerful of all of us," Nicki said with a challenging look that made Alex feel very nervous. "I bet you'd be an awesome healer."

"I- I'd rather not," Alex stumbled to say, flinching at how that sounded. "You're the healer because you're the best at visualizing what you want your magic to do."

"You'd better have a better reason than that." Nicki arched an eyebrow, and the tension in the room returned with a vengeance.

"Look think about how my power seems to work, Nicki. Sure, I can do the charge balls of magic and lightning bolts, but most of the damage I've done has been from turning magic against its user. I took over the Sídhe magical orbs in the tunnels, and I killed Chernobog's shadows by pulling their magic right out of them." Alex was waving her hand about wildly, begging Nicki to understand. "I'm just worried that if I tried to heal, I'd pull on their magic or life essence instead of sharing mine."

A snort escaped Nicki as the other mage kept herself from laughing, but she inclined her head after a moment. "Alright, Alex, I supposed that's rational for now, but once you have more control, you're learning to heal," she said in a voice that left no room for argument.

"We'll see what Morgana thinks," Alex offered. "She'd probably have the best sense of if I could do it."

"Don't go hiding behind your big sister."

"Don't call her that!" Alex crossed her arms and gave Nicki a stern look. "It's weird."

"I think you'd best get used to weird," Nicki reminded her. There was a hint of a smile on her face again. "That's your life now. You're the main hero in this warped story: you're the one who'll get thrown in front of the biggest monsters."

Alex tried to think of what she could say to that, but her brain didn't seem to be in proper banter mode right now. What she said was true to a certain point. As a basic mage, she hadn't really had much of an option to walk away, and if she tried to now, well, she probably couldn't period. And even before she'd known she was the Iron Soul, she had been the one to be captured by the Sídhe and begun a unique escape. Plus, she'd killed the Old One Chernobog when he'd attacked Ravenslake less than a week ago. It was crazy to even think about.

"Shit," Alex cursed. She lowered her head into her hands to muffle the next few curses.

"And it's sinking in," Nicki chuckled.

"You're evil; you know that, right?" Alex demanded. She looked back up at Nicki sharply.

"A little bit," Nicki agreed with a lazy shrug. "Consider it my revenge." A deep sigh escaped Nicki, and she looked over towards the window. "We really need to work on your education, though, just in case. Your genre savviness needs some improving."

"Do I even want to know?" Alex asked, rubbing the right side of her head. "Time is limited."

"Maybe, but we're up against a lot of nasty things that bend the rules of physics. I think making sure you know some of the core tenets is a good idea." Nicki licked her lips before she added, "And Jenny and Lance too if they're going to be sticking around in this fight. They don't have powers, and right now, we haven't got any iron swords available to us."

"I don't know if they'll be sticking around once Aiden is alright. Jenny was talking about transferring."

"I think it'll depend on what happens when we find the Chalice," Nicki said. "They clearly care about each other, no matter how weird that might be. This might be good for them." Nicki turned to look back at her. "Or would that bother you?"

Alex paused at the question, a bit surprised by it, but she shook her head a moment later. "No," she replied calmly. "I'd be relieved, I think, that if all of... everything at least managed to lead to a couple of people being happy."

"You are such a sap," Nicki teased.

Frowning, Alex opened her mouth to argue with that, or at least defend it as not being a bad thing when a knock on the door made them both look toward it. The door opened a few inches a moment later, and Lance tentatively peered in at them. He looked a bit worried, and Alex wondered if he was expecting bloodshed or something. Then he eased the door open enough that he could lean into the room.

"Ah, excuse me." Lance looked a bit embarrassed as he glanced between them. "Jenny found something that might be helpful."

"What did she find?" Nicki asked as she stood up from the bed. She swayed slightly, and Alex jumped up and grabbed her arm to steady her. "Thanks."

"Well, we were working on dinner, and she just decided to start doing some searches online, and something came up."

"Dare I ask what her search words were?" Alex asked. Releasing Nicki's arm, she quickly crossed the room with Nicki a step behind her.

"I think this search was Celtic mythology, skull, and cup," Lance informed them with a shrug. "It brought up information on Bran the Blessed."

"Bran the Blessed?" Alex repeated. "That sounds familiar."

"We glanced it over when we were doing a Celtic mythology assignment," Nicki reminded her. Lance turned, and they began to head downstairs. "But it was more Welsh than Irish, so we left it alone. What about it?"

"Well apparently one, it is Welsh, two, the guy had a magic cauldron." Lance stayed in front of them as they reached the bottom and positioned himself to catch Nicki if needed. "And three, his head was cut off and buried to protect something."

Nicki suddenly stopped on the stairs in front of Alex and turned to her with a small smile. As Nicki raised an expectant eyebrow, it occurred to Alex that she probably looked stunned. Nicki shrugged at her with a teasing smile before she followed Lance down the stairs, leaving Alex standing on the small, wooden staircase by herself for the few seconds it took her to gather her wits. Shaking her head, Alex followed the others downstairs, trying to keep the hope bubbling in her chest in check.

14

Bran the Blessed

Alex was trying to remember the paragraph or so that she'd read on Bran the Blessed as they headed down the hostel hallway to the kitchen. Around them, she could hear the sounds of other guests moving about, and based on a couple of shouts, there was a group preparing for a pub crawl. Unfortunately, she didn't have the best memory for what she read, which was sad given that she was the literature major. The story hadn't been about the Sídhe and thus had been largely ignored by the group except for Aiden pointing out that Bran's nickname matched the figure's name. She glanced over at Nicki, who had a thoughtful expression on her face and wondered if the other girl thought this might be helpful.

As they approached the open kitchen doorway, Alex could hear fragments of a conversation between Jenny and Bran. An odd feeling of confusion swept over her. It was odd to suddenly have Nicki being friendly towards Lance, and now apparently, Bran and Jenny were having a conversation on their own. She was happy, of course, but the notion had an otherworldly feel to it that made her feel a little bit suspicious.

"I've met other hapas who have the 'Asian glow,' and I've met a few that look more European than I do," Bran's voice said with a hint of amusement from inside the kitchen. "I'm at least lucky that I can recognize my dad in me thanks to getting his eyes."

"Yeah, I've got to be honest, I've been trying to figure out what it was about you-" Alex heard Jenny start to say.

"The cheekbone structure and brow shape. A lot of people don't even notice, but I've gotten the 'what's your mix' question more than a few times."

"Have you ever gotten crap about it?" Jenny asked.

Alex glanced towards an equally befuddled Nicki, who shrugged. They reached the doorway, and Alex glanced inside to find Bran and Jenny seated at one of the two small round tables in the room. Three of the four walls were lined with cabinets and appliances with bright, colorful posters of London, Edinburgh, and Cardiff covering almost all the blank space. A pot of water was bubbling on the gas stove, but neither Bran nor Jenny seemed to have noticed as they chatted.

"No not really; keep in mind the Asian stereotype tends towards smart, disciplined, good at math, and such things. There're a few people I've met who don't like biracial, but most of them haven't really caught on that I'm mixed."

"I remember when I started middle school, someone asked me if my mom could come and clean his house," Jenny said with a clear tone of lingering annoyance.

"Ouch, what I always loved was when people assumed that my Korean mother was my nanny, but I think that was the worst I ever got."

"Lucky." Jenny sipped at her glass of water. "Do you identify much with your Asian side?"

"Not really, I mean, my family lives here now, and they were pretty determined to start over in the US. I've never been to Korea and only speak a few words of the language."

Lance coughed to announce their presence, and both Jenny and Bran turned in their chairs to look over at them. Jenny's eyes darted between Nicki and Alex with a hint of worry that gradually faded as they moved into the small kitchen and dining area. Lance slipped past them and went to the boiling pot of water on the stove.

"So, what's your dad?" Lance asked as he dumped a bag of noodles into the hot water.

"He was German, Polish, and a couple of other things," Bran said. "Bit of a classic American mutt."

"Okay, I've got to ask." Nicki looked between Bran and Jenny in confusion. "What the hell brought on that conversation?"

"Well, I found a page on Bran the Blessed." Jenny turned her tablet so they could see the screen. "And it was kind of funny, so I asked Bran if he was Irish or anything like that, and he laughed and told me he was half Korean." Jenny giggled at herself. "It really wasn't that crazy or random, I promise."

"Apparently Bran the Blessed is a Welsh figure who went to war with Ireland," Bran explained, looking a bit too amused by the situation. "Now that's probably only semi-historical or a later addition, based on our experiences thus far with how accurate these things are." Bran licked his lips and seemed to struggle for words for a moment. "The thing is that Bran the Blessed apparently had this cauldron that could heal; some stories give it other abilities, but the thing was powerful."

"One of the linked articles was about how the cauldron might have been one of the mythological items that inspired the Holy Grail," Jenny admitted with a conflicted look.

"Plus, Bran the Blessed's head was supposed to have been cut off and buried," Bran finished. "Actually, the myth says it is at the white hill, which some think is the modern Tower of London."

"Bran means raven," Jenny added quickly.

"Yeah, so that's part of the whole 'if ravens ever leave the tower' thing probably," Bran said. "But the point is that this is a Welsh figure that actually might link to the Iron Chalice."

"The Iron Soul's name was Gofiben," Alex said with a small frown. "But you might be right about this being a clue. It's at least in Wales." Alex set the tablet down. "Anything else?"

Nicki reached forward to grab the tablet and scrolled through it, nodding her head a few times. "Okay, Bran the Blessed is from the Second Branch of the Mabinogion. His cauldron can resurrect the dead, though those revived cannot speak. He gives it to the King of Ireland when the king marries Bran's sister, but war breaks out." Nicki's eyebrows went up, and she glanced towards Bran before continuing. "He is wounded in the leg, and the cauldron is destroyed. Bran's head is severed, and his followers take it back to Britain, leading to its eventual burial to protect Britain."

"This is why I've never been big on mythology," Lance said with a disgusted look. "They cut off his head?"

"In Celtic tradition, the head was the seat of the soul, emotion, and strength," Nicki explained. "It's one of the reasons for them taking the heads of warriors they slew in battle."

"Okay, gross," Lance remarked with a shudder.

"Additionally, well more amusing than anything, is that the Bran myth is also linked to the Fisher King myth of Arthurian legend. You noticed the whole leg injury thing," Bran told Alex with a pointed look. "Maybe I'm overly optimistic, but three strong links to the legends connected to what we're looking for makes me wonder if this might not be the right research path to take."

"Fisher King?" Lance repeated with a frown. "I'm not familiar with that."

"Well, it's a lesser-known part of Arthurian lore," Nicki explained. "It's not a popular story like the sword in the stone or Lancelot and Guin-" Nicki stopped herself sheepishly. "Never mind."

"The Fisher King, or the Wounded King, is a weird figure in the Grail story," Bran said, drawing attention away from the blushing Nicki. "He changes a lot depending on the writer of the Grail myth, but he's usually the last in a long line of grail keepers, sort of like the knight in the Indiana Jones movie. Anyway, he's a king who has some kind of injury, usually the groin though the medieval text said thigh, and is incapable of moving on his own. Due to this, his connection to the land is weakened, and his kingdom starts to become a wasteland. All he is able to do is fish near his castle, where he waits for someone to heal him. In the Grail stories, the knight who is seeking it uses the Grail to heal the Fisher King."

"Uh... if he was the guardian of the Grail, why didn't he heal himself with it?" Lance asked. He was pouring cans of sauce into another pot and turned to look towards them. "What?" he asked at the weird looks.

"It's a valid question," Jenny said in his defense. She sent a warning look towards Bran that made Alex smile.

"I think some stories say that he got the wound because he tried to use the Grail," Nicki answered carefully with a thoughtful look. "At least in some versions. In other versions, one of the Knights of the Round Table was the one who hurt him. There are a ton of variations."

"Really, a Knight of the Round Table hurt him?" Lance asked with a frown. "I thought they were supposed to be the good guys?"

"Well, medieval knights: nice to certain classes of people, douches to others and jerks who disobeyed the tenets of being a knight," Nicki offered with a shrug. "We tend to make myths nicer in our modern retellings."

"We're off-topic," Alex interjected.

"Yeah, back to the Grail issue," Bran reminded them all with a roll of his eyes. "Though it's not the Holy Grail we're after: we're after the Chalice that inspired the story of Bran the Blessed's cauldron and those later myths."

"The source of the archetype," Alex said with a nod. "Okay, it looks like we've got something at least to go on, but is there really any chance that Bran the Blessed's head is under London, or are we thinking it's in Wales somewhere? We're still lacking a real idea of what we're looking for."

"Yeah, and there isn't a location given in the Fisher King myth that I put any faith in for a possible site of the Chalice and... Bran's head."

"Wait," Jenny called out, fixing a curious look on Bran. "Isn't your last name Fisher?"

"Yeah, it is," Bran agreed with a nod and slight blush. "Bit weird, I know. My nickname being Bran and Fisher being my last name, but it's just a coincidence."

"Do you actually believe in coincidences?" Jenny raised a beautifully shaped eyebrow.

"Sure." Bran shrugged and gave Jenny a look of his own, "Though in some cases, I'll admit that magic probably has an impact and there may be a bit more going on than we know so far, but yes, I'm completely okay with the idea of a coincidence."

Jenny looked like she wanted to say something else, but thought better of it. Alex held back a sigh of relief. Everyone seemed to be doing alright today, and she could only hope that it continued for a couple more days, at least. Lance glanced her way as he brought a stack of mismatched plates over from one of the cabinets, looking a touch worried. A moment later, he brought over the forks, which clanked loudly in the quiet room.

"I think we need to talk with Morgana again," Alex suggested. "Maybe this will spur some kind of memory."

"If she knew about it, don't you think she'd have said something by now?" Bran asked.

Nicki frowned, her lips twisting unpleasantly. "Or maybe she's withholding information to see what we can find."

"Don't be unkind, Nicki," Bran told her sternly.

"Morgana said that she and Merlin weren't present during that last bit with the Chalice, so this may just be a mess of stories to her as well," Alex reminded Nicki. "The person who took the Chalice to hide and maybe… Bran's head," Alex flinched when she said that, feeling a bit ill, "Well, they died before they reported where they hid it, so this is all second-hand at best for her too."

Bran sighed and shrugged while Nicki begrudgingly nodded at Alex's words. "Well, then I think we have to call her." Bran chuckled and glanced towards Jenny. "And this is why you should actually be grateful that you've got the phone that works over here. I don't think Morgana has your number."

"Oh, I bet Morgana does," Alex said. "It's probably more like she'd keeping Merlin from finding out what it is."

Jenny appeared more than a little uncomfortable at that idea but was distracted by Lance bringing over a steaming pot of noodles and pasta sauce with a little cheese sprinkled on top. He handed Nicki the oversized spoon and a plate with a tentative smile that the redhead returned. For a moment, Alex wished she could take a picture of the group to send to Merlin and Morgana, probably with a caption like 'see you didn't have to talk about killing them.' It was probably just as well that her phone couldn't access a network right now.

"Alright so Alex will talk to Morgana after dinner," Bran said, pulling her attention back to the here and now as she was dished up a plate of pasta. "And the rest of us will hide from her just in case Merlin is also present."

Alex sat down at the table and grabbed one of the forks, trying to ignore the odd churn in her stomach at the idea of talking to Merlin about everything that was going on. Sighing softly, Alex leaned her face against her left hand as she slowly began eating, and listened to the others try to find a topic they could all discuss that had nothing to do with Arthurian lore or Celtic mythology. They had to settle on school and their classes for next semester; the hint of awkwardness still hung in the air around them, but not as thick.

After they finished dinner, Alex noticed that Nicki was moving rather sluggishly. Her usual energy was absent, and she'd been quiet the last half of the meal. Sharing a look with Bran, Alex silently agreed that Nicki needed rest after dinner. Jenny and Lance seemed to catch on as well. Once everyone was finished, they gathered up the plates and flatware while Jenny started the dishes, and Lance began cleaning up the kitchen.

"We have to leave early in the morning," Bran told Nicki conversationally. "How about showers tonight and turning in early?"

"Yeah," Nicki agreed weakly with a small smile. "Sounds like a plan, uh, anyone mind if I go first?"

"No," Alex agreed quickly. "Go for it. I need to get set up to call Morgana." She picked up the tablet. "Thanks for taking care of dinner, Lance, Jenny. See you upstairs."

"Yeah," Jenny said. "We'll be up later." When you're not talking with the scary history professor went unsaid, but Alex nodded her understanding.

Nicki made it up the stairs without Alex's help, but it was a near thing. Alex almost suggested that Nicki skip the shower and just crawl into bed, but her friend's expression was firm and determined. She glanced towards Bran, who shrugged as Nicki grabbed her small toiletry bag and vanished into the bathroom.

"I'll watch the door." Bran sighed as the bathroom door closed with a firm clicking sound. "Good luck."

Putting down the tablet, Alex logged in and scrolled down her list of contacts. Morgana was logged on, and Alex exhaled in a blend of resignation and relief. The call connected almost instantly as the sound of the shower turning on hummed in the room.

"Hello, Alex," Morgana greeted pleasantly with relief on her face. "I'm glad you called."

"What time is it there?" Alex asked with curiosity as she recognized that Morgana was in her study at her home with a tall bookcase behind her. The professor was dressed in a university sweatshirt with her long dark hair hanging loose. "I didn't wake you, did I?"

"Relax, dear, it's just after three in the afternoon." Morgana smiled warmly. "How are you? Are you alright? What about the others?"

"Well, we're okay, we're in Cardiff right now and heading for the coast tomorrow, but we were attacked by more creatures. These ones had red caps and didn't seem to be bothered by blood."

"Did they hurt you?" Morgana asked with narrowing eyes. "Bloody red caps."

"Uh no, they got Lance, not me, but Nicki took care of it," Alex explained in a rush. "But yeah, we thought they might be Red Caps. Are they immune to iron?"

"Not fully, but they are close to it. From birth in our world, they expose their young to human blood, so they build up a resistance to it. Nasty little creatures, usually found in big cities. I don't think they actually go after humans as the myths suggest, but they do like to collect spilled blood." Morgana shuddered with a look of distaste. "Most of the refugees don't bother me much; their ancestors were slaves and couldn't go back to their homeworlds, but Red Caps I hate."

"Okay..." Alex was unsure of the look on Morgana's face. "So, no news on how the Queen is getting them to attack?"

"No: that kind of magic is just... Merlin and I can't comprehend it." Morgana shook her head with a deep frown. "We've had a few attacks here as well, I'm afraid, which is really putting Merlin on edge. With the winter solstice approaching, things should be calming down, but they're not."

"You don't have any ideas, nothing at all?"

"Alex, the Queen is taking control of creatures that by rights should be trying to kill her, not us; they might not love the Iron Realm as it isn't their natural home, but we as mages don't go hunting down the peaceful refugees. We're actually allies with some of them, so this... this whole situation is just wrong."

"Anything on Arthur, what he was... how he pulled everything off?"

"Nothing there either," Morgana said. The woman shook her head dejectedly. "And trust me Merlin is trying to figure that out. Our current theory is that Arthur is some kind of hybrid like Merlin or myself made by the Queen from a natural mage. He did have magical powers, but his Connection was shaky. Merlin and I made excuses for his lack of a

Connection, which was a mistake on our parts, but now it seems obvious it was because he wasn't loyal to the Iron Realm."

"Then why did I have a Connection with him?" Alex asked sharply with a frown. "He had enough magic tied to Earth for that."

"Or perhaps it was some kind of recognition on your part since you were related in a previous life."

Alex shuddered, and whined, "Please don't mention that. I was sleeping with the bastard."

"You were cousins three thousand years ago," Morgana reminded her with a sympathetic smile. "And you were male then if it helps."

"Doesn't really," Alex muttered before she shook her head. "Okay, so we've still got a lot of mysteries, but we had a thought tonight-"

The bathroom door opened, and a damp Nicki came stumbling out. She glanced towards Alex with glassy eyes and gave her a small wave. Without a word, Nicki climbed into her bunk and pulled the duvet over her head.

"Alex?" Morgana called.

"Uh, right, sorry. Nicki was just going to bed," Alex informed her with a forced smile. "She's very tired."

"Healing is exhausting," Morgana agreed carefully. "But if she wasn't unconscious right from the start, she'll be fine. Just let her take it easy tomorrow if possible."

"We will," Alex promised before she licked her lips. "Okay, my question is, what do you know about Bran the Blessed?"

"Bran the Blessed," Morgana repeated with a tight frown. "I suppose I should have expected that question."

15

The Dead Aflame

7 21 B.C.E. North Pembrokeshire Coast

It was the smell of smoke as thatched roofs caught fire and the sounds of people screaming that hit Merlin first. The terrible familiarity of it made his body ache before years of habit activated, spurring him into action. Merlin pulled on the small flickering force below his heart and was rewarded with magic flowing through his body. Morgana was already rushing towards the screaming as another explosion rocked the hill. Chunks of flaming wood fell around them.

Merlin could see part of the outer wall crumbling in the light of several burning roundhouses as he began to move forward. The roundhouses and walls kept him from seeing outside the village and confirming if Badb was attacking. Green sparks of magic flickered across his palm as Merlin scanned the area for any sign of the enemy. The smoke was thickening and reflecting the light of the flames, making it difficult to see as Merlin sought to navigate the unfamiliar network of paths.

People were yelling and screaming as bolts of dark-red energy zinged through the air. Eyes widening, Merlin swept his magic forward around a small girl running up the hill. Green sparks surrounded her in a cloud blocking one of the dark-red bolts, but another struck a nearby man in the back, throwing him to the ground. His skin darkened, and he struggled for air, collapsing as the little girl screamed. Pulling back the magic, Merlin gathered it in an orb grasped in his right hand. The little girl ran as Merlin scanned the smoky sky.

Laughter echoed out of the smoke, and the fires parted as a female figure stalked out of the haze. She stopped just beyond the burned-down ruins of the outer wall and smirked as she fixed her eyes on Merlin with Cathanáil still strapped to his back. The thin circle of red in Badb's eyes was glowing in the light of the fires, and the tips of her long black hair were aflame as she laughed. Her feathered cloak slipped off of her shoulder as she sent a wave of dark-red magic hurtling through the air, revealing a bony shoulder with tightly stretched gray skin over it.

"Give me the Sword, mage, and I will depart." Badb's expression was smug. "Or this little blight of a town will burn to ash."

"Never!" Morgana shouted, coming up behind him.

Silver magic lashed through the air like a whip as Morgana stopped beside him. She moved her hand sharply to direct the magic as it struck Badb in the chest, forcing an animalistic cry from her. A wave of dark-red magic rippled out and vanished as it connected with Morgana's whip, making both dissipate. Large gray wings unfolded from behind Badb's back as she turned towards Morgana and hissed. Her teeth lengthened, and the red of her pupils bled over her entire eye. Merlin felt a shiver run up his spine at the gleeful expression on her face. Badb raised her right hand, and wisps of dark-red magic shifted and spun around her fingers as her eyes glowed.

"She can't keep this up too long," Morgana hissed next to him. "This isn't her world; she doesn't have Cyrridven's link to the Iron Realm."

Merlin wasn't sure about Morgana's assumptions, though he had to admit that she had a point. The Sídhe's magic was limited in this world, and while the Old Ones were powerful and could generate large amounts of magic themselves as beings of pure power, they surely had limits. He was just less certain of those limits than Morgana. In the corner of his eyes, he could see her gathering an orb of silvery magic that flashed between her fingers. She was about to throw it when a man dressed in a long brown robe rushed past them, crying out to Badb with a worship chant spilling forth from his lips.

"Please, Great One!" The druid fell to his knees, the iron decorations on his belted sash jangling softly. "Please, what have your servants done to anger you?"

Morgana shouted something that was lost in the sound of Badb's laugh before she opened her hand. Dark fire spilled forth from her fingertips and enveloped the man, who screamed in agony. His form withered as he fell to the ground and attempted to put out the flames, but the magical fire could not be extinguished. Merlin summoned his own magic in a quick bolt of power that he threw at Badb. It struck her, and a snarl escaped her as she spun towards Merlin.

"Give me the Sword, or I shall burn them all!"

"You will never hold Cathanáil!" Merlin shouted.

He pulled forth his magic frantically. Beneath his feet, he could feel the ground pulsing with power and pushing raw magic up his body. His legs trembled from the force, but he smiled softly as his hands glowed brilliant leaf green. Moving his hands, Merlin released the magic into the trod down earthen paths of the village. The ground shook, and Merlin pulled on it harshly. In the corner of his eyes, he could see a few people falling to the ground and struggling to crawl away from the fight, but he didn't ease the spell.

Green magic burst up as cracks formed in the ground and around the humans running for cover. Across the village, the glow of the fires dimmed as mounds of earth washed over the flames and smothered them. Morgana moved away from him, sending bolts of silver magic against Badb, who swept her arms to create a shield of her dark-red magic. The two colors clashed against each other until both faded away in the dark air.

"Do you think it is that easy, you pathetic little iron children?" Badb sneered.

She twirled her hands, gathering dark-red magic that sparked around her, casting twisted shadows. Before Merlin could move to stop whatever she was planning, Badb laughed gleefully and tore her hands apart, sending her magic crashing all around them. Shapes of dark-red swarmed through the air surrounding them too fast for Merlin to see anything clearly. They surged over the bodies of the fallen on the ground and seeped into the corpses through mouths and eyes. Merlin stopped in his tracks, completely stunned as the corpses began to glow dark-red. Then one of them moved its arm, sending Merlin stumbling back in shock. The arm shifted, and its hand clawed at the ground as it began to sit up.

The horrific burn marks on its face, the still-burning clothes on its body, and the smell of cooking flesh made Merlin gag as the corpse rose up from the ground. Others around it followed, all with the same magic pulsing beneath their skin. Screaming erupted anew throughout the village as more of the bodies began to rise up. Some were burned up and still on fire, some had been crushed by the explosion of Badb's magic, and some had been trampled by frightened animals, or worse, their own neighbors. Yet they all stood.

The corpses began to move with slow steps and outstretched hands. Dead eyes gazed at Merlin while sparks of Badb's magic flickered from within. Merlin's mind raced as he tried to understand what he was seeing and what to do. Dark-red magic flared off of one of the corpses as it stumbled past a roundhouse and flashed into flames, setting the house ablaze. As they shambled towards the living, the grasses and fences were catching fire, and the screaming was getting louder and louder. A sharp cry of alarm from behind him cut through the din as Merlin recognized the voice of Gofiben. Releasing a burst of magic, Merlin forced the earth beneath the dead to rise up sharply, sending them tumbling to the ground.

Badb laughed as he turned his back, and he knew she'd be upon him in moments, but he rushed up the slope of the hill and looked around for any sign of Gofiben. In the smoke and waves of heat, Merlin feared that he would lose his way back to the young man's roundhouse, but he kept moving. The screams were growing softer as people fled the village, and Merlin found himself hoping that Gofiben had done the same. Yet he had an instinct that the smith hadn't gone anywhere. He caught sight of movement in the corner of his eye and turned sharply to the right, barely missing a blast of dark-red magic, but he spotted Gofiben still near his home.

Anger and fear flared in Merlin's chest as the walking dead closed in around the smith, his brother, and his friend. Only Galath was armed and swung his axe into the skull of one of the corpses. It collapsed to the ground as Galath roughly tugged his axe from its head, but then began moving again. Gofiben reached out and pulled his brother back from the creature just in time to keep the thing from tripping him as he swung at another corpse.

"Gofiben!" Merlin shouted as he tugged the Sword off of his back.

As the boy turned to look at him with wide eyes full of terror, Merlin almost changed his mind. This was just a young man: he wasn't a warrior. That was his elder brother. Apparently, he was just a smith. Then again, he conceded as he ripped away the bindings on the sheath and threw it through the air towards Gofiben; that was what he'd once been training to be.

Gofiben jumped to catch Cathanáil in both arms, hugging the sheathed blade to his chest with a stunned and confused look. Around him, the corpses glowing with magic began to move towards him. Gathering more magic in his hand, Merlin shoved it harshly through the air. It sparked and swirled violently before striking one of the corpses and bouncing against another. They both fell to the ground with a fleshy thud that made his stomach turn and did not move again.

Gofiben tugged the Sword out of the sheath clumsily, but within moments the blade was exposed to the night air and the light of the fires. The blade was just over two feet long with an elegant golden hilt that had been crafted with the help of Cyrridven. Cathanáil gleamed brightly and began to glow a faint orange color as Gofiben's magic connected with the Sword. For a moment, Merlin couldn't breathe as he saw sparks of magic begin jumping off the Sword as Gofiben stared at it in shock.

One of the corpses stumbled towards Gofiben, its leg mangled from being trampled. Sending a blast of magic down into the ground, Merlin pulled the earth beneath the reanimated creature up around its legs. As the mud hardened and sealed it in place, Gofiben swung the Sword at the body with his eyes closed tightly. Magic flashed off the Sword, and as Cathanáil sliced into the flesh, Merlin could see the orange of Gofiben's magic flashing against the dark-red of Badb's.

Then the corpse fell to the ground with the long groan of a dying man. Gofiben opened his eyes and Merlin saw him tremble, but he kept a tight hold of Cathanáil as another corpse lumbered towards him. Merlin barely moved before Gofiben tensed up and swung the Sword again. His brother was rushing up next to him, hacking at the corpses with his axe and a terrified expression as he kept glancing towards his brother.

Assured that Gofiben was safe, Merlin spun around and released a wave of green magic down the hillside. It rolled down the gentle slope towards the fires and walking dead like the tide and washed over the flames. The dead stumbled as the magic struck their feet, causing small flashes as Badb's magic pushed away his own. But it slowed them down. Silver magic flashed as Morgana swung her magic around her like two thin, deadly whips, striking at any corpse that came too close. Pausing in her defense, she gathered a sparkling cloud of silver magic above her head and sent it spinning through the air towards Badb.

A scream of frustration drew Merlin's attention back to the Old One, who summoned her own magic to block Morgana's attack. Several of the corpses fell to the ground as she changed her focus, and Merlin could see Morgana's smirk of triumph illuminated dangerously by the flames. Merlin felt his breath catch in his throat, feeling a rush of excitement and vindication. He twisted his own magic tightly in his hands, willing it to condense. The shimmering green sparks solidified in his grasp, forming a solid spear of glowing rock.

Morgana risked a glance towards him before unleashing another wave of silver magic. Her moves and attacks were wild and uncontrolled, but they were keeping Badb busy. Merlin inhaled quickly as his magic settled into the spear before he raised it. Summoning even more magic, Merlin pictured the spear striking Badb and called on the magic to keep his aim true. He threw it forward.

The spear shattered on contact with her form into hundreds of small earthen fragments that latched onto her. They began to expand even as Badb screamed and began tearing the largest pieces. Merlin smiled as several of the fragments connected across Badb's chest and right arm. The Old One's shriek of anger turned into one of terror as her long taloned fingers clawed at the stone skin encasing her. Her magic flared wildly over her limbs to fight back Merlin's. Silver magic swirled around her head, and Merlin gasped softly as he saw the right side of Badb's gray face begin to collapse under the pressure of Morgana's magic.

A scream filled the night as dark-red magic exploded around Badb in one giant burst of power. Merlin felt himself being pushed back by the force and watched his magic crumble away from her. Then everything went still, and he could hear pained sounds escaping Badb. Around them, he heard bodies hitting the ground and saw the flicker of dark-red magic in the air vanishing.

The smell of wood smoke, charred fabric, and cooked meat filled the air, making Merlin feel ill, but he kept his eyes locked on Badb. Screaming, she swept her feathered cloak around her body. It shifted violently in a swirl of her dark-red magic, and a gray and black bird swept up into the sky. Raising his eyes, Merlin summoned more magic on a swell of anger and released it as a leaf green bolt. Badb, in her bird form, released a sharp cry and dove to avoid the blast before vanishing into the pillars of fiery red smoke.

Merlin frowned and examined the fallen corpses, one of them had fallen into the burning remains of a roundhouse, and its clothes caught fire. It was such a waste, and he looked towards Morgana with a heavy heart. His counterpart had a look of barely contained rage and disgust on her face as she looked down at the corpse of a young girl. Then she closed her green eyes and shook herself quickly before she stepped away from the corpse.

Morgana hummed softly as her silvery magic spun around her hands, her eyes closed in concentration. Her magic swirled together to form an orb that slowly transformed from light into water as a drop of sweat ran down Morgana's cheek. With a soft grunt, she opened her eyes and tossed the water orb into the nearest fire. Steam rose out of the flames with a hiss, and Morgana released another burst of magic as water to extinguish another fire. Merlin nodded in silent agreement and glanced towards Gofiben only a few feet away. To his relief, the boy appeared uninjured.

His own magic resisted the transformation into water more than Morgana's, but he finally managed enough water to splash out a few of the fires. Around them, the survivors were rushing about with jars of water to put out the flames and salvaging what they could. The walls of the village were all but gone with people vanishing into the night with tears and cries of sorrow. It was all too familiar.

Merlin caught sight of Bran tending to a wounded woman and directing the efforts to put out the fires. He felt a small burst of pride in his chest at the realization that the young man had not just taken off. Gofiben at least had Cathanáil to help him fight: it seemed that somehow the Sword knew its own power and could pull on the power of the Iron Soul even if the Iron Soul was not yet trained. But Bran had not had any such advantage, and despite the horror of the situation around him, Merlin gave a satisfied nod.

He busied himself with his magic to put out the fires and caught sight of Morgana kneeling next to an injured child with glowing hands. He frowned and told himself to remind her to be cautious with healing. They could not afford to lose her to a mistake. Still, he smiled indulgently at the sight of Morgana speaking with the frightened little thing until a crying woman rushed over and swept the girl into her arms. As the fires were extinguished, those that had fled began to trickle back into the village with shocked and pained expressions.

Merlin turned and began to head towards Gofiben, noting that Bran was gone. It only took him a few moments to find the young men together near Gofiben's roundhouse. Bran stepped up next to Gofiben and said something to him in a voice that Merlin couldn't hear. The young smith was shaking, and it was only his brother's hand on his shoulder that was keeping him steady. Merlin paused to give them a moment as Bran hugged his friend and spoke to Galath. Morgana did not wait and swept up to them with her cloak flaring behind her. Shaking his head, Merlin joined them at the entrance to Gofiben's roundhouse, which was one of the few unharmed by the attack.

"Was that?" Bran turned to look at Merlin and Morgana, his eyes wide. "Was that-"

"Yes," Morgana informed him with a nod as she wiped the sweat from her brow with an unscorched corner of her cloak. "That was Badb, the Old One that attacked us a few days ago."

"She wanted that Sword," Galath observed with a frown as he pointed towards the blade in Gofiben's hand with a hesitant look. "Is that Cathaburn?"

"Cathanáil," Merlin corrected. There was a rush of irritation in his chest. How soon people forgot, but he recovered quickly. "Yes, she wants the Sword for some reason."

"And you can't give it to her," Galath clarified with a worried look at his brother's face.

Gofiben was still holding the Sword with both hands on the hilt and looking at the polished surface of the metal with awe. He didn't seem to notice them, and Merlin wondered if it was the smith or the Iron Soul that was captivated by the blade. The pulse of magic was receding, but Merlin couldn't help but think that Cathanáil looked a little brighter now.

"And you want my brother to fight her." Galath stepped protectively between Gofiben and Morgana.

Merlin expected anger from Morgana, a sharp outburst of frustration, but instead, she looked at Galath with soft, understanding eyes. Then her gaze shifted to Merlin as she waited to see what he would do. Swallowing, Merlin stood there in silence, trying to organize his thoughts. There had been no time to process Cyrridven's revelation of Gofiben's true nature. The boy was a young man, not a child that he could raise for his great responsibly. And the way Morgana was looking at him... he could see her as a conflicted young woman as he took her brother away after the Sídhe attack. She'd betrayed him to the Sídhe, but even then, she'd loved Arto, and now she was in the same position he had been then.

"It's alright, Galath," Gofiben announced. He sounded calm as he set one hand on his brother's shoulder. "Look around, brother." The boy's expression was mournful as he nodded at the carnage around them. "This can't... I can't just let this go on. She'll come back if I just stay here."

"Yes," Merlin agreed. He felt a twinge of guilt for putting so much on the young man. "She will."

Gofiben released a long breath and swallowed thickly as his gaze dropped to the blade in his hand. "And you don't know why she wants the Sword so badly?"

"We do not," Morgana agreed with a nod and a softer expression. "But there is power in the blade; you have not been trained, and yet with Cathanáil, you were able to cancel out Badb's magic."

"Any chance that will dissuade her?" Galath asked. He was still standing protectively by his brother.

"Doubtful," Merlin said. He shook his head gently, wishing once more that he had his staff to lean on. "I'm afraid that she has decided it is time for another war."

16

Fog of Myth

E yes widening at Morgana's statement, Alex waited impatiently for her to say something more about Bran, but instead, the professor looked mildly confused. Alex supposed that she was trying to organize her thoughts to explain, but Alex found it difficult to wait.

"Was he based on a real person?" Alex asked. She fidgeted in the uncomfortable chair. "Someone you knew?"

"Bran was a rather gifted young mage who grew up with Gofiben," Morgana explained. "While his magic took the form of power over plants, he also had visions similar to your Bran."

"And that doesn't strike you as strange?" Alex asked only to have Morgana chuckle.

The ancient mage brushed a strand of her long dark hair behind her ear and regarded Alex with warm green eyes. "You are not the first Alex that I have known. There have been many Alexanders, a few Alexandrias, a couple of other Alexandras, and even an Aleksander or two. Names don't have the power that you think, and Bran is a shortened form of Brandon. It didn't seem that important in the grand scheme of things. I'm three thousand years old; I'm a bit past jumping to conclusions and chasing every ghost that I think I see."

"Okay... so what happened to Bran, the ancient one then?"

"He died in the final confrontation with the Old One Badb's forces," Morgana informed her gently, watching Alex's face carefully. "Merlin and I had been.... lured away, leaving Bran and Gofiben facing off against Badb. I don't know much about how everything happened as both Gofiben and Bran died that day." Morgana paused as guilt flashed in her eyes for a moment. "Merlin and I returned after some time, and Galath wasn't interested in telling us what had happened."

"What happened to lure you away?" Alex tried to ignore the sick feeling in her chest. "Why did you leave them alone?"

"We were retrieving Cathanáil from Badb," Morgana replied. "She was, unfortunately, able to take the Sword and use it to a limited extent. That is why we gave Cathanáil to Cyrridven once it was all over. We had to accept that she could hide Cathanáil's power and keep it safer than we ever could." Morgana shook her head sadly. "Believe me, Merlin and I were distressed to learn that our students had been killed. We'd had very little time with them, and they were good men."

"But Bran... our Bran, there's so many little things. Didn't you ever think, I mean, didn't you ever wonder during the last year and a half? Even Jenny noticed the strong connection between Bran and the myth! Jenny! Why didn't you tell us about Bran the Blessed?"

"Alex, please keep in mind that the myths and legends that you children can read up on are merely those that have survived. People die, people forget, and people make things up. Stories change, especially stories that are passed down orally. After Merlin and I found out about Gofiben's death, we tried to find out what happened, we did, but there were already different stories circulating. Rumors that would later turn into different variations on what would become a myth." Morgana rubbed her eyes and said, "And to be honest, your former brother Galath was of no help. He blamed Merlin and I for Gofiben's death, and while he did tell us about the Iron Chalice, he refused to ever reveal its location to us."

"My brother," Alex repeated weakly.

"At this point, Merlin and I have been exposed to hundreds of tales about Bran and Gofiben. If you think there are too many different versions of fairy tales from the Middle Ages, then imagine how many different rumors Merlin and I heard about what happened to the Chalice, Bran, and Gofiben."

"I suppose but-"

Morgana shook her head and gave Alex a pointed look. "We don't tell you those stories because they are meaningless to us, and if we told you one, then we'd be reciting stories to you for days on end, days that, I will remind you, we have never had the luxury of. Remember, Alex, that most of human history is lost to us; it precedes writing and all oral traditions. Myths and legends are the scraps of human stories and experiences in the past that survive. You cannot count on receiving truth from them." Morgana chuckled, and her gaze softened. "It's a bit like history."

Alex hummed to herself but didn't disagree with Morgana's statement, as much as she hated to acknowledge the point. Morgana was watching her with an amused expression but pressed her lips together thoughtfully a few moments later. "That being said, perhaps looking at the myth has something to it. I never put much stock in the idea that Galath cut off Bran's head and buried it somewhere, but your Bran's vision seems to suggest that it is what happened. It seems odd, but perhaps under the right circumstances, he might have been convinced that it would help."

"Could... well, scrying for the Chalice doesn't work, but maybe you could scry for Bran's head, the ancient Bran's head. If you know who it is, could that help find the Chalice?"

The look Morgana gave her was strange even by Alex's standards. It was a look of almost horrified consideration as the older woman tilted her head slightly. "An interesting thought," Morgana agreed slowly. "I'll certainly try it, but I'm not sure what the magic would have to latch onto. Since the head was buried underground, there might be enough DNA left that the magic could still recognize it as Bran, but I've never scryed for a dead body before."

"But you'll try?" Alex pressed nervously. "I'm afraid that despite looking at the Bran the Blessed story, we still don't have a location to go on. The only real other thing that we're looking at is the potential link between Bran the Blessed and the Fisher King."

"The Fisher King?" Morgana laughed. "Really, Alex, you're looking at the myth of Bran and the Fisher..." Morgana trailed off as her eyes widened and her face went a little pale. It was all Alex could do to keep from smirking as the professor got it. "Bran... Fisher..."

"Like I said, Jenny brought up the connection. Do you think it means anything?"

"I..." Morgana shook her head. Her eyes were still wide and shocked. "I don't know, Alex. Part of me knows that trying to find meaning is dangerous; it'll have you jumping at everything, but then again... it is a bit much, isn't it."

"Morgana?" Alex hoped that the professor wasn't too swept away by the overwhelming oddness of the situation. At the sound of her name, Morgana's eyes cleared, and she looked back at the laptop screen with a small hum. "Is magic... I don't know, sentient?"

"Oh.... That question...." Morgana paused and licked her lips. "I don't know, Alex, not for certain, and not to what extent. Somehow the Iron Soul was created... something in the Sídhe invasion, in the Queen's plans, triggered the creation of your soul and your unmatched connection to the Iron Realm. Somehow Cyrridven became trusted by that same magic despite not being of our world. I've never been inclined to believe in any gods: I wasn't raised in that sort of a culture, but I was raised to believe that power had a flow to it and that everything had a place."

"So, you don't really know?"

"No, I don't," Morgana replied. "There are many things I don't know, Alex. Merlin and I are three thousand years old, and we don't fully understand what a soul is, but we've observed Jenny and Lance coming back time and time again. We don't really know how the Iron Soul was created, but here you are. We know there are other worlds, but Merlin has never left this one, and I haven't left since I was made a Changeling. I don't have a good answer for you, Alex." Morgana paused for a moment. "And if there is something intelligent behind all of this, some force pushing things into place, keep in mind that it might not be the same force that grants us magic and created your soul. Don't assume anything."

Alex heard a knock on the door that made her instantly go silent. Morgana raised a hand at the screen and looked away from Alex. "It's Ambrose; stay quiet, Alex, or else he may demand your location." Morgana informed her with a slight chuckle before calling back, "Come in, Ambrose."

"Is that a good idea?" Alex whispered to Morgana, unable to ignore the sudden nervous knot forming in her stomach. She liked Merlin, but they hadn't really spoken since Arthur had stabbed her, and this mess had begun. "Didn't you say-"

"Hello, Ambrose," Morgana greeted, ignoring Alex and looking past the laptop screen. "How was the hospital?"

"Fine. Aiden isn't doing any better, but there hasn't been any magical interference from the Queen or that bastard." Alex could hear Merlin clearly even if she couldn't see him.

"I doubt the Pendreds will put their efforts into killing Aiden at this point." Morgana's expression was too calm, but Alex stayed silent. "They seem to be focusing their efforts in another direction."

"Indeed, I haven't had any luck with contacting Shiva. I'm not sure if he's awake right now or not."

"That's unfortunate; we don't have many allies amongst the Old Ones. What about Sif?"

"Nothing. I'm not even sure how to contact her or Odin. The Norse that are awake are rather content to blend in with humans whenever possible." Merlin sighed loudly and then gave a strained chuckle. "Don't tell me you're working on next term already."

"I was working on researching Elaine Pendred if you must know," Morgana said. "She has a full history including medical records from before Arthur's birth, though since then she hasn't been to see a doctor. Her husband passed away shortly before Arthur was born in a car crash, though I wonder if it was an accident."

"How much of this do you think is true?" Merlin asked, and Alex heard the shuffling of papers.

"Difficult to say, but I am inclined to believe that Elaine Pendred was a real person once. Perhaps some form of possession is at play here; Scáthbás' body was destroyed, but she..."

"She was against the forming Iron Gate when you killed her." There was a hint of disapproval in Merlin's voice. "Terrible to think that she survived in any form through Arto's magic."

"It is just a theory, but Medraut was there as well. Perhaps she captured his soul, and when she escaped, she took over a pregnant woman in order to bring Medraut back to life." Morgana's fingers toyed with her pendant.

"How did she know that Elaine's child would be a mage?" Merlin asked. "I think the boy may be a hybrid now like us, but to keep the charade of him being the Iron Soul going, it would be important that he have some sort of link to the Iron Realm."

"But then we're back to the problem of how could he use magic," Morgana agreed with a nod. Then a sad sigh escaped her. "I lost the ability to use my powers as a young woman when I was conflicted."

"Indeed: it is a puzzle, but that is not why I'm here," Merlin said. Alex heard the sound of a chair moving. "Have you been in contact with Alex?"

"She's checked in occasionally to let me know that she is safe."

"I still disapprove of you letting Alex leave Ravenslake." Alex could hear him pacing. "If she'd merely returned to Spokane then one of us could have stayed close in case of trouble, but sending her after the Iron Chalice-"

"Save your breath, Merlin, I didn't apologize yesterday, and I won't be apologizing today. Alex isn't alone. She has Bran and Nicki with her."

"And Jenny and Lance."

"Where is your optimism, Merlin?" Morgana teased with a hint of bite in her voice. "They betrayed Arthur already, and Alex knows who they are. I do believe that we dodged the metaphorical bullet this time; it seems you were right to be optimistic at the start of last year."

"They betrayed the person we thought was Arthur, who used them as part of his grand show. I do feel sorry for Jenny having been manipulated for so long in order to help that little bastard with his deception, but they could still-"

"Merlin! Listen to yourself," Morgana snapped, and Alex could see a flush of red working its way up her teacher's neck. Merlin stopped pacing, and Morgana exhaled slowly to calm down. "I'm worried too. I know I'm hard on the reincarnations of that pair, but they know what they are now. Besides, I've noticed no lesbian tendencies in Alex that lead me to be concerned about she and Jenny starting a doomed romance in this life."

Alex kept herself from making noise at that statement. She slipped a hand over her mouth to muffle any giggles and noticed Morgana glance towards the screen with a tiny smile.

"Perhaps it could go the other way this time!" Merlin still sounded agitated.

"Well, our observations of Lance are that he is a very polite, compassionate, and intelligent young man, but he has been infatuated with Jenny since they first met, despite her dating Arthur," Morgana said. There was a hint of a smile on her face. "For once those two actually seem to be making an effort at behaving like adults. Besides, Alex is fond of them, and it is her decision if she wants to have them accompany her. Under the circumstances, I highly doubt romance is on any of their minds."

"Morgana... how can you be so calm about this? This is Alex; you were fond of her even before we knew she was the Iron Soul. That should have tipped us off; you were so fond of the girl. Why are you behaving so calmly like this?"

"We do seem to have traded roles," Morgana agreed. "But to quote someone I know, 'we can't keep her under lock and key. Need I remind you of how much some of her incarnations have chafed at the very idea?"

There was an odd note in Professor Cornwall's voice, and Alex was certain that it was Merlin that Morgana was quoting. Morgana had a pleased little smile on her face, and it was difficult for Alex not to giggle, but the revelation that they were talking about her and her other lives helped still the impulse. Alex could hear Merlin huff and then sigh loudly.

"Touché, Morgana," Merlin agreed, still out of view. It was silent for a moment before he asked, "Do you think they can find it? You and I accepted the Iron Chalice lost to us a very long time ago."

"That's not entirely true; you did go on that three-year quest for it back in the 14th century, or was it the 15th century?"

"There was nothing important going on then, but I searched across Wales and even down into Devon. Galath hid it well."

"Perhaps we lack the right perspective," Morgana suggested. The professor leaned back in her chair and had a sharp look on her face that made Alex wish she could see Merlin's expression. "Have you given much thought to the old stories surrounding the Iron Chalice?"

"Not recently, not since my rather ill-fated attempt to find some trace of it," Merlin replied in a tired voice. Alex thought she heard him slump into a chair. "Dare I ask what you are thinking, Morgana?"

"Bran Fisher has a great seer talent." Morgana brought her hands up in front of her and folded them neatly. Her eyes were fixed on Merlin, and Alex once again really wished she could see the other mage. "And there is the similarity in his name that makes me a little curious."

"His name?" Merlin chuckled warmly. "I won't argue with his talent as a seer; if the boy was better at scrying then he'd be an immense force for our side. I can only hope that he'll find the right medium for himself soon. But really, Morgana, it is just a name, and a nickname at that."

"Bran the Blessed and the Fisher King." Morgana raised an eyebrow. "I can't help but wonder. The story of the Fisher King has always been hard to trace. Perhaps magic played some role in how that tale began." They were both silent, and Alex was almost afraid to breathe.

"We need to be worried about protecting Alex," Merlin finally said. "Arthur is out there, and I fear he has some strange magic that he and his ... mother are using to achieve these strange happenings. Alex is in danger out there alone. If Arthur finds her-"

"I half-hope he does," Morgana countered sharply. "It would be interesting to find out which one of the girls would do the most damage: Alex, who he tried to kill after seducing, Jenny, who he used for years as a pawn, or Nicki, whose friend is dying in the hospital." Morgana glanced towards the screen and Alex. "Speaking of the hospital, Merlin, I'll guard Aiden tonight. I think your talents would be best spent trying to get more information on the Pendred family. Maybe their financials will reveal where they might be hiding."

"Morgana?" Merlin sounded tired and shocked. "Are you truly placing greater value on saving Aiden then the life of the Iron Soul; on Arto's current life?"

"Alex isn't Arto," Morgana's eyes were locked on Alex's through the computer screen. "She is the Iron Soul, but she is herself as well. We made so many mistakes with Gofiben because we were more concerned about protecting Arto's legacy than him. I know we needed to save the Sword, but we should have been worried about Gofiben too. If we had been, if one of us had stayed with him..." Morgana looked back towards Merlin. "Then maybe Alex wouldn't be in this position."

"You didn't answer my question," Merlin said after a long moment of silence. "Do you think they can find the Iron Chalice?"

"I don't know, Merlin, I honestly don't know, but I know that Alex needs to try."

A deep sigh escaped Merlin. "Very well. You take the hospital tonight, and I'll see how far I can get with my magic on the mystery of the Pendreds."

"Thank you, Merlin."

There was the sound of someone crossing the room, and then the door opened and closed. Morgana turned her attention back to the screen with a neutral and suddenly unreadable face. The professor gave Alex a small smile. Alex wanted to ask why Gofiben's brother had been so angry with them and what Morgana had meant by her statements to Merlin, but she had no words.

"Trust your instincts, Alex. I hope for Aiden's sake that whatever theory you've got forming in your mind about Bran is accurate, and that it is enough to lead you to the Iron Chalice."

"Thank you, Morgana," Alex forced out. Her mouth was dry, and her throat strangely sore despite her silence for the last part of the video call. "We'll be careful," she promised.

Morgana's face softened, and she smiled more warmly at Alex. "I'd be most grateful if you would, Alex. Stay in touch just to let me know you're safe. A simple text will do if you can't manage anything more or an email."

"I will," Alex heard herself promise once again. "Thank you for your honesty."

"Even when it isn't useful, I will always try to be honest with you," Morgana assured. "And who knows, maybe you're right about this."

"Don't forget to scry for Bran's head," Alex added quickly, only to make a horrified face. "I can't believe I just said that."

Laughing, Morgana shook her head with a real smile on her face. "Get some rest, Alex, and remember to follow your instincts, and if you are right, then focus on following Bran. I'll email you or call Jenny's phone if I come up with anything."

The video call ended, and Alex collapsed back in the uncomfortable metal chair with a deep sigh and stared up at the ceiling unsure of how to feel about her life.

17

Welcome to Pembrokeshire

This train was not as nice as the other trains. It felt smaller and more confined, even though Nicki was pretty sure it was the same size. While the other train had lots of tables with four chairs around it so passengers could do things, this train had only one table in the whole car and was surrounded by those irritating traditional front-facing rows and rows of uncomfortable plastic chairs. Bran and Lance were on one side of the table with Alex and Jenny across from them. She was the odd one out sitting in one of the terrible forward-facing seats across from them. Five wasn't a good number to travel with.

"So, we're heading for the biggest town in the area, but it's still only like 13,000 people?" Lance gave them a dubious look as he shifted in the small seat. "Seriously?"

"This is Wales," Bran said. "Europe really does have small towns, you know." He flipped through a couple of pages in the tourist guide he was holding.

"Anything in there we actually need to know?" Nicki leaned into the aisle, trying to catch a glimpse of the pictures on the glossy pages of the guide.

"Well, Haverfordwest is the administrative center of Pembrokeshire; it's the retail center of the area and has some distinct bluffs in the area. Oh, a village just to the south is called Merlin's Bridge, interesting, but I don't think anything there is helpful to us." Bran scanned through the page, his lips moving as he read through the information. "It's a traditional market town, and lots of the transit comes through there. The history of the area is a bit fuzzy as it's a strategic location, but there haven't been a lot of archeological digs in the area. Though there are traces of Iron Age and Roman occupation. The Iron Age stuff is a good sign for us."

"I doubt this was where Gofiben lived," Alex pointed out carefully. "Morgana probably would have been able to keep track of that with the landmarks."

"Probably, but we might be nearby." Bran shrugged a little. "I picked this as our first destination because it connects via train and bus to a lot of the other towns in the area."

Nicki tried to ignore the hint of helplessness in Bran's voice. She reminded herself that this wasn't anyone's fault and felt the knot trying to form in her chest loosening. Being so angry all the time was quickly becoming exhausting. Looking up, she caught Alex glancing her way and gave the other mage a reassuring nod. Bran kept flipping through his book on Wales, and Nicki forced back a sigh as silence reigned in the car.

"This is so nice." Jenny was looking out the window at the dark sky where only the faintest traces of sunrise were visible. "I wish we had more trains at home. Wouldn't it be great if we could jump on a train to go to Portland from Ravenslake?"

"Sadly, the United States is an automobile country," Nicki said. She chuckled a bit, finding herself rather enjoying the relaxed smile on Jenny's face. The other girl was really very beautiful, but she stopped that train of thought immediately. That was a can of worms they didn't need opened. "I doubt passenger trains will ever be as important for transit back home as they are here."

"There's a lot to be said for both," Bran added. "Trains obviously have the advantage of people not needing cars and not having traffic issues, and depending on the train, they are more environmentally friendly. Cars, on the other hand, provide more independence: trains can't get you to really rural areas, and you can set your own schedule with a car. I'm not sure that I'd prefer trains over cars, to be honest."

"Uh, do you even have a car?" Nicki asked in surprise as she looked at Bran. "You always seem to ride with us... how has this never come up?"

Bran laughed. "I do have a car: Mom hated letting me drive in high school, but I was able to convince her that I needed to be able to drive myself with Aunt Haeun's help. I don't drive it much since it gets uncomfortable after about half an hour." Bran gave her a look and asked, "How did you think I was getting groceries all last year?"

"I kind of just assumed that you only ate on campus," Nicki admitted. She could feel herself blushing. "Okay, it was a bad assumption, apologies."

"Accepted." Bran looked like he was trying not to laugh.

"I'd still like to see more trains," Jenny insisted stubbornly. "I don't care much for flying and airport security, so if trains were more convenient, I'd probably take them more often than not for long trips."

"Speaking of trains, whose idea was it to take the 5:30 AM train?" Alex asked as she rubbed her forehead. Sighing, she leaned against the window. Jenny patted her arm with an amused little smile. "I mean, what have you got against sleep?"

"It's December 18th," Bran said. He still gave Alex a sympathetic look. "We've got to focus on finding something that can help us."

"I know," Alex said. "Sorry, I just didn't sleep well last night."

Nicki could believe it. She'd been awake for part of the phone call with Morgana despite her exhaustion. The chance to overhear whatever information Morgana had was just too tempting to resist, so she'd stayed silent underneath the blanket. Now she kind of wished that she hadn't listened in. Her exhaustion from healing Lance had ensured that she'd fall asleep eventually, but Alex had dark rings under her eyes and a far-off dazed expression.

"Right there with you." Bran closed the book, using his thumb to keep his place. "I had a hard time sleeping myself after someone put some very worrying notions in my head," he said pointedly with a look at Jenny.

"What?" Jenny huffed with a small pout. "You can't deny that it's a pretty serious coincidence. Too much of one!" Jenny looked at Alex. "What do you think, Alex?"

"I don't know," Alex replied. "I was up for hours thinking about it, questioning what I'm prepared to believe about magic, but... I just don't know. It seems a bit much to hope that things would align like that for us, but at the same time, it is hard to ignore that Bran seems to be a walking reference to the Fisher King myth."

"Speaking of references," Nicki said as the tension became a little too much, "I've got some homework for you, missy." She opened up her backpack and pulled out the sheets of paper. "I printed this off at the hostel this morning; start reading."

Nicki handed the pages across the aisle to Bran, who took one look at them and snorted. He handed them to Alex with tightly pressed lips as he struggled not to laugh. Leaning forward, Nicki positioned herself at just the right awkward angle to see Alex's face as she read the first lines of the printout. The blonde's expression was a mix of amusement, disbelief, and curiosity as her gray eyes widened just a bit. A loud giggle escaped Nicki, and she settled back in her chair properly with a smug smile.

"Really, Nicki?" Alex asked pointedly with a dramatic roll of her eyes. "I really don't think this is going to help me."

"Genre savviness is important, Alex," Nicki informed her, maybe feeling a touch too smug. "That's simply the combined knowledge of the mistakes that villains and heroes make most frequently. The Evil Overlord List!"

"I can't see the Sídhe Queen putting me in a death trap rather than just killing me," Alex replied.

"But isn't that why you got out of the tunnels last time?" Bran pointed out. He was smirking, and Nicki sort of wanted to give him a high five or a fist bump. "They left you alone, and you escaped."

"No, I fought my way out, thank you very much, and there was a guard!"

"Do I even want to know what that stuff is?" Jenny questioned. She looked at the grinning Bran and pointed at the papers in Alex's hand.

"Not unless they try to make you read them," Alex muttered, though she did drop her eyes down and start reading the list.

"Okay then, have fun with that." Jenny sent a cautious look towards Nicki that just made Nicki smile. It pleased her in a small, nasty way that the other girl was still nervous around her.

Then Jenny looked away and turned her attention to Lance, who gave her a warm, soft smile. For a moment, the pair seemed content to just stare at each other. Nicki might have felt her heart beat a little faster and her cheeks heat up a tiny bit at the look. There wasn't anything sexual about the look, just... supportive. Lance was looking at Jenny like he had the entire trip; softly and affectionately, but now Jenny was returning the look. It set off a bunch of emotions that Nicki wasn't sure what to do with.

"So do we have a plan once we get to… Havers- the town?" Jenny asked. "Or do we have a timeframe for heading north?"

"Actually, I'm thinking I'll try meditating," Bran said. He shifted nervously. "It helps us connect with our magic, so if we're in the general area of something useful, then maybe it will trigger a vision." He shook his head in frustration. "I was so optimistic in Cardiff when I saw… well, I'm not sure what. I don't know how useful the town proper will be to us."

"What about the general area of this town?" Lance asked. "Anything useful there?"

Bran opened the guidebook again and flipped through a few more pages. "Well, the coastal regions of the area pretty much make up Pembrokeshire National Park. The north section of the park has some Iron Age sites that might be useful to us. If Haverfordwest is a bust, then heading north will probably be our best bet, but after that, I'm not sure."

"So, we really are just relying on your visions?" Lance grimaced and shook his head. "No offense, man, but that's a little unnerving."

"I don't know," Jenny said as she toyed with a strand of her hair. "I bet that Bran's supposed to find the Chalice; maybe that's the reason for the similarity between him and myth." Jenny paused and looked a bit conflicted for a moment. "Maybe he's even a reincarnation of Bran the Blessed."

"So, you think I'm seeing my own head?" Bran sounded like he was trying to tease, but his voice came out too weakly. "Bit creepy."

"We don't know anything on that front," Alex cut in, giving them all a look. "Morgana said she'd try to uh… scry for Bran the Blessed's head. She'll let us know if she finds anything."

And the silence returned with Jenny looking out the window as the beginnings of the sunrise appeared on the horizon. Lance watched Jenny and looked like he wanted to say something. Alex was leaning over the printed sheets Nicki had given her, and a few chuckles escaped her from time to time. They'd gone from almost happy comradery back to awkward silence, and Nicki was aware of the ache at Aiden's absence. She'd been surprised at how smoothly Jenny and Lance were beginning to fit in with their little ragtag team and couldn't help but believe that if Aiden was here that these silences wouldn't happen.

A groan made Nicki look at Bran in alarm. He was clutching the edge of the table with a pained and frustrated expression. His eyes were squeezed shut, and he was breathing hard. Alex reached across the table towards him as she swung her legs out into the aisle with a worried look.

"Bran? Are you okay?" Nicki asked, beginning to shift out of her seat.

"Did I knock your leg?" Alex frantically moved her hands, reaching towards him.

"No, vision," Bran grunted, and they all straightened up around him. "Shit, it's gone!" Bran slammed his hand on the table. "I thought I had something; I saw... I'm not sure; it was so fuzzy."

"That's fine," Alex assured him with a forced smile. "We're heading towards Pembrokeshire, and you having visions trying to form is a good sign."

"Maybe being on the train interfered with it," Lance offered quickly. "Your magic comes from the Earth, but right now, you don't have a solid connection; you're moving over it, so it's not even like a building."

"Yeah." Jenny nodded and gave him a smile. "As Alex said, it's a good sign. Probably means that when you try to meditate, it'll all come together."

"Maybe." Bran forced his fingers to relax around the edge of the table and slumped back against his seat. "We'll see."

It was obvious that he didn't want to talk about it, and Nicki couldn't blame him. This whole quest was basically hinging on his powers, and worse, the one that he couldn't control. Everyone fell silent and looked away from Bran to give him some space, but Nicki couldn't help but sneak glances towards him. Bran was looking down at his leg. His hand was settled on the brace that supported him when he walked.

Nicki studied it for a moment, noting the form-fitting plastic sections that tied in with the metal skeleton structure. When she'd first met Bran through Aiden, she'd gone online to learn more about how leg braces worked, so she didn't say anything stupid. She knew that it helped keep Bran's joints in position so that he could stand and walk; she knew that it didn't really support him, but instead allowed his body to support itself, but he'd never been clear as to why he needed it. She knew about the accident when he was fifteen when Bran's vision had caused him to grab the steering wheel from his mother and turn the car enough to save their lives, but Bran had never gone into detail about the extent and type of his injuries.

He had to be thinking about the Iron Chalice. Jenny pointing out the similarities between Bran and the Fisher King must have gotten him thinking about it, and Jenny hadn't even pointed out the biggest similarity between Bran and the Fisher King. It wasn't about the name, not really: it was about the injury. Bran had an injured leg, he could stand and move around, but running was hard, and combat always left him exhausted if he had to dodge. A terrible little voice in Nicki's head pointed out that Bran's injuries from the car crash might be a lot more severe than just the leg.

Nicki almost blushed at the line of thought she was on. She was a lesbian and thus didn't think much about what men got up to, but the Fisher King's injury had been to his groin. Sure, the medieval writers hadn't wanted to be clear about that, but it was generally accepted to be the case. So maybe it hadn't just been his legs that had been hurt... she couldn't remember Bran going on a date once since they'd met. Aiden was still dating Sarah even if she doubted that was going to last much longer. Alex had been hung up on Arthur since she met him, which was a tragic mistake, and she'd had more than a couple of dates and flings, but Bran.... Nicki did blush now and rubbed her fingers against her forehead.

"I'm going to Hell," she muttered in despair.

Yeah: he had to be thinking about the Iron Chalice and what it could mean for him. Nicki's heart jumped a little at the idea of Bran not having to worry about his leg anymore. To be able to play soccer like he used to, or not have to rely on them so much to watch his back in fights. Nicki shifted uneasily in her chair. Was it wrong to hope for a disabled person to get better; was it an insult to their journey and the things they'd been through? Was it an insinuation that he wasn't good enough? Would he see it that way? Was it wrong for her to be hoping that Bran would be healed? She wasn't sure what to think or how to feel.

Eventually, the others stopped watching Bran with small sideways looks. Alex focused on her reading as the train rolled on towards Haverfordwest while Lance and Jenny tried not to stare at each other. The sun climbed above the horizon, washing the gently sloping fields that were still remarkably green with light. Then the train slowed to a stop in Haverfordwest, and they gathered their things. Nicki followed the others off the train, inhaling the fresh air though she couldn't keep her eyes from dropping down to look at Bran's brace once more.

"Shit!" Bran cursed as he began to sway in place.

Nicki jumped forward and grabbed his shoulder to keep him steady as she shifted beside him so he could lean against her. In the corner of her eye, she saw Lance move, and the large football player placed himself behind Bran, letting the smaller man lean back against him. Easing her grip on Bran's shoulder, Nicki stepped around Bran and gasped softly as she looked at his eyes. His pupils had almost vanished and narrowed into tiny pinpricks with his green iris blown wide and glowing a soft golden yellow. He was panting as his lips moved in soft, barely audible words.

She was vaguely aware of Jenny calmly telling other people on the platform that Bran would be fine and that they knew what to do while Alex stepped closer to him. Alex reached out and touched his shoulder, a flash of dark gray magic shimmering over her hand. Then Alex's gray eyes darkened in color.

"Not you too!" Nicki slipped her head beneath Alex's arm to keep the other girl steady.

"The sun... it's in the wrong place," Bran intoned in a far off voice, almost devoid of emotion. "Sun rises in the east, but there's the ocean."

Alex's hand slipped from Bran's shoulder, and she slumped against Nicki with a groan. Nicki looked at Bran in mild alarm but relaxed as his eyes shifted back to normal, and he blinked.

"What the-" Bran raised a hand and gripped his head gently. "That felt a lot more real than usual." He looked over at Alex, and Nicki dropped her gaze to the blonde as she shifted against her and began to stand up. "Alex, I think you helped me control the vision."

"Well, I didn't mean to!" Alex groaned as she rubbed her eyes. "Everything's too bright."

Lance slowly released Bran with a hesitant expression, but Bran's eyes were wide and bright. He didn't look exhausted or irritated. In fact, he looked excited. Behind them, the train began to pull away from the platform, leaving the group alone in the early morning light.

"What did you see?" Jenny asked.

"I was in a village, but not here. I had enough control that I was able to look around; it was almost like really being there." Bran shook his head, and his expression turned more serious. "The sun was rising, but I could see the ocean in the distance from the top of the hill: it was to the north. We're not in the right part of Wales." Bran pointed off in a direction that Nicki guessed was the north. "We have to go north. The village wasn't too far from the ocean." Then Bran turned his eyes towards Alex and gaped at her in shock for a moment. "Alex... I think I saw Gofiben."

"Really?" Alex asked in a thin strained voice. "Are you sure?"

"No, but he had a smith's hammer, and I just got the sense that's who he was, and Merlin and Morgana were there." Bran paused as a look of surprise took over his face. "They really haven't aged at all, maybe twenty years tops."

"Was there anything else?" Alex stepped closer to him with wide eyes. "Anything about the Chalice?"

"I... I don't think I heard anything, I just saw things," Bran explained nervously. "It looked like there had been a fire, Morgana had one of her light orbs in her hand, and Merlin was talking with Gofiben. There was another man there, sort of looked like the smith."

"Galath maybe," Alex suggested with a nod. "He was... Gofiben's brother."

Nicki glanced between the two of them, noting that Alex looked pale and ready to be sick again. Bran was almost vibrating with nervous energy and whatever magic Alex had given him. She looked over at Jenny, who was watching Alex with no small amount of worry. Just as Nicki was about to speak up, Lance cleared his throat.

"Why don't we go into town for breakfast and get information about how we can head north? We need more details about possible locations for this village."

"Took the words right out of my mouth," Nicki agreed as she reached over and gripped Bran's arm to keep him steady.

Alex's legs began to buckle underneath her, but Lance stepped over and offered her his arm. Nicki watched as Alex gave him a shaky smile, and slowly and carefully the group gathered up their bags and headed for the exit; a new destination already in mind.

18

Fire and Sight

⟶ ⟨⟩ ⟵

721 B.C.E. North Pembrokeshire Coast

From here, he couldn't see the ocean. The rolling hills between them and the coast made it impossible, but the villagers were uncomfortable with them practicing magic within the new walls. The survivors of Badb's attack that remained in the area regarded Merlin and Morgana with suspicion and concern, and Merlin was certain that if they hadn't been so afraid, they would have insisted he and Morgana leave. It didn't seem to bother Morgana, but Merlin had to admit that he was uneasy being viewed with such distrust.

Still, a small valley near the village provided a decent place to work with their young mages. The rocky slopes provided plenty of targets and helped to keep out any wild animals or wandering livestock. At least, it would have if Gofiben had managed to manifest his magic in any form except through his hammer and Cathanáil.

"That's it," Morgana said. She was sitting across from Gofiben, both of them on thick furs. His eyes were closed, and he was breathing deeply. "Relax and turn your focus inward. Below your heart, just above your stomach, there is a spark, a tiny flame waiting for you to build it up."

Shaking his head, Merlin turned to look towards Galath, who was seated on one of the smoother rocks with a scowl on his face. His arms were crossed, and he was keeping a close eye on his younger brother. Merlin was tempted to chuckle at the childish behavior that Morgana and Galath tended to fall into whenever Gofiben was involved.

"Why is this so hard?" Gofiben whined. The boy's fingers twitched toward the axe he'd made only a few days ago. "You said I keep putting magic into my ironwork."

"You are." Morgana reached out with glowing fingertips and moved them along the iron head of the axe so Gofiben could see sparks of orange magic reacting to her. "Only a little bit, it won't linger long. Only a few years I expect, but when you are smithing, you are pouring magic into what you do."

"So why is this so difficult?"

"Gofiben, I need you to relax," Morgana said sternly. Her voice left no room for argument. "Try to imagine that you are in your forge and working on a new project. Think about how you feel then; how you're thinking when you're working." Morgana's voice softened. "Try to put yourself in that state. That's how you access your magic. That's you when you are calm, centered, and most connected. Please try."

Something about Morgana's words or tone seemed to calm the young man. Gofiben pulled his hand away from the axe and folded his hands together in front of him. Morgana resumed her instruction, and Merlin felt a little more optimistic about their ability to teach the young man. Gofiben needed to learn how to do more with his power, and they couldn't trust that he'd always have a hammer in hand.

He turned his attention towards Bran, who was seated away from Gofiben and having a great deal more luck. Merlin smiled when he caught a glimpse of the dusty green magic swirling around a few of the smaller stones. Slowly a hint of green appeared around them as a small bit of weed began to poke its way up between the rocks.

"Bran's magic has the potential to be very useful," Galath noted behind him. "And not for combat: imagine being able to harvest the crops early or even have fresh produce in winter."

"He's a long way off from being able to affect plants on such a massive level," Merlin replied, but he couldn't help the smile on his face. "But it certainly has potential. His time in the fields with the livestock seems to have given him a strong link to the earth. I'm just hoping that he finds a way to use it to protect himself. I doubt you want them depending on you forever."

"You've been training them for almost a month now." Galath frowned for a moment, but his expression softened when he looked at his brother. "But Badb is attacking villages all across the land, and she's coming closer." Galath made a frustrated noise. "I know the walls don't mean much to her, but giving an enemy time to rebuild is foolish. What is she waiting for?"

"Cyrridven hasn't been able to tell us much. The reason for Badb being banished to our world is unknown, but she rejected all attempts by others of her kind to help her hold onto her sanity. She seems to have embraced the madness our world inflicts on those who do not belong here," Merlin said uneasily. "But we must try to get Gofiben and Bran ready to fight; they will be needed. Badb's magic may only be useful for short periods of time, but it is brutal and terrifying. As for why she hasn't attacked yet... I'm as worried as you are about what her reasons might be."

"Can't you do something about her?" Galath asked urgently. "During the last clan battle, she arrived and used her power to bring back the fallen." Galath shivered at the memory of the battle. "It was horrible, Merlin. We barely escaped."

"It did stop a rather pointless battle, even if that was not truly her intent," Merlin reminded Galath with a disapproving look. "Your brother needs you here; he and Bran lack the control needed to protect themselves from all but the most basic of threats."

A shout of excitement made Merlin turn to look at Gofiben and Bran. Morgana was on her feet with her hands clasped together. Her eyes were wide, and she beamed down at Gofiben, whose orange magic was swirling around his right hand. Sweat was dripping off of the boy's forehead as he stared down at the glowing orange orb in his palm. Merlin couldn't help but smile at the look of awe that was shining through Gofiben's exhaustion. A sigh of relief bubbled up in Merlin's chest, but he held it in. Morgana caught his eye, and he could see a similar feeling in her eyes. Gofiben had proven himself a highly intelligent and determined lad over the last few weeks, but without a hammer in his hand, he never seemed to know what to do with himself. This was a reassuring sign.

"Wonderful." Merlin grinned at him.

Morgana pulled Gofiben to his feet and pointed at one of the larger stones. The orb in his hand was beginning to glow and spark off embers. Grinning, the boy threw the orb towards the rock, but it arched too much in the air and crashed down almost two feet short. Flashing brightly on impact, the magic flared, and a wave of heat flooded the valley as the energy left a crater in the hard ground. Dirt flew into the air over Gofiben and Morgana with a few pebbles landing near Merlin's feet.

"Ah... oops," Gofiben offered weakly.

"I think that perhaps the boy's talent will be for iron and fire." Merlin chuckled. "And perhaps that is enough for the day."

"Sorry about that." Gofiben sheepishly looked down at his hand. Despite his embarrassment, Merlin noted that the boy couldn't keep the smile off his face.

"I feel like I should be worried," Bran remarked as he moved over to join them with a smile on his face. "I've got plants, and you have fire. It doesn't sound like a good mix."

"Could be interesting," Morgana said. Her eyes were brighter than Merlin had seen in some time. "Let's have Gofiben try it one more time, Merlin: I'd hate for him to lose his progress."

Before he could say anything on the matter, Gofiben nodded eagerly and stepped away from them. Galath gave Morgana a look that she merely ignored. Shaking his head at them both, Merlin moved a bit to the right so he could watch Gofiben's face. His features were relaxed as Gofiben unclenched and clenched his hands a few times. Then orange sparks of magic began to appear around his hand, flickering like embers on the wind. For a moment, Gofiben just grinned at the sight of them. He shifted his hand, and the tiny glowing sparks of magic swirled around his fingers and followed his movement. Sparks spun together to form a ball of fire in his hands.

"Lovely," Galath said. "My brother can set things on fire."

Morgana laughed at the remark, and Merlin allowed himself to chuckle but didn't take his eyes off of Gofiben as the young man toyed with the fire. The flames danced across his fingertips, and he was studying it the way that only one who lived by a forge could. After a few moments, he seemed satisfied and allowed the flames to collect into a small pulsing orb of barely constrained power. Gofiben threw it at another boulder, this time with his aim holding true. There was a flash of fiery light, a wave of heat, and a rolling crash as the boulder broke apart. Rock dust and tiny fragments of stone rained down around them, and Merlin smiled as the cloud of debris began to settle. The rock had been blown apart, and he beamed at Gofiben.

"You see?" he said happily. "You can do it."

"Is it bad that I have fire powers like Badb?" Gofiben asked as an odd, worried expression crossed his face.

"No," Morgana interjected before he could say a thing. "To start out with your magic will take a form comfortable to you. My easiest form of magic is light, but I can move objects, scry, and do all sorts of little things like fixing broken items. Magic is ever-changing; you'll learn how to do other things with it, but for now, your power takes the form of fire and heat."

"Indeed, you'll find that the Old Ones like Badb have magic that they generate while in our world, but they are not as versatile with it," Merlin explained with a nod. "But I believe we agreed it was time to return to the village," he added, gesturing over his shoulder towards the village in question.

"Good ide-" Bran stuttered before his voice faded away, causing them all to turn and look at him.

Bran stumbled to the ground, his eyes wide and his breathing erratic. Merlin reached him first, dropped to his knees, and gripped the boy's shoulders. He was at a loss for what was happening, but then he noticed the slight shine of Bran's dusty green magic in his brown eyes. Reaching out, Merlin brought the boy's face up and watched his eyes begin to clear back to the natural shade.

"I... I saw," Bran stuttered.

"What did you see?" Morgana demanded with a curious, almost eager look.

"I'm... I'm not sure," Bran replied as he slumped down on the grass. His fingers dug into the dirt as he sought to ground himself. "It was like

I was there, watching through someone else's eyes… there were these tall shining buildings, but not like roundhouses. They were like standing stones, but people were going inside them through odd openings. They were shining in the sun- I've never seen anything-"

"Did these people look human?" Morgana asked with a softer, but still curious tone. "Or were they something else?"

"I think they were human," Bran told her hesitantly with a glance in his direction. Merlin nodded for the boy to continue. "They looked like us, but some had dark skin, and their clothes were strange."

"There are people with much darker skin to the far south," Merlin explained. "Not too long ago, when we traded with the Romans, you might have even seen one." Merlin eased himself down onto the ground next to Bran and laid a hand on the boy's shoulder. "Take a deep breath."

"Do you think he saw something in the distance?" Morgana asked as she stepped back, allowing Gofiben to shift closer to his friend.

"Perhaps," Merlin replied. He hummed thoughtfully for a moment. "I'm afraid that I cannot see the use of such a vision to us at this time."

"Nothing's wrong with him though, right?" Gofiben asked. The boy was looking between them and Bran with worried eyes.

"No, not at all. He hasn't hit his head or eaten anything disagreeable," Merlin assured both of the young men. "Thus, I assume it to have been a magical vision, something that the flow of magic is sharing with you."

"Do you have visions?" Bran asked. He slowly climbed to his feet while leaning on Gofiben for support.

"On occasion; in fact, I had a vision of the Iron Soul before Arto was born. It was magic's way of informing me of my destiny."

Given the way that Gofiben glanced towards Morgana, who was lingering behind him, Merlin was fairly certain that she'd made a face at his words. She disliked the general notion that they had a destiny; her half-Sídhe nature was the result of the Queen's plan rather than a natural or unnatural occurrence of birth like his own. Still, the discovery of Gofiben had brought a spark back to her that he was grateful for. Reaching down, Merlin picked up Cathanáil and secured the Sword in its sheath once more. Gofiben's eyes lingered on it, and Merlin knew that the boy had to be wondering when they'd hand the Sword over to him now that he'd summoned his magic away from his forge.

"I think we've done more than enough for the day," Merlin announced as he stretched out his arms. "I know that you all have chores in the village."

"Yes, in the village that is now unsure of us all," Galath remarked as he strode over to his brother. He gave Bran a look over and nodded in the satisfaction that he was alright. "You both look tired."

"A bit," Gofiben agreed with a grin. "But I also feel energized like I could work at the forge for hours without rest."

"Well, take it easy, but I'm sure the villagers would be glad to have the backorders filled soon," Galath teased with a softening look.

Gofiben jostled his brother's shoulder as he and Bran followed Morgana up the slope of the valley. Galath fell into step behind them, keeping an eye on Bran, who was shakier on his feet than he probably wanted them to notice. As he followed them up the slope and the young men started talking about the things that needed to be done in the village Merlin found himself wondering about Bran's vision. It was an odd thing, and he couldn't see the value in it, but he supposed that in time things might become clearer. Magic had its own reasons and ways.

They reached the village far too soon for Merlin's taste, and he forced himself to nod in greeting to the solitary guard at the gates. In return, the man glared at him but pulled open the right side of the gate to let them enter. People were moving about, but they gave the group distance.

Gofiben nodded and waved to a few people who acknowledged him with quick looks before rushing off. Thankfully the lad had been protected from the fallout at least a little bit as the local blacksmith. In a small village like this, they couldn't afford him being angry.

The village was roughly half the size it had been before the attack. Several of the original roundhouses were still standing with five new ones having been recently completed. Only some of the fencing had been repaired, and the empty spaces where homes used to stand had become communal work yards.

"Do you ever miss the reverent looks?" Morgana asked. They watched Gofiben go over to the doorway of a nearby roundhouse to speak with an older man.

"More and more each day," Merlin admitted with a sigh as a woman tugged her child away from them. "Reminds me a little too much of when I was a child."

Morgana gave him a sympathetic look; his half-Sídhe heritage had been well known in his home village, and it had only been his mother's status as a priestess that kept him safe until he was an adult. Most people still didn't know that Morgana was half-Sídhe, though he imagined that the longer their lives went, the more rumors would be born about them both. He sighed and shook his head, looking towards Gofiben's roundhouse as the three young men spread out into the village to talk with the locals. Merlin jumped as Morgana suddenly reached over and tugged on the straps holding Cathanáil in place.

"Morgana, what are you doing?"

"Just checking," she replied. Crossing her arms over her chest, Morgana glanced back towards Gofiben. "Are we doing right by him? Is this really the right thing?"

"He has to be trained-"

"But he's twenty-two years old, and his magic hasn't caused any problems; maybe it never would have," Morgana protested, and she looked towards the young man in question. "He's just…"

"He's not Arto, Morgana." Merlin reached over to touch her shoulder. "You accepted Arto's destiny."

"Not really," Morgana informed him with a dangerously arched eyebrow. "But by the time I was part of his life again, he'd accepted his destiny."

Sighing, Merlin nodded in vague agreement with her statement. He dropped his hand to his side and looked over to where Gofiben was collecting a basket of produce with a smile and talking animatedly to one of the local warriors. The boy certainly had a talent with people as he watched the distrust melting away. A shout from the gates made them both turn sharply, and Merlin summoned his magic on reflex. Green magic swirled around his hand as he and Morgana rushed down the path.

People were shouting, and the locals were gathering in curiosity rather than fear as they reached the gates. Merlin released his magic carefully before it could draw any attention. The gate was pushed open, and the guard appeared with an unfamiliar man that he half carried and half dragged into the village. He was roughly forty with dusty gray hair and wide, almost wild brown eyes. All of his limbs were shaking, and he jumped back when a woman stepped forward to offer him some water. Then he recovered enough to grab the water skin and empty it into his mouth and over his face. Another person draped a blanket around the man's shaking shoulders.

"What happened to you?" Someone in the crowd asked, and Merlin vaguely realized that people were crowding in around him and Morgana, seeming to have forgotten their fears.

"Did someone attack your village?" Another voice called from further back.

"Are you alone?" Yet another person demanded with a gruff tone in their voice.

"The goddess Badb," the man cried. Curling his legs against his chest, he tightened the blanket around his shoulders. He either ignored or didn't hear Morgana's snort of derision. "She came to my village and unleashed a plague upon us."

Many people in the crowd drew back quickly at the words, which allowed Merlin to slip forward. In the corner of his eye, he saw most of the crowd retreating to their homes and pulling their children in after them. Kneeling down next to the man, Merlin studied him carefully and frowned. The man looked fairly healthy aside from his exhaustion from fleeing from whatever Badb had done.

"What happened exactly?" Merlin asked. "You don't look ill."

"No one did." The man looked between Merlin and Morgana. "It was a dark red fog; it filled the village and made everyone ill. It hung over them; their veins turned dark red," he insisted frantically. The man gestured towards the blue veins in his arms. "I was out moving livestock most of the time, so I wasn't as affected as the rest. When the others started dying, we left, started walking." He shuddered, and dry heaved for a moment, making pained sounds. "The others started to drop dead; I'm the only one left."

"Get him out of the village," a voice hissed behind them. Merlin turned to see a man poking his head out of his roundhouse with dark, angry eyes glaring at them. "Get him out of here; we've suffered enough of late. We don't need the goddess's wrath on us anymore." He narrowed his eyes on Merlin. "You've brought doom on us, Merlin."

"He can stay in my roundhouse," Galath offered. He crossed his arms and studied the man. "With all of you, Gofiben's home is getting too full."

"Thank you, brother," Gofiben replied.

Bran clasped Gofiben's shoulder, and Merlin noted that the smith looked ill. Inwardly he sighed in frustration. It seemed that Badb had decided on a new course of action and that the question of if Gofiben and Bran were ready had been taken out of their hands.

19

Fishguard

"So, is this going to be a new thing?" Lance asked. The bus lurched forward out of the small Haverfordwest bus station. Alex was blinded by the low-rising sun before they turned and began heading north out of the city. "Us leaving as soon as we get somewhere?"

"We didn't have much of a choice," Nicki said with a smug little smile. "We're just lucky we were able to catch the 8:22 bus north."

"Still, I would have liked more than a muffin from a coffee shop to eat," Lance countered. He looked a bit put out. "We could have at least hit a supermarket first."

"I'm not sure where we could have found one," Jenny said. She gave his arm a soft pat that made his entire body relax. "Not unless we wanted to explore the whole town."

"Yeah, the whole town of 13,000 people," Alex countered with a chuckle.

At least there was a very convenient bus system that could get them north in less than an hour, Alex reminded herself. None of them could rent a car here, so they were limited to public transportation options. They were the only large group on the bus and had taken over the back couple of rows. An older woman was sitting near the front with some shopping bags and chatting with the driver. Two guys a little older than them were slumped near each other in the middle of the bus texting away with their phones.

The whole bus was fairly cold even though she could hear the heater running full speed at the front. At least it wasn't as cold inside as it was outside, and the roads were clear of ice and snow. Alex glanced out the window at the rolling hills of Wales and wondered what it looked like in the spring and summer. There was a thin layer of snow on the ground, but it was so slight that Alex, with her northwestern USA upbringing, almost hesitated to call it such. Patches of grass were peeking through, and the trees were bare against the gray sky. Scattered across the landscape were farmhouses, beautiful short stone walls, and pastures of sheep. Everything seemed peaceful and tranquil.

"We can eat when we get to Fishguard," Lance agreed. "It'll only be a little after nine when we get there. Should we get a place to stay for the night?"

"Yeah..." Alex agreed tentatively. "Just to make sure that we have a roof over our head."

"Probably," Bran agreed. "Even if I have another vision, we'll need to see if we can narrow it down some." He toyed with a tear in the fabric cover of his chair nervously. "And maybe if we do find a market or something, I should look around for a small mirror. Morgana didn't have much of a chance to teach me how to scry, but I could give it a try."

"Doesn't she use that bronze disk, though?" Nicki asked. She was absentmindedly braiding a small section of her red hair.

"Yeah, but I haven't got anything like that." Bran shrugged. "Maybe it will help me control the visions a bit more."

"Speaking of Morgana and scrying," Alex interjected. "Maybe Morgana's had some luck scrying for the skull," she suggested with a smile and held out her hand. "Jenny, can I borrow your phone?"

"International, right?" Jenny asked. Shaking her head, she handed it over with a resigned sigh. "I'm tempted to submit a bill to the Professors for the expenses. At this rate, my dad isn't going to let me go shopping for at least a year."

"Give it a shot," Nicki suggested with a mischievous look. "They're pretty smart immortals who keep savings and investments. They can probably cover it."

"They do fake their deaths routinely," Bran said. Jenny pressed her lips together in consideration, making Bran chuckle. "I always imagined it as being very orderly."

"Sounds lonely to me," Jenny said softly.

"At least they have each other." Alex thought back to the recent conversation she'd had with Morgana. "But yeah, I think it gets a bit lonely."

Alex entered Morgana's phone number; a bit surprised that she could remember it. The phone rang, and with a glance at the other passengers, Alex set it on speakerphone as the others awkwardly leaned in.

It rang twice before Morgana's voice answered calmly, "Professor Cornwall."

"Morgana, it's me, I'm on Jenny's phone," she explained quickly. "I called to see if you've had any luck with your scrying?" Alex glanced around, but none of the other passengers paid her any mind.

"Where are you, kids?" Morgana asked.

"We just left this town called Haverfordwest in Wales," Alex said. "We're on our way north towards uh... Fishguard Harbor. Bran had a vision of seeing the ocean in the north, so we thought-"

"Yes, Gofiben's village was in the north of modern Pembrokeshire. Why didn't you head there from the start? That's where Pembrokeshire Park is."

"Uh, Morgana, the national park curves around the whole coast," Bran informed her dryly. "Sure, the north part is the biggest section, but you didn't really narrow it down much for us."

"Ah... my apologies, apparently I don't pay as much attention to modern geography as I thought." Morgana actually sounded a little embarrassed to Alex. "But keep in mind that the Chalice may not be anywhere near the village."

"Yeah, but my vision was really clear, I couldn't hear anything, but I could see this village with roundhouses and some people," Bran said.

"Interesting..." Morgana trailed off for a moment. "Well, as for why I asked where you are, it's because my attempt to scry for Bran's head as you requested, Alex, hasn't gone very well."

"Can you not get anything?" Alex slumped back in her seat, trying not to sigh in disappointment.

"Not exactly... the problem is that it keeps moving. When I scryed yesterday, it registered Cardiff, but two hours ago, it was in the middle of the lower Welsh peninsula. I'm afraid that I'm scrying for your Bran instead of the ancient one."

Alex and the others all glanced over at Bran with small, curious looks. Jenny frowned and tilted her head, and Lance's eyes widened slightly. Nicki stared at Bran before her mouth began to form an oh shape, and her eyes glinted almost dangerously.

"Uh... I feel like I'm missing something."

"Well, part of Celtic tradition was that the soul was connected to a person's head," Morgana explained tentatively "So the fact that I'm picking up our modern Bran rather than the ancient one does seem to indicate-"

"Welcome to the reincarnation club," Lance cut in. He raised an eyebrow and reached past Jenny to offer Bran his hand. Bran took the offered hand with a stunned look, and Lance shook it while Jenny patted Bran's arm with a strained smile.

"You think I'm a reincarnation?"

"Really?" Alex asked. She turned in her seat, so she was looking right at Bran. "Is that what you're suggesting, Morgana?"

"I didn't really consider it seriously until I had problems scrying," Morgana said. "Over three thousand years, you come across a lot of coincidences, so I tend to dismiss them."

"Did he have visions too?" Bran asked in a tight voice.

"On occasion, but they never seemed to make sense," Morgana answered carefully. "I'm trying to remember, but ... well, it was two thousand years ago."

"You said it wasn't anything important," Bran pressed, "but why would a vision not be important?"

"He was seeing strange buildings and people I think," Morgana muttered, sounding rather frazzled and frustrated. "Like I said, nothing that was relevant at the time. We were fighting Badb, and it was about the time she released her plague."

"Plague?" Nicki cut in, "Wait, what? Badb, the Celtic goddess of death?"

"One of them, but yes, that's how she's remembered, and believe me, she earned that reputation," Morgana growled. "She created a magical fog that tormented and killed those caught in it. Then she would animate their corpses for a short time."

"She made zombies?!" Bran shouted a little too loudly, causing the other passengers to look at them. "Uh, sorry," he called to them with a small wave.

"I suppose yes, but they were usually fresh bodies, so decay wasn't really an issue. Anyway, she did that as a distraction and stole Cathanáil from Merlin and me."

"What did she want it for?"

"That's... impossible to say," Morgana said. "Badb said something about ripping open portals when Merlin and I were recovering Cathanáil from her, so Arthur isn't the first being to think it is a key. As to if it worked, I can't say that for certain, we left Gofiben and Bran to chase after Badb. All I know is some of the rumors about what her magic did with the Sword."

"How long had you been training them?" Bran asked nervously. "I mean, didn't they die in that fight?"

There was a long pause on the other end before Morgana answered, "Not long: barely two months if I recall. They were talented, but to be honest, they weren't ready. Gofiben... well, he was an artisan by nature, not a warrior. But Merlin and I wanted to retrieve the Sword and stop Badb before she tried anything else."

"So, you don't really know what happened?" Bran confirmed. "And you think I might be the reincarnation of the original Bran?"

"You might be," Morgana corrected. "I'm not saying that you are, it's just that things seem to be pointing that way. Even if you are not, whatever connection your visions are giving you to the Chalice and the original Bran's head are interfering with my scrying."

"But couldn't that have been the point?" Jenny said only to get odd looks. She blushed and pushed some hair behind her ear. "I mean that, well, you can't scry for the Chalice, right?"

"Correct," Morgana replied, sounding a bit curious as to where Jenny was going with her observation.

"Well, was it normal for a dying man to request that his head be buried with a magical object?" Jenny asked. "I mean if that was common-"

"No, it wasn't normal," Morgana agreed before she hummed in thought. "You think Bran had Galath bury his head with the Chalice as a way to find it?"

"And I'm feeling even more creeped out," Bran whispered, looking a bit pale and ill.

"It is an interesting theory, but how would he have known to do that?" Morgana questioned out loud. "Maybe Merlin remembers more about Bran. I admit that I paid far more attention to Gofiben than Bran."

"Wow, you paid more attention to the reincarnation of the Iron Soul than the other mages," Nicki chimed in with a smirk as she gave Alex a pointed look. "What a shock."

"In other news," Morgana continued as if Nicki hadn't said anything. "Everything is magically quiet here, and Aiden is still stable, though his parents are meeting with more doctors. Merlin has some concerns over how long they are going to keep him on life support." Whatever jovialness had been in the back of the bus faded, and Alex bit her bottom lip to keep herself from making any noise. "I'm sorry to tell you that," Morgana added in a softer voice. "But you need to know."

"Yeah," Alex agreed a moment later. "Well, you have Jenny's number now, so keep us informed. We'll be in Fishguard in less than an hour and go from there."

"Understood, be careful," Morgana replied gently. "All of you."

The call ended, and Alex handed the phone back to Jenny, who slipped it into her pocket and looked out the window. Nicki slumped back in her seat and closed her eyes. Her breath danced in the air as a wispy cloud, and Alex wasn't sure if it was really that cold inside the bus or Nicki using her ice magic. Looking over at Bran, Alex found him looking down at his hands with a strangely blank look. She reached forward and put a hand on his shoulder, giving it a small squeeze. For the rest of their trip, all of them were lost in their own thoughts until their bus pulled to a stop in Fishguard.

They were in a round, open area surrounded by buildings with streets heading off in different directions. The bus followed the curve of the empty street and parked with a soft thump and hiss. Everyone seemed to move as one as the doors opened, releasing a burst of cold air into the bus along with a thick, salty smell. Grabbing her backpack, Alex led the others off the bus and gave a quick thanks to the driver. The other passengers all took off in various directions, seeming to know exactly where they were going. Alex moved away from the bus to let the others follow her as she looked around the area.

The buildings were small and old looking with some made of stone, some having a bit of the Tudor style, some standing alone, and others forming a long string of buildings. Modern signs and streets contrasted with buildings of mixed styles. There was a squat stone building that looked like it was probably a restaurant or bar. Alex nodded towards it to the others, and they got out of the road. Alex glanced towards Bran, both hoping for and dreading him having another vision so quickly, but he didn't seem to be reacting to anything. She realized that the others were looking at him too and waited before he gave a helpless shrug.

"Well, what do you think?" Nicki asked. She looked around doubtfully. "I'm not sure if a town this size would have a hostel or not."

"I don't know," Bran admitted. "I wasn't expecting us to come this way, at least not today."

"Guys," Jenny called with a small chuckle. "Tourist information right there." She gestured towards a green two-story building with a weather vane on the top of the roof and a flag hanging out over the door up the street from them. There was a small sign listing the various things in what was apparently the town hall, including tourist information and the library.

"Yeah, that works." Nicki stepped around Alex and headed up to the door. "Come on!"

They followed her inside only to find that the older exterior did not match up with the sleek look of the information desk. Alex hung back and looked at a series of brochures on display, grabbing the couple that referred to the national park and any of the Iron Age sites.

Jenny did the talking, turning her charm up to a high level with a fun story of a Christmas break trip to see Wales. Within a few minutes, she had a local map with the town hostel circled on it, and thankfully it was just around the corner. The information attendant even called over to see if someone was available to check them in, informing Jenny gently that they usually only did check in at night. Alex tuned out the conversation and instead stared at the picture of a recreated Iron Age village in her hand with an odd churning feeling in her stomach. She glanced over at Bran to see him looking at a photo of the same attraction with a nervous expression.

"Alex," Lance called. "Come on." He gestured towards the front door, and Alex hurried after the others.

"So, get a room for the night?" Jenny asked as they stepped outside. She pulled her rolling suitcase along behind her. "Or do you want to wait?"

"I haven't seen anything," Bran said. He nodded towards the brochures in Alex's hand. "We should check into our options to visit some of the Iron Age sites and do some research on the area. So far, we've just been running from point to point and depending on luck."

"Okay then," Alex agreed with a nod. "Let's make sure we have a place to stay, and then we can start seeing what more we can find out."

Outside, the weather was turning dark and damp with small, scattered raindrops falling down on them. Alex tightened her coat around her shoulders and hoped it would hold up against the Welsh rain. They followed Hamilton Street down and around as it looped back towards the main street. The hostel was a stone building that Alex didn't linger in looking at as the chill of the rain drove them all inside. Thankfully the entry was warm and comfortably large. As Jenny moved forward to the main desk, Alex glanced into the living room with a longing look at a rather comfy looking sofa.

As it turned out, the hostel didn't have rooms large enough for five people; only reinforcing Alex's opinion that five was an awkward number. Thanks to it being a rather slow season, they were able to get rooms arranged despite the early hour of the day. They waited as another group was checked out and gave them an odd look on their way. Alex's stomach grumbled in disgust at having been denied breakfast. The lodge only had three rooms, so alone, they almost filled the thing, and the receptionist left to copy their passports humming.

"So, what have we got?" Bran asked, leaning forward to see over Jenny's shoulder.

"We're in rooms 1 and 3, so a total of seven beds," Jenny said. "We can do a boy's room and a girl's room."

"Okay, stow our stuff and then get some food," Alex announced as the receptionist returned, handed over their keys, and pulled a stack of linen out of a cupboard.

They waited out in the hall as the staff cleaned out the vacated room for the girls and showed the smaller three-bedroom to the boys. Alex glanced inside to see a small space with one bunk bed and one single. Lance tossed his backpack up onto the top bunk without even a glance towards the single. Bran set his own stuff down and pulled out the Wales guide book to begin flipping through it.

"Alright," the lady called to them with a smile. "Sorry, things are a bit rushed."

"No, thank you for taking us so early," Alex replied gratefully. "We've been more than a little disorganized."

"You're lucky that we didn't have any groups rent the hostel for the week," the receptionist informed them seriously. "But I'm afraid you'll have to be out before the 20th."

"I'm sure we will be," Jenny said. She stepped into their room and nodded in satisfaction. "Thanks again for making arrangements for us."

"Well..." the woman seemed a little put off by them but recovered quickly. "I'll be around the hostel if you need anything. You've got your key and a map of town, but do you need anything else?"

"I think we're good," Alex said. "Thanks."

As their hostess left, Alex stepped into their room and sighed. It was only morning, not even 10 AM yet, and she was already exhausted. Their room was pleasant with a window overlooking the street at the foot of one of the single beds, and a bunk bed was up against the wall. The roofline was slanted, and Alex set her bag up against the wall with a soft sigh. Briefly, she was at a loss for what to do, but then her fingers tightened around the brochures about the Iron Age sites. Nicki walked past her and tossed her backpack on the bottom bunk while Jenny claimed the middle bed without a word.

"Okay: we have the whole day ahead of us." Alex shrugged out of her coat and hung it up on a small set of hooks near the door. "Let's get the boys and get some breakfast, then see what we can find."

A knock on the door made Alex smile as she turned to open it, expecting to find the boys on the other side. Instead, there was a pair of unfamiliar figures a little shorter than Alex with bright purple eyes looking right up at her. They were dressed in baggy hoodies pulled over their heads that mostly hid their silvery-white hair, but the dark color made their translucent skin stand out all the more. For a strange moment, Alex wasn't sure what she was looking at; they looked like Sídhe, but-

One sprang forward, its pale palm extended towards her with sharp talon-like nails reaching for her chest. Its eyes flashed a strange shade of dark gray as it clawed at her. Alex jumped back on impulse, almost tripping over her own luggage as her legs collided with it. Half falling and half rolling to the side, Alex tugged at the spark under her lungs as her hands hit the floor. Her dark gray magic sparked around her hands as Alex began to roll back on her knees. At the door, the two creatures were hissing long and slow like some kind of snakes.

"Stay down!" Nicki shouted, and Alex glanced over her shoulder to see shards of ice flying over her head.

The first of the Sídhe-like creatures jumped out of the way, grabbing at the frame of the bunk bed to avoid the ice shards. They collided with the wall but dispersed as water with a soft splashing sound. The second Síd stalked into the room. This one looked a bit more masculine, and his purple eyes flashed strangely as he looked towards Alex.

Rolling back and turning, Alex brought up her left hand and pushed the gathered magic at the creature. It tried to move out of the way, but Alex twisted her hand angrily, and the magic rolled in the air. The close quarters of the room limited where the creature could go even as it tried to back out through the doorway and out of the path of her twisting bolt of magic. As it turned to run, Lance and Bran stepped into the doorway and nearly collided with it. The bolt of magic hit it in the back, and the creature hissed in pain.

It tried to claw at Lance, but the large man grabbed its arms and pinned it against the wall. Alex blinked in surprise but stepped forward while charging more magic. Another snarl to her right made her turn and barely miss another set of talons slashing at her as the other creature attacked. Yellow magic surged in the corner of her eye, and the creature was knocked back hard against the bunk bed.

"I've got it," Nicki snapped as blue magic formed in her hand. The creature struggled against a band of yellow against its neck holding it tightly against the bunk bed. It thrashed, making the bunk bed rock and knock into the small side table next to it. Jenny fell back on the twin bed as she scrambled away from the creature, fleeing behind Nicki, who smiled. "I've got some aggression to get out."

Alex looked back at the one Lance was keeping pinned. It was lashing back against him and even brought a knee up into the wall, cracking a hole in the plaster. She stepped forward urgently, glancing towards the hallway with worry. Behind her was the sound of panting just before a wet slicing sound reached her ears. Alex ignored it and summoned her own magic, concentrating it into a solid, pulsing form in her hand. It shifted into the shape of a dagger, part of the magic staying tight between her fingers. It wasn't solid but didn't slip away from Alex as she moved up beside Lance and the creature.

The creature threw its head back, striking Lance's chest, and he almost lost his grip. There was a moment of sympathy as Alex wondered if this was another creature under the queen's power. But as its violet eyes narrowed on her and it tried to twist away from Lance, Alex brought the cracking magical construct forward and sliced it into the creature's chest before it could escape and attack again. It went limp in Lance's arms, and he released it, stepping back as it fell to the floor. Alex flinched as its head collided with the bunk bed frame and almost sighed in relief as Bran firmly shut the door of the room. In her hand, the magic pulsed, and Alex allowed it to form an orb. Exhaling let the magic slowly dissipate.

"Curse you." The creature stared up at Alex with silvery blood spilling from its wound and vanishing as soon as it hit the ground. "Curse you, Iron Soul, for what you wrought!"

Then its eyes rolled back in its head, and it gurgled in pain. Alex stepped back, almost colliding with Lance as the creature's form vanished, leaving them alone in the room once again with small piles of clothing.

"What do you think it meant by that?" Jenny asked after a long moment of tense silence. She frowned distastefully, but bent down to scoop up the various piles of jeans and hoodies and tossed them into the corner.

"I don't know," Alex answered. She turned to the look at the others. "But let's get the damage fixed before the staff comes up here again."

There was a moment of silence. No one knew what to say, and Alex felt some reassurance that she wasn't alone in her discomfort. Lance moved back from the wall and went over to Jenny, who hugged him. It was Bran who finally went to the wall.

"What were those?" Yellow magic ran down his fingers as he touched the wall, and it began to reform beneath his hand. "They didn't look like normal Sídhe."

"No, they didn't," Alex agreed. "They were smaller and didn't seem to have any magic." Alex rubbed her hands together and looked out the window. "Maybe descendants of the Sídhe who were trapped in our world after the earlier Iron Gates were made. If they've been in our world a long time, that might explain why they seemed smaller and weaker."

"Maybe," Nicki said. She slid her hands into her pockets and watched as Bran repaired the wall. "So, we've got more creatures to contend with. What now?"

Alex felt them all looking at her, waiting for her to do something. "We still have a mission," she said. "Let's get some food and try to figure out what to do next."

Nicki nodded in agreement and headed for the door with Lance and Jenny following. Bran looked her way for a moment before glancing down at where the Síd had been. There was no trace, but Alex wasn't sure she'd ever get used to this. She shuddered, trying to throw off the messy emotions. They had to survive, and the thing had been trying to kill her. Trailing after the others, Alex told herself to stay calm and keep focused on the Iron Chalice. They'd deal with the rest later.

20

The Iron Age

Four roundhouses made of wood, mud, and thatch stood around them, apparently built on the preserved foundations of ancient ones. The smell of the mud and rain overpowered the musty scent of wood as Alex stepped over next to one of the buildings. A few feet away was a large fire pit carved into the ground with rocks piled up to create a windbreak. It was cold and bare now, and the silence of the small reconstructed village felt heavy and unnatural. Alex could understand them being the only ones here; winter wasn't the best time to visit an outdoor attraction, especially not with Christmas only days away.

Exhaling, Alex watched her breath curl through the air like the morning mist. She shifted and almost bumped into the bottom of the thatched roof of the nearest house. It was an odd-looking thing to her: the steep thatched slope went almost to the ground. They were larger than she'd thought based on the pictures, with large square doorways under a curve in the roof to allow access. Alex stepped away from the house and almost ran into a wooden post in the ground that marked the outline of some sort of yard, probably for livestock.

She sighed; she'd been expecting to feel something among the round-houses. Sure, they were modern construction, but they were made of the same sort of materials and built the same way. They were even in the exact same positions they would have been thousands of years ago. This probably hadn't been Gofiben's village; the odds against that were huge, and she couldn't really see the ocean from the hill. Still, Alex had thought she'd feel something being in a place like this. Maybe some sense of familiarity or a feeling of loss or just... something.

Grumbling, she kicked at the ground dejectedly only to hit her toe against a rock. Alex grit her teeth and forced herself to stand still, waiting for the pain to ease. Shoving her hands into her pockets, she glared at the nearest roundhouse a bit tempted to experiment with using a fire spell. It wasn't her natural area of magic certainly, but Morgana and Merlin kept promising that they could do more. With how she felt right now, it wouldn't be difficult to visualize a ball of fire setting the place aflame.

The knot in her stomach felt like it was being suspended over an empty pit as she looked around at the buildings. She knew it was her own fault: too many stories about reincarnations, and even the short taxi ride had given her more than enough time to envision something important happening here. This was just disappointing, and the frustration crawled up her back to her shoulders, making Alex feel like she was carrying something heavy and inflexible.

She looked over at the others; Nicki was studying the pamphlet in her hand and wandering between the roundhouses with an interested expression. It was nice on some level to see Nicki calm enough to actually be capable of enjoying being here. After watching her for a bit, Alex noticed that Nicki was glancing towards Bran eagerly every few moments. Apparently, she wasn't as calm as she seemed and was instead eagerly waiting for something to happen.

"I bet this place is nicer in the summer or spring," Lance observed in a low voice as he and Jenny moved over to join her. Alex noted with a slight flicker of cheerfulness that Jenny had her arm through Lance's even if they didn't seem to realize it. "The forest just looks dead."

Alex nodded in agreement, glancing into the woods that lined one side of the village. Large grayish-brown trunks with bare branches were all she could see, along with a scattering of rocks and a layer of dead leaves visible between patches of snow. There wasn't even any wind to give any sense of life to the forest. The rain had stopped and left a wonderfully clean smell, but it didn't seem to reach the forest.

"I don't think they get a lot of winter visitors." Alex tore her eyes off of the forest, disliking the melancholy feeling trying to take her over.

"Yeah," Jenny agreed softly. "It's a pretty area, though, even with everything so gray."

"Made for a nice little walk." Lance's smile was rather forced as he watched Alex's face. "You still worried about what that thing said?"

"I guess." Alex shrugged helplessly. "And you know, everything else."

"Aiden will be okay," Lance promised gently. He reached out and put a hand on her shoulder. "We'll find the Chalice, and I can't believe that his family won't at least wait through Christmas, so we've still got a few days."

Christmas: she'd almost forgotten. Her mind had been set on Aiden and the knowledge that the winter solstice might be able to help them find the Chalice if they could get close enough. It was funny in a way; a few weeks ago, when they'd been concerned about Chernobog, she'd actually also been worrying about getting home for Christmas. Now instead of being stuck in Ravenslake waiting for a dangerous Old One worshiped as a god by ancient humans, she was running around Wales following old legends and vague visions.

"I'd sort of forgotten about Christmas with everything going on," Alex admitted.

"Do mages celebrate something else?" Lance squeezed her shoulder again before letting his hand drop.

"Well, I guess it's mostly about the culture you grow up in," Alex answered in surprise. "Morgana doesn't seem to like Christmas much while Merlin loves it. As for if we have an actual holiday, then I guess it would be Winter Solstice, you know, the longest day of winter. It marks a day when the alignment of energy is at its best for mages." Alex gave them both a slightly sheepish look. "I'm afraid I don't understand it very well, but we're more powerful, and creatures from other worlds are weaker. We're usually safe that day."

"So, if you're more powerful, then maybe that can help you with the Iron Chalice!" Jenny's eyes widened in excitement. "Isn't that in only a few days?"

"December 22nd this year," Alex said. "We got lucky; we have an extra day to try and find the Chalice, but if not, then I'm hoping we might be able to do something to help Bran have a vision of it."

"Or maybe you'll be able to scry for it yourself," Lance suggested. "After all, you are the Iron Soul, and it doesn't make much sense if you don't have the ability to find it."

Alex frowned; that was actually a valid point. Morgana and Bran had both been trying to find it, but she hadn't tried yet. At least not with magic. Maybe as the current incarnation of the Iron Soul, she would have the power to find it, and if that were true, then maybe she could find Cathanáil too. Her thoughts were interrupted by Jenny's phone ringing. The sound cut through the silence, and everyone jumped with Nicki sending a dark look towards them. A cry of alarm escaped Jenny, and she dropped the phone into the soft mud beneath their feet. It sloshed as it hit the ground, and Alex bent down to pick it up. She heard Lance ask

Jenny what was wrong, but their voices faded away as she wiped away the mud and read the screen. It said one word: Arthur.

"Oh god." Alex's legs buckled, and she fell to her knees. The cold mud squished beneath her, and she heard someone shout her name. A hand slipped under her arm and hauled her off the ground as the phone kept ringing.

"What is it?" Nicki asked. There was a flash of red hair in the corner of her eye as her friend tried to see the phone. "Shit."

It stopped ringing, leaving them all in silence as the others crowded around Alex. Then the phone began to ring again with the soft series of chimes that seemed far too innocent for someone so dangerous. Jenny whimpered and drew back from the phone as if it was threatening to burn her. Looking over at her, Alex felt her stomach turn at the devastated look on Jenny's face even as Lance wrapped an arm around her. Jenny spun in his arms and buried her face against his chest.

"If she answers it, then he can find us, right?" Lance looked down at Jenny with a helpless expression on his face.

"That's not how cellphones work, Lance," Bran said with a strangely neutral expression as he eyed the phone. "No, if her phone is working and he has access to the phone company, then he already knows where we are. That's how the GPS works in the first place."

The phone stopped ringing again as everyone crowded around. Nicki pushed up beside Alex, glaring at the phone with blue eyes that were cold as ice. Alex hoped the other girl didn't lose control of her magic. Then it rang again, and Alex answered it before she could change her mind.

"Hello, Arthur." Alex tried to sound calm, but her heart threatened to beat right out of her chest.

"Alex, alive and well it seems," the very familiar voice of Arthur Pendred cooed. Some little part of Alex melted a bit at the sound of his voice, but then the memory of him stabbing her with Cathanáil and collecting her blood in vials rammed its way to the front of her mind. "And Aiden, lying in the intensive care unit. His loyalty is to be commended."

"While yours leaves a great deal to be desired."

"And you're answering Jenny's phone. That must mean that despite knowing the truth, you've decided to keep the ex-wife with you. Tell me, is Lance there as well? Aren't you even a little concerned about the betrayal?"

"I'm not worried about them."

"You weren't worried about me." Arthur sounded far too smug. "You were far too busy damn near falling over yourself for me. Remember that night we-"

"What do you want, Arthur, or did you really just call to gloat?"

"You wound me, Alex; perhaps I was merely concerned over Jenny and Lance. After all, she was family in another life. I was always very polite to my cousin's wife." Arthur chuckled. "Oh, and doesn't that put a rather incestuous twist on some of the things we got up to."

"You are a bastard, Arthur!" The anger flared up stronger than the shame and regret churning in Alex's stomach.

"No, you'll find that isn't true. My dear mother Elaine was married before she became the vessel of Queen Scáthbás."

"So, what are you then?" Alex demanded sharply. "You're not really an Earth mage, you're something else."

"I'm a half-breed, just like your bitch of a sister and the old abomination. I'm the Prince of the Sídhe," Arthur answered in a sing-song voice. "Come on, Alex, it's not going to be that easy. Well, maybe it would be if you could remember your old lives."

"Do you remember Medraut?" Alex asked before she could think better of it.

"That would be telling, my darling Alex. It really was a little disappointing that you were the Iron Soul; I might have enjoyed trying to win you over to my side. But in the end, you're just a little too... well, boring, I suppose."

"So, you did just call to gloat."

"Actually, I'm curious as to what it is that you're in... Wales looking for? Why would you leave a friend who is lying in a hospital dying for you to run off to that backwater?"

Alex pulled the phone away from her ear and switched off the call in one fast movement. Before the others could say anything, she pressed the power key and waited for the phone to shut down. "He knows where we are," she said in a shaky voice. "And he knows that it's Aiden who is hurt. I don't think he'll go after Aiden, though. I don't think Arthur cares about that."

"Or he knows I'm already plotting ways to kill him," Nicki growled.

"Get in line." Anger flashed in Jenny's eyes as she let go of Lance and straightened her hair self-consciously.

"We'll kill him together when we have the chance next," Alex said, turning to look at Bran. "What do you think?"

"I haven't seen anything." Bran dug into the black shoulder bag he'd picked up that morning and pulled a small round mirror out of it. "But I could see if I can get anything."

"Yeah..." Alex trailed off as she thought back to the earlier conversation with Jenny and Lance. "Uh, do you want to try here?"

"Sure," Bran agreed as he looked around. "The setting couldn't hurt."

"Can you guys combine your magical power?" Jenny asked from behind Alex only to get the attention of all the mages on her. "I mean, Alex was thinking that maybe since she made the Chalice, you know in another life, that maybe she could scry for it?"

"Except I've never scryed before," Alex said.

"But you've had dreams," Nicki reminded her quickly. "You had dreams about the tunnels last year before you were captured."

"And we did make the Iron Gate in Ravenslake together, so we can combine our powers, at least to a certain extent," Bran added with a thoughtful look that began to morph into excitement. "Let's give it a try."

He stepped away from them and found a drier patch of grass on the ground. Alex hesitated and glanced nervously towards Nicki, but her friend's face was brighter than she'd seen it for a while with a blend of cautious optimism and curiosity. Then there was a hand on her shoulder, and Lance was leaning over her from behind.

"Give it a try," Lance said gently. "It's worth a shot."

Forcing a smile and trying to look more confident than she felt for Bran and Nicki, Alex stepped forward and followed Bran over to the spot he'd chosen. Bran arranged his legs carefully and settled onto the ground with a barely contained shiver. He dropped one hand and touched it to the ground. In his other hand, he gently held the mirror and lowered his face, so he could view it easily. From her position, Alex could see the reflection of Bran's Ravenslake sweatshirt and the gray sky in the mirror. She sank to the ground in front of him and put her left hand over his before placing her right hand on the ground. The mud felt cold to her bare fingers, but Alex could feel a slight hum in the earth that seemed to be reaching for the spark of her magic.

Closing her eyes, Alex tried to envision what the Iron Chalice looked like. Unfortunately, her mind instantly provided a golden grail with small gems in the base that was completely wrong, and Alex inwardly cringed. She felt utterly lost, suddenly unsure of how to reach for the Iron Chalice. Magic responded to a mage's desires, but it had to be directed, and the easiest way was visualization. The problem was Alex had no idea of how to visualize the Chalice. She felt the warmth of Bran's hand beneath her own and forced herself to relax. Tightening her fingers around his, Alex reached for her memories of Morgana's meditation lessons and focused on her breathing. Slowly and gradually, the growing fear began to ease, and she could think a bit more clearly.

She remembered how Cathanáil felt in her hands; the strange instant burst of energy that had traveled through her whole body. At the time, she'd just assumed it was the power of the Sword before she'd handed it to Arthur, but maybe it hadn't been. The Sword had somehow fit in her hand, somehow hadn't felt heavy or awkward, but like an extension of herself. The magic of the Iron Soul had been bound up in that metal, in every strike of the hammer that had shaped it, and in every act that Arto had used it for. Three thousand years later and she'd still been able to feel it. Maybe she could feel the Chalice too.

It was a long shot, a really really long shot, but Alex inhaled slowly and tried to remember what holding Cathanáil had felt like. She tried to envision a simple-looking Chalice made of iron that looked like a bowl on a wide iron base. How would it feel in her hands? Alex swallowed and sent a small burst of her magic into the ground through her hand, along with a wish for it to find the Chalice. The wish kept repeating in her head over and over again.

A sudden roar in her ears threatened to deafen Alex and shook her whole body. Alex was about to open her eyes in alarm when the darkness behind her eyelids vanished in a flash of red quickly followed by a flash of white. There was a blur of two battling colors and another roar, this one at a lower pitch. She couldn't see anything for a moment, but everything around her seemed to tremble and shake.

A red dragon rose up in front of her out of a crumbling hillside on four legs, fierce, sharp dark-red talons digging into the stone beneath it. Then it looked right down at her with glowing, golden eyes that seemed to flash as they met hers. Long red horns formed crests atop its head. It roared, opening its mouth and exposing rows of vicious-looking teeth right before spreading blood-red wings and casting a dark shadow over her. Another roar made it look up, and a white shape came crashing down at the red dragon.

Her eyes opened on instinct, and Alex gasped for air, suddenly feeling like her lungs had been compressed. Forcing herself to calm down, she looked at Bran, who was staring at the mirror in his hand with wide eyes as his hands shook. Pulling her hand off of his, Alex swallowed thickly and shook herself as if she were a dog trying to shake off water.

"Alex? Bran?" Jenny called from next to them. "Did it work?"

"Yeah... yeah, it did," Bran replied slowly with a growing smile. "At least I think it did; I saw something really wild, though. It might not have anything to do with the Chalice."

"It does, it has to," Alex insisted as she blinked her eyes and tried to process what she'd just seen. Her heart was racing, and she was fighting a strange sense that she'd forgotten something that she should know. "It has to," she repeated.

"What did you see?" Nicki almost shouted as she dropped to the ground beside them both.

"Dragons!" Bran grinned. "Real dragons: one of them was white, and the other was red. They were fighting, and there were flashes of another battle, but it wasn't as clear. Then they both fell to the ground, and the earth shook. It was intense."

"A red dragon," Lance repeated as he bent down and pulled the book on Wales out of Bran's shoulder bag. "That sounds familiar," he added as he offered his arm to Bran and helped the other young man to his feet.

"It should," Nicki declared as she held out a hand to Alex and tugged her to her feet. "It's a myth about Wales and the Saxons. The Welsh were represented by the Red Dragon; it remains the symbol of Wales to this day while the Saxons were represented by a White Dragon." Nicki frowned, pressed her lips together, and tilted her head thoughtfully. "They were battling underground, and their battle kept causing a castle to collapse over and over again. A king was told to find a boy with no natural father and sacrifice him to stabilize the castle." Nicki, realizing that she had everyone's attention, shrugged. "That boy, according to the myth, was a young Merlin."

"I remember that story," Alex added with a nod. "We went over it in our King Arthur class, but Merlin said that it never happened. That the story wasn't real."

"Maybe not to him," Jenny offered, "But if you heard a story about a wizard back then, you'd probably assume it was about Merlin."

"Besides," Nicki added with a nod. "Morgana said that she and Merlin had left Gofiben and Bran. Maybe something big happened."

"But dragons?" Alex asked with wide eyes. "You think dragons happened?!"

"It's right here in the book," Bran said. He held up the guide book and started to read. "Dinas Emrys: near Beddgelert in Wales, has the remains of a fortification on the hill. Site of a 1st or 2nd century Iron Age settlement and is the site of the legendary exchange between Vortigern and a young Merlin. Legend says that there were two dragons battling deep beneath a pool, one white and one red."

"Where is Beddgelert?" Jenny asked softly.

"To the north, outside of Pembrokeshire," Bran answered with a frown. "A long way outside of Pembrokeshire."

"Morgana said that Gofiben lived in this area." Jenny tugged at the hem of her coat and bit her lower lip. "That's why we're here."

"Just because this is where he lived doesn't mean that it's where the final battle took place," Alex said. "But where the hell would the dragons have come from? Morgana didn't mention dragons."

"Maybe she thought the dragons were made up," Lance suggested. "As for where they came from, maybe, they were summoned somehow."

"Look, that doesn't matter right now," Nicki cut in. "The question is, do we head for Beddgelert?" She pulled the book away from Bran and showed the map of Wales. "It's all the way up here." Nicki pointed to a place in the northern bit of Wales before she pointed to the southern tip. "And we're down here. If we get there and we're wrong, then we lose time."

Above them, the sky rumbled, and cold raindrops began to fall. One hit Alex and rolled down her cheek, sending a shiver through her body. Closing her eyes, she pictured the red dragon. She could see the long curve of its neck with the small dark gold-red spikes, its wings rising out from its sleek scaled body, and the long whip of its tail. Alex exhaled and opened her eyes. The others were watching and waiting.

"We didn't see the Iron Chalice." Alex turned to look at Nicki. "What do you think?"

Nicki's eyes widened, and she swallowed as she took the book from Bran, holding a side of her coat out over it. Frowning, she looked down at the pictures, including the one of the Welsh flag. After what seemed a very long time, Nicki nodded.

"Yeah," she said. "You and Bran were focusing on the Iron Chalice, and the dragons were what the magic showed you. Maybe the Chalice is there, and the dragons were just magic showing us the way."

"Okay then, let's see if our taxi is still there and get back to Fishguard. We've got a train to catch."

"Actually, I'll be impressed if we can get a train from Fishguard tonight," Bran muttered behind her. He pulled his hood up against the rain and shoved the book back into his bag. "But let's give it a shot."

21

Crack in the Mountain

721 B.C.E. South of Mount Yr Wyddfa

Gofiben had never been so far from home. Gone were the rolling hills and pasture lands he'd grown up with. Here there were high mountains, rocky slopes, and hill valleys cut by rivers. The mountains above were still capped with snow, despite the flowers blooming on the hillside amongst lush green grasses. They hung ominously over the valley. There was still a chill in the air, although winter was behind them.

Swallowing thickly, he tried to distract himself and looked down the hill to where two of the rivers joined in a swirl of water and dirt before raging on down the valley. Yet the sight wasn't calming in the least. It all seemed so wild, so untamable, and yet here he was, suddenly feeling very small as he watched the rays of the sun creep up over the hill. He wanted so much to be brave, to relish these new sights, but it seemed every time he saw something new, his mind flashed back to those terrible animated corpses.

"I wish we were back home," Bran admitted. He climbed up next to Gofiben and sighed. "I miss home."

"Me too," Gofiben said. "I miss my forge: I miss feeling like I know what I'm doing."

"And they won't even give you the Sword," Bran added with a frown as he glanced at the axe in his hands.

"To be fair, I was pretty bad at using it."

"Hit the other guy with the sharp part," Bran huffed as he sat down on one of the rocks that made up the slope of the hill. "It's not that hard."

"I'm used to hammers," Gofiben defended, even as a blush crept up his face. "Besides, I'm not good with combat in general." It was an understatement, and Bran nodded his understanding. "Do you think anything will happen this time? Badb's just run the last three times we caught up with her."

"Merlin and Morgana seem to think that something is going to happen."

"They always think something is going to happen."

Bran opened his mouth to say something, but the clear voice of Morgana called up the hill, "There you are! Gofiben, Bran, get back here this instant!"

"Yes, mother," Gofiben grumbled. None the less he began to slowly make his way across the hill on a small game trail with Bran following along behind.

Morgana was standing on a clear spot overlooking the rivers, Cathanáil grasped tightly in her hands and the blade shining in the early morning light. She didn't turn to them as they reached her, and Bran stayed behind Gofiben, pushing him towards the older mage.

"Beltane," Morgana observed. "And another confrontation with Badb."

"Maybe not," Gofiben suggested as he took a tentative step forward. "She keeps retreating each time we catch up with her." He kicked at a rock, sending it tumbling down the hillside. "Morgana, isn't there more we can do about the plague? It's terrible here and that last village-"

"Gofiben…" Morgana interjected with a shake of her head, tightening her grip on Cathanáil. His eyes were drawn to it, and he felt a slight hum in the air that made his heart beat faster. "Contrary to what you think, I'm not denying you Cathanáil because you're not ready or bad with a sword. You haven't practiced with a blade, so its only natural that you'd be a bit clumsy."

"Do you not trust me then?" Gofiben asked, only to flinch at the brash words.

Morgana, however, merely turned to look at him and shook her head before answering, "No, Gofiben, I don't want you having the Sword because you're safer without it. Right now, Badb isn't interested in you; she doesn't care much about the Iron Soul, and that keeps you safer." Morgana shifted to face him. "I know you want to stop the plague, but Cathanáil doesn't have that power."

"Maybe I can make something that does!" The words spilled out of Gofiben's mouth before he considered them, but he liked the sound of them. "I'm a smith by trade, Morgana, and I was using my magic while smithing before you found me. Surely I can-"

"Cathanáil was made by Arto after years of preparation," Morgana reminded him. "It exhausted him even with the help of Cyrridven."

Their conversation was ended by an explosion rocking a hillside just up the valley. Morgana turned sharply and growled as dark smoke began to curl up into the sky. Gofiben's mouth went dry as he saw flashes of dark red magic arch into the air. Down the hill, he saw movement and green magic spinning into the air. The green magic swirled out over the river and up the hill before transforming into a rain cloud that began to downpour over the flames.

"Remember," Morgana said sternly. "Today is a season day; we are at a disadvantage against Badb. The defenses for our world are at their weakest when the seasons change. You cannot count on your magic to protect you from her."

"Do we have to fight her today?" Bran asked in a softer voice. He looked around the sloping hills of the valley. "This feels like a trap."

Morgana frowned: Gofiben wasn't sure if she was worried about the observation or Bran's reluctance to fight. Gofiben understood both and wanted to be brave, but the last few seasons of chasing Badb further and further north as more villages fell ill had left him exhausted. They weren't ready for this, and his own fear must have shown as Morgana's expression softened.

"You'll be fine, just stay together," Morgana told them as she lifted Cathanáil and looked back towards the pillar of smoke. "Keep your distance from Badb, but keep an eye out for any of her tricks. If something goes wrong, Galath is in the village waiting for you."

Then Morgana took off, rushing down the hill as she released small blasts of silver magic to keep herself steady. Her magic formed into a bridge across the river, and she vanished into the trees.

"I hate this part most." Bran tightened his cloak nervously. "What do you think?"

"Let's cross the river, at least." Gofiben took a tentative step down the hill. "So, we're close in case they need us."

Bran clearly didn't like the idea as his eyes widened, but he nodded. Slowly they made their way down towards the river, having to watch their steps while also glancing towards the churning flashes of dark red, green, and silver up the valley. Gofiben's heart was pounding by the time they found a good crossing point, but he felt the fear threatening to turn to panic when he heard a scream echoing down through the valley.

"We'll just cross the river," Bran said behind him. "Just in case."

They crossed quickly; icy water splashing them. Gofiben called forth his magic in a whirl of orange sparks that glinted like embers around his hand. Closing his fist, he concentrated on heat rather than the flame and smiled in relief as waves of warmth rolled off his fingers over Bran and himself. Reaching out, he touched his friend's shoulder and commanded the magic to dry their clothes, careful to keep the heat from becoming too much.

Thick greening trees surrounded them, celebrating spring, but they did little to muffle the shrieks and sounds echoing amongst the hills. Gofiben flinched back and lowered himself against a rock when a blast of fire erupted ahead of them and shook the valley. Water splashed out of the river and over their feet. Something was definitely happening today: Badb was not running. He looked over his shoulder at Bran, who was pale with his freckles standing out starkly against his skin, but the other young man nodded, and they resumed their hike.

"How close should we get?" Bran asked as they ducked behind a large outcropping. "Merlin and Morgana can probably handle her themselves but-"

Another explosion sent small rocks pouring down through the valley, followed by the bang of trees snapping. They could hear more crashes and a loud groan of pain that sounded like a male, which meant it was Merlin. Gofiben licked his lips and glanced at Bran, who was eyeing the hill around the outcropping nervously. He dearly wished that mage or no mage, his brother was here; he could use the reassurance.

"It doesn't sound like it's going well," Bran said. "I suppose we could..."

"Yeah," Gofiben agreed with a nod and swung himself out from the outcropping before he could change his mind.

Moving faster now, they could both see the battle up ahead of them. Badb, Merlin, and Morgana were fighting on the eastern bank in a burned-off patch of the hill. Gofiben straightened as he saw a dome of silver form around the battlefield, blending with green magic and holding back a stream of dark red power. Unease churned in his stomach. Badb seemed more powerful than before. Bran's concerns about a trap suddenly seemed much more real.

Trees were downed in the water, some drenched and some aflame as dark red magic clashed mid-air with green and silver. Part of the hill had been wrenched up by Merlin's magic, but Badb did not seem concerned as she laughed and more dark red magic glittered around her. Turning back, Gofiben peered at the small village near the joining of the rivers with a sympathetic grimace. He hoped those who were still free of Badb's plague were fleeing and that his brother was keeping things calm.

Then Badb screamed, released a wave of her dark red magic that flooded the battlefield in a thick red fog. Morgana and Merlin's dome flickered as the green and silver glow was consumed in the fog. Gofiben started to run up the shore; his heart pounding as he summoned his magic once more. Burning trees were uprooted and scattered around the battleground as thick black smoke rose into the air, and the hissing of steam filled Gofiben's ears as the fires met lingering patches of snow and wet ground.

He brought up his hand and pushed back the red fog in front of him with a shimmer of orange magic. Next to him, Bran released a wave of his own magic, clearing a small patch of the shore. Through the red haze, Gofiben caught sight of green magic flashing, followed by a pillar of silver forming. Grinning in relief, Gofiben stepped back and watched as the red fog began to recede.

He could see Morgana and Merlin again now. Both were panting and covered with mud even as their magic glowed brilliantly in their palms. Badb dodged a bolt of lightning flying from Merlin's hand, and Morgana's silver whip lashed at her arm. A howl of pain escaped Badb, but she just grinned at Morgana with flashing red eyes.

Gofiben saw the magic strike Morgana in the chest; saw the dark red magic run over her exposed neck, and Morgana's mouth open in a silent cry. She was thrown back against a tree with a loud echoing crack while Badb laughed. Cathanáil tumbled from her hands and hit the ground with a soft clinking sound. In the corner of his eye, Gofiben saw Merlin throw a blast of magic into the ground, but Badb leapt forward and changed in a swirl of magic, feathers, and the sound of cracking bones into her crow form. Jagged rocks erupted from the ground where she'd been. The bird twisted in the air and, in another swirl of magic, hit the ground in human form and lunged forward. Badb grabbed Cathanáil and spun around, sending another blast of magic towards Merlin.

The Sword flashed in her hands, and a pained screech escaped Badb, but she held tightly to the hilt. Morgana groaned and started to pull herself up just as Badb's eyes returned to her. Cathanáil flashed, and Badb's hand shook as she fought to keep hold of the Sword. A wave of red magic collided with Merlin's green magic in mid-air as he tried to distract her. Gofiben gasped and jumped forward to run to Morgana as Merlin was pushed back.

"Gofiben!" Morgana shouted in warning as she started to sit up, "Don't!"

There was a strange song in the air, a few long and haunting notes that reached his ears before a sharp pain in his side sent him rolling to the right. He curled his arm against his side on instinct and looked up in alarm. Badb was holding Cathanáil only a short way from him, and red blood was dripping from the tip into the muddy snow. His blood, he realized with a sharp pang of fear.

Badb cackled as she held Cathanáil aloft. Gofiben watched in horrified silence as his own blood gleamed red on the blade and began to drip down the hilt. Dark red eyes fixed on his own, and Badb smiled a twisted, sharp grin. Then she screamed, the sound echoing through the valley and making Gofiben flinch back as his chest began to ache. His body shook, but he forced himself to look back up at Badb only to gasp in alarm.

Her body was dissolving into smoke. Her long dark cloak was swirling behind her and becoming long streams of smoke dancing in the air. Long dark hair flew around her only to gradually shift into wisps of black smoke. Badb's eyes were glowing dark red, almost black, and in her hand, Cathanáil was glowing a sickly shade of blood red.

"Yes!" Badb laughed wildly. "I've done it!"

She raised her free hand, and dark red magic swirled around her like a tornado, sending chunks of snow, rotting leaves, and dirt flying all around them. Gofiben covered his eyes and crawled towards Morgana. A warm hand caught the back of his neck and tugged him toward her. Then there was a hand at his side over the wound. He could feel something flowing over the wound that felt like warm water as the pain eased.

"Stay still!" Morgana shouted over the deafening wind.

In the river, the water churned and splashed high into the air as waves began to form. High overhead, the gray clouds darkened as the wind sped up around them. Gofiben turned his head enough to see Badb still holding the Sword, though she looked strange, like a black, smoky version of herself as her body shimmered and faded. Cathanáil was pulsing with a strange, dark red and black energy, his blood stain along the blade glinting in the low light.

Badb lowered her eyes and met his. Her dark eyes were gleaming with excitement that sent a shiver rolling down his spine. There was another flash of magic from Merlin, but it swirled harmlessly and was dispersed by the cloud surrounding Badb. With a laugh, she turned the Sword in her hand, pointing the blade towards the ground. Dark-red magic billowed around her like a storm cloud, and flashes of blood-red magic sparked and crackled around her form.

Thrusting Cathanáil into the ground, Badb released an animalistic scream. The Sword flashed blood red as it struck the stone, which began to crack and crumble on contact. Cathanáil shuddered, and the red energy streamed into the ground, causing the rocks around the Sword to turn a dark, bloody red. Everything started to shake, and Gofiben froze in terror as the ground around Cathanáil began to split open. Red light spilled forth, casting the whole valley in a terrible fiery glow.

Morgana's hand tightened on his shoulder as she tried to shift towards Cathanáil. Gofiben grimaced at the pressure against his chest. Morgana slowly brought a hand up, and silver sparks danced around her palm, but she couldn't seem to do anything. Gofiben's eyes were drawn back toward Cathanáil, and the dull ache in his chest became a sharp pain right over his heart.

Then everything went still. Badb collapsed forward against the Sword and wrenched it out of the ground with a puzzled expression twisting what remained of her features. Badb clutched at the Sword, her body swirling back together, though she looked pained and frail now. A furious mix of emotions took over her features as she stumbled away from them all. Gofiben turned towards the sound of Merlin groaning and found the eldest mage clawing at a rock to help him stand up from the mud. With a shout, Merlin took off after Badb with green magic running up his arm. Morgana released Gofiben, pausing only for a moment to look at his face and then at his side before she hauled herself up and began to pursue them.

The pain in his chest made it hard to move, but Gofiben grit his teeth and grasped at the badly bent tree he and Morgana had been all but pinned to. His fingers searched his side, but thankfully found a closed wound and drying blood. Hauling himself up, he stumbled and turned around. Bran was at his side in an instant and helped him down the slope of the hill as Badb continued to stumble her way up the valley.

"What did she do?" Bran called after Merlin and Morgana. "What happened?"

Neither of them answered, and Gofiben rushed after them, his side and his teeth aching. Bran called his name, but he didn't stop his pursuit down the hill. He stopped only when he caught sight of Badb running into the river. She screamed something, and dark red magic flowed out of her body, seeming to shrink her form, but she still clung to Cathanáil.

Water erupted out the river, forming a wall of liquid right in front of Badb. Gofiben drew back in shock as the water began to swirl as if pulled by a strong current. The whole river suddenly seemed to be spinning, and Badb fell forward into the water. She vanished into the waves just as Merlin reached the portal of water with Morgana close behind.

"Gofiben!" Morgana called. She glanced between him and the water tunnel where Merlin was gesturing for her frantically. "We'll be back," she promised quickly. "Be careful and go back to your village to wait for us."

He nodded: he couldn't think of anything else to do. Every instinct was screaming at him to stop them, but he didn't know why. Morgana's eyes lingered on him a moment longer, but then Merlin called her name. She turned and rushed toward the wall of swirling water that was shrinking with every second. Merlin grabbed her hand, and the pair vanished into the vortex, which spun for only one more moment before all the water splashed back into the river.

Gofiben stared into the water of the river as it began to calm and run normally. Silence hung over the valley, and he realized distantly that there were no birds chirping, and even the wind seemed to have died. There was also a strange, faint smell in the air that was growing stronger, but he couldn't place. Swallowing, he struggled to find his voice and looked towards Bran, who appeared as shocked as he felt.

"What do you think she did?"

"I have no idea," Bran admitted with a pained laugh. "Merlin and Morgana didn't even stay to check on what it was."

Gofiben nodded and looked around at the unfamiliar valley. He knew if they went downstream, they'd come to a village, but part of him sparked in anger at just being left behind.

"They'll catch her." Bran squeezed his shoulder, but it didn't reassure him. "They'll get the Sword back and... well, it was their own fault that she got the Sword."

"Maybe." Gofiben sniffed at the air. "Do you smell that?"

Bran paused, tilting his chin up thoughtfully. "Yeah," his friend agreed after a moment. "Like... something burning."

"Maybe the trees lit something-"

The ground heaved, shaking so violently that both men fell. Gofiben groaned in pain as his knees hit the rocks of the shore, but he looked around frantically. He tried to call on his magic, but the shaking was making it impossible for him to stay calm. Struggling to regain control, he looked around as part of the hillside crumbled away. The glow of flames lit up the valley, and smoke began billowing up into the air once more. Then there was a deafening roar unlike anything he'd ever heard before, and a harsh wave of heat swept through the valley.

Closing his eyes, Gofiben brought his hands up to his ears at the horrible sound. Everything kept shaking, and the roaring grew louder. Then there was an echoing swishing sound like a leather door flap being caught in the wind, but so much louder. The roaring died down, and the shaking stopped. Gofiben forced his eyes open even though the rest of his body still felt frozen. Looking up, he gasped as he caught sight of a huge, white, winged creature flying off into the sky towards the south.

His surprise turned to alarm when he managed to climb to his knees and look towards the hillside. There, under several large rocks, was a massive creature at least two hundred feet long. It shifted, sending more rocks rolling down the hill, and turned to look at them as it stood. The creature looked like a giant lizard with shimmering red and orange scales and long horns on the top of its head. Massive wings rose out of its shoulders that it folded down against its body as it eyed them.

Sharp golden eyes met Gofiben's as the creature opened its mouth and exposed rows of sharp glittering teeth with flames dancing at the back of its throat. But then it flinched and stumbled on the rocks. Gofiben grabbed Bran, and they both rushed back into the river as the creature fell forward with a long, sad cry of defeat.

22

Legend of Dinas Emrys

The bridge was out of a fairy tale, with a soft arc across the river and made of fitted stone. Two arches supported the bridge with the central pillar in the middle of the water. Snow-dusted ivy climbed up the bridge, and below them was the soothing sound of the burbling water. It was the sort of bridge that Alex liked to draw when she was young and envision when reading fairy tales, but this wasn't a fairy tale, and she tightened her coat against the winter chill.

In front of her were the Snowdonia Mountains. Many of their peaks were hidden by thick gray clouds with rolling rocky hills between them and the small town. Somewhere up there was the clue they needed to find the Iron Chalice, or at least that was the hope. Alex swallowed and set her hands on the cold stone wall of the bridge, looking down at the cheap watch she'd picked at the Swansea train station on their way north. It was early afternoon, but they'd still burned almost a whole day just getting here. The late December chill and the already sinking sun served as reminders that the winter solstice was drawing closer with every moment.

Around them, the locals of Beddgelert were going about their lives. People wrapped up against the winter cold moved between old stone buildings that lined the streets on either side of the bridge. Alex looked around as Bran stepped up next to her.

"What do you think?" Bran asked as he gazed out at the mountains.

"Bit late to ask me that given we just spent five and half hours getting here," Alex said.

"At least we caught an early train," Bran reminded her. "And we had some time to research the area in Fishguard." He gestured around at the village. "Beddgelert: population roughly 450 and purported to be the home of the legendary hound Gelert. I admit before reading up on it, I'd never heard the story, and won't repeat it now as things are depressing enough as is." Bran waited a moment in silence, but Alex said nothing. He sighed and pointed towards the river sweeping under the bridge. "The River Glaslyn and River Colwyn join just upstream, and they have a local meteorite."

"We should have been here yesterday."

"Trains only run at certain times; you're on their schedule." Bran set his hand on her shoulder. "It's okay, Alex. We still have time: Aiden's parents aren't going to give up on him so quickly."

Alex nodded and tried to dispel the tension that had been creeping up on her the whole trip. She couldn't shake the growing feeling that they were chasing ghosts. Dragons, she reminded herself as she looked at the hills. There couldn't be dragons in those quiet hills, and if the Chalice wasn't here... Shaking her head, Alex forced down that train of thought and focused instead on the river.

"Here come the others," Bran warned.

Jenny, Lance, and Nicki were crossing the bridge with exhausted expressions. Lance had his backpack slung over one shoulder and looked the most alert of all of them. Alex noted with a frown that Lance was walking between the two women like a barrier. Nicki sped up and moved ahead of the other two, nodding to Bran and coming around to Alex's other side.

"Anything?" Nicki asked in a low voice as she eyed the hills.

"No visions if that's what you're asking," Alex replied. "I'm afraid that we're hiking."

"Well, I got some information at the hotel," Nicki said. "But we have to follow highway A498 to get there."

"Stuff is stashed." Jenny collapsed against the side of the bridge. "And locked up," she added.

"Sorry, there wasn't a hostel," Alex apologized. She tried to smile, but couldn't manage it. "But since we're going up to the hills to poke around, it's probably for the best."

"It's fine. We just don't have time to go around to the guesthouses. I'm going to send Merlin a bill since he hasn't even been helpful," Jenny huffed as she tightened her scarf around her neck. She looked down at her boots with a slight pout. "I did not bring the right footwear for this."

Lance chuckled and knocked his heavy boots against the side of the bridge with a smile, which earned him a glare from Jenny. Instead of shying away, he smiled and shrugged at her. Then he caught Alex's eyes, and his smile vanished.

"You okay, Alex?"

"Just tired," Alex assured him. "Just like the rest of you."

Lance's frown deepened at her words, but he nodded and stepped closer to her as he moved around Bran. "Come on," Lance said, gently touching her shoulder. "It's a mile up to the trailhead and then two miles to the hill itself, and we'll be hiking around the area for a while. We need to get moving now if we have any chance of finding something today."

There were nods of agreement, and Nicki pointed to one of the roads off the bridge. Alex listened to the rhythmic click of their feet against the road and let her thoughts drift off. They walked along the road in silence, with everyone minding the traffic that kept breezing by. As they drew closer and closer to the rocky slope of the hill, Alex felt her chest getting tighter and tighter; her mouth drier and drier. She snagged the water bottle in Bran's bag and took a greedy gulp that didn't help much. Her fingers clenched and unclenched painfully in the cold air, and she took a moment to pull on her gloves with awkward movements. There was a sense that she should say something, but the others were all walking along in silence. Alex wondered if they all felt the same urge and were ignoring it as well.

Overhead the gray clouds were beginning to clear off a bit, and patches of blue sky were appearing. Around them were tree-covered hills and open fields with earthen walls covered with grass and dusted with snow. Houses were scattered about; some of them looked very modern while others were built with dark stone and looked old. One of the rivers, Alex, wasn't sure which one was off to their right, twisting and turning along with the road.

"This is it," Lance announced as he came to a stop and pointed towards a tall hill around the curve of the road. "And here's where the trail starts," Lance added, pointing to the small parking lot just off the road next to them.

"Can't we just go to the hill?" Nicki protested, "It's right by the road."

"These are volcanic mountains," Lance explained. He nodded towards the parking lot. "Dinas Emrys is famous because it was a fortress hill in addition to the dragon legend. It's high and steep with a large stone face on the roadside. The trail is two miles, but it is designed to be something a person can get up." Lance glanced towards Bran but didn't say anything. "Besides, what we really need could be in the area around the hill."

"He's right," Alex said before Nicki could protest further. "Let's stick to the safe path for now. We'll probably have to climb all over the thing before we're done."

Lance didn't look too happy with her endorsement but nodded, and they headed into the parking lot. A large sign with a map showed the area and the various trails that spread out across it. Pulling out a small map, Lance studied it and touched a few places thoughtfully. Alex grimaced as she looked at the 'strenuous' rating for the Dinas Emrys hike and risked a glance towards Bran. He was turned towards the east near the trailhead and looking at the hill across the fields and old stone walls that crisscrossed. Worry began to churn in Alex's gut that there was no way they were going to finish this hike anytime soon.

"Okay." Lance swung his backpack off his shoulder. "Just to be on the safe side, I grabbed some flashlights, batteries, granola bars, and a couple of whistles." He opened the backpack and began pulling out the items in question and passing them around. "If we're lucky, the sky will clear a little so we can get some moonlight."

"Where did you get this stuff?" Alex asked in surprise as she slung the whistle around her neck.

"There's a sporting store down by the hotel: I went there while Jenny and Nicki got us checked in," Lance explained with a shrug. "I was a bit surprised there was one here." He tossed a bottle of water to Bran, who slipped it into his shoulder bag with a smile. "I've also got a couple of emergency ponchos and blankets just in case."

"How long do you think we'll be out here?" Jenny asked. Her expression was uneasy. "It's a two-mile hike."

"Distance changes when you're talking about a steep climb," Lance explained. "But look, we stay together and try to stay on the path. If we're lucky, we'll find what we came here for quickly. We only have a couple hours of daylight left, but it's this or waiting until morning."

Nicki snatched the offered flashlight from his hand but took a bit more care in putting the whistle around her neck. Lance looked a bit uneasy as he shouldered his backpack and looked at the trailhead. Alex couldn't blame him; nothing about this was particularly smart, but it was still early afternoon, and they had to try. Glancing towards her one more time, Lance nodded and stepped out onto the trailhead to lead the way. He stopped only once more to grab a tall, heavy stick off to the side and pass it back to Bran to use instead of his cane.

The trail was still in pretty good shape despite the weather. It was wide and well-trod, following the natural slope of the hills. Trees lined the area to the west of the trail while the open fields with the small stone walls were to their east and Dinas Emrys across the way. Had it not been for the river that cut through the lower area, she would have been tempted to run across it, but the steep slopes of the distant hillside also served as a reminder of why that was a bad idea. It was a pity really that they were in such a rush, and everyone was moving as fast as they could to get as much out of the daylight as possible. They crossed a small babbling stream, and despite the chill of winter and the lack of green on the hillside, their surroundings really were beautiful, patches of dark rock contrasting with the vegetation.

Twilight fell, and the flashlights came out as they were passing over another stream with the sounds of a waterfall thundering down into the valley. The little remaining light cast strange shadows across the trail and the hills that their small flashlights did little to dispel. Time dragged on as they were forced to slow and take more breaks as the danger of accidents became all too real. No one was talking except in low whispers, and Alex kept reminding herself that wild predators like wolves and bears were extinct in Wales. Alex couldn't ignore the way that shadows seemed to jump around them as the last rays of the sun vanished and left them alone in the dark.

"God, I hope there aren't any more Sídhe around here," Nicki muttered behind her. Alex nodded in agreement.

"Easy guys," Lance called from the front, "We're doing okay."

"Bran," Jenny asked in a soft voice. "How are you doing?"

"I'm still here," Bran answered in a tight voice. "But I'm considering using magic to help me," he admitted with an exhausted sigh.

"You have telekinesis, right?" Jenny asked, a note of disbelief still ringing in her voice. "Then, you should."

"We have limited magic," Bran said, sounding pained. "When we get to the main part of Dinas Emrys... maybe."

"Then start." Lance shined his light on a small trail sign. "Cause we're officially on the hillside now." He turned and shifted his light, so his features were illuminated. "Now I know you mages really want to find this thing, but if you need to stop, then stop. We've got blankets and water: it won't be pretty, but we could take shelter in the ruins up here if need be."

"We'll tell you if we need to stop," Nicki promised, her flashlight beam already shining on the path ahead. "But please, let's keep moving."

Lance shook his head, a weary and worried sigh escaping him, but he turned and began to lead the way up the slope of the hill. A soft sound of pain escaped Bran and Alex began to turn around. Then there was a flash of yellow magic that spun off of Bran's hand and shimmered around his leg.

"Are you trying to levitate?" Nicki asked eagerly.

"No." Bran laughed a little. "Nice idea, but there's a lot of hills to go for that. I'm just trying to ease the strain on my brace a bit." He sighed and started walking again, a faint glow of yellow magic around his leg. "That's a bit better; I'll be alright."

Turning back towards the path with a nod, Alex nibbled at her lip. She wondered if they should have told Bran to stay in town; he could have kept doing research, but if this wasn't the place, then they'd need his visions. The knot of frustration was back in Alex's shoulder, even stronger than before, making every step ache. Exhaustion was beginning to make her body feel heavy and awkward. It was getting hard to feel her feet between the cold, the slush, and the layers of mud caking over them.

Parts of the hillside were solid rock, while the rest was forested all the way up the summit. The soft dusting of snow did nothing for traction, and the group had to give each other plenty of room for flailing about. Lance led them up the hill slowly, finding them good footholds or sturdy branches to hold for balance and illuminating them with his light. It was a constant process of finding a path, stopping, and illuminating it for the next person. Alex was behind Lance with Bran and Jenny next, and Nicki bringing up the rear. Yet they kept moving, and Alex kept focusing on how Lance was climbing to keep her mind from wandering to uncomfortable places. Over their heads, the clouds cleared away, and the moon, which was a little over half full, appeared. Silvery light illuminated the hillside, and Alex could see Lance's shoulders relax a little.

Alex lost track of time as she focused on putting one foot safely in front of the other. Her feet and legs were aching from the incline and frequent stops to check on the others. She thought she could see the summit of the hill up ahead of them, and Lance stopped to shine his light on what looked like part of an old wall. A sudden breeze ripped through the thinning trees, and her teeth chattered loudly.

Then as the wind died down, she heard the soft chime of a bell. It was low and soft but echoed in her ears with a sweet high note. Blinking her eyes, Alex looked around for any sign of a camp where another group might be, but the only lights she could see were their own. She followed Lance up a few more steps only for the chime to reach her ears again. This time she stopped and shined her flashlight around in the trees.

"What is it?" Bran asked, giving her a worried look even as he panted softly.

"It's a bell, I think," Alex said. The soft chime echoed around them once more. "Can you seriously not hear it?" Spinning around, Alex searched the hillside for any sign of a bell only to get blank looks from the others. "It's there, I swear!"

"Calm down, Alex," Nicki ordered, reaching out and grabbing her arm. "Take a breath."

"Nicki, I swear-"

"We believe you," Bran cut in quickly, reaching up to wipe the sweat off his forehead. "You're hearing a bell?" he asked as he began to dig into his bag. Bran shoved the bottle of water at Alex, who took a tentative sip. "I think that was in the book." He pulled out the guide book, and Nicki stepped up behind him, shining her flashlight down at the pages. "Okay, on the page for Dinas Emrys, there is a reference to a local legend that Merlin hid a treasure in a hidden cave." Bran moved his lips as he silently read something, and even in the low light, she could see his eyes widening. "And when the right person comes, someone with blonde hair and blue eyes, they will hear a bell and be led to the hidden cave."

"Or maybe gray eyes," Jenny offered. "Close enough."

Alex heard the chime again and turned towards the left where it seemed to be coming from. Licking her lips, Alex took a careful step off the path and shined her light in the direction of the sound. She heard the others move behind her, and a large hand caught her shoulder to keep her still.

"Let me go first," Lance suggested next to her as he came around her side. "There's no path here." Snow slushed beneath his feet, and mud squished as he took another step. His light swept the side of the hill, but there was no sign of a cave. "Nothing."

Alex heard the chime again. "There it is again!" She looked hopefully out into the darkness. "I'm not sure how far."

"Yeah, okay," Lance conceded as he gestured to Alex to step forward. "But be careful: this slope hasn't been cleared as a trail."

The ringing got louder and louder as they moved along the hillside. Jenny slipped twice, and Bran had to be helped down a particularly uneven and wet drop. Lance was making worried sounds about them getting back on the trail, but Alex was finding it hard to focus on anything but the chiming sound that seemed to be echoing in her head. Stumbling forward as another chime rang somewhere very close, Alex completely ignored Lance, trying to grab her arm. Thankfully her feet didn't slip in the mud as she rushed forward to the source of the ringing.

Except that it was a patch of dark, exposed stone with only a few plants around nearby trees. Thankfully, there was an empty patch of ground in front of the area, and a few large and jagged rocks provided the space with some protection from the night wind. Alex's feet crunched the patches of snow into the ground as she studied the stone.

"Alex?"

"It's... it's through here." Alex reached out a hand to touch the stone quickly. She pulled her hand back right away, but nothing happened. The others came down onto the small ledge, crowding around Alex with looks of confusion. Taking off her right glove, Alex tentatively touched the stone again, but nothing happened. "Right here," she said.

"So, what now?" Jenny asked as she touched her hand to the solid stone side of the hill. "Do you think you're supposed to do something magical to unlock it?"

"Speak friend and enter," Nicki said. She came up around Alex and tapped at the stone with a suspicious look. "I don't know, maybe try to use magic to shift the rock."

"I'm not so good at the elemental stuff," Alex admitted with a grimace, looking at the stone wall doubtfully even as the chime once again seemed to echo out of it.

"Maybe any kind of magic will do," Bran suggested. Alex glanced over at him where he was all but collapsed against the rocky wall. "You know if done by the Iron Soul. Just try something."

They were all looking at her expectantly with flashlights both on her and the wall. Alex's hand tightened around her flashlight to keep from shaking until Nicki reached over and tugged on it. Alex forced her fingers open and allowed Nicki to take the light, catching a glimpse of Nicki's expectant expression. Looking back at the stone, Alex considered it carefully. She had to admit that it did sort of seem like a wall, even if it blended in with the surroundings. Touching it again, Alex leaned against it, but it seemed solid enough.

"Just give it a try," Jenny whispered. "Something small to see if it recognizes your power."

"I'm still wondering who set all this up," Alex said. "I mean, Morgana said that Galath hid the Chalice, but he was Gofiben's brother and not a mage, so how?" She looked back at the wall now, feeling confused. "How could a magical lock have been created? Bran was dead, and so was Gofiben."

"We won't find that out without getting inside," Bran pointed out.

Nodding, Alex closed her eyes. She could feel the spark of magic grow-ing stronger as she pulled on it, but the nervous flutter in her stomach was hard to ignore. The ringing sound still echoing in her head wasn't helping either. Alex licked her lips and swallowed. This shouldn't be harder than fighting a Sídhe in battle or destroying an insane Old One, and yet it felt like it was.

She pulled harder on the magic and sighed in relief as the warm tin-gling rush began to spread through her chest and down her arms. Her legs felt a bit stronger, and the aches eased as the magic made its way to her fingertips. Opening her eyes, Alex looked down at her hands and watched as the dark silver sparks began to manifest. They glittered in the light of the moon and the flashlights, swirling around her fingers and waiting for instruction. Reaching out, Alex set her palm flat against the rock, letting the magic brush across the cold stone. A hiss escaped her, and she shivered at the sudden icy feeling spreading up her arm. It was a little too familiar, reminding her of her brush with death. Alex bit her lip and commanded the magic into the rock, forcing it to sink deeper into the stone.

It seemed to warm up beneath her fingers and take on a soft gray glow, though Alex wasn't certain if that was her or the moonlight. Still, nothing happened. Alex could feel the eyes of the others on her and hear the chiming of the bell in her head. It was becoming infuriating: the constant sound was almost taunting her. Holding back a groan, Alex pulled at her magic and shoved it into the stone. Beneath her hand, the wall vibrated, and Alex almost jumped as she felt feedback from her own magic.

She reached out and tugged at the magic a little uncertainly only to see the stone in front of her tremble and shift, creating a small hole. It didn't go all the way through, but focusing on it, Alex told herself to ignore the bell and willed the hole to go deeper. The rock shifted again, almost looking like ice melting under hot water as it rippled away from the point of heat. Alex couldn't see anything through the wall, but carefully slid her hand up to it and slipped in a finger. There was stone around her finger, but then she felt air at the tip of her finger. A soft gasp escaped Alex, and she pulled out her finger, reaching out to trace the faint streams of her magic that she could feel in the rock. Closing her eyes, she could almost see them as glistening strands running through the rock, just waiting for her.

Alex grasped at the magic and imagined the stone shifting all the way, so there was a hole big enough to step through. She envisioned it melting away to leave them a path into the hollow space beyond. A strange rumbling noise made Alex open her eyes right before the stone wall slipped away under her hand, sending her tumbling forward into the new opening. She hit the ground with a soft huff, her wrists protesting the fall and her knees aching. Groaning, she started to get up only to stop as the rumbling ceased, and she realized that she was inside the hillside with moonlight spilling in behind her.

"Well," Nicki chuckled as she helped Alex to her feet. "Merlin didn't exactly open the door, but close enough."

There was a long path of dark rock stretching out in front of them, rough and shimmering in the glow of their flashlights. Up ahead, it opened up with a strange mound of rock blocking their view. Alex was unsure about how far down the hill they'd ended up but took a cautious step forward. The tunnel didn't provide much space above their heads, but it was wide enough that they could almost go two by two. Inhaling carefully, Alex tested the air only to discover that it smelled a bit sweet rather than stale. This place wasn't natural at all.

Everyone was quiet, with a charged sense of excitement hanging around them. Her heart was pounding with the growing certainty that they were finally in the right place. Alex forced back the sense of relief trying to flood her system, reminding herself that they didn't have the Iron Chalice yet. As they walked forward, with Alex leading the way, the beam of her flashlight caught on something metal, and Alex picked up the pace only to freeze as she reached the end of the tunnel.

The rock floor continued in a rough half-circle shape into an empty space where Alex could see nothing, like a balcony off a cliff with no railings. Alex raised her flashlight off the floor and back to the mound of rock she'd noticed earlier. It was a rough, raised area like a pedestal carved out of the cavern. Alex's heart raced as she looked at the two items on it: an old skull stripped bare by time with its teeth still firmly in place and a rusting Chalice. As Alex stepped forward, her eyes lingered on the Chalice, and she swallowed thickly.

It was, in truth, more of a small, deep cauldron on a thick stand. The bowl was a little larger than her hands cupped together would have been and almost as deep as her fist. The Chalice was very plain, save for a small band of iron wrapped tightly around the joining between the bowl and stand. Leaning forward, Alex gasped softly as she made out the shape of the triskelion engraved in the metal. This was the Iron Chalice, but it was rusting with flecks of red showing along the rim rather than the magical item untouched by time that Alex was expecting.

"Thank god it's been sealed underground." Bran carefully came up beside her. "But Cathanáil wasn't rusted, right?"

"No, it wasn't," Alex agreed uneasily. "But Cathanáil was with Cyridven, so her magic might have kept the magical protection against rusting active longer."

"Okay, we've got the Chalice!" Jenny was clutching at the rocky wall with an almost panicked expression as she eyed the empty space below them. "Let's go then," she hissed.

Lance reached over and took her other hand as he stepped closer to her. He said nothing, but Alex didn't think she imagined a softening of Jenny's features. Satisfied that Jenny was okay, and feeling a bit silly for only finding out now that she had a problem with heights, Alex turned back to the Chalice. She picked it up but frowned in confusion.

"What is it?" Bran asked. "What's wrong?"

"When I picked up Cathanáil... I felt something," Alex struggled to explain. She used her teeth to tug off her other glove and shoved it into her pocket so she could put her other hand on the Chalice. "I'm... I'm not sure."

Alex took a deep breath as she called on her magic once again. Her hands glowed, and the Chalice began thrumming softly in her hands. Tiny flickers of magic illuminated it. Alex raised her eyes to look at Bran. For a moment, she couldn't speak, but then her gray eyes caught his wide green ones, and she managed a small smile.

"Hey, Bran, wanna try it out?"

23

Emrys

Alex's question was both expected and a shock all at once. Nicki couldn't believe that Alex had phrased it that way, but on the other hand, she couldn't imagine how a person could calmly present such an idea. Her eyes shifted from the Chalice to Bran, and any witty remark she might have been tempted to make died on her tongue. Bran was staring at the Chalice with a hopeful yet lost expression, his fingers holding his cane so tightly his knuckles were white.

The darkness around them and the tension were getting to be a bit much for her. Nicki's hands were shaking as she looked down at them and pulled her own magic forth. They'd found the Iron Chalice, so maybe they could afford to use a bit more magic. Icy blue sparks shimmered around her hand, and Nicki concentrated them into an orb. Closing her eyes, she focused on making a light, on the orb's magic becoming light instead of water or ice. It thrummed in her hand, and then through her closed eyelids, she could see the glow. Opening her eyes, Nicki smiled at her little achievement and carefully lifted it into the air. She concentrated on it staying afloat without her hand and pushed it a little further up.

With more of the cavern revealed, Jenny made a small displeased sound behind her. The dark local stone shimmered in the soft bluish light of Nicki's magic. It was a fairly small cavern in all truth: the ceiling was only a short way above their heads, and the floor they were on extended out a few more feet in front of the pedestal. The beams of her light reached down several feet, illuminating another large ledge on the other side of the cavern, but the bottom of the cave was nowhere in sight.

"Bran?" Alex called nervously. "I didn't- I didn't mean to pressure you; it's totally up to you if you want to use-"

"Yeah," Bran said. He was still panting, but he nodded. "I've been thinking about it since we left Ravenslake and, well, especially since we had that Fisher King talk."

"Right." Relief was obvious on Alex's face. "Uh, I think we need to put some liquid in it. Then I'll see if I can activate it or something."

The nervous expression was back on Alex's face, but Bran nodded and pulled out the water bottle. Pouring what was left into the Chalice seemed to take forever. Alex looked lost for a moment, and Nicki noted that a bit of the rusting rim seemed to have washed off into the water. Bran was pale and staring at the Chalice with a look that was a mixture of hopeful awe and resignation. Nicki couldn't blame him; the dull rusting thing in Alex's hands didn't exactly inspire her. Nonetheless, Alex closed her eyes, and her magic began to swirl around the Chalice. The sparks seeped into the iron, and it began to look a little brighter. Bran gently took the Chalice when it was offered to him, and after a beat raised it to his lips. No one moved as Bran gulped down the water and drew the Chalice back from his mouth.

"Did you feel anything?" Alex asked. Her eyes darted between his face and his leg. "Any magic?"

Bran swallowed with a blank expression but shook his head. "No, I didn't."

"Let me try something else," Alex said. She took the Chalice from him and placed it back on the pedestal of rock carefully. There was an almost frantic expression on her face. "I just need a minute."

Nicki frowned; she couldn't help but feel concerned over the odd tone in Alex's voice. Magic burst from Alex's hands and swirled in the air, illuminating her face and casting eerie shadows upon the walls. Alex grimaced, confusing Nicki until the dark gray magic spun down over its owner's hands and sliced one of them. Red blood began to pool in Alex's left hand, but she only smiled as she reached for the Chalice. Grimacing in sympathy, but unable to look away, Nicki watched Alex spread her blood across the Chalice. Then the blonde mage closed her eyes and poured more magic into the Chalice. The blood seeped into the metal, and it once again looked a little brighter, but Alex was beginning to shake.

Bran plucked the Chalice away from Alex, glancing towards Nicki with lost green eyes. Lance reached forward and handed her a bottle of water. Sharing another look with Alex, Nicki poured some of the water in, and Bran again took a deep drink while Alex watched with wide, hopeful gray eyes. But then Bran lowered the Chalice and slowly shook his head. He was watching Alex with worried eyes as she took in his expression. Defeat took over her face as she looked at the Chalice and slowly took it out of Bran's hands. The glow of her magic had faded, and she turned with shaking hands to put the Chalice back on the pedestal.

Nicki's eyes widened as Alex stumbled back from it, her breathing uneven and loud in the cavern. Alex turned to look at them, her eyes wide and her face pale. For a moment, she looked like she was going to say something, but then the tremors in her body took over, and her knees gave out.

"I'm not the Iron Soul." Alex's face was in her hands, and her whole body was shaking. "This proves I'm not."

Bran was looking at the Chalice and skull, a confused and sickly expression on his face. Nicki began to reach for him, but he shrugged his shoulder and twisted away from her. Nicki turned to look back at Alex only to find Jenny kneeling down and wrapping an arm around her. Above Nicki's head, the magical light flickered as her own desire to see what was happening began to fade.

"You are the Iron Soul," Jenny assured Alex. A dry sob escaped Alex, and her shakes got worse. "Alex, honey, breathe!" Jenny looked up at Nicki with a wide-eyed, worried look. "This doesn't mean anything, not really."

It was all coming down around them, Nicki realized in the back of her mind as she clenched her fists. She wanted to say something, but the anger was building in her chest again, and she dared not. Alex was shaking against Jenny and staring off into the distance. Blood was dripping from Alex's cut hand onto the dark stone. Was she back on that beach with Arthur, Nicki wondered? Or was she replaying that promise she'd made back in Ravenslake to be worthy of the sacrifice that Aiden had made for her? Nicki felt bile rising up in her throat as guilt warred with anger.

"Shit," Alex swore. "What did I do wrong?"

"Nothing," Jenny insisted. "Alex, the Chalice has been inactive for two thousand years; maybe you just need to-"

"I didn't feel anything, Jenny!" Alex snapped, looking up at Jenny with wide gray eyes. "I don't know what I'm doing. We've been wrong about the identity of the Iron Soul before; maybe we are again."

"I don't believe that," Jenny said. "I don't, Alex. We'll sort this out: maybe the Chalice needs a certain liquid or spell to reactivate it." Jenny glanced towards Nicki, her mouth moving as she tried to think. "Let's just get it out of here, and then we can call Morgana."

"Morgana..." Alex repeated the name, but her face lost all color, and for a moment, Nicki believed that she was really going to be sick. "Shit!" Alex hissed as she pulled away from Nicki and lunged towards the edge of the ledge.

The sounds of Alex getting sick over the side didn't help as Nicki tried to think of what to say. Jenny started shaking as she tried to crawl over to the edge, but she stopped and looked pleadingly towards her. Moving before she'd even thought to, Nicki knelt down by Alex, mindful of the edge, and pulled back her blonde hair to keep it out of her face.

"We'll sort this out," Nicki promised, rubbing Alex's back gently.

Fear for Aiden and doubt was prickling over her like an icy chill, and Nicki struggled to ignore it. She forced herself to think back to her parents' attempt to return to her life. Alex had been with her through that: she'd been there when her Gran called and had driven her home rather than have her drive across town upset. It had been Alex that sat with her while they waited for Aiden. Alex, who grew up in a sitcom home with two well-employed parents and healthy brothers, who comforted her when her own shit parents came back to see her after abandoning her because they 'weren't ready for the responsibility.'

"It's okay, Alex," Nicki said. "I think you're wrong– whatever is in your head that makes you think it isn't you is wrong." Alex gagged, and Nicki looked back at Bran, but he was staring at the Chalice. "Look," Nicki tried again, struggling to find the right words. "It wasn't me or Bran or Aiden who turned around when we were almost out of the Sídhe tunnels to go and rescue some kids we didn't even know. That was you, and despite the crap you're going through now, thanks to Arthur, you came here to find the Chalice."

"But I can't make it work," Alex protested weakly. Nicki was just grateful that Alex was moving away from the ledge.

"We'll take it with us and try again on the Solstice; maybe it just needs more juice to start working again than you can use." Nicki released Alex's hair and gripped her arm. "You've only had your powers for like a year, so of course there are going to be some problems along the way."

"But Aiden needs the Chalice."

Nicki's heart ached at the reminder. She dropped her forehead down to touch Alex's shoulder as helplessness poured through her. There was nothing to say that could make this better. She had no idea what was wrong with Alex's magic. Part of her wished that she could believe that Alex wasn't the Iron Soul, but Arthur had been so sure, and Cyrridven, Merlin's ally of three thousand years, had died to protect Alex from Chernobog long enough for Alex to use Cathanáil. No, there was no doubt in her mind, but there was a dark fear creeping through her about just what that meant. Turning her head slightly, she looked towards Jenny, who seemed just as lost as she was.

Nicki froze as a strange scraping sound, echoed up the cavern from below. Jenny stiffened sharply, looking around nervously and starting to crawl back towards the tunnel. Lance reached out and helped her up as he searched for the source of the noise. Then the sound grew louder with an odd groan accompanying the scraping noise. There was the loud echoing sound of something catching the air. The sound grew louder and louder, and Nicki could tell that something was coming up from below them. Nicki barely had time to tug Alex to her feet before something large and red reached the light of her magical orb. It landed at the far outcropping with a thump, and Nicki forced herself to look.

It was a Dragon. A real dragon. Nicki's brain must have gone offline for a moment because the next thing she was really aware of was that the dragon had stretched out on another rocky ledge across the chasm. He-she-it was over a hundred feet long, and that wasn't counting the long red tail tipped with spikes that it calmly curled around its body. Large wings were folded neatly against its shimmering scaled back.

"Wow." Nicki was suddenly aware that her mouth was hanging open a little.

"Run," Lance hissed. He reached for Jenny and Alex.

"No, wait!" Bran said. "Guys, it's not attacking."

Indeed, the Dragon was just watching them calmly. Its red horns scraped at the top of the cavern when it shifted its head. To Nicki's shock, it turned its golden eyes towards the ceiling with a disgruntled look. Then its gaze swept over them, lingering on Bran for a moment with its eyes widening as its nostrils flared. The long red-scaled snout with hints of orange and gold came closer and sniffed again as they all stood frozen.

"Hello, Bran," the Dragon greeted in a deep rumbling voice. It drew back its nose. "Or do you have another name now?"

It sounded calm and merely curious. Nicki sucked in a deep greedy breath, suddenly feeling faint. The Dragon glanced at all of them once more, but it quickly looked back to Bran. Her friend's expression was cautious, but curious mixed with fear.

"No," Bran said slowly. "Do you know me?"

"Indeed, I believe I do," the red Dragon answered in slightly accented English. "Your magic smells the same as it did long ago, and I have always had a good memory for smell." The red Dragon looked towards the pedestal, and then back at Bran with a curious expression. "Do you know me?"

"I'm afraid not," Bran admitted. Nicki was impressed by how calm he was. "Are you an enemy or an ally of those that put the Iron Chalice here?"

"I was a friend," The Dragon's voice rumbled around them. "You called me Emrys."

"Emrys," Bran repeated doubtfully, but he didn't look away from the beast. "That was your name?"

"The names of my kind are not something you could pronounce." Emrys tilted his head and revealed his teeth in what Nicki almost thought could be a smile. "You and Gofiben insisted that you needed something to call me." The Dragon shifted on its front legs, giving another dirty look towards the ceiling, and extended his nose once again. He sniffed at the air once more and fixed his eyes on Alex. "I believe I smell another familiar scent." Heart pounding and hearing a sharp inhale from Alex, Nicki gently pushed her forward. She had to keep both hands on Alex's shoulders as the blonde tried to back away from the Dragon's nose. "Interesting," Emrys said. "I recognize your scent as well, Gofiben. It is good to see you as well."

Nicki could hear a collective sigh of relief and risked a glance back at Lance and Jenny, who were in the tunnel staring at Emrys with wide eyes. Chuckling to herself, Nicki turned back and grinned as she took in the Dragon. He was gorgeous, with shimmering scales and an air of dignity that even his obvious discomfort in the small space couldn't hide.

"I am the Iron Soul?" Alex asked.

"Indeed," Emrys answered with a hint of confusion. "Were you not aware of that?" Then his gold eyes traced Alex and then went to the Chalice. "Ah... then it was you who was ill." Emrys chuckled when Alex tensed up and made a tiny sound of fear. "Thankfully, you missed me, but the smell did wake me up. I was not expecting company."

"What are you doing here?" Lance asked curiously, only to flinch back once he realized he'd spoken up. "I mean with the Chalice and underground."

"I have little choice in the matter, I'm afraid." Emrys considered Lance for a moment. "The Old One Badb pulled me and my prisoner, the White Dragon, into your world a very long time ago." Emrys nodded his head down towards the cavern below. "Not far from this cavern in fact. Unfortunately, even once Badb was dead, there was no way to return home, and I still had the duty of keeping my prisoner confined."

"Why not just kill him?" Nicki asked. She looked towards the edge of the ledge, wondering if there was really another Dragon down there.

"I tried that," Emrys confided, "But alas, the nature of Dragons combines with the nature of your world in... odd ways."

"Odd ways?" Bran pressed. "What do you mean?"

"Dragons have iron blood," Emrys explained. "Unlike most other... guests to your world, we are not naturally incompatible; many of the creatures from worlds on my branch of the Tree of Reality are like that. The problem is that it is still not our world, and the nature of life and death for Dragons is different. We are reborn a short time later into a new body, and slowly regain our old memories."

"Seriously?" Nicki gaped up at the Dragon. "So, what happens here?"

"Our souls, our essence, cannot take on a new body as there are not Dragons being born. Instead, our bodies slowly heal our injuries, but our souls cannot move on. We are essentially immortal," Emrys informed them before nodding into the cavern below. "Which is why I remain here to keep the White Dragon contained."

"It's the legend!" Bran looked over at Nicki with wide eyes. "It's true."

"Ah, yes, the legend." Emrys chuckled, and his horns scraped the top of the cavern. "Parts of it are correct."

"If you don't leave here, then how are you aware of the legend?" Alex asked with a frown.

"I have a little magic," Emrys informed her with a soft huff. "There is water far below here that I stay in to keep myself cleansed of any other side effects being in your world might cause, but there is a small side pool through which I can view parts of the world, or at least the BBC."

"You watch television?" Bran asked with a slack jaw.

"Sadly, I cannot view any areas where magic is very active," Emrys admitted with a sigh. "That is a veil I cannot pierce, so I've been isolated down here. Television has been a joy in the last... oh, sixty or so years. It is actually worthwhile to stay awake and check on the state of the world."

The idea that Emrys watched the BBC using magic nearly short-circuited Nicki's brain. "Don't you want to leave?" Nicki asked. She was deeply confused by how calm the Dragon was after being underground for two thousand years.

"And do what, young mage?" Emrys turned his eyes on her. "Fly out into the sky and alarm the humans? Leave the White Dragon to wake up? I was a law keeper and was entrusted with tracking him down and stopping him. That vow has not faded simply because of my circumstances here." They all shifted uncomfortably, and Nicki was aware that the temperature in the cave had become much warmer. She desperately hoped that wasn't a bad sign, but then Emrys shook his head and looked back to Bran. "Do you not remember?" He looked at Alex. "Do neither of you remember me?"

"I'm afraid not," Bran answered. "We found our way here because I had a vision of the skull and Chalice, but I didn't see you."

"Dragons are not easily found," Emrys chuckled, but his amusement faded as he looked at the Chalice. "I helped Gofiben make the Chalice," he explained in a softer voice. "After I was pulled into your world, the

White Dragon got the better of me and left me for dead. As I said, we cannot truly die in your realm, and Gofiben helped me. Badb's plague was overtaking the region; his teachers Merlin and Morgana were far away and unaware of what Badb had done, so he asked me for help."

"And that's why you guard it?"

"No, once I realized that I could not return home, I carved this chamber with my magic and Gofiben and Bran's help. I defeated the White Dragon and trapped us both inside to keep him contained. And as a result of keeping the White Dragon from destroying your world, I was not able to help Gofiben and Bran against Badb's forces." Emrys lowered his head and shook it sadly. "I only learned of Gofiben's death from Galath when he brought the Chalice and Bran's head here to hide. The Iron Chalice had already lost its power, and your brother was in a rage."

"And you put a spell on the cave so that Alex could find it?" Nicki asked.

"No, Gofiben did that himself. We kept the cavern sealed when he was not here to prevent... accidents. The chiming was something he did so that he could find the entrance again. Only he could hear it."

"I guess the blonde and blue eyes thing was just a coincidence," Bran said. "Or another mage had a vision of Alex finding this place one day. Gray eyes are sort of a shade of blue."

"But enough of the past: something is wrong now," Emrys said. "Magic is spreading across the world once more, and you stink of distress."

"We need the Iron Chalice, but it isn't working," Alex explained nervously. "I even tried using my blood, but I couldn't restore its power. Did Galath tell you anything?"

"Your brother told me only that Badb was dead, and there was still no sign of Merlin or Morgana. He was very angry with them, and I believe he blamed them for Gofiben's death. He used Gofiben's blood to enter this cavern and asked for permission to leave the skull and Chalice here. That was the last time a human has been in here."

"Why the skull? The Chalice sure, but why the skull?" Bran looked over at the skull with a morbid, but curious expression.

"Bran had requested it: Galath did not know the reason, but he followed his wishes."

"So, you don't know how to restore the Chalice?" Alex stepped towards Emrys. "You helped make it."

"I do not know," Emrys informed her sadly. "I long assumed that Gofiben's reincarnation would be able to use it. My old friend, you are so changed and yet..." Emrys sighed and examined Alex as Nicki stepped to the side, trying not to be alarmed at the sight of Alex right in front of the nose and mouth of a Dragon. "You still lack faith, even after all these years. Why?"

His question made Alex stutter, and Nicki grimaced at the defeated expression once again, claiming Alex's features. Guilt hit Nicki again, and she looked away. Bran was standing by the pedestal with a thoughtful look. She wondered what was going through his head and hoped he could say something to reassure Alex. Then, Bran shifted his hand, touched the skull, and brushed his thumb thoughtfully over the brow of the empty eye socket.

"Bran?" Nicki asked. She took a step closer to him. "Hey, are you okay?"

Bran finally turned to look at her, lifting his hand off of the skull. Gasping softly, Nicki had to force herself to stay still when the skull crumbled into dust. Bran exhaled and turned his palm to inspect it. Emrys made a strange sound and shifted on his ledge, stretching out his body so he could look at Bran.

"Bran?" Nicki's eyes darted between him, the pile of dust, and Emrys. "What happened?"

"I'm..." Bran leaned against the pedestal with a dazed expression. "I'm..."

"Your scent is as I remember," Emrys declared with narrowed golden eyes as he re-examined Bran. "Do you know me now, Bran?"

"No," Bran replied. Then he shook his head. "And yes. I... it's like a dream, but yes."

"What?" Nicki demanded, reaching towards Bran while Emrys chuckled.

Then the Dragon threw back his head, carving deep gashes in the stone as he laughed. The cavern shook around them, and Alex tumbled back from the ledge, falling on the ground. Bran grabbed the Chalice and pulled it close to his chest while Nicki dropped to the ground to avoid falling the wrong direction. Gripping Alex's shoulder, she looked over at Bran and watched the confused, but stern expression on his face.

"Emrys!" Alex shouted; her voice barely heard in the dim. "Emrys!"

The laughing ceased, and the Dragon shifted his head, catching his horns on the deep grooves he'd carved, forcing him to duck his head down. Nicki watched the movement with an odd blend of amusement and irritation growing in her chest. This Dragon had clearly gone insane due to his isolation, television, or not. But after two thousand years, television in the last 60 years had probably been far too late.

"I just realized something amusing; I am sorry if I frightened you," Emrys apologized. He settled on his ledge again with a slight smile. "But I remember now something Gofiben told me after I discovered that I could not properly die; the soul is stored in the head."

Nicki looked at Alex in confusion, but she only managed a weak shrug of bewilderment while Bran looked thoughtful. He turned towards Alex and appeared to be pondering something before he turned back to Emrys.

"You think I regained my... I won't say memories because that's not accurate, but... awareness because I touched the skull?"

"You now remember me, she does not," Emrys pointed out with a shrug. "I will not claim to know how your human souls work, but perhaps finding her previous life would be of use."

"Which one?" Alex asked, spreading out her hands in a helpless gesture. "I'm not even sure how many lives I have had, let alone where to find their remains."

"You were not the first," Emrys said. "I do not know the details, but Gofiben was not your first life. Perhaps you should start at the beginning to find the answer."

"Arto." Alex's expression was strange, thoughtful, and disappointed all at the same time. "He was the first Iron Soul."

"And perhaps a part of you lingers with him still." Emrys sniffed at the air. "You are the Iron Soul, but you are... lacking something."

"Tell me something I don't know." Alex looked over at the Iron Chalice that Bran was still holding close.

"Your brother loved you very much," Emrys told her. "But he allowed his grief and anger to color his actions. Never in two thousand years have Merlin or Morgana come here seeking the Iron Chalice. I am aware of many of the modern stories surrounding you, and I find it ironic that your warrior brother Galath is remembered as Galahad, who found the Grail, while in truth, it was he who hid the Iron Chalice beyond the reach of anyone save the Iron Soul."

"He never told Merlin or Morgana where it was," Alex admitted as she climbed to her feet and rubbed her arm self-consciously. "We only found you thanks to old myths and Bran's visions."

"And perhaps that is the answer to why Bran asked to have his skull left here; to provide a link for those that followed into the past."

"'Does sound like something that you would do," Nicki told Bran with a weak smile; to her relief, he chuckled.

"Then take the Chalice with you. The winter solstice approaches, and you may find what you need on that night."

"It's our best chance," Bran agreed. "Morgana and Merlin can tell us where to find Arto's remains, and hopefully, that will give Alex the boost she needs."

"And if it doesn't?" Alex asked.

Nicki flinched at Alex's question and shared a helpless look with Bran while Emrys watched Alex with displeased eyes. "What is your name in this life?" Emrys suddenly asked. "I did not think to ask before for the names of you and your companions."

"Uh, this is Nicki, that's Lance, and that's Jenny," Alex introduced them all in a rush. "And, I'm Alex."

"Alex," Emrys repeated. "It means defender of mankind," he observed calmly as he stretched out his wings carefully and shifted on his ledge. "I can help you no further, old friend. My post is here, but I wish you luck."

Then, before any of them could say or do anything more, Emrys slipped off his ledge and allowed himself to fall into the darkness. They could hear the flapping of his large wings, but that too soon faded away. Nicki risked a glance towards Alex's face. She looked lost and nervous, but her lips were thin, and her gray eyes were staring sharply ahead.

Alex stepped towards Bran and carefully took the Iron Chalice from his hands. She studied it for a long moment before a deep exhausted sigh escaped her. Watching in silence, Nicki waited for Alex as Bran reached out and squeezed her hand. A soft gasp escaped the young man, and he stumbled. Alex gripped his arm tightly, nearly dropping the Chalice.

Bran lowered his head and rested it on Alex's shoulder while they all waited.

"I hope that doesn't happen every time I touch you," Bran groaned, rubbing at his temple. "Well, the good news is I know where to go."

"And the bad news?" Lance asked from the tunnel as he stepped out onto the ledge and offered Bran an arm.

"We've got a ways to go to get there. I saw Stonehenge."

24

Birth of a Myth

7 21 B.C.E. South of Mount Yr Wyddfa

The sunrise cast warm rays over the hills and spread long shadows into the valley. Green leaves rippled in a soft breeze alongside the babbling river below. Everything seemed calm and peaceful until a loud flapping sound echoed down the valley, and the trees swayed from the force of huge wings. Gofiben looked up sharply from his small fire and jumped to his feet. Behind him, a small recently built roundhouse shuddered in the gusts, and the animal pelt hung over the door flapped in the wind. Raising his eyes, he grinned as the red Dragon flew into view. Its right wing was no longer ripped from its battle with the White Dragon, and slowly it rose through the air. A loud laugh escaped the Dragon and echoed down the valley to where their small group had made camp.

He glanced down the valley towards the village and grimaced at how they might react to a Dragon in the air again. Their attempts thus far to keep the villagers calm without Merlin and Morgana had not gone well. Frowning, Gofiben glared at the red mist he could see a hint of in the air. It was like that in almost all the villages in the west now: a veil of plague hanging over human settlements. Attempts to move never seemed to work; the plague latched onto groups of people, and the villagers were too afraid to leave the perceived safety of their homes.

The sound of someone behind him drew Gofiben's attention, and he turned around to greet them. His brother was dressed in a heavy tunic with a fur draped across his cloak despite the warming weather. His axe was strapped to his back, and Gofiben noted the extra dagger secured in his boot. Galath was frowning at the rising sun and the glimmer of red dancing through the sky.

"Galath," Gofiben greeted with a smile, but his brother went back to looking towards the mountain with a frown.

"So, the Dragon is flying again." His voice was tight as a flash of red appeared above the trees and then dove out of sight.

"Yes, he went out today to check the area." Gofiben tentatively looked towards his brother. "You don't like him, do you?"

"I wish that beast had died when it collapsed," Galath growled. "I don't wish to be cruel, but something like that, something of that size is a danger."

"He hasn't harmed any of us," Gofiben protested. "And besides," he added in a lower voice. "He can't die."

"Doesn't that bother you?" Galath gave him a sharp look. "The way he keeps coming right back, the way his injuries keep healing?"

"Of course, it does," Gofiben said. His stomach turned at the memory of watching the Dragon's flesh slowly knit itself back together. "But he can't help it, and trying to kill him would only make him our enemy," he added weakly, moving his hands and clenching his fist in an attempt to steady himself.

"You keep toying with your hands," Galath observed, turning his brown eyes to him. His expression softened, and he sighed. "You miss your forge, don't you?"

"Feels like years since I worked iron," he admitted. Gofiben slumped down on the pelt covered stone that was serving as his seat. "I do miss it."

"Still no news from Morgana or Merlin?"

"No," Gofiben sighed, knowing that Galath had already known the answer. "I wish I knew where they went. That... water tunnel was terrifying, but they didn't seem that worried."

"In theory, they have encountered such things before," Galath pointed out before he too sighed and sat down. "I confess that I'm grateful they didn't take you with them."

"Do you regret coming with us?" Gofiben asked, forcing the words out. "I mean... you don't like Morgana or Merlin, and you don't have magic, so you usually get stuck hunting or patrolling the area-"

"You're my brother," Galath cut in with a small smile, reaching over and clapping him on the shoulder. "With mother and father gone, it's just us, and I consider it my responsibility to take care of you."

"I'm hardly a child."

"No, but you left your village, your home, and your livelihood to travel with a pair of mages that you still barely know," Galath countered. "What did you expect me to do? Morgana knows that's why I'm here; at least, she did." Galath muttered something under his breath. "How long are we going to stay here? It's been two weeks since they vanished. We've built a shelter for goodness sake. Doesn't it make more sense to go back to the village, as Morgana said?"

"I'm worried about the Dragon," Gofiben admitted with a shrug. "He's out of place here. When he first came through... I thought it was dead, and then the white one took off."

"It's better now, and it isn't your responsibility."

"I'm a mage, and he isn't from this world; that makes it my responsibility. And he's not that bad."

"How much have you been talking with that thing?" Galath asked sharply.

"Not often," Gofiben rushed to assure him. "But I mean when it started breathing again and opened its eyes... what else was I supposed to do?"

"Hit it with a rock in the head," Galath answered bluntly.

"Hitting things is more your skillset."

"And trying to make them or fix them is yours," Galath countered with a pointed look towards the Dragon. "What do you really think is going to come of this?"

"I don't know," Gofiben replied with a weak sigh. "But he can't die, and his injuries have healed. You didn't see him, Galath. He died and then just came back again over and over until the wounds from his fight with the White Dragon healed. It was horrible."

Gofiben shivered and focused on a tree on the other side of the river. The memory of the red Dragon collapsing was so very clear. He'd crept up to the thing with Bran, motivated by curiosity, once he was certain it was dead. There'd been long slices in its hide, and its right wing had been in shreds with rocks crushing its side. Yet it had suddenly stirred and awoken with a pained groan only to die once again in only a few moments.

Each time it woke up, it stayed alive a little longer. Four days later, it managed to speak, its words sounding odd and strange until he'd summoned his own magic and begged it to help him understand. The Dragon hadn't spoken long and had released a pained cry at the news that the White Dragon was gone. It had tried to stand and fly, only to die a short time later with a terrible, pained scream.

He felt sick and shook his head to clear away the terrible images and sounds. Galath was silent next to him and sighed, turning to watch the

Dragon. It was circling in the air, going higher and higher as it became accustomed to flying once more. Briefly, Gofiben wondered if there might be some way to kill the Red Dragon; perhaps Cathanáil could. The Sword, along with Badb's power, had brought both Dragons here, but the idea didn't sit well with him.

"Good morning," Bran's sleepy voice greeted behind them as he stumbled out to join them. "Oh wow, it's flying."

"Yes, his wings were almost healed yesterday," he answered without turning around. "How'd you sleep?"

"Fine," Bran replied with a shrug as he took a seat on his own low rock and rubbed his hands together. "I'm surprised it took his wings so long to heal."

"Probably healed the injuries that were killing him first," Gofiben offered with a shake of his head. "I still can't believe I'm saying that."

"Well, you see a creature die and come back again and again..." Bran trailed off and shuddered. "I wonder if the White Dragon was doing the same."

"Maybe; neither of them looked all that good when they came through."

Galath hummed loudly on his other side. Bran gave him a sympathetic look, and Gofiben relaxed. At least he wasn't alone in this decision. He loved his brother, and he was grateful for him, but he didn't understand his warrior mindset. There was a reason he'd preferred to stay in his forge. Things were simpler, and if he made a mistake, all he had to do was reheat the iron and try again.

"Gofiben," Galath started to say as the Dragon swooped towards them. Then he sighed and shook his head. "I hope you know what you're doing."

The Dragon landed with a crunch of trees on the far hill, and there was another laugh of triumph that made him feel both relieved and worried all over again. Galath stood up with a huff and touched his axe before he shook his head again. Gofiben listened to his brother's footsteps as they moved away and tugged at his hair in frustration.

"What do you think?" Bran asked finally, nodding towards the hill. "Should we go and talk to it?"

The unease that Gofiben was feeling wasn't enough to keep him from nodding. Galath was nowhere in sight, though Gofiben suspected that his brother might have expected this to happen. They took a moment to bundle up and grab some provisions before heading down towards the river. Warm sunshine was quickly causing the shadows to retreat and making the day much more pleasant. Gofiben hoped that the weather and the flight would mean that the Dragon was in a good mood.

It was hard to miss, a huge creature perched on a flatter part of the hill. Gofiben was certain that it was visible for miles and wondered what the folks in the village might be whispering about the beast. The Dragon noticed them coming up the hill and lowered its head. With a small blast of fire, it heated a patch of the ground and then lowered its belly onto the warm earth with a happy huff. Folding its wings and legs against its body, it calmly watched them as they came up the slope.

"Hello?" Gofiben greeted nervously. "Do you remember us?"

"I do." The Dragon nodded to them. "I trust you are well."

"Yes," Bran answered. He was standing stiffly next to Gofiben.

"I'm Gofiben," he offered with a smile. "And this is my friend Bran. We're glad that you're alright..." he trailed off hopefully.

The Dragon answered with a series of clicks and sounds that not even his magic could make sense of. Exchanging a glance with Bran, he found his friend looked just as confused as he. A chuckle escaped the Dragon, and he shook his head.

"Forgive me, it appears that even with magic, my name isn't something that translates to a human tongue," he informed them before stretching out his legs. "My name is rather traditional, I'm afraid; a burden even on a Dragon tongue."

"Well, is there something else we could call you?" Bran suggested carefully.

"Nothing comes to mind," the Dragon pondered with an odd expression on its face. "But I suppose you need something to call me."

Gofiben considered the question for a moment. It was an odd request, but he supposed the Dragon was trying to make them more comfortable. He nearly laughed; it was already working as he was focusing much more on the question at hand rather than the Dragon. Licking his lips, Gofiben had to admit he didn't know how to feel about that even as his eyes landed on the small scar that was healing on the Dragon's upper chest.

"How about Emrys," he suggested before his brain had a chance to process what he was saying.

"Emrys," the Dragon repeated doubtfully. "Why that name?"

"It means immortal," Gofiben offered with a sheepish smile, suddenly afraid that the name would serve as more of a bitter reminder than anything else.

"I suppose that fits my identity in this realm," Emrys agreed with a sad note to his voice as he stretched out his healed wings. "Still, I wonder if time will prove to be my undoing. Hopefully, not before the White Dragon."

"May I ask what he did that was so bad that, even when trapped in another realm, you still want to capture him?" Bran shifted nervously, but seemed determined.

"He is a murderer; contrary to what our teeth and claws might suggest, we Dragons have firm rules about dealings with each other. He went on a rampage and killed over a dozen of our fellow Dragons. I was, but part of a team ordered to find him and bring him to justice," Emrys explained. The Dragon flexed his wings. "Normally I would avoid killing him, but I think I must try it at least once before I declare it a lost cause."

"Then what?" Gofiben asked. "You have no way back and unless Merlin and Morgana return and they know how to use Cathanáil to get you home.... What will you do with him?"

Emrys hummed in thought and looked out towards the nearby mountains, his eyes tracing up the slope of the highest peaks. Gofiben had a strong sense that Emrys was seeing something that he was not and shifted uneasily. "These mountains and hills were birthed in fire," Emrys finally answered. "I will carve out a prison for us both." He turned his eyes back to Gofiben and tilted his head with a flash of his great white teeth. "You and Bran's magic could help me. With your power behind mine, I could bind him beneath the surface."

"Aren't you even going to try going home?" Confusion welled up inside of Gofiben. "Then you could get help and take the other one back."

"Tell me, Gofiben, do you know much about what happens to beings who cross between worlds?" Emrys asked him gently. The Dragon crossed his front legs calmly with his talons delicately touching the ground.

"Merlin and Morgana explained a little about the Old Ones: they are like living lightning and force themselves into the same form as us to survive, but being in our world slowly drives them insane like Badb unless they stay in water which cleanses them."

"Indeed, my people have explored our own branch of the tree somewhat. Our worlds are inhabited by great beasts such as ourselves, and over time many of them have shifted from realm to realm. Within the same branch, it usually isn't a problem, but beyond..." Emrys shook his head and lowered it. "Travel beyond our branch is forbidden. For us, the worst changes occur not when we leave, but when we try to return. Though the White Dragon and I did not come to your world willingly, we are barred from ever returning home."

"They've exiled you, and you'll still hold the White Dragon for them?"

"He is a murderer of his own kind; what do you think he will do to yours?" Emrys countered seriously before chuckling wryly. "Makes me grateful that I was an old bachelor. It's my own fault in a way; I was fighting the White Dragon, quite valiantly, I might add, and the portal just appeared. Rather than pull away, I chose to be stubborn and didn't stop fighting even as we both rolled through it."

"Still," Gofiben said. "I'm sorry."

Emrys looked at him in silence, giving Gofiben the feeling that the Dragon was seeing much more than he could realize. Then Emrys nodded his head. "You are a good one, Gofiben. You have nothing to fear from me, but I need to find the White Dragon. I hope that you will not try to stop me."

"I'm not sure," Gofiben admitted. "I don't want it out there, especially if it is as dangerous as you say, but... well, I don't know you, Emrys. I know you didn't try to kill Bran and me while you were hurt, but I have a responsibility to my realm. I'm not sure if just letting you fly about is a good thing."

A sharp, high-pitched roar rolled down the valley, making Gofiben jump in alarm and pull his dagger. A harsh growl escaped Emrys as he stood up and sniffed at the air. Bran gripped his friend's shoulder and began to pull him away from the huge beast. Looking up, Gofiben saw a white form moving rapidly towards them. His throat closed up as Emrys growled; Bran pulled him harder, and they began to rush towards the river. The air pressure around them plummeted, making his ears pop as Emrys spread his wings and took off into the sky. A wave of heat rolled over them, and Gofiben struggled against the urge to look back. As his feet hit the cold water and a shudder raced through him, he shook off Bran's hand and looked up into the sky.

High above them, the White Dragon was circling the area, its pale scales glittering brightly in the sunlight. At this distance, he could see a slight blue tint to its underbelly scales and that it had larger wings than Emrys. It opened its jaws and released another blast of fire that Emrys swept around. The beam of flame struck the hillside again, igniting the few trees that hadn't already been on fire. Emrys flew straight at the White Dragon and released a blast of fire from his mouth, striking the other Dragon in the left wing. It spun through the air but quickly recovered and closed the gap between them.

The White Dragon was aggressive, lashing out at Emrys with its teeth, talons, and tail in brutal movements, but Emrys was faster. The large red Dragon dodged the attacks and slashed at the White Dragon's wings and long throat each time it attacked. Bursts of flames rained down around them, there were snarled shouts to each other, and the White Dragon tried twice to circle around behind Emrys.

The larger Red Dragon was on his guard, lashing out with his tail and spinning each time to slash at the White Dragon. Gofiben and Bran both dropped into the water as the Dragons unleashed their fire at the same time. The walls of flame collided, washing the whole valley in heat. Gofiben swore that he could feel the water lapping up against his arms, getting warmer as he lowered his eyes from the inferno.

There was a cry of pain, high pitched, and throaty that sent shivers down his spine. The heat was easing, and he looked up, gasping at the sight of Emrys with his front talons buried in the chest of the other Dragon. His tail lashed up and sliced brutally at the wide white wings. They both began to tumble out of the sky with the red Dragon continuing his assault. Brilliant red blood spun through the air, falling down from the sky like glittering red stones. Gofiben and Bran turned and began running back up towards their encampment.

The earth shuddered when the dragons hit the ground, sending both of the mages to their knees. Looking back over his shoulder Gofiben's jaw dropped: Emrys had the White Dragon pinned with his front left talons sunk into its flesh. Red blood was running down the hill towards the river, and before Gofiben could consider what he was doing, he started to run up the shore towards the dragons.

"Gofiben!" Bran shouted in alarm behind him. Moments later, Gofiben could hear his friend splashing through the shallow water after him. "Gofiben! What are you doing!?"

"He might need help!" Gofiben began to climb up the slope between the Dragons and the river. "He wants to imprison the White Dragon!"

"Are you sure about this?!"

No, he wasn't. He had no real idea if this beast was friend or foe, just an instinct. But Merlin and Morgana weren't here, half of the nearby mountains were already on fire, and Badb was still somewhere out there. She might be summoning more Dragons, or something else at this very moment. Or she might be dead at Merlin and Morgana's hands with them working their way back towards his home village. He had no idea, but right now, there were two Dragons fighting each other. Neither could die from their injuries, and the scale of what they might do was frightening to even imagine.

"No." He watched Emrys slash violently at the White Dragon's chest as it clawed at his leg. "But at least there will be one fewer."

Flames burst from Emrys' mouth, striking the side of the mountain in a wave of heat and fire. The forest exploded into an inferno, but Emrys didn't stop, and slowly, his breath narrowed into a beam that struck the dark rock of the hill. Beneath his front leg, the White Dragon started to stir as the wound in its head slowly knitted back together. With a roar, Emrys smashed his leg down on its skull, knocking the creature out again or maybe killing it. The hillside began to melt away; a large opening was being burned into the rock. Gofiben could barely believe what he was seeing and heard Bran inhale sharply. Emrys stopped producing fire and swayed on his feet. His golden eyes moved towards them.

"Mages, I need to contain him," Emrys shouted between deep gasps. "Help me shape a chamber to hold him. Use your magic so he cannot leave it. I will take him into the cavern and hold him there myself."

Gofiben felt panic shooting through him at the suggestion and looked towards Bran who was clearly just as uncomfortable. Emrys began to breathe once more, his flames melting the rock away. Nibbling at his lower lip, Gofiben raised his hand and closed his eyes. Around him, he could feel the world becoming silent, and the spark in his gut expanded as magic raced up his body. Gofiben envisioned a deep pit beneath the mountain while the cries and snarls of the White Dragon resonated around him, and with a grunt, pushed the magic into the hill. Despite Morgana and Merlin's lessons on the truth about the Old Ones, he found himself whispering a soft prayer that this was the right course of action to anyone or anything that might be listening.

25

Shadow of Stonehenge

The bus was chilly despite the crowd of bodies as the gray sky overhead threatened rain or maybe even snow. Nicki held back a sigh and glanced over at Bran across the aisle, who was searching the horizon in earnest for any sign of their destination. Alex's head was on her shoulder; the exhaustion of the last few days had not been dispelled by a single night's sleep in Salisbury.

"Winter solstice at Stonehenge, isn't it exciting?" asked an overly-chipper female voice behind Nicki. Her question was answered by a sleepy grunt from her male companion.

Winter Solstice; Nicki breathed out slowly in recognition of the day. Time was slipping through their fingers at an alarming rate. Of course, wandering down from Dinas Emrys had taken them into the early hours of the morning, and they'd slept through the train departure they needed to get to Salisbury. They'd only managed to arrive on December 21st, dealing with heavy Christmas traffic and lingering exhaustion. Straightening up, Nicki told herself to stay calm. There was no reason at all to think that Aiden's parents would take him off life support before Christmas.

The bus turned again, and they entered a reasonably-sized parking lot. Between some of the people ahead of her, Nicki caught sight of the gray stones. Even with the circumstances and questions hanging over them like a Sword of Damascus ready to drop and slice off their heads, Nicki couldn't help her excitement. They came to a slow stop, and the doors opened. All around them, people rushed off the bus, and Nicki gently shook Alex awake.

"What?" the blonde mage asked in a groggy voice.

"We're at Stonehenge; time to wake up," Nicki told her kindly.

Alex raised her head off of Nicki's shoulder with an apologetic look and rubbed at her neck with a grimace as they stood up and took their place in the line to leave the bus. Glancing back, Nicki saw Bran managing his way in the line and noted the protective way that he was holding the bag with the Iron Chalice. Lance and Jenny were a bit further back, but slowly coming forward.

"There are more people than I figured there would be this close to Christmas," Alex muttered as they moved towards the doors.

"Well, Stonehenge was built in astronomical alignment with the solstices." Nicki reminded her. She stretched her arms with a soft groan. "That trip felt a lot longer than I figured it would."

"It's eight in the morning," Alex grumbled, "Of course it did."

They stepped off the bus and quickly moved away from the rush of people heading for the hill. Around them were rows of cars and a few other buses dropping people off. Nicki could see part of the site from the car park, and her body trembled with excitement. Then she felt a flash of guilt that Aiden wasn't here, that he wasn't seeing this. Nicki shifted to the side as Bran joined them, and they let the tourists push ahead of them. There was a layer of snow on the grass, but the pavement was clear if a little damp. Nicki tugged on her gloves and licked her lips as Lance and Jenny finally climbed off the bus.

"Okay," Bran called as he began to unfold a map of the area. "We're here in the Stonehenge parking lot," he explained as he pointed to the map. "Now, the whole area has a bunch of old burial sites, and here is Woodhenge." He pointed at another point on the map.

"Woodhenge?" Alex asked. "What's that?"

Bran raised an eyebrow at the question; they'd gone through it on the train, but Alex had been a mess since leaving Dinas Emrys. He glanced towards Nicki, and she made a tiny nod, forcing a smile for Alex.

"It's a Neolithic henge circle about two miles that way," Bran explained before pausing and looking down at the map again. "No, more that way," he corrected. "Unlike Stonehenge, as the name suggests, it was actually built out of timbers instead, in a big circle formation. It was found by aerial photography in the 1920s and is believed to be over four thousand years old. Dating puts it at being built around the same time as Stonehenge."

"There's only been limited archeological digs there," Nicki added, picking up the explanation. "It's not as sexy as Stonehenge, but over the last few years, there has been a greater focus on looking at Stonehenge and other sites in the area as a part of a whole rather than just stand-alone sites."

"And since I saw Stonehenge at a distance in my vision, that means that what we're looking for could be anywhere around here," Bran interjected. He pulled out the map and a brochure, running a finger down the glossy page. "Woodhenge is now believed to have been connected with Stonehenge as a burial site. Some theorize that it was actually a large building for preparing the dead and that they were then taken from Woodhenge down the River Avon, where they were floated down to another older stone circle now called Bluehenge. It connects to Stonehenge via a long processional avenue that they've found. It's just a theory, but from the bits and pieces that Morgana and Merlin have revealed, it seems possible."

"Sort of a journey between life and death," Alex muttered with understanding dawning in her eyes. "So Arto could be near Stonehenge or Woodhenge or even this Bluehenge."

"Exactly; it all depends on how far Merlin and Morgana took him through whatever ritual was in place here," Bran agreed with a nod.

"Recent excavations have begun to connect Stonehenge more with the Winter Solstice, rather than the Summer Solstice," Nicki added quickly. The eager excitement was building, and she started rocking on her feet. "They've even found signs of cremation here and burials!"

"And if Arto was buried instead of cremated like we're hoping, then he'd be one of the older burials in the area," Bran finished. "His burial might have even started the shift from cremation to burial."

"I hadn't considered that," Nicki said with a little smile. She was pleased to have someone on the same history wavelength as her. Even if only temporarily.

"So, what did Morgana say?" Jenny asked in the same nervous tone that she always did when Morgana came up. Nicki wondered at that: did Jenny know that Morgana had considered killing her, was there some kind of residual fear from her previous life, or was she just afraid of her as Professor Cornwall? "Did she tell you where Arto was buried?"

"Uh...I didn't actually tell her that we were coming here. I just emailed her that we were okay and left it at that," Alex answered with a nervous look.

"Alex!" Nicki scolded sharply.

"She's weird about anything related to Arto," Alex insisted with a pleading look. "Since we're thinking that we have to get to his body so I can touch his skull, I figured it was safer not to tell her that." Alex shuffled and kicked lightly at the pavement. "I'm not sure that she'd allow it, even if it meant getting the Chalice working." Alex swallowed and lowered her eyes, and added, "Especially since we aren't sure if it will work."

"It'll work," Bran answered calmly. He was standing straight, leaning slightly on his cane for stability, yet he seemed more in control than usual. Nicki realized that Alex was looking at him too, although Bran didn't seem to be concerned with the staring and kept studying his map. "Honestly, with it being the Winter Solstice, I think we should start things off by trying to trigger a vision like we did in Wales. There is a lot of ground to cover here, and I don't think we want to start trying to use magic until we have to."

"I hate to point this out," Lance cut in, "I really do, but say you find the place where Arto is buried, then what? I mean, are you going to just dig him up near one of England's most important tourist destinations?"

"He's right," Jenny said. "That's going to attract a lot of attention, and we're already walking around with an ancient chalice."

"Thankfully, the Chalice doesn't look ancient thanks to the magic in it," Nicki pointed out with a sigh, though she did have to nod in agreement. "They're right, though: this isn't a place that we can just dig up."

"We can try casting a spell to keep people from noticing us," Bran suggested quickly. "Like Merlin and Morgana use, just enough to make sure that people don't pay attention to us. If we can find the right spot, then our magic should help us get down there."

"Okay...." Alex agreed slowly. "Okay, let's give the vision thing a try. But I don't have the Chalice to focus on this time, Bran; what should I try to connect to?"

"Well, if Emrys was right and a part of your soul or an imprint of Arto or whatever it was in Bran's skull is still in Arto's body, then you should be able to connect to that. It's supposed to be part of you after all," Bran reminded her with a confident nod. "If you focus on that, my gut tells me that this will work."

"Your gut," Alex repeated doubtfully, licking her lips before she nodded. "Okay, we'll try it, but maybe we should let the crowd disperse a bit more," Alex suggested. nodding towards the other visitors. "Come on, let's go around the stones and see if that triggers anything."

The hopeful, almost desperate note in Alex's voice was hard to miss. Nicki noted with a frown that Alex's hands were trembling as she shoved them into her pockets. Maybe while the rest of them had been collapsing with exhaustion, Alex had been lying awake fretting. It would explain how she managed to fall asleep during a short bus ride. Holding back a worried look and a sigh, Nicki started walking up the paved trail around Stonehenge with the others following along behind.

Stonehenge was smaller than Nicki had always imagined it. Over the years of learning about it and wondering when she'd finally get to see it for herself, she'd never really understood the size. Not that it wasn't gorgeous even with all the people milling about and taking photos. White pristine snow surrounded the stones that stood high over her head and gleamed in the early morning light. There was nothing fastening them together, no cement or even mortar, and Nicki allowed herself a moment of awe for the sheer ability of humans: people who learned to carve small notches into the stones, so they fit together, to bury one end into the ground so that the earth itself kept them aloft, and to lift the massive stones high into the air to create the famous arches.

Even with the noise of the crowd all cooing over the alignment of the stones on the solstice, there was a sense of magic that Nicki could feel in the air. She wasn't sure if it was real or just her imagination. Nicki thought that she could feel her own magic flaring and glanced towards the others. Alex had a nervous look on her face as they followed the circle around the stones, and Jenny looked uneasy. Nicki raised an eyebrow as Jenny suddenly reached over and gripped Lance's hand tightly.

For a moment, Nicki couldn't help but wonder about the whole reincarnation thing. She'd avoided thinking about it too much as even Merlin and Morgana didn't have much to go on. They'd never died and had only come to the conclusion about reincarnation being real after observing the Iron Soul, Jenny, and Lance come around again and again. The way the three of them were reacting to Stonehenge seemed a bit odd, like they were feeling something that they didn't understand. Maybe they'd been here in that first life and laid people to rest, and it was still inside of them somewhere.

She glanced towards Bran; he didn't seem to be affected and was instead looking at the stones with interest and using his phone to take some pictures. Nicki chuckled and pulled out her own phone. No signal, no coverage, but the camera did still work. As she snapped a few photos, she wondered if reincarnation was something common or if it was rare. If Bran was a reincarnation, did that mean that she and Aiden might be too? Had they known the Iron Soul in another lifetime? Nicki found herself hoping not as they watched the crowd begin to clear off.

"Anything, Bran?" she asked calmly without looking at him.

"No," he admitted with a sigh. "I think we're going to have to connect to our magic directly if we want to find Arto."

Bran shifted his weight onto his cane, and his brace squeaked slightly as he began to stride towards the parking lot again. Sighing, Nicki took one more photo of Stonehenge and followed, promising herself that she'd come back here as soon as she could with Aiden. The thought made her stand up a little straighter and move a little faster after Bran. He led them off to the side of the parking lot behind a large parked tour bus.

Feet crunching in the snow, Bran looked around and then nodded in satisfaction. He tugged off his gloves and shoved them into his pockets, gesturing for Alex to do the same. Bran didn't bother pulling out the mirror this time and instead held out his hand for Alex's. With his other hand, he pulled off his shoulder bag and held it out for Nicki to take. She accepted it with a nod and opened the top flap quickly to confirm that the Chalice was still in one piece. Then Bran turned his attention back to Alex and closed his eyes.

It was strange watching them as they stood there facing each other. The wet ground and the presence of so many people nearby were a problem that had Nicki wondering if Bran wasn't being too optimistic about them hiding themselves. Her fingers twitched with the desire to test that theory, and she could feel her magic beginning to flow into her torso. She stilled the impulse, reminding herself that exhaustion was very real, and they had a long way to go.

For a moment, nothing happened, but then the faint gray glow of Alex's magic became visible around their joined hands. Alex shifted her free hand to touch Bran's shoulder, and her chin fell forward slightly as Alex squeezed her eyes tightly closed. The sound of the cars on the nearby road suddenly sounded much more distant, and Nicki shivered, feeling a slight change in the air. Nicki noted the gray glow of Alex's hand pulsing softly and Bran's bare hand shimmering in Alex's grip. Then Bran opened his eyes though Alex didn't react at all. Bran looked around with a confused gaze only to have his eyes become fixed on the field beyond the parking lot. He started to move and nearly caused Alex to slip in the snow as he held tight to her hand.

"Okay, it's uh this way, I think," Bran said nervously. He pointed out into the snowy landscape. "Come on." Alex released his hand, and Bran suddenly stopped. Before anyone could say anything, he grabbed Alex's hand again, tugging her up next to him. "Shit, use your magic again," Bran ordered. Gray magic flared around Alex's hand once more, and she looked out over the snow-covered field in confusion. Bran relaxed and looked over at Alex with a sheepish smile. "I need you to keep holding my hand, okay?" he muttered urgently. "My ability to direct my magic towards visions seems to be letting me see the way."

"Alright then," Alex replied with a faint smile. "If you say so."

"You do have nice hands, though," Bran assured her with a small smile.

A real laugh escaped her, and Alex fell into step with Bran, minding his pace as she walked along on his left side. Bran gave Nicki a smile of triumph over his shoulder, and she grinned in return, pleased to see some life in Alex. He quickly turned his attention back towards whatever it was he was following while she looked towards Jenny and Lance. A soft relieved smile was on Jenny's face, though she still seemed very nervous. Nicki was tempted to suggest that they just wait there, but without working cellphones that they could safely turn on, it wasn't a good idea to split up.

They moved northeast away from the main road and Stonehenge. They were in a field of some kind, and Nicki's eyes were drawn to the small mounds of earth scattered here and there that she knew from her research were ancient burial mounds. Silently she reminded herself that they all were surely from after Arto's burial and that he was most likely somewhere else, somewhere much deeper. Her eyes went back to

Alex, and Nicki had to admit that she understood her reluctance to call Morgana. Bran had his gut instinct, and she had hers. Arto was buried deep; Merlin and Morgana had magic and knew how to use it. They could have put him a hundred feet down near the sites used to honor the dead so that he was close to them. They might not have even broken a sweat doing so.

Shaking herself out of those thoughts, Nicki looked around and noted that she could now see the River Avon off to her right, though it was hard to see past a row of tightly packed houses. Apparently, riverside suburbs weren't just a problem in Ravenslake. She looked back towards Bran as he adjusted their trajectory and squinted her eyes, hoping to catch a glimpse of whatever he was following.

"Uh, Bran?" Nicki asked carefully. She looked into the empty space in front of them. "What are you following? And before you claim otherwise, you are definitely following something."

"It's hard to explain..." Bran moved across the snowy landscape slowly. "It's sort of like... I don't know."

"Bran?" Alex questioned sharply as Bran almost slipped in the snow. Nicki gasped, but Alex kept hold of Bran with her softly glowing gray hand. "What is going on?"

"I think the magic created a guide," Bran offered as they moved around one of the small burial hills. "It's funny; another point on the side of magic having some kind of sentience behind it. I'm not sure I feel about that. I guess using a vision wasn't going to be clear enough."

"A guide, huh?" Lance repeated as he and Jenny kept following them, still hand in hand. "And it couldn't have guided us to the Chalice from Cardiff?"

"Yeah," Jenny muttered as she almost fell in the snow. "That would have been a lot faster."

"Alex and I weren't combining our powers then," Bran replied quickly. He sounded a touch embarrassed. "And I don't know if that would have worked; after all, Alex was focusing on the Chalice, and I was focusing on his- my- the skull."

"Bran?" Alex asked seriously. "What are we following? Are you sure it's on our side?"

A deep, suffering sigh escaped Bran, and for a moment, Nicki thought that Alex might drop it, but the girl suddenly seemed alert again. It was a nice change after having a basket case on their hands for the last twenty-four plus hours.

"Bran?" Alex pressed.

"It looks like a will-o-wisp," he admitted with a small grimace. "Sort of gold in color and just hovering in front of us."

"Will-o-wisp," Nicki repeated doubtfully. "Uh, Bran, those are usually-"

"I know," Bran sighed, though it looked like he was tightening his grip on Alex's hand. "Lights that lead travelers to their deaths, but this... this feels right. I can't explain it-"

"Okay," Alex assured him quickly. She looked over her shoulder towards Nicki and shrugged. "We'll hope that it's not some Sídhe creature."

"I didn't see it until we used our magic, and it's... sort of shimmering. Like a mirage, not really there, you know?" Bran struggled to explain. "I think it's just a manifestation of some kind. Maybe people just had will-o-wisps wrong or didn't follow them right."

"Alright, alright," Nicki called to them. "Let's keep moving. We're on a schedule, remember."

The ground sloped down in a very small gentle hill with Stonehenge still in sight. Nicki felt a bit bad for stomping across some farmer's land,

and up ahead, she could see a road and collection of buildings. In the snow, Nicki could see a round imprint just off the river ahead of them and noted the small poles rising out of the ground.

"Here!" Bran called out as he led Alex down the slope. She shifted her weight in order to keep them both from slipping in the snow. "It's right here; the light disappeared into the ground!"

Alex nearly slipped on the slick ground but caught herself as Bran suddenly released her hand and reached down to brush away the snow. Underneath were only thin wild plants that had managed to grow between the harvest and the frost. Coming down behind the others, Nicki noted that Lance and Jenny stayed at the top of the small hill and were standing close together.

"What do you think?" Alex asked as Nicki stepped up on her left side. "Maybe under the hill?"

"You didn't see anything else, Bran, just the will-o-wisp?" Nicki pressed.

"There was not a vision, just a strong sense that the magic was responding, and when I opened my eyes, the guide was there," Bran explained. Nicki noted that he didn't sound sure himself.

"Maybe you have to open the hill like Alex opened the cave," Lance called down. A moment later, he and Jenny descended the gentle slope to join them.

Nicki nearly jumped when she felt Alex take her hand and looked down to see a soft gray glow encompassing their hands. Leaning forward, she could see that Alex had done the same with Bran. Alex's eyes were closed, and she was breathing deeply, yet it was just on the edge of frantic. Each deliberate breath sounded too loud, but Nicki closed her eyes and let her own magic blossom in her chest. The warm feeling of it running through her eased the tension in her shoulders, but then she paused in surprise as she felt her magic smoothly shifting out of her hand and into Alex's.

"Alex?"

"I know, I feel it too," Alex whispered back, "But I think I need the help."

"Focus on the hill," Bran told them both. "Direct everything there: focus on Arto and finding him; focus on us needing a way to get to him."

Nicki dared not open her eyes but called upon every film or TV episode that she could think of to help her visualize a tunnel opening in the hill. All she could see was the dark gaping tunnel of the Sídhe, but she repeated the name Arto again and again in her mind. She felt her magic shifting around her; some still flowing into Alex, but her left hand began to feel hot as icy blue magic swirled off her fingers and into the hill.

"Keep us hidden," she whispered to the wind as it breezed across her cheek. "No one notices us." She pushed her magic out into the air, willing the sparks, the energy to follow the words on the wind.

"Come on," Alex grunted as if in pain. "It has to give. It has to."

Nicki's right hand, held captive by Alex, felt hot as if it was too close to a burner. Nicki hissed as the magic began to slip away from her like melting ice. With one final push, she shoved everything she had left towards the hill. The ground beneath her feet rumbled. Everything went black, and she was dizzy. Then she was aware of arms holding her up and opened her eyes. In front of her was a long shallow slanting tunnel leading deep into the ground with darkness looming before her.

26

Funeral Rites

The opening they'd created radiated with their magic. Alex wasn't sure how, but as she walked down the long tunnel through the dirt and rock, she felt encased in warmth and wasn't reminded of the Sídhe tunnels. The musky scent of dirt surrounded her, and she could see the layers of the earth around them as they followed the shallow slope into the hillside. The tunnel gradually turned to stone, yet the reassuring smell of earth remained.

Then the tunnel ended at a strange alcove that was at Alex's waist height and went a couple of feet deeper into the hillside, forming a large shelf. Alex forced herself to bend over and look into the alcove. It was carved from the rock with smooth walls, and she could almost feel Morgana's magic. The whole little chamber was oval shaped with a flat floor where a skeleton was stretched out neatly.

Her brain stopped for a moment, along with her heart and lungs. Her eyes still worked just fine, and she took in the small items around the skeleton. An iron sword that had left a red stain on the rock as it rusted away, a string of jet beads, small pots, and things that were so old she had no idea what they might have once been. A hand on her back spurred her to suck in a deep greedy breath. She almost choked on the stale air but trembled as she stumbled back to full awareness.

"Okay," Bran whispered in a soft voice that resonated through the tiny chamber. "Touch the skull."

She didn't want to touch the skull. She really didn't, but Alex began to reach into the alcove. Alex trembled as she felt tiny electric jolts run up her fingers and around her forehead. A burning headache was forming between her eyes, and she struggled to not just curl up right there. Then her fingers brushed over the skull, and the ache eased. Alex sighed in relief even as a strange warm feeling moved up her arm.

"Alex?" Bran called softly, but then his voice faded away.

Closing her eyes, Alex leaned her head down against the rock and fought back a shiver as the ache in her chest eased a little. Her spine tingled with the odd sense that her father usually called someone walking over your grave. She opened her eyes and looked up the line of her arm to where her hand was resting on a three-thousand-year-old skull. Alex's eyes widened as she saw what at first glance, she thought was smoke seeping out of the skull and into the air. It shimmered and glittered with white sparks as it swirled towards her. Another jolt of magic jumped up her arm, and she started to pull her hand back. Tiny threads of magic formed between her fingertips and Arto's skull, moving with her and keeping them connected.

"Alex?" Bran called softly. "Are you okay?"

The magic threads shuddered in the air as Alex readied herself to try and explain what was happening when the walls around them began to glow. She heard Jenny gasp and the sound of a flashlight hitting the ground behind her. Thousands of tiny streams of glittering magic poured out of the walls like a million falling stars.

"Alex?" Jenny asked in a weak voice that sounded torn between awestruck and frightened. "Where's the light coming...?"

Her voice trailed off, and the tunnel went silent as the tiny sparks of magic danced around them. Alex felt her whole body relaxing despite the lingering pain in her head. Breathing was easier, and the tension in her shoulders was fading away. There was a whisper at the back of her mind, followed by brief flashes of faces, places, and things. She saw a younger Morgana with fewer worry lines and Merlin, staff in hand, near a large wooden structure at the bank of a river.

Then it changed: she could see the river. She was flying down it. There was a small circle of standing stones, and a long road leading towards a pristine Stonehenge. Gleaming rocks stood tall with the upper rocks all carefully perched at perfect right angles. A ditch surrounding the large inner stones and a circle of smaller stones around the perimeter were clear. Footpaths had been carved into the landscape through use and stretched out from the monument toward the river and another circle in the distance.

Alex was jarred back to the present by her head, slumping forward. There was a moment of clarity that something was pulling at her, and probably at all of them. Some magical force much more potent than anything she'd ever felt before was tugging her like a strong hand on the shoulder. This wasn't Morgana or Merlin's power, and she didn't think that it was Arto's either.

Yet there was a sense of peace slowly washing over her, gently pulling her back into the dreamlike state. Alex felt the tug of the magic as the vision replayed in her mind. No, she realized, as she felt her own magic link with the swirling power around her and pull it inside. This was something else; this, she realized with a small giggle, was whatever force had created the Iron Soul. Her soul.

Alex moved her fingers and pushed some of the magic building up inside of her outward. Gray sparks swirled through the air lazily. She wasn't sure what she wanted them to do and felt the magic lashing back against her chest as it wildly spun in the air. Untamed and undirected, like a lightning bolt in a storm. Then she heard a whisper in the back of her ear, a soft, smooth thing that she didn't understand. Her magic flared, sweeping itself together like a wisp of smoke and spun through the air towards Arto's body. It began to encircle the bones.

Blue and yellow streams of energy drifted past her, and Alex was vaguely aware that Nicki and Bran must have been releasing their magic as well. She wondered if they were even aware of it or if the magical pull was guiding them too. Their magic joined hers in spinning around the laid-out bones. The magic spun tighter and tighter around the bones, wrapping them in a veil of shimmering colors. Then the mass of magic and bones lifted off the bottom of the alcove wrapped up gently in magic.

Alex blinked as the streams of sparkling light shimmered through the air around her. She could only sort of see them; they were vague and hazy like a vanishing sunbeam, but she was certain they were there. It was like the magic she'd pulled out of Chernobog's creations, she realized, except she wasn't pulling the magic towards them... or was she? Glancing towards Arto's body, Alex felt her stomach flip and reached towards the cocoon of magic with a shaking hand.

Magic rippled over her skin, sinking into her body and swirling through her veins like it was her own. Beneath her feet, Alex could feel a soft and steady pulse of energy being released and pulled in. Her fingers brushed through the magic, keeping the body afloat, and touched one of the long delicate bones of Arto's leg. A sharp flash erupted in her head, making her unsteady, but she kept moving.

Alex felt the fluttering little spark of magic beneath her lungs jumping about as if dancing with excitement. Alex began to fall, but she caught herself with her left hand, gripping the edge of the shelf where Arto's bones had lain. Beneath her fingers, she could feel an electrical charge that made her shudder. Her brain began to feel heavy as if a dream was pulling her back into the gentle embrace of sleep.

She started to move back, the cocoon with the bones following her as she began to walk. Passing the others, Alex was aware of the vacant, slumbering expressions on their faces. They were all sleepwalkers now, playing through some magical dream. She wanted to protest, but the steady hum of magic seemed to calm her. Reassured her, it was okay. This was her magic, Alex told herself, surely it wouldn't harm them.

No one said a word as they moved back up the tunnel. Bran led the way with Alex behind him, feeling magic spilling out of the walls and flowing towards Arto's bones. Nicki was behind the body with Lance and Jenny at the back. The ground trembled softly, and Alex didn't have to look back to know that the tomb was closing up behind them. Magic sparked around her, filling the air and her lungs with energy as they returned to the surface. The press of magic down on her shoulders felt even heavier than before, but Alex managed to turn and look back at the tunnel. As Lance stepped out onto the hillside, following them with a dazed expression, the earth began to shift and fill in the tunnel. A moment later, there was no sign of it except a bare patch of dirt in the snow.

Below them was the circular outline of Woodhenge, but Alex could see the streams of magic around them already flowing down the hill. Her feet began to move again, and Bran stepped up even with her as the magic-encased skeleton floated between them. Snow crunched underfoot as they all moved towards the circle. The world around her blurred, shifting out of focus as the wave of magic rippled outward. Near her feet, the concrete posts set into the ground to mark out the circles of Woodhenge shimmered as the magic flowed into them. She heard a gasp, unsure if it came from her or the others as the posts began to transform.

Glowing white magic swirled up around them. The concrete posts faded, turning to wood, the gray vanishing into a warm brown. They grew towards the sky as one, stretching up as magic rolled across their surface. Suddenly they stopped far over the mages' heads and branched out, joining together to form a roof. Shimmering walls stretched forth, enclosing them in a large wooden building. It was ghostly; there, and yet not there at the same time. She could see the sky, and yet she could also see the roof. Alex swallowed nervously, uncertain if they were walking through a memory or time itself.

Her feet kept moving: she kept walking through the building as it formed around them. In the corner of her eye, Alex could see the others still keeping pace with her, strange awestruck expressions on their faces. Above their heads in the center of the structure was an open area through which she could see blue sky scattered with clouds. Magic was pulsing around them, pounding in her veins and rushing towards them, swirling in a mass about their small group.

Looking back at Lance and Jenny, Alex's eyes widened. Both of them were walking alongside Arto's body with wide glassy eyes. Magic was spinning around them both. Alex could see different faces and forms interposed over them. One second, Jenny was a young Hispanic woman, but the next, she saw a white woman with long brown braided hair. Then it was gone, and she closed her eyes as the dull feeling clawing at the back of her mind returned. There was too much: the magic swirling and spinning around them, the way it was infusing everything, was making it hard to see anything else. Alex's brain ached, her body felt exhausted, and she couldn't feel her limbs properly anymore.

Woodhenge towered around them with magic whispering and tugging at them. The road between them and the river faded away like mist as the magic thickened. Looking back, Alex could see the great wooden structure vanishing as the magic followed them, leaving only the concrete posts behind. She felt a hint of fear pushing its way up her chest as they stepped out into the road. Bracing herself, Alex pushed against the magic surrounding her with her own. Instead of it doing anything, her own magic just joined the storm around them. A car came zooming towards them: a gasp escaped her, but the car just sailed through them like it was a ghost. Or like they were ghosts.

The Avon River wasn't impressive given the places that Alex had seen in the United States. It wasn't that wide or, judging from the flow of the water, that deep. She was at a loss as her legs stopped being compelled, and Alex almost toppled over in surprise. She had a chance to breathe and consider the river, but the release from the magic was short-lived. Magic swept around the group with the small streams of colors twisting together over the water. Alex's eyes widened as the shape of a boat began to form. It settled on the surface of the river, sending out a rush of ripples as a shallow boat rocked gently and waited for them. Alex had just a moment to note that there was no rudder or paddle before the magic sank into her limbs once more.

As her legs jolted forward, Alex remembered that they weren't supposed to control it. The boat rocked gently on the water but stayed perfectly still as the group climbed into it. Then it slowly rolled forward, carrying them down the river and following the gentle curves of the shore. Swallowing, Alex looked down at the bundle of magic that was holding Arto's remains. She was suddenly reminded of the myth of King Arthur's remains being carried away by a magical boat and almost chuckled. This was a bit of the opposite now.

"What is going on?" Jenny asked in a tight soft voice. "I feel…"

"It's magic," Bran whispered. "It's guiding us."

"I'm not a mage," Jenny whimpered, and Alex fought off the weight of the magic enough to look back at Jenny.

Lance had his arm around Jenny and looked just as distressed as he stared down at the bones in their midst. He raised his brown eyes to meet Alex's gaze, and she flinched as they suddenly changed their shade and shape. It passed quickly, but she had to take several deep, almost pained breaths and looked forward again.

"No," she said weakly. "You aren't mages, but you were connected to this man."

"What are we doing?" Lance pressed. His voice was shaky but stronger than her own.

"Giving Arto his funeral rites," Nicki offered softly. "That's why it's affecting you; you knew him, and without Morgana here, you stand as his family."

"That wasn't us," Jenny whimpered. "That was our previous lives."

They were coming around another bend, and the magic began to swell up around them once more. Up ahead, the ground was shimmering, and glistening stones were rising up with a swirl of golden light.

"I don't think that matters to the magic," Alex forced out just before the magic pressed down on them again.

The stones were smaller than the ones at Stonehenge as the boat slowly came to a stop by the snow-covered shore. Alex felt the fire of the magic settling onto her again, and tiny electrical jolts jumped through her body. Shuddering, Alex tried to fight it, but the whispers were back, and she couldn't bring herself to fight when the small spark inside of her was humming happily at the connection. She stood up, and with small steps, climbed from the boat with Arto's bones floating behind her.

White magic streamed in front of them, seeping up from the ground and dancing in the air. A circle of twenty-seven standing stones stood near the shore to greet them. In the soft winter light, the stones shimmered a soft blue color as magic jumped from stone to stone. Each step in the snow made Alex feel lighter as if she could float off the ground at any moment.

The avenue stretched out before them with small standing stones lining it. Mounds of earth marked out the course which went northwest from the river and then turned twice on the way to Stonehenge. As they followed the avenue across the snow-covered fields, more ancient stones appeared alongside them only to vanish once they'd passed. Alex wanted to speak with the others, but her body wasn't fully her own anymore as magic flowed through her and kept her moving.

People were milling around Stonehenge, taking photos and talking happily even as they were bundled up against the winter air. Was it cold, Alex wondered as her feet crunched down on the snow? She couldn't feel it. No one was looking at them, and the itching in her skull was getting stronger. None of the tourists seemed to see them. As the magic rolled over the area like a fog, they all began to move away from the path around Stonehenge as if in a trance.

The stones in front of them shifted, magic overlaying yet another image of what it once was before them. Alex could still see the fallen stones on the ground, but then they were tall and proud, with the outer ring standing complete. Each step brought them closer and closer. As the magic settled, the present condition of Stonehenge was a mere ghost to the stone circle waiting up ahead for them.

In her head, the faint whispering was getting louder. Forcing her head to move, Alex looked down at her hand and saw the glistening streams of magic connecting her hand to Arto's skull were still there and pulsing, even as her gray magic continued to swirl as a part of the cocoon. They followed the avenue amongst the stones, and Alex noted that the area was still and silent without any tourists.

Shuddering, Alex's legs finally gave out. Cold raced through her body as her knees collided with the snow. Everything was white and gray in a blinding swirl of magic and colors. Then there was a rush of heat and a flare of fire before her eyes. She could see Bran again, standing by the altar stone with Arto's burning body floating in the air before it. He was stumbling back from the burning bones with a stunned expression. She heard a soft sound of surprise from Jenny and an aborted question.

Fire suddenly flowed into her veins, hot and powerful. The threads of energy linking her and Arto exploded into a brilliant rope of light and wove its way up her arms and curled around her neck. The cocoon of magic was opening slowly, allowing the flames to leap and jump into the air. Embers fluttered into the sky, and Alex trembled as another wave of magic crashed over her. Throwing her head back, she focused on a dull gray cloud directly overhead, but arches of white, green, violet, blue, and many other colors were forming around her. Colors were streaming through the air like a hundred tiny rivers and swirling around her, cutting off the rest of the world.

There were faces: dozens of faces flashing before her so quickly that she couldn't really see any of them. All male, but with every tone of skin on Earth, every shade of brown, blue, and green eyes within humanity and every build. Some were scarred, some had beards, some were clean-shaven, some were smiling, and some were frowning. All of them were staring at her as she flew past their faces. Their eyes, whatever shade or color they were, were all locking with her own gray ones. The vision ended as quickly as it began, leaving her reeling.

She was moving, stumbling in the snow blindly. Alex could feel the heat of the flames but was too preoccupied to consider what she was looking at. Someone was shouting; they sounded frightened, but even that didn't cut through the sense of desperation and purpose. Her fingers clawed rough fabric, and then she was on the ground again, something cool grasped between her fingers.

The Iron Chalice began to glow in her hands. Alex felt the magic settle over her body like a warm cloak. Then the Chalice begin to pulse and connect to her own magic with tiny sparks running up Alex's arms. Her hands began to glow a soft gray color that seeped into the relic: the rusty patches that had remained faded away, and the worn bits of metal knitted back together. For a moment, it shone so brilliantly in her hand that Alex had to slam her eyes closed. Everything stopped around her. The frantic hum in her bones turned soft and soothing.

Then the magic that had been thick around them like a fog lifted, like a tide going back out to sea. Alex opened her eyes and looked down at the artifact in her hands. It was gleaming like it had just been polished. Turning the Iron Chalice slowly in awe, Alex stopped as the triskelion came into view. The small symbol had a glow all its own that twinkled up at her before slowly fading. Alex basked in the warm presence of it in her hands and the tingling sensation running over her skin. Raising her eyes, she found a pile of ash in front of her that was already beginning to blow away in the cold winter air, and the others staring at her with shocked and exhausted expressions. She was about to say something when screams suddenly erupted around them as the last of the magic slipped away.

27

The Chalice

721 B.C.E. South of Mount Yr Wyddfa

It had been fifty days, Gofiben reflected as he surveyed the area around the small roundhouse that had been home for almost a season. Galath had begun storing food for the winter, and there was now a small yard with livestock. They really should return to the south: these mountains were becoming too familiar to them all. It wasn't home. Yet home was an uncomfortable place now, a place with whispers and frightened looks.

Gofiben sank down by the fire pit with a sigh and rested his chin on his knees. With each passing day, he worried more and more that Morgana and Merlin were dead. Midsummer had come and gone with no news, no attacks, and no changes. Badb's plague was weakened in her absence, but many of the victims were still feeble and in pain. The dead may not be walking, but the effects of Badb's magic were still present.

Looking down towards the village, Gofiben rubbed the back of his neck in aggravation. They did what they could to help, but also retreated back into the hills to avoid the lingering plague. Around him, the wind blew through the trees, sounding like the waves upon the cliffs not far from his home village. He felt so very homesick for the place, if not for the people. Meanwhile, the two people whose advice he needed most were gone.

Gofiben shook his head and stood up suddenly, unwilling to just sit and wallow. He started marching towards the distant hill, his eyes fixed on a bare slab of exposed rock. Putting one foot in front of the other, the sounds of the forest hills around him and the happy bubbling of the flowing river helped steady Gofiben. The steepness of the hill slowed him down, but he reached his goal before midday.

He licked his lips and followed the soft chiming that was ringing in his head with a smile. It had been a clever idea on Galath's part; a way to find the new entrance into the cavern without leaving it too exposed. It took him only a moment to open the passage and step into the warm, dark cavern. Calling on his magic with tightly closed eyes, Gofiben formed a small orange orb of light to illuminate the path.

"Hello, Emrys," Gofiben called out, his voice echoing down into the darkness below.

He stopped a few steps away from the sharp drop. It was a dizzying thing for him, being so high with nothing beneath. A brand new and frightening experience, but his life had been full of those lately. With a roar of his great wings against the air, the Dragon rose into view and landed on the far ledge that he'd made for just this purpose. His horns dragged along the cavern roof, and Gofiben held back a smile.

"Morning," he greeted quickly, hoping to hide his amusement.

"Good day, Gofiben," Emrys answered with a nod. The Dragon lowered its head.

"I'm a bit sorry we already sealed the cavern," Gofiben offered with a smile, which earned him a stern look.

"I will manage," Emrys replied, crossing his great clawed feet in front of him. The Dragon tilted his head slightly and narrowed his eyes. "You are distressed, Gofiben."

His mouth opened, but no words came out. It was upsetting to realize just how transparent he was. Suddenly grateful that he hadn't met his brother or Bran that morning, Gofiben swallowed and licked his lips. Emrys was silent, merely watching him and swinging his tail below the ledge.

"I don't know what to do," Gofiben finally spit out, pacing on the small ledge as Emrys watched him with sympathetic gold eyes. "There is no sign of Merlin and Morgana. I know I should probably go home, but there's a pair of Dragons under a nearby hill."

"Gofiben," Emrys called gently to draw his attention. "Yes, there are Dragons here, but we will be here for a long time. Neither of us can return home."

"That's not fair," Gofiben sighed, collapsing to sit on the ground. He buried his hands in his hair and groaned. "Emrys, it feels like I'm supposed to be doing something more. The plague is still making people sick across the land, yet I was barely trained as a mage."

"You and Bran helped me make this prison," Emrys reminded him as he tilted his head and made his horns drag along the rock. "Carved in Dragon fire, but sealed with the power of mages. Neither of us will escape from here."

"Wait," Gofiben suddenly cut in with a frown. "You mean... you can't leave either?"

"We sealed the mountain after I pushed the White Dragon in," Emrys reminded him gently. "You and Bran used your magic and followed my instructions to make the stone immune to Dragon fire. Unless the power of the Iron Realm fades away, I do not believe that it will be possible for a Dragon to leave this hill for thousands of years."

"Then why did you- Emrys, couldn't you have just thrown the White Dragon down here and left it at that?"

"I cannot leave him alone," Emrys answered sadly as if regretting the current conversation. "I can keep him asleep: that is safest for us all. Hunger afflicts neither of us in your realm, so not even that shall wake him."

It was tempting to look down into the great cavern hidden out of sight and attempt to catch a glimpse of the terrible white Dragon. He felt a bit sorry for the thing; wondered if it had gone through as much pain as Emrys when it came through. True, it had been able to fly off, probably believing Emrys dead, but he couldn't help but wonder. Emrys' comment about no longer feeling hunger made him relieved and sad at the same time.

"You'll trap yourself here too," Gofiben finally said, looking back at Emrys. "Why? Don't you trust yourself?"

Emrys breathed out slowly through his nostrils, sending a wave of warm damp air over him. The Dragon's face tensed up, and Gofiben believed that he'd pushed this tentative friendship a bit too far. He opened his mouth to apologize, but Emrys spoke first.

"No, I do not," the Dragon admitted softly, dropping his eyes. "There are stories of the effects of traveling to other worlds. Without your magic, you and I would be unable to understand one another; I would just be a great fear-inspiring creature that cannot die. Perhaps in the future, I will be: perhaps after being in your world too long, I shall lose my mind and become something quite unlike what I am now."

"I don't believe that," Gofiben insisted, speaking up before he'd thought about it. "You're not like that, Emrys. You crashed into our world by no fault of your own and have been nothing but kind and good to us."

"The White Dragon was free while I recovered," Emrys reminded him, his voice deep and rumbling in the cavern. "I have no doubt that he caused damage, nor should you. Perhaps he did not fall under the power of this Badb as she might have intended, but I failed to protect your world from him."

"You put too much on yourself."

"We are both defenders," Emrys answered with a softening look. "You speak to me of feeling like you must do more: I understand, Gofiben. That is why I become a defender of my own realm; that is why I refused to stop fighting the White Dragon even when he slashed my wing. It is a part of me, and should it ever be stripped from me by the flaw of being trapped in your world. I would rather have myself locked underground than above with your fragile fellow humans."

"I don't think that could ever happen to you."

"Gofiben, the only constant in all the worlds is change. It occurs whether we like it or not," Emrys informed him sadly, curling his tail up on his ledge. "It is why even though Dragons are reborn with our knowledge, we are never the same. Death transforms, and each moment of a new life changes us. We embrace this change, perhaps too much in some cases," he added with a dark look into the vast blackness below. "And even I too, in this darkness, may change."

They sat in silence after that for some time, and both were lost in their own thoughts. Gofiben was strangely comforted by Emrys' words and wondered if he would be reborn again as someone else. He'd been Arto before, so who would he be next?

"You spoke of a magical Sword that brought us here; forgive me, but you seemed concerned about it," Emrys questioned suddenly.

"Cathanáil; the first Iron Soul made it. Badb stole it, and that's why Morgana and Merlin ran off after her," he muttered more bitterly than he wished to. "It's very powerful: I don't think they knew it could do something like that."

"It sounds as if the Sword is attuned to the fabric of your world," Emrys pondered, "I suspect that power was imbued in it by your predecessor."

"I suppose."

"Have you considered trying to replicate it?" Emrys asked curiously. "From our conversations, you have a solid understanding of the magical basics of your realm, and you are the Iron Soul's current form."

"You... you think I could make another Cathanáil?" Gofiben asked before he stepped back from Emrys, a dark thought flooding his mind. "So that you could go home?"

Emrys straightened up and snorted, looking offended, but he shook himself lightly and relaxed. His talons scraped at the rock, and Gofiben gave himself and the Dragon a moment to center themselves.

"No," Emrys finally answered, "I cannot return home, and there is no need for you to make a sword, Gofiben." Gold eyes met his own brown ones, and he had the distinct sense that Emrys was rather excited. "You are a smith, are you not? I suspect that you could make whatever you wished."

"I don't have a forge here," Gofiben protested even as he felt his mind lighting up at the mere possibility of what Emrys was talking about. "There's no way to achieve the heat necessary at the roundhouse, and I'm not sure I want to try infusing magic into metal down in the village." He rubbed the back of his neck as his excitement turned to frustration. "I can't do it without traveling."

"Or perhaps Dragon fire might be of use," Emrys suggested, lowering his head down to the ledge where Gofiben was standing. "I am able to control it."

Gofiben stared at the Dragon, trying to process the words. Then they all snapped into place, and he stumbled back with a stunned, awestruck, and exhilarated expression. Dragon fire: he could remember the flames that burned into the mountain in a small precise stream. The power and raw heat had so completely dwarfed his own magical flames that he hesitated to even think of them as anything alike.

"You... you would do that?"

"This realm is now my home," Emrys replied with no small amount of resignation. "And the sad truth, Gofiben, is that I expect there to be many days in the future without any company. I would help you while you are still here for me to help."

Swallowing, Gofiben nodded and stepped back. Mortality was something that was becoming increasingly difficult to think about. His new friend seemed unable to die and would linger for eternity, much like Merlin and Morgana, he supposed, while he would die and be reborn into yet another life. Another life that would never be as important as his first one. He shook his head and looked back to Emrys.

"I'll need to get some things, and we'll need iron," he explained as he looked around the cavern. "This isn't ideal, but with Bran's help, I think we can make it work." Emrys nodded, and Gofiben smiled as he turned back to the tunnel. He raced down to the opening only to turn back around. "I'll be back soon, Emrys!"

"I thought as much," the Dragon laughed behind him as Gofiben began racing down the hillside, not even bothering to close up the tunnel.

He made it back to the roundhouse without even tripping once. Bran and Galath were both awake by the outer fire and looked up in surprise as he came barreling past. Galath was on his feet first, drawing his axe and looking around for a threat while Bran stumbled after him into the roundhouse.

"Gofiben, what is going on? Are you alright?"

"I'm better than alright," Gofiben answered with a laugh as he began to look through the iron they had available. "Can't use Galath's axe, but we've got those two daggers," he muttered to himself as he sorted through one of their bags for the spare weapons in question. "And that extra clasp too."

"Wait, what are you doing?" Bran asked in confusion. "Gofiben, slow down, and explain."

"Emrys brought up an interesting possibility this morning." Gofiben forced himself to slow down. "He's offered to help me forge my own magical item as Arto did with Cathanáil."

"You're making a sword?"

"No; not a sword, something else, something new!" He picked up his hammer and grinned at it. "I'm not sure what yet."

"Wait, so you're just going to take the iron and go to make something?" Bran laughed. "Gofiben, you aren't even going to plan it?"

"I'll plan it when I get up there, but I need to do something."

"But without Merlin and Morgana to help-"

"I've been infusing magic into my work without meaning to, Bran; if I'm trying to, then I know I can do this," Gofiben shouted as he shoved everything into a bag and slung it over his shoulder. "I just can't..."

"Okay," Bran offered with a hesitant smile. "Let's go then," he paused and chuckled. "But you know that Galath is going to insist on coming."

"Yeah, I doubt we can give big brother the slip."

"He'd start banging all over the hill until he found you."

As if summoned by his name, Galath stepped into the roundhouse with a serious expression. "What happened?" he asked as his eyes swept over Gofiben, checking to make sure he was okay.

"I'll explain on the way!" Gofiben stepped around his brother to get outside.

"Wait," Bran called out to him. "This may take some time; you explain to Galath, and I'll grab us some food and water."

He couldn't argue with the point and quickly informed his confused brother of the rough plan he had. Galath looked worried by the time Bran came back with a couple of rolled-up blankets and his bag filled with rations. Unsure about facing more of his brother's questions, Gofiben rushed out and began to lead the way back towards Emrys' cave.

They didn't talk much on their way up the hill, or rather he didn't talk much though he could hear Galath and Bran speaking behind him. Gofiben paid no mind to what they said; he knew what he was like when a new project sparked in his mind. Their concerns, in this case, were probably warranted, but he wasn't going to stop. They reached the tunnel, which had closed itself up; had Morgana or Merlin been here, he would have asked about how that worked.

Putting his hand on the wall again, Gofiben pushed his magic into the stone and smiled when it melted away beneath his palm. The light orb he'd created was still shining, and Emrys was still lounging on his ledge with an amused expression. Fighting down embarrassment, Gofiben walked out onto the ledge and set down the bag of iron. He glanced over his shoulder to find Galath positioning himself at the mouth of the tunnel and watching Emrys with a very stern expression. Behind him, the tunnel was still open, and Gofiben dashed out to collect some smaller stones.

"So, what do you want it to do?" Bran asked curiously, staying in the tunnel and glancing towards the edge nervously. "Have you got a plan yet?"

"Badb's plague isn't going away," Gofiben replied as he laid out the stones they'd brought in to make a fire ring. He'd need a secure place to heat the metal for this, and while it wasn't a forge with Emrys' flame, he was confident they could manage something. "Even with her gone and who knows how far away, its effects are still lingering. The dead may not be walking, but we still need to do something."

"Merlin and Morgana-"

"Aren't here," Gofiben interrupted. He shook his head dejectedly. "And, to be honest, I'm getting frustrated waiting for them." He licked his lips and sighed. "I'm just... Bran, we're mages too. I know they weren't able to train us for long, but we're supposed to be doing something. Do you think the people weakened by the plague will make it through the winter?"

"It's not bad in most places," Galath said behind them. "I've been out checking, remember? The worst area is here in the valley. Whatever magic Badb used here seems to have kept her spells strong."

"Then we can at least help the valley," Gofiben muttered as he reached for the bag of iron, causing it to clang against the rocks. "I don't know; I need to make something that can help them."

"A healing artifact then," Emrys suggested in a warm voice. "You'll need to have a way for the item to direct its power, a way for it to transfer the magic to the subject."

"Transfer the magic..." Gofiben repeated with a frown. "You mean like touching it, or something more?"

"Healing is dangerous; Morgana taught us that," Bran reminded him, though he hummed in thought. "Maybe if you made it something that could... No, that's no good."

"Weapons are out of the question, but what might work?" Gofiben asked as he reached for his water skin. He took a long drink and then stopped. "Wait, what if I made a chalice? It could put the magic to heal into the water, and then the person could drink it."

Bran paused and looked up at Emrys with an uncertain expression. "I suppose that could work," the other mage said. "In theory, it makes sense from what I know about magic."

There it was again; that lingering reminder that their teachers were missing. He wanted to believe that they were trying to return, but he couldn't help the hurt and anger churning in his stomach. Morgana had at least shouted instructions back to them, and he felt a little guilty at not following them. But no part of him believed for a moment that Morgana and Merlin were in his home village waiting for their return. Without a word, he dumped out the bag of wood chips he'd brought and called on his magic.

It surged through him, and he opened his palm as orange sparks began to dance around it, releasing the magic in a burst of fire and heat. A burning orb danced in his hand, and he lowered it to the wood, lighting the small circle of kindling in an instant. He pulled the wooden handles off the iron daggers and tossed them into the bed of fire. Then he moved back a little way and set his hammer and tongs to the side before shoving the first two pieces of iron into the fire. Looking up at Emrys, he nodded. Dragon fire spun in the air, and Gofiben couldn't help a surge of fear. He nodded to himself as Emrys began to focus the flames onto the small pit of coals. This would be the strangest forge of his life. Intense heat was rolling around them, and smoke was beginning to fill the cavern. Emrys unfolded his wings and pushed much of it out of the tunnel with one large flap of his wings.

Gofiben didn't hesitate once he saw the iron turning that beautiful hot orange hue. He pulled the first piece out of the fire with the tongs and moved it over to the top of the flat stone pillar at the end of the ledge. It wasn't an ideal anvil, but it would do the trick. Magic seeped from his fingertips into the warm metal of his hammer. He brought it down on the iron with a crash, twisting the smooth dagger to create a slight curve. Then he did it again twice more before placing it back into the fire and pulling out the second piece.

As the magic flowed into the fiery orange metal, Gofiben paused in his mechanical actions. The hammer in his right hand was glowing as fiercely as the bed of coals in front of him. His makeshift anvil was beginning to chip, and by rights, he knew he should have been worried about what he was doing. Yet he felt only exhilaration: his mind was racing, and he could feel the pulse of magic inside of him more strongly than he ever had in the past. It was suddenly so much easier to believe, to understand, and to accept that he was the Iron Soul.

Time slipped away from him. Gofiben only paused for a short time when Bran begged him to drink something but refused to eat after a few gulps of warm water. In the back of his mind, he was vaguely aware of Galath pacing nervously in the tunnel, and Bran lingering just out of his way. His senses were focused on the stream of Dragon fire melting the iron together. He could feel the power pulsing just at the edge of his senses each time he brought his hammer down and pushed his own magic into the metal. It was humming beneath him, twisting more to his will than to the force of the hammer as the small bowl began to take shape.

Someone moved up beside him, and water splashed onto the rocks as Bran set down a large jar of water. He nodded shortly to his friend but said nothing as he watched the bowl glow in the dim light. Setting it aside, he pulled the last piece of iron from the flames with the tongs and began to twist it as well. With every hammer strike, he could see more of his magic rippling across the surface. It was like being next to Cathanáil except better, so much better. Soon enough, the base was complete, and he submerged both pieces into the water with a sharp hiss.

Both pieces were still shimmering with magic, making the metal glow like it was gold rather than iron. He tapped them both carefully, but they were merely warm. Licking his lips, Gofiben pulled harshly on the magic he could feel pulsing through the ground beneath his feet, pulled it from the air around them, and pushed it hard into the Chalice. It was hot and warmth tingling across his skin like a hot summer breeze. His fingers traced the place where the base met the bowl, and harsh orange magic surged into the iron. It began to melt the two pieces together as he traced his finger around the circumference. Pulling his hand back, Gofiben inspected the small band of glowing iron he had created with a smile. Then with one final push of magic into the metal, he moved his finger over the band, calling on all his magic and the fire he could still feel thrumming in his limbs, to create a small triskele symbol.

28

Battle for Stonehenge

The first scream was followed by another, and Alex tore her eyes away from the Chalice to look around in confusion. Tourists in the distance who hadn't already wandered off were pointing at something and moving towards the parking lot. Others who were closer were running away as the magical bubble encasing the landmark faded. There were more screams, and Alex found herself struggling to reorient herself to reality.

Her hands were warm, both still clutching the glowing Iron Chalice, but Alex quickly shifted the Chalice into one hand. Alex climbed to her feet only to almost stumble over the altar stone. There was a pile of ash that was quickly being blown away and a few fragments of charred bones. People were running towards the parking lot with expressions of fear and confusion. Alex didn't see anything and wondered if this was some delayed reaction to the high levels of magic. Looking towards the others, she noted that Nicki and Bran were both on their feet looking a bit shaky and exhausted, but functional. Jenny was on her knees on the ground with a lost expression on her face with Lance in a similar state next to her. Whatever they'd seen and felt hadn't fully passed yet.

"Nicki," she called over to the redhead, "Stay with Lance and Jenny."

As Nicki nodded, Alex moved around the stones. Her feet kept trying to slip on the snow as she focused on Bran. His green eyes were moving across the landscape with a stern and worried expression. She forced herself to look at Lance and Jenny again as she moved towards them. Reaching Lance, Alex called his name, but only got a weak groan in response as the man shook his head like he was trying to clear a fog. She bit her lip in worry, but another scream made her look around in alarm. Alex shifted around Lance and unzipped his backpack, reaching inside and moving her hand around until she found one of the spare bottles.

Moving quickly, she marched towards Bran while people continued to rush past them like they weren't even there. Then she heard strange crashing and crackling sounds from beyond the visitors' center. It sounded a bit like electricity and heavy things moving. Alex rushed to Bran and uncapped the bottle of water with her teeth.

"Alex? What-"

She spit the cap out and began to pour water into the still glowing Chalice. A soft gasp escaped Bran and Alex watched the water in the Chalice shimmer and ripple. Bran glanced towards the horizon for a moment before taking a deep breath to calm himself. Moving closer to him, Alex let Bran lean on her as she handed him the Chalice. He felt light against her, thanks to the adrenaline pumping through her veins. She risked a glance towards Nicki, who was standing in front of Lance and Jenny. Thankfully they were on their feet now.

Grunts and growls from a distance made Alex look up. The air rushed out of her body as she saw a number of creatures rushing towards them, surrounded by a black mass of energy. There were more of the same beings they'd seen in Fishguard: they looked human at first glance, but their eyes were too purple, their skin too translucent, and their nails too much like claws. Around them were more of the small pixies, redcaps, and many more strange and twisted looking beings of many shapes and sizes. Some were crawling on the ground like animals, some seemed to float through the air like ghostly figures, and some marched like human soldiers to war. Alex's head ached, and her vision went fuzzy as she focused on the black fog of magic circling and seeping into all of them.

"Shit," Alex hissed without taking her eyes off the approaching legion. "We let them all know exactly where we were," she said with a look towards the glowing Chalice that was still in Bran's hand. "Practically put up a beacon." He was staring at the Chalice in shock with a far off look in his eyes. Shoving down a jolt of guilt, Alex bumped him gently. "Bran, not to put too fine a point on it, but we're being attacked, so you kind of need to decide if you're drinking now. If not, then get ready for a fight."

Her words spurred him into action, and with a shaky hand, he reached down to undo his brace. Alex helped him hop over to the nearest standing stone and then leaned him up against it. Part of her rallied against the disrespectful action; she wondered if that was her own inner little girl who'd always wanted to see Stonehenge or something much newer, or perhaps much older. Shaking her head, Alex banished the thought.

The spark beneath her heart that connected Alex to her magic throbbed painfully. Reaching over, Alex placed her hand on one of the standing stones and tried to keep her heart rate steady even as the animalistic creatures began to rush ahead of the others. She felt a trickle of magic flowing through her body and willed it to manifest in her right hand. A strange large black cat-like creature was almost upon her when Alex snapped her hand forward and released a bolt of lightning that hit it in the chest.

It yowled and hit the ground with a thud as Alex looked over her shoulder to check on Bran. A spear of glistening ice from Nicki shot past Alex and struck another one of the advancing creatures. Bran took a deep drink from the Chalice as Alex summoned forth more magic. She could feel the spark in her chest humming and pulsing with a dull raw pain. Her body was already protesting at her, trying to use magic after so much had been conducted through her. A desire to shout at the sky that it wasn't fair surged through her, but Alex shoved it down and focused on the approaching horde.

A small groan next to her made Alex whirl around to find Bran slipping down the weather-worn standing stone with pain etched on his face. He was breathing hard and clutching at his leg with the Chalice grasped tightly in his other hand. Glancing between him and the horde, Alex forced her magic to manifest, groaning in pain at the harsh ache that spread through her chest. Dark gray energy spun in her hand, and Alex watched it ripple around her fingers like the aura of a flame.

Snow surged up around them like a wave, drawing all the powder near them together into a wall. Nicki's blue magic rippled across it, and Alex flinched in automatic sympathy as she realized what was about to happen. The snow exploded in a shower of icy spikes into the rows of creatures creating a cacophony of pained screams. For good measure, Alex released a few quick blasts of energy, striking down a few more of the creatures.

Bran kicked the brace away and uneasily stepped forward as yellow magic licked around his hand. He joined Alex and pushed his hand forward, sending yellow magic blasting through the air. It rained down over the creatures as tiny sparks, making them jump back, though not killing any of them. Alex was confused for a moment before the yellow sparks hit the ground, and the newly exposed brown grass twisted upward. The blades of grass lengthened and tangled around the feet of the creatures, causing many of them to stumble.

One of the humanoid beings snarled, purple eyes flashing with rage. The dark aura around it flared wildly, and it lunged forward with three more of its kind on its heels. Silver magic exploded in front of Alex and the others, forming a wall of fire that flared out towards the creatures. Stumbling back, Alex pulled Bran with her and looked around frantically. The color was familiar. She spotted a pair of figures running towards them across the main road.

Green magic erupted around them, shaking the ground: Alex looked frantically towards Stonehenge, but the stones remained upright as small chunks of earth surged up and grabbed three of the cat-like creatures. It was Merlin and Morgana. Not waiting for Merlin to finish the job, Alex reached out her fingers and beckoned the black magical energy towards her. It spun in front of her, the dark color fading away, and she shoved it back at the creatures as three bolts of lightning.

Morgana reached her first, raising her hands and placing them firmly on either side of Alex's face. Intense green eyes met her own, and she watched Morgana's face run through a gambit of emotions. The professor looked her over quickly and frowned in worry.

"You're exhausted," Morgana said. She turned to look at the magical creatures still advancing. "Stay behind us."

Alex was gently pushed behind Morgana as another of the humanoid creatures lunged for her. Morgana and Merlin began slinging magic all over the area, forcing the horde back. Alex scanned the creatures quickly, trying to count them. There were at least twenty of them left with the corpses vanishing all around them in flickers of magic and rapid decay. The creatures that remained were clumsy and stumbling, surrounded by the inky black magic that clung to them like a slime.

One of the humanoid creatures dashed forward from Morgana's right, slashing at Alex with a long knife. Ducking out of the way, Alex moved back and grimaced in pain as she pulled more magic into her hand. It pulsed wildly, and Alex shoved it hard towards the creature. The magic exploded outward as a bolt of lightning, and Alex closed her eyes against the sudden brightness. It screamed only to have the sound cut off as its body dissolved. Alex opened her eyes and turned her attention to Bran, who two of the creatures were attacking. He blasted one with a bolt of yellow magic, sending it flying back several feet.

Stumbling towards him, Alex pulled on the black thread of magic around the other creature. She felt it fight her for a moment before it streamed towards her easily as if she'd pulled out a blockage on a river. Spinning around her hands, the magic turned dark gray and glinted in the low light, but most surprising was that the being in front of her stumbled back with a frightened expression. Its violet eyes were wide and confused until a blast of yellow magic struck it in the side. Mouth open in a silent scream, it collapsed on the ground and shuddered as its body began to dissolve.

Staring at the spot where it had vanished, Alex felt a heavy weight in her stomach and cold confusion sweeping up through her chest. A sharp cry of alarm pulled her back to the fight, and she turned to see Lance and Jenny dodging away from a group of dark, quickly moving shapes. The energy in her hands reacted before the thought had fully formed, responding to her intentions automatically. Magic leapt from her hands as a bolt that curved around Lance and Jenny to strike the first of the creatures, only to turn into a cloud of lightning that caught the others.

"Lance!" Merlin shouted, swinging a scabbard off his back and tossing it to him. "Defend yourself and Jenny!"

Alex spun to watch as Lance pulled an iron sword out of the scabbard and held it awkwardly in front of him while Jenny stayed behind him. She didn't know if Merlin had brought the sword for them, but she felt a swell of gratitude rising through her as the mage pulled a dagger from the inner pocket of his tweed coat. He handed it to Jenny as he moved over to them for a brief moment before summoning a swirling cloud of green sparks. They spun in the air above his head briefly before crashing down on the creatures as balls of green fire. Crashing into the snow with sharp hisses, they sent up wisps of steam as more of the faeries fell.

The creatures' numbers were thinning, but they weren't stopping. In the corner of her eye, Alex saw Lance swing the sword at one, slicing into its flesh and Jenny poking the dagger at another that was coming too close as the pair retreated. Alex glanced over towards Morgana only to see the older mage blasting another pair of creatures into dissolving mounds of magic and flesh as she started backing up. Morgana's arm came out, shifting in front of Alex to keep something between her and their attackers. In any other situation, Alex might have been touched, but both her magic and her emotions were a little too raw right now, and she moved away from Morgana.

Everything became a blur of movement. The dark, malformed creatures attacked them in a rush of claws, growls, teeth, and snarls. Alex felt almost consumed by the black aura as it swelled thicker and thicker around her. Gasping for air, she pushed out her hands and curled her fingers, willing her magic to grab as much of the aura as she could. It sprang to her with only a little resistance, lightening to her own magical shade in an instant. She waited for a heartbeat, letting the creatures get closer before she released it as a blast of raw magic. It zinged through the air and struck three of the creatures at once, taking out a humanoid, an odd floating one, and a redcap.

"How did you know?" Alex called over to Morgana as she moved closer to the professor, eying the ten or so remaining creatures.

"Are you joking?" Morgana released another flurry of silver magic around their group. "The level of magic released by whatever happened here could be felt in Oregon."

"We had to get Arto's body," Alex admitted as she pulled at another black thread of magic. "We uh... cremated it."

Morgana was silent, only grunting softly when she released another wave of magic that swept the remaining snow around them off the ground and threw it up against the creatures. A wave of light blue magic from Nicki transformed the snow to spikes of ice that dug into the attacker's flesh.

"Why?" Morgana finally asked in a softer voice.

"Part of my soul or something was still with him; I don't know why. Maybe it had something to do with his mental state or something magical that the Queen did to him," Alex explained in a rush. The black magic spun through the air and turned dark silver as she collected it in her hands. "But when I first tried to use the Iron Chalice, I couldn't; nothing happened."

"You found the Chalice then?"

"Yeah," Alex laughed. "That would be why Bran is beating pixies off with his brace."

"We will discuss your grave desecration after we've dealt with this," Morgana shouted in a tight voice. Alex caught a glint of moisture in the woman's green eyes before she spun a whip of silver magic and lashed it out at the nearest Fae creature. "Get back!" she shouted at their attackers. "You do not have the magic to face us! Retreat and live!"

They didn't listen, and the last few remaining creatures sprang towards Morgana. Bolts of green magic collided with two of them, knocking them to the ground as dirt washed up and over them, pulling them down. The last creature made a strange, mournful cry as it leapt towards

Lance, only to be run through by the iron blade in his hands. As it dissolved, Lance took a few steps back and gasped for air as he clutched the hilt tightly.

Panting, Alex looked around the area to see if there were any more Fae creatures. They seemed to be alone, though she could see cars on the road and a few pulling into the parking lot. Apparently, they'd moved a few feet away in the course of the fight, and Stonehenge stood to their right, looking the same as ever. Alex's heart fluttered slightly at the sight of the stones, and she looked over at Merlin and Morgana. They were both staring at the tiny pile of ash and bone in the center of Stonehenge with broken expressions.

29

Long Overdue

The only sound was the soft howling of the wind across the plains. The stillness that had surrounded them prior to the attack returned, and Alex found it difficult to breathe as she watched Merlin and Morgana's faces. They both moved towards the center of Stonehenge slowly, and Alex shook herself, trying to break out of the strange spell that had fallen over them. Alex couldn't bring herself to look away as Morgana and Merlin moved slowly towards the pile. With a wave of his hand, Merlin released a cloud of green sparks that danced around Stonehenge even as tourists began to return to the site, all with dazed expressions on their faces. They looked past the little group, smiling and pointing at the monument as if the mages weren't even there. Focusing on Merlin and Morgana, Alex pulled up her hood just in case and tried to ignore the returning crowd.

Merlin and Morgana stopped near the altar stone; their eyes still fixed on the ashes. Neither of them spoke, and Morgana licked her lips and began to move them as if trying to form words that just wouldn't come. The green magic around them hummed softly in the air, muffling the sounds of the tourists, and letting them linger in their own little world for a moment longer.

"I'm sorry," Jenny said suddenly, drawing everyone's attention. She lowered her face for a moment. "I know I'm not really the one who should be saying it, but I suppose maybe I'm here to say it for her." Jenny shifted nervously and continued quickly. "I don't really know your story... Arto, but based on how much these two loved you, I'd say you were pretty amazing. I... I never meant to hurt Arthur; I know he wasn't really the Iron Soul, but I was still cheating. I knew it was wrong, but I felt-" She glanced towards Lance, but quickly averted her eyes. "I'm sure it tore her up too and that she carried that guilt for a long time, probably the rest of her life. So, I'm sorry. I'm saying it for the person who never got to say it."

"Me too," Lance offered when Jenny's voice faded. "I don't really have anything to add to that except that I'm sure he never forgave himself, but I'm sure he spent his life trying to find ways to make it right." His brown eyes shifted to Jenny, and he swallowed before forcing out, "And I'm sure that he hoped you'd understand his loving her. I hope you were able to forgive him, and on his behalf, I'm sorry that you were the one who suffered that betrayal."

They both stepped back, sending little looks towards each other, and Alex thought that just maybe they were both standing a little straighter. She didn't want to make guesses as to why they'd been reborn over and over again and kept getting stuck in the same situation, but the literature student in her, the girl who loved a good ending, really hoped that this was some kind of closure. It took her a moment to realize that Merlin and Morgana were staring at them, surprise evident on both of their faces. Morgana recovered first, a soft chuckle escaping her as her eyes fell closed for a moment and a sad smile appeared on her face.

"Arto." Morgana looked down at the small bone fragments with tears gathering in her eyes. "You'd think after three thousand years I'd know what to say, but I still don't. I'm still trying to forgive myself for the danger I put you in, and the danger that I keep putting your new lives in." Morgana laughed bitterly, wiping at her eyes. "It's difficult sometimes to separate them from you; some of them are so much like you, but other times I... other times I can't see anything of you in them. I'm sorry if that disappoints you, but I keep trying." Morgana paused, and a soft smile appeared on her face before she added, "And I rather like your current life: about time you came around to being female." Holding back a snort, Alex looked towards Morgana and shook her head. "I'm sorry if I haven't behaved towards... Jenny and Lance, as you may have wanted in the past." Morgana licked her lips and nodded to herself. "Goodbye, little brother; thank you for everything."

Merlin stared down at the pile with a blank face, as if he was searching for something to say. He swallowed thickly and began to speak in a soft, rhythmic language that Alex didn't understand. His tone was soft and soothing, and she looked towards Morgana to find the woman gazing at Merlin with soft watery eyes and nodding slightly. It occurred to Alex that Morgana's words had been meant for both Arto and for her, but Merlin's words to his former... student, or in a way his son, were private. Under other circumstances, he might have avoided sharing them with even Morgana. Somehow that made her feel a little happy, instead of the sadness she'd been expecting.

Then both of the elder mages moved their hands, magic spinning around them. Silver and green wound through the air and collected what little remained of the bones. Brilliantly colored flames then burst to life and quickly consumed it all, letting the wind carry the ash off. Whatever the magic had wanted to occur was finished, and it was time to move on.

"Come," Merlin called in a thin voice, his fingers twitching in the air. "We shouldn't linger. I can't keep them from noticing us much longer."

"Uh, we can take the bus-" Nicki started to say.

"No, Nicki," Morgana interjected gently, her tone sad and resigned. "Too much magic has been used here today. Let's not risk another attack by staying in the area."

"Water travel is our best option," Merlin added with a nod, gesturing towards the river. "This way."

"Water travel," Lance repeated cautiously. "Is that how you got here?"

Merlin paused and looked over at Lance, who was still clutching at the hilt of the iron sword. He nodded calmly and shrugged the scabbard off his back, handing it over to the young man. Taking it with a hesitant look, Lance glanced her way and waited for Alex to nod before he put it on. It felt a little silly, but she could sympathize with Lance being afraid of Merlin.

"Yes," Morgana sighed with a shudder. "I hate water travel, but there are moments when it is the best option."

In the corner of Alex's eye, she saw Bran moving and turned her attention towards him. The rest of the world fell away; even the odd blend of emotions burning through her chest from Arto's funeral. Bran's leg brace was gone: he was standing differently and had a look of barely contained shock on his face. She lowered her eyes for a moment, feeling unable to look at the vulnerable expression. Licking her lips, Alex repeated Merlin's warning about lingering to herself and looked up.

"Bran?" Alex asked as she moved towards him while he pushed himself off of the standing stone and took a few careful steps.

His legs stayed straight, and Bran exhaled slowly as he straightened up completely. The absence of his cane and brace made him seem taller, and Alex just stared at him. His brace was on the ground from where he'd used it to hit a particularly violent pixie, and the Iron Chalice was still in his hand. Nicki moved past her, brushing their shoulders, and stepped in front of Bran.

"It worked," Nicki declared with a happy, relieved smile as she bounced over to join them. "Oh, it worked!" She reached over and gently took the Chalice from Bran's hand, cradling it against her chest. "It worked!"

"So that is the Iron Chalice then," Merlin pondered as he paused and looked towards Nicki. "I've often wondered..." He reached out and touched the Chalice carefully as if afraid it might shock him. "There were times I wondered if Galath just invented the whole story."

"He wasn't happy with you, was he?" Alex asked as she stepped up next to Morgana. It didn't feel as strange talking about him now; something had changed, though Alex wasn't sure how much. "Sorry about that."

The older female mage shook her head sadly and replied, "No, and he was right to be angry. We were not the guides and protectors of Gofiben that we should have been."

"Well, we've got a lot to catch you up on." Alex chuckled, reaching over and patting Morgana's shoulder a bit awkwardly. "Cause apparently there is the magical cave in Wales that opens to the Iron Soul, and there are Dragons inside of it."

"Dragons?" Merlin repeated, straightening up and looking at her in alarm. "In Wales?"

"Yeah, you know the story that is about you in your youth with the dragons?" Nicki laughed, her thumb caressing the Chalice softly. "Apparently, there some truth in it."

"There is some truth in almost everything," Morgana cut in with a shake of her head. "But come along, we can talk while we walk."

Bran fell into step beside them as they quickly moved away from the monument, letting the sounds of normal everyday life surround them. Crossing the road took a bit longer than Alex expected with heavy traffic making them wait for a few minutes. She could feel questions and things she wanted to say to him, sticking in her throat. It wasn't until they were hiking across another field that she finally summoned the courage to talk to him.

"So, Bran, how do you feel?" Alex finally forced out, trying to sound nonchalant, but finding it difficult not to stare. His brace was in his hand, and his cane had been left behind it seemed. "Everything feel alright?"

"I'm a bit sore," Bran replied in a strained voice. "Uh... parts are a bit achy. I suppose that's from being knit back together after all these years." He blushed a little bit and shrugged before adding, "Haven't had a chance to look at everything yet."

"I knew it," Nicki chuckled in front of them, which only made Bran turn a bit redder.

"And how do you feel?" Alex pressed, licking her lips. "You okay with this?" She gestured nervously at his leg. "I'm sorry if I was pushy earlier-"

"Alex, I'm fine," Bran interrupted, looking her way with a soft expression. "It's weird, sure, and it's going to be... impossible to explain, but I can walk without a brace or worrying about a cane." Bran swallowed thickly. "But I... this is good. This is something I'm happy about."

He smiled at her, reaching over and squeezing her cold hand in his with a soft expression. Bran was right, of course, this would be complicated to try to explain, but it boded well for Aiden. The Iron Chalice was working again, and she felt her own heart lighten. Nicki was all but skipping in front of them, urging the group to move faster. A soft laugh escaped Alex at the sight, and she felt her lips turn into a smile.

"We have the Chalice," she whispered mostly to herself.

Bran leaned over to nudge her shoulder and softly whispered, "Yeah, we do. We actually finished the Quest for the Holy Grail."

"With plenty of peril along the way," Alex added before she rolled her shoulders and groaned. "God, I hope things calm down a bit."

"Probably not," Bran sighed with an angry expression flickering over his face. "We still have a lot of questions that need answering."

"And Arthur is still out there," Alex agreed. "Yeah."

"But not today," Bran told her as he gave her a somewhat stern look. "We'll get back and take care of Aiden and go from there."

"No," Alex sighed. She rolled her shoulders and grimaced at her achy body. "Not today."

"Although, it's only like two in the morning in Oregon," Bran reminded her with a yawn.

"Good; we can heal Aiden and then crash," Alex grumbled, moving her head as they went down a slight slope to the river.

Before them, the waters of the river Avon lapped softly against the grassy bank, the rush of the water having melted away the thin layer of snow. Merlin and Morgana exchanged a look, and then Merlin stepped forward. He closed his eyes and took a deep breath, which he slowly released as his green magic appeared around both of his hands. Below them, the water of the river began to churn and splash up into the air, and Merlin hummed softly in concentration.

With a nervous look, Lance packed the Iron Chalice into his backpack and handed it off to Alex with a soft 'just in case.' Jenny was eyeing the portal with a look of near terror, her eyes darting towards Morgana and Merlin. Alex knew that she should ask if water travel was safe for non-mages, but the words stuck in her throat. Morgana looked down the line and nodded in satisfaction.

Water suddenly blasted into the air as a fast-moving column. It turned and twisted violent, beginning to spin. More and more water was pulled up from the river and gradually expanded, creating a hollow space between the curved edges of the vortex. Green magic rippled across the water and pushed the tunnel further and further back, creating a long passageway before them.

Grimacing at the water tunnel, Alex's mind went unbidden back to the sight of Arthur vanishing into it, and leaving her to die on the rocky shore of Ravenslake. Morgana reached over and took her hand with a reassuring nod and a slight squeeze. Merlin's left hand was hovering in front of the portal, his green magic spinning across the surface of the rushing water. The sound of it was tremendous up close, like a waterfall only a few feet away. Merlin took Alex's free hand, putting her firmly between the two most experienced mages. The others formed a line off of Morgana's other side. With the Iron Chalice in her bag and Merlin and Morgana hovering nearby, Alex knew that she should feel safe, but their protectiveness was putting a bad taste in her mouth.

"You'll look after them too, right?" she asked Morgana in a soft voice, drawing the older woman's attention. "Please?"

Morgana's green eyes softened, and she nodded gently, her thumb rubbing the back of Alex's hand. "I will," she promised quickly as her hand began to glow a soft silver. The glow traveled down the line of friends, though the others didn't seem to notice. "That will help everyone hold on."

"You need to hold tight: if you are separated, then it is all but impossible to follow someone through a water portal," Merlin lectured calmly as the water swirled in front of them. "I will guide our passage."

"Merlin and I learned that when we chased Badb," Morgana observed. "Thankfully, Merlin had my hand, but we had almost no control over following Badb when she left the water portal." There was a hint of frustration and regret in Morgana's voice, beneath her usual casual tone. She squeezed Alex's hand again. "Just focus on holding on; close your eyes if you have to, and we'll keep you safe."

"I hate to point this out now," Jenny called out. "But our stuff is back at the hostel…"

"We'll take care of that," Morgana promised, quickly giving Jenny a much gentler look and even a reassuring smile. "The priority is getting all of you out of this area before more Sídhe relatives show up."

"Okay, if you say so," Jenny replied, seeming more than a little thrown by Morgana's suddenly warmer behavior.

Then Merlin moved forward, his hand reaching out to touch a stream of water. It spun around his hand. He looked nervous, Alex realized with a sharp twist in her gut, but it was too late as he stepped into the portal and pulled her along behind him. Everything around her became a wild blur of waves, brief flashes of shorelines, and the sounds of the world moving quickly, like a room full of televisions all on fast forward. Alex was aware of a strange pressure on her body, and her ears popping painfully. She couldn't see anything except Merlin in front of her and the steady glistening of his magic around them now. It was getting harder and harder to breathe as the pressure on her body forced the air from her. On instinct, she kicked with her legs and tried to move them, but there was resistance as if she was truly submerged.

Then the tunnel gave a sharp turn making the bottom of her stomach drop. She was floating as the sounds around her suddenly vanished. Around her, the brief sights of other places suddenly slowed, and she glimpsed a dark moonlit beach with rolling waves. Then a rush of cold hit her like she was being dumped into an icy swimming pool, and her vision went white.

Panting for air, Alex nearly collapsed to her knees. She was disoriented for a moment but forced her head up. The fast rush of water was gone, and she was amongst a collection of bare trees. Behind her were the sounds of the others coughing and moving, and the soft lap of water against rocks. Looking around, a soft sigh of relief escaped her as she recognized the nearby path that she was fond of jogging through in the spring and autumn. They were on the southern shore of Ravens Lake in the university arboretum. They were home.

30

Goddess of Death

7 21 B.C.E. South of Mount Yr Wyddfa

It was beyond reassuring to watch the soft glow of the Iron Chalice illuminate the water within as he handed it to the little girl. Gofiben forced himself to smile despite the exhaustion weighing down on him and avoided looking at the others who were gathered around. They were many, and the number was growing each day as people traveled to the village. While the worst of Badb's plague had faded away, people had been quick to bring those weakened by it here.

They'd finally moved down to the village just past the confluence of the rivers after the Chalice had allowed them to heal what remained of the population. It was unsettling to be around people again, to not be so isolated, though it had been necessary when they first arrived. Yet the looks he received each time he used his magic to awaken the Iron Chalice were all unnerving. There were whispers spreading amongst the healed, and he dreaded just what kind of stories might get back to Merlin and Morgana.

Shaking his head, Gofiben took a drink from the water skin on his belt. He didn't smile at the next person he came to, but then the older man didn't look like he particularly wanted a smile. Instead, he took the

Chalice from his hands with a suspicious look and drank it down with a few gulps. Almost instantly, his pale cheeks began to turn a healthy pink color, and his breathing evened out. Gofiben turned to Bran, who refilled the Iron Chalice from a jug of water, and they moved to the next person.

They were near the end of the day's group who had come up the river when Bran stumbled slightly. Twisting around, Gofiben was able to catch the jug of water and set it on the ground with one hand and take hold of Bran's arm with the other. A little boy was left holding the Chalice with a surprised look for a moment as Gofiben got Bran settled on the ground leaning up against the fence. He then turned and retrieved the Chalice, holding it close as he turned back to Bran, who was panting a little and looked dazed.

"What is it?" Gofiben asked. He knelt down and put a hand on his friend's shoulder. "More of those visions?"

"Yes, but this one was different," Bran began to explain with a thoughtful and worried expression. He looked at the Chalice in Gofiben's hand and reached out to touch it gently. "I saw the Chalice with those strangers I keep seeing."

"You sure?" Gofiben straightened up in surprise. "My Chalice?"

"I'm sure it was," Bran assured him, pointing to the small triskelion on it. "One of them, a man a bit younger than us, had a bad leg." He shook his head and groaned in frustration. "Fisher: I didn't understand most of it, but he was the fisher."

Gofiben was suddenly all too aware of the curious eyes on them. He sighed in relief when Galath placed himself protectively between the crowd and the two mages, allowing them a moment to catch their breaths.

"We both need a rest," Gofiben told Bran gently.

"But there are still people waiting-"

"There will be people waiting later, too," Gofiben reminded him with a sad chuckle. "We've only been at this for what... seven days, and somehow it seems everyone in the whole mountain range has shown up."

"Can you really blame them?" Bran chuckled as he stood up, and the two shrank back into the roundhouse they'd been given after first healing the villagers. "Suddenly, there's this cup that heals all their wounds."

Groaning at Bran's words, Gofiben stretched his arms and sighed as his muscles protested, but then eased. He collapsed on his bed and threw an arm over his eyes, causing Bran to chuckle. There was a peaceful quiet save the muffled sound of voices outside and the soft noises that Bran made as he sat down. Gofiben exhaled softly, allowing himself to slip towards a restful state, though he did not allow himself the luxury of a nap.

Finally, he forced his eyes open and brought the Chalice, still held in his left hand, up so he could see it. The glow of magic had faded, but he could still see a slight shimmer on the surface. There was a warmth in the metal that he was inclined to attribute to Emrys' fire. His fingers brushed over the metal, and he could see the tiny sparks of magic below the surface following his fingers. He knew that it wasn't as potent as Cathanáil: even now, that Sword amazed him, but in a way, he liked the Chalice more. A person had to want to help another when they used the Iron Chalice. Hopefully, that meant that it would never be turned against them like Cathanáil had.

Suddenly the noise outside exploded. There were shouts and worried murmurs that made him sit up sharply. He glanced towards Bran and confirmed that he wasn't just hearing things. They both jumped up, and Bran strode towards the doorway with a grim expression. Setting down the Iron Chalice in the small basket by his bed, Gofiben followed Bran outside and looked around. A pillar of smoke was rising from a hillside just up the valley, and there was already the smell of burning vegetation on the wind. People in the village were pointing towards it with low murmurs of worry.

The villagers turned to look at them, expectation written on all of their faces, and it was all Gofiben could do not to sigh. Nonetheless, he glanced towards his brother, who was frowning at the hillside while Bran merely shrugged. Holding back a weary sigh, Gofiben began to walk towards it, keeping an eye on the wind and the thickening smoke with Bran at his side and his brother rushing to get in front of him.

It didn't take long for them to reach the burning area, and Gofiben took it in with a frown. Smoke was billowing forth, darkening the sky, and he could see the flames high in the trees. He stopped and looked down towards the river below, wondering how much water he could bring up with his magic. It wasn't something he'd done before, but Merlin and Morgana had assured him such feats were possible.

"Can you stop it?" Galath called over his shoulder, shifting and turning to face them.

"Maybe," Bran answered before turning towards the river. Bran closed his eyes in concentration, and his magic began to spark around his arms and hands. "Let me give this a try."

They had no warning; only the sharp sound of a crashing tree and a familiar laugh echoing down the hill. The wave of dark red magic knocked them all off their feet, and Galath groaned in pain as his axe tumbled out of his hand. Groaning himself, Gofiben looked at his brother and froze for a moment in panic at the sight of red blood trickling from a cut on his head. A bloody sharp rock was right next to him and added to Gofiben's panic. He crawled over to his brother and sighed in relief when he confirmed that Galath's breathing was steady. Gofiben grabbed his brother's axe and jumped to his feet.

Badb stepped out of the flames, her gleaming black eyes moving between the two mages for a moment before settling on him. Her eyes narrowed, and she bared her teeth at him. Higher on the hill, the flames burst into the sky, forming pillars of fire and thickening smoke, darkening the hillside.

"Where is the Sword?" Badb demanded hotly, her dark red magic flaring around her dangerously. "Where is it!?" Gofiben couldn't keep his confusion from showing on his face at her question. His eyes searched her, but she didn't have Cathanáil, and he felt his heart beating a little faster. "You don't know," Badb realized with a snarl. Then she turned her head and unleashed a blast of dark red magic across the hillside. "Where are your keepers? Where is my Sword!?"

Her words sent a hot bolt of anger through him, snapping Gofiben out of the confusion and unease. There was a surge of relief at her question about his 'keepers': he knew she meant Merlin and Morgana. Had they recovered Cathanáil from her? Where were they then? Magic was sparking around his hand before he'd even fully processed calling it forth.

Badb laughed; it was a high-pitched sound that vibrated through him. His bones ached, and a feeling of absolute dread was seeping into him. Fire exploded all around them, raining down from the swarm of dark magic billowing around Badb. Gofiben feared that his heart had stopped, but then felt the spark of magic in his chest singing. It spurred him to action as he conjured a ball of his own magic, focusing on keeping it from becoming fire, and blasted it towards Badb.

It did little good but was enough to distract her. With that terrible cry of hers that reminded him too much of a crow, she spun back to face him. Her face twisted into a sneer, and he lifted his brother's axe. Looking back towards Galath, he almost collapsed in relief when he spotted Bran dragging his brother further down the hill.

His moment of distraction gave Badb a chance to send a stream of dark red magic flashing through the air. It struck his chest. Screaming, Gofiben's knees shuddered as he felt her power attempting to burrow into his chest. Bringing up his hand, Gofiben felt his own exhausted magic push violently against the attacking presence. The orange glow overpowered the dark red, but he was left shaking badly. He barely had the chance to look up and dodge another blast.

Badb was smirking: her face was excited and smug as her magic danced around her fingers. Rage flashed through him. She was enjoying this. She didn't see Bran or him as a real threat. Merlin and Morgana had apparently gotten Cathanáil away from her, but they hadn't destroyed her, so what could he and Bran do? Gofiben didn't even try to control the anger. Instead, he let himself drown in it, feeling his connection to his magic flare with energy as his emotions overcame his exhaustion from a day of healing.

He swung at her, pushing magic into his axe head. The wooden handle in his hands resisted the flow of his power for only a moment before the iron head began to glimmer with an orange haze. Badb dodged his wild swing with a laugh and brought up her hand with black fire licking around her fingers. Suddenly she stumbled with a look of shock on her face. Glancing down, Gofiben nearly cheered at the sight of small summer flowers curling up around her bare ankle. He slashed forward with his axe, but Badb shifted back and avoided the blow as her hand moved and sent a bolt of dark red magic hurtling towards Bran.

Bran hit the ground with a sharp crack. Around them, the fire was spreading from treetop to treetop in the wind, casting a horrible glow across the hill. On instinct, Gofiben moved towards Bran, reaching out a hand for him. Bright red blood was flowing from a wound on his friend's head down onto the rocky soil. A groan escaped Bran, and he began to move. Gofiben almost turned his back on Badb, but a sharp cry made him look back at her with wide eyes.

Lashing out at him, Badb's talons scraped across his chest. The thick layer of coarse cloth dulled the blow, but Gofiben could feel the sharp fire of his skin being sliced open. Badb pulled her hand away sharply and twirled it with a vicious little smile as dark red magic flared around her fingertips. Gofiben's heart seized up in his chest as a terrible sense of certainty that he was about to die set in. The blast of magic hit his chest before he could move. A soft crunching sound echoed through his body, and he couldn't manage anything more than a pained whimper.

A nearby tree swayed in the wind only to suddenly bend down with its branches reaching for Badb. Branches grew and groaned, twisting around her body. Screaming, Badb shifted her hands and began to burn away the offending plants. It was the opening Gofiben needed, and with a shout, he threw his entire weight into the swing. A blast of fire ripped through his side, and he caught the horrible smell of burning fabric, hair, and flesh. His swing connected, and the sharp blade of his axe flashed brilliantly as it collided with Badb's head. Her body flickered black and turned smoky for a moment, but his axe glowed and remained in place. A pained cry was torn from Badb's lips as his legs trembled, but he dared not let go of the weapon. Dark red magic flashed against his own as her magical body struggled to pull away and stay together.

Gofiben struggled for air, feeling his side burst with pain, making it feel like he had been shoved into a fire pit. He grasped desperately at the magic he had left and pulled sharply on the soft, gentle pulse of it beneath his feet. Badb clawed at him, her flickering, screaming face full of terror and shock, all traces of arrogance and malice gone. Then like a pillar of dark smoke, Badb dissipated into the wind, her glowing, terrified eyes were the last part of her to be seen.

Collapsing to the ground, Gofiben barely felt his knees scream in protest over the absolute agony that the rest of his body was in. Everything hurt, and he could see his own blood beginning to pool on the ground. He tried summoning his magic once again, but the connection felt weak and low like a dying flame. Gofiben chuckled at his poetic thought only to grimace at the pain the laugh had sent through his body. He coughed and felt blood pour into his mouth and begin to seep out from between his lips.

Bran was still on the ground not far from him, but Gofiben's attempt to move only sent a bolt of pain through him that made his vision go white. Breathing was hard enough as it was, but now he could only smell and taste smoke. Distantly he felt some concern for the fires around them and was almost amused by the notion of a smith dying in the smoke and flames. Someone called his name: Galath, not Bran. It was getting hard to focus; he felt light-headed and exhausted.

He wondered what Morgana and Merlin would think. They'd found him less than a year ago, but he'd created another object that might not rival Cathanáil, yet was wondrous in its own right, and he had killed an Old One. A feeling of guilt surged through him, along with painful resignation as his brother dropped down beside him. Galath's hands moved hesitantly while his brother's horrified face peered down at him. There was dried blood all across the right side of Galath's face; he was ghastly, but alive and moving. Tears were running down his cheeks, and Gofiben reached up towards him. Galath took his hand as a pained sob escaped him, and Gofiben felt himself smile as he used the last of his strength to squeeze his brother's hand in return.

31

Return to Ravenslake

She'd lived in Ravenslake for years, but in the early morning hours of the Winter Solstice, it felt dangerously quiet to Nicki. As the group worked their way up the arboretum path towards the dorm parking lot, Nicki looked around nervously. Around them, the lampposts of the university campus were glowing softly and illuminating the freshly fallen snow. Above their heads, the inky black night sky was filled with stars.

Nicki had trouble shaking off the odd realization that they'd gone from England to Oregon in... she frowned and wondered how much time had passed when they were in the water tunnel. It had felt almost instantaneous, but maybe it hadn't been. Alex shifted in front of her, pulling the backpack off and opening it. A look of relief took over her friend's face before she swung the backpack up onto her shoulder once again.

They had the Iron Chalice. She almost laughed and jumped around. They'd found a magical item that had become the Holy Grail in human mythology. It had been a long eight days. Nicki nearly tripped as she repeated that in her head. It had only been eight days since they left Portland for Wales. Shaking her head, Nicki focused her gaze on the backpack and Merlin's protective stance next to Alex.

"I'm parked nearby," Merlin told them, breaking the silence. "But I can't take everyone."

"I'm coming," Nicki insisted sharply, glaring at the back of Merlin's head at the very notion that he'd try to stop her.

"Me too," Bran added with a nod. "I think we all want to be there when Aiden wakes up if possible."

"My car is in the student lot," Jenny pointed out with a nod towards the illuminated rows of cars near the dorms. "I can take Lance and someone else."

"I'll go with you then," Bran offered with a small smile to her. "I don't think Nicki wants to be out of sight of the Chalice."

Lance chuckled behind her, but Nicki didn't turn around. To her surprise, Alex slowed down for a moment, so they were side by side and snagged her hand. Tightening her fingers around Alex's, Nicki hoped that her gratitude could be felt. Merlin glanced back at them, his eyes focusing on Alex for a long moment causing him to almost trip.

"Ambrose, pay attention," Morgana chided with a small chuckle before she looked back at Bran, Lance, and Jenny. "Drive safe; we will see you at the hospital."

Morgana fell into step beside Merlin as they split off into their two groups. Nicki focused on the back of Morgana's long dark blue coat as nervous energy and exhaustion warred within her. She saw Morgana turn her head to look back at Alex with a soft worried look. Sighing, Nicki squeezed Alex's hand a little tighter as the cold chill sank into her. They stepped into another parking lot, and Merlin pulled out a key fob. A moment later, an SUV nearby was running and, Nicki hoped, with the heater going.

"Are you alright, Alex?" Merlin asked in a soft, but urgent voice as they settled in his SUV.

"I'm fine," Alex assured him. She hugged the backpack on her lap. "Just tired."

"Perhaps this can wait-"

"Merlin," Morgana interrupted in a warning voice. "They found the Chalice so they could help Aiden: you won't win this argument."

Nicki could hear Merlin's leather driving gloves tighten around the steering wheel before a soft sigh escaped him. Then he nodded, and they were moving out of the parking lot as Nicki tried not to vibrate out of her seat. Merlin took them south to highway 20, and Nicki craned her head to look out of the front window. They weren't far from the hospital, and the streets were empty. Christmas lights were strung up across windows and around trees, but Nicki paid them little attention.

Finally, the tall hospital surrounded by warm white lights came into view. She wanted to leap out at once, but Alex gripped her hand. Turning to look at her, Nicki noted that in the lights of the parking lot, Alex looked more pale than usual and a little frightened.

Nicki glanced toward Morgana and Merlin before leaning over to whisper, "It'll be alright. It'll work."

Alex looked over at her as they came to a stop and managed a quick nod. Nicki hesitated to let go of Alex's hand and instead gave her a smile as they slid out of the SUV on Alex's side while Morgana watched them. The older mage reached over and set her hand on Alex's shoulder, squeezing it gently while Alex cradled the backpack. Merlin came around to them as Jenny's car pulled into a spot only a couple cars down from them. Bran was out of the car first and jogged towards them with a grin on his face. His expression made Alex giggle softly, and he grinned triumphantly. Jenny and Lance were a few steps behind him, both shivering slightly in the cold night air and looking nervous.

"Come on," Morgana said. She guided Alex forward by her shoulder.

Ravenslake Hospital felt far too empty with a vacant front desk and their footfalls echoing on the tiled floors. Morgana confidently led them deeper into the hospital and up the stairs to the second floor. Around the corner to the right was the Intensive Care Unit, and this time Nicki didn't feel her stomach aching as they approached.

Everything was quiet, and the front desk nurse was over in one of the other rooms just visible through the doorway. Morgana led them towards Aiden's room; the nurse stationed there looked up in surprise and jumped to her feet. Merlin stepped up in front of the nurse and waved his hand in front of her. Green sparks shimmered around her head, and Nicki watched in fascination as the woman's eyes glazed over. She seemed unsteady on her feet, and Merlin gently took her hand and moved her over to the desk. Helping her sit down, Merlin glanced at the computer screens and nodded in satisfaction, waving for them to come forward.

Sliding back the curtain that separated Aiden's room from the nurse's little cubby, Merlin waved them inside. Alex finally released her hand and stepped through, wrapping her other arm around the backpack. Nicki followed her inside with Morgana right behind them. Lance and Jenny lingered by the nurse's station, watching with odd expressions as the nurse ignored them and calmly went to check on another patient. Merlin nodded to himself, and Nicki barely held back a nervous giggle.

Walking over to the glass side of Aiden's ICU room, Nicki made sure that the heavy curtains were pulled shut. Bran switched on a small set of low lights above Aiden's bed. The television was on some hospital channel with pretty videos and soft music playing. By the large windows and sliding door, out towards the main room were counters stacked with towels, bedding, and a tower of latex gloves by a sink. A well-worn copy of The Phantom Tollbooth was on the edge of the counter, and Nicki smiled softly at the sight of Aiden's childhood favorite.

Then she turned to look at her best friend. He looked like he was sleeping, but his skin was too pale and his face too neutral. There were a bunch of tubes linking up to his IVs, a feeding tube going in through his nose, and a ventilator that filled the room with a deep breathing and humming sound. It was disturbing, but Nicki smiled as Alex set the backpack down on one of the chairs and pulled out the Iron Chalice.

Turning on the sink, Alex allowed the tap water to spill into the Chalice as Nicki tried not to shift impatiently. They were all exhausted, but Nicki noticed that it showed far more on Alex. She hadn't been sleeping, and whatever had happened with Arto had knocked her friend for a loop. Still, Alex hadn't suggested they wait until morning, and Nicki felt nothing but gratitude for that. Dark gray magic, the same color as the Iron Chalice, began to shimmer around Alex's hands and flow into the iron metal. Slowly the Chalice's surface began to ripple, and a soft glow spread across its surface.

"What do you think?" Alex asked, looking towards Morgana. "Should we try to make him drink it or put it in the IVs or-"

"Certainly not," Morgana cut in with a dubious look towards Alex. "He has a ventilator, so we have to be careful in the amount put into his body through his mouth at once." Morgana looked towards the IVs and shook her head, "And I'm afraid that my medical knowledge is growing more and more out of date, so I don't want to meddle with his IVs."

"So..." Alex trailed off, looking between the glowing Chalice and Aiden. "Uh..."

Morgana moved over to a rolling cart by the door with a series of drawers. She opened a couple of them and then withdrew a handful of small wrapped sponges that were hooked onto a white stick. She handed them to Nicki with an expectant look before she moved to the doorway. Nicki was stunned for a moment but shook herself gently. She ripped the wrapper off of the first of the sponges as she inspected it with a jolt of understanding. These were perfect for putting in a patient's mouth to give them some water without interfering with their tubing.

The Chalice glowed softly in Alex's hands and cast a warm golden-orange light through the dark room. She set it down on the rolling tray table by Aiden's bed and moved up next to him, placing a hand on his head for a moment before collapsing into the second chair. Nicki watched Alex for a moment, just to make sure that she was alright. Then she dunked three of the sponges into the water. A giggle escaped Nicki, which made Bran and Alex look over at her while Morgana raised an eyebrow from the doorway.

"Sorry," Nicki sputtered, shaking her head and moving the sponges against the side of the Chalice to help them absorb more water. "It's just... I put a bunch of sponges in the Holy Grail."

Alex began to giggle, and Bran put a hand over his mouth to muffle his own laughter. Morgana shook her head, glancing between them with an oddly affectionate smile. Merlin stepped into the room a moment later with Jenny and Lance trailing after him nervously. They filled the small room well beyond its usual two-person limit, but everyone quickly quieted. Bran moved to stand beside the bed and, after a moment of hesitation, set his hand on Aiden's shoulder.

Everyone else seemed to have decided that she should be the one to do this. Nicki braced herself even as her heart pounded with excitement, and told herself that Aiden was going to wake up now. She pulled out one of the sponges and carefully maneuvered it into Aiden's mouth, letting the liquid drip onto his tongue. Feeling a bit weird about it, Nicki pressed it up against the roof of his mouth and then his teeth. Nothing happened: she put the sponge back into the water and pulled out another one.

She repeated the process for what seemed like hours, trying to figure out how much a person had to drink for the magic to work. Bran had gulped down the whole thing to heal his leg, but that might not have been necessary. Outside, the nurse continued to check on the other patients, and when one of Aiden's machines chirped, she glanced inside but didn't notice them at all. Nicki looked towards Merlin and found the older man wiping a bit of sweat from his forehead and looking worn down. Morgana set the backpack on the floor and pushed Merlin down into the chair with a firm hand on his shoulder.

A soft groan escaped Aiden and Nicki did her best to repress her fast-beating heart. She exhaled slowly and pulled another sponge out of the water with one hand while gently holding his hand with her other. Her thumb brushed over the warm skin of his hand as she slipped the sponge into his mouth around the ventilator. Aiden suddenly shifted on the bed, his legs stretching out. His hand twitched around hers, and she looked towards Morgana with wide eyes. The older mage stepped over to the screen by the nurse's station, her eyes searching it carefully as a slow smile began to appear on her face. She turned back towards Nicki and gestured towards the Chalice with a nod. Then she waved for Lance and Jenny to come over to her.

"We can't all be in here," she whispered softly to them. "Doctors and more nurses will arrive soon."

"Okay," Lance whispered back with a nod, putting a hand on Jenny's back. "We'll... uh, be in the waiting room, I guess."

Morgana nodded, and the pair slipped out past the nurse towards the main doors. Morgana gave Merlin a pointed look, and he groaned as he pulled himself out of his chair. Then Morgana hesitated, glancing between Nicki, Bran, and Alex before she moved over to the window and pulled back the curtain a tiny amount. Then she slipped out of the room and moved to the window, watching them from outside.

Alex stood up with a soft grunt and walked over to join Bran. She weakly leaned against the railings of the hospital bed but reached down with one hand to take Bran's hand. His fingers twitched and tightened around hers. Nicki slipped another sponge into Aiden's mouth without removing the one still in. She kept her left hand firmly entwined with his right hand the whole time, afraid to let go for even a moment. Nicki waited a few minutes and then slipped one of the sponges out and tossed it into the trash, ripping open another sponge packet and dunking it into the water before putting it into Aiden's mouth.

There was a sudden cough from Aiden; his whole body was shifting and bouncing on the bed. His breathing changed, becoming faster and uneven. He made an odd choking sound, and Nicki reached down to pull out the two sponges. One of the machines beeped, and he groaned. Then a pair of familiar brown eyes fluttered open with a soft groan of pain. They softened as they met her eyes, and she could hear soft sighs of relief from Alex and Bran as a sob of the same escaped her. Squeezing Aiden's hand, Nicki felt tears slip from her eyes as she smiled like an idiot.

32

Intensive Care

Somehow there was no rush of doctors or nurses: whatever Merlin had done seemed to stick. Aiden was looking up at Nicki with dazed, but open eyes. Beside her on the tray table, the Chalice's glow was dimming, and Alex felt her knees tremble in raw relief. A warm arm wrapped around her waist to help keep her upright.

"Easy," Bran said softly. "It's okay; he's okay."

Alex tore her eyes away from Aiden as Nicki carefully slipped another sponge into his mouth while she whispered something to him. Alex turned and looked up at Bran. His green eyes were watery as he stared at Aiden before he turned and looked down at her.

"Thank you," he whispered in a voice thick with emotion. "It's amazing to be able to stand."

"I wouldn't know right now," Alex giggled, feeling a little faint and unsteady. "I mean... shit."

Bran chuckled, and the sound caught Aiden's attention. He turned towards them slowly, still clinging to Nicki's hand. His brown eyes focused on them, and even around the tube in his mouth, he smiled slightly. There was confusion on his face, and he looked ready to fall back to sleep.

"Easy, man," Bran told him, patting his shoulder. "You're safe; everyone's safe."

Aiden's brow furrowed, and his eyes cleared a bit more as he looked right at Alex. Already, some of the color was returning to his cheeks, making him look more like himself. Alex shifted uneasily under the gaze, wondering just how much Aiden remembered. She didn't want to put him into shock. Then Aiden's hand, which she'd almost forgotten she was holding, tightened almost painfully around her own.

"I'm okay." Alex whimpered as a rush of tears, blinded her, and her throat tried to close up. "You saved me," she whispered. Bran's arm came up around her shoulder, and he hugged her gently. "You saved me."

Aiden's grip loosened, and he managed a tiny nod right before several of the machines started beeping. There was a sudden rush of footfalls outside, and Alex reached forward with her free hand to grab the Chalice. Less than half an inch of water at the bottom sloshed around. Alex was about to move to dump it into the sink regardless of what a waste that would be when the curtain was pulled back, and the night nurse was suddenly staring at them all in absolute shock. Alex gulped it down quickly and shuddered as it slipped down her throat.

"Oh, my!" The nurse murmured as she looked at Aiden and around at them. It took her a moment to recover, but she straightened up and firmly said, "I'm afraid I need you to wait outside. I've summoned a doctor who needs to check him."

Alex nodded and moved away from Aiden's bedside. Bran gently pulled Nicki away from Aiden, and they stepped out of the small room just as another nurse rushed inside. They avoided colliding with any of the staff rushing to Aiden's room and joined the others. Leaning back against the main desk, Alex watched eagerly through the open curtain as Aiden nodded at one of the doctors. A nurse checked the machines around him for a moment before the doctor began listening to Aiden's chest with a stethoscope.

They watched for some time as Aiden was checked over. His face was tired but animated as he answered questions and spoke to the doctors. A frown crossed his face at one point, and he peered out of the window for a moment, his eyes landing on Alex. Straightening up, she forced a smile and nodded to Aiden. She wondered how much of that night he remembered. Aiden's expression certainly suggested that he remembered at least part of it.

Noise from the hallway as the staircase door was pushed open with a bang drew her attention. The Bosco family was rushing down the hallway right towards the ICU, and Alex relaxed in relief. Aiden's mother, Shannon, looked grayer than the last time Alex had seen her with her long, light brown hair in wild disarray. Professor Bosco's usual clean-shaven face had gray and black stubble on it, and he was dressed in sweats, something Alex had never seen him wear before. Aisling looked the most alert and at ease, her smiling preteen face looking at Alex and the others with a strange expression of comprehension. At that moment, Alex wondered if their grandfather hadn't been right when he said that Aisling's brush with death, thanks to cancer, hadn't made the girl more sensitive to the truth.

Yet Aisling merely waved to them as the Boscos rushed past and into the ICU room. Relief was fighting against lingering worry on their faces. It twisted in Alex's chest as she imagined how her own family would react. There was a doctor in a lab coat marching towards the room with a clipboard in hand and a pair of nurses talking in rapid shocked voices. Alex could feel that the energy in the ICU was suddenly very different, and many members of the staff looked beyond surprised.

They lingered longer than they probably should have. None of the staff tried to stop them as they calmly watched the proceedings through the opening in the curtain. Shannon almost collapsed in relief over Aiden when he gave her a small weak wave. Professor Bosco started crying as he gripped his son's hand, and Aisling jumped around eagerly just out of the way of the doctors. Alex felt tears gathering in her eyes at their happiness and struggled to contain her own churning emotions.

"He'll be here a few days more," Morgana announced, breaking the silence. "While he hasn't been in a coma long and they've been moving him to prevent bedsores, he's still going to be shaky. And there will be a lot of tests to make sure that he's really alright."

"Morgana and I have already made a donation to Aiden's care," Merlin added in a soft voice. "His family will be just fine."

"And we'll reimburse you for the costs of getting everyone to Wales," Morgana informed Jenny with a small smile that was a little strained, but genuine. "Thank you for helping them," Morgana told her sincerely.

Jenny looked over at Morgana with obvious surprise but managed a quick little nod. Morgana's eyes moved between Jenny and Lance, who was still standing right by her side for a moment before she chuckled softly. Alex smiled at them until her knees began to tremble. Whatever temporary boost the Chalice had given her was wearing off fast. Merlin caught her elbow and steered her into the waiting room with the others following behind.

"I'm glad he's going to be okay," Jenny offered with a small smile as she looked towards Alex. "I know there's still a lot to worry about, but he's okay, and Alex is okay."

"You're right," Nicki agreed with a nod. "And we have the Iron Chalice now in case of emergency."

"Let's avoid using that too much," Alex huffed as she collapsed into the waiting room chair. She shrugged out of the backpack and set it down by her feet. "I'm not good at gauging how much magic to give it, and I'd rather people just avoided getting hurt in the first place."

"Agreed," Bran chuckled, "But obviously, I'm not going to argue with the outcome of our trip." He tapped his foot on the floor with a ridiculous smile.

"Aiden's going to be so upset," Nicki laughed as she slumped into the nearest of the hospital waiting room chairs. "He missed the Quest for the Holy Grail! He'll be so disappointed!"

"There would have been a lot more references," Bran agreed as he stretched out his arms before leaning against the wall with a soft smile. "But what now?"

"I just want to sleep," Alex groaned. The noise in the ICU was dying down slightly, and she took that as a good sign. At least it meant that they weren't rushing equipment in to check every little thing. She could still distantly hear Aiden's family and licked her lips thoughtfully. This could happen again. To any of them. "Tell your families the truth," Alex announced seriously, leaning forward with her elbows on her knees.

"What?" Nicki asked in confusion.

"I'm going home for Christmas," Alex told Nicki, rolling her shoulders carefully. "It's barely December 22nd, so I have time to get to Spokane and see my family, hopefully before the next crisis starts. I intend to tell my family about magic, about being the Iron Soul, and what has happened."

"Alex," Merlin chided as he moved towards her. "That isn't wise: the modern world-"

"I could have died, Merlin," Alex cut in, feeling her heart beating a little faster and a knot in her stomach turning over. "If Aiden hadn't arrived, then I would have been dead on the shore, and Arthur would have escaped with Cathanáil."

"I understand that you are upset-"

"I'm not upset," Alex interrupted, shaking her head. "And let me finish, Merlin." He looked surprised and stepped back a bit. "Arthur is still out there and is allied to the ancient Sídhe Queen that you and Morgana fought with Arto. They know about all of us and our lives in Ravenslake, and worse, they seem to have a way to control the modern descendants of Sídhe creatures in our world. That isn't a mild threat. We had enough time to find the Chalice and save Aiden, but who knows what happens next." Alex shook her head and sighed, "No, I'm not going to make my family wonder what I died for. It won't be an easy conversation, but they're my family, and I won't act as if silence will keep them safe from the Sídhe. We both know that it won't."

"And if they don't want you in this battle?" Merlin asked gently with a sad look in his eyes. She knew he was thinking of Galath and the families of other Iron Souls. "Then what?"

"It won't change anything: I know I'm part of this," Alex promised as she lowered her eyes and studied her hands. "I know that now, Merlin, in my bones. This is who... what I am."

"Well," Morgana said with a shake of her head, breaking the tension. "There is much to do, is there not, Ambrose?"

"Indeed, there is the matter of the children's things in Salisbury to attend to," Merlin agreed, though his attention did not move away from Alex.

Morgana waited a beat and then shook her head. She brushed off a fleck of dust from her coat and reached down to put a hand on Alex's shoulder. "I'll take care of things then. Alex, do get some rest. You've done remarkably well; all of you have," Morgana added as she looked at all of them, even Lance and Jenny. "Aiden is in good hands, and I suspect the greatest danger he faces at this point is curious doctors."

Alex managed a weak chuckle, and Morgana squeezed her shoulder before heading out of the room. Pausing for a moment, Alex licked her lips before pushing herself out of the chair and stumbled after the woman. She heard Merlin move behind her, but he said nothing as Alex stepped out of the waiting room.

"Morgana?" Alex called after her as the woman started to move down the hall. Morgana stopped and turned back around as Alex left the others to walk up to her. "Thank you for helping us."

"You don't need to thank me for that, Alex," Morgana sniffed, making Alex realize that there were tears gathering in Morgana's eyes. "It was overdue. I- Merlin and I both owed Gofiben and Bran a great deal. I dare say that they would have been thrilled that you found the Chalice. Gofiben would have been especially happy that it was used to save the reincarnation of his best friend. He was a very... compassionate young man."

It wasn't as weird now hearing about another life. Instead, the small spark in her chest seemed to warm at the sound of his name. Before she could overthink it, and knowing that she could always use her exhaustion as an excuse, Alex stepped forward and wrapped her arms around Morgana. The older mage didn't push her away or try to move away herself, but instead brought her arms up around Alex and set her head against Alex's shoulder.

"Why are you always taller than me?" Morgana asked with a chuckle. "Every time. Even as a girl."

"I'd say because you're short, but you really aren't."

"No, I'm not," Morgana agreed with a snort as she released Alex and stepped back. She reached up and tucked a strand of Alex's blonde hair back behind her ear. "I'd say try not to worry, but I know that's not going to happen." Morgana studied her for a moment with a small smile and then softly said, "You've had many lives, Alex, and I daresay you will continue to learn more about them as we move forward; some have been good, and some have been bad." Morgana cupped Alex's cheek softly and rubbed her thumb over her skin. "But when I look at you, I see the best of all those you've ever been." Morgana stretched up and kissed Alex's forehead with a warm smile. "I'll be back in Ravenslake soon, I promise. Just let the others know that I'll be keeping their things at my home for the time being."

"Okay," Alex whispered as Morgana let her hand drop away from her cheek. "Just be careful in case there are more of the creatures about... you don't really have to go, you know."

"You kids left the United States and haven't officially re-entered it," Morgana pointed out with a chuckle. "So yes, Alex, I do need to go and recover your passports and use a little magic to make sure there aren't problems down the line. Besides, there is also the pressing issue of dealing with what may have been seen at Stonehenge." Morgana sighed dramatically and shook her head, "It's much more complicated than it used to be."

"Sorry about that," Alex chuckled, ducking her head slightly. "But thanks for taking care of this."

"Merlin is going to want to stay close to you for a while," Morgana cautioned her with a sympathetic smile. "Just be warned that he will probably follow you to Spokane. He won't interfere... just stay close."

"Okay," Alex agreed with a resigned nod. "Are you flying or water traveling?"

"Water traveling," Morgana informed her with a small shudder. "Not really any other option. I'll fly back if I can. Hopefully, it won't take long, but I will be gone for a few days."

"I'll be careful," Alex promised softly, hoping to reassure her.

"I know, but remember today is the solstice, and they still attacked, so be vigilant." Morgana paused and shook her head. "I hope that you're right about telling your family, Alex; I hope it goes well, but if you-"

"If I need you, I'll call."

"Then happy Winter Solstice," Morgana said warmly. "And good luck."

Morgana turned and pushed open the door to the stairwell, leaving Alex standing alone by the ICU doors. Taking a deep breath, Alex glanced back over her shoulder to find Merlin leaning calmly in the doorway of the waiting room, giving her some space, but still staying close. She held back a sigh and shook her head as Jenny stepped out past Merlin. Her keys jangled in her hands as Lance handed her the backpack with the Chalice.

"Come on, Alex, I'll take you home."

"It would be better if a mage was with her," Merlin interrupted, looking uncomfortable. "Perhaps you should stay at my house."

"I'll go with her," Bran offered as he came out into the hallway. "Nicki wants to stay, but gave me permission to crash in her room tonight."

"I'm leaving in the morning, Merlin," Alex repeated firmly, giving him a look that she hoped showed her determination. "I don't need a babysitter."

"I'm not trying to be difficult," Merlin sighed with a shake of his head. "But... you're a good person, and your power is impressive, Alex. Reincarnation or not, you can't just be replaced."

Alex smiled slightly at the words and nodded to Merlin. This was all still so new; there'd been no time for adjustment, but it would come. But not tonight or this morning. Shifting the backpack, Alex unzipped it and pulled out the Chalice. It had reverted to its normal iron color, though it appeared to be highly polished in the white hospital lights. Alex could feel a soft, comforting hum beneath her fingertips as she held it out to Merlin. A look of surprise crossed his face as he carefully took the Chalice in both hands.

"Take care of this for me," Alex told him solemnly. "And please stay here a bit longer with Aiden and Nicki, just to be on the safe side."

Merlin swallowed, then looked at Alex like he hadn't seen her before. At first, it made her want to blush and back up, but she met the gaze. Then Merlin nodded, breaking the eye contact and dropping his gaze to the backpack in her hand. Alex handed it to him and said nothing as Merlin gently placed the Chalice back inside to keep it out of sight. He turned to walk back into the waiting room with it cradled in his arms. When he was gone, Alex felt her legs tremble, and she felt a rush of vertigo. Lance caught her gently around the waist and propped her up against him with a soft chuckle.

"Come on, Jen, let's get this one into a bed," Lance said as he led Alex towards the elevator. "Have you got your keys?"

"Yeah," Alex managed with a weak nod. "I've got my keys."

Everything was a little hazy as Lance got her into Jenny's car, and Bran slid in beside her. Alex's legs hit the discarded brace on the floor of the backseat, and Bran offered her a sheepish smile. She was vaguely aware of Jenny promising to drive Lance up to Portland to get his truck since she was going to the airport tomorrow anyway. As they pulled into the deserted student parking lot and Bran helped Alex out of the car, Alex looked back at Lance and Jenny. They were both standing by her car in the light of a street lamp, talking in low voices.

Grabbing Bran's shoulder, Alex pulled him to a stop and watched. She couldn't hear them, and despite her great desire to curl up in her bed with her plush dog Galahad, Alex couldn't bring herself to look away as Lance reached up and touched Jenny's cheek. Jenny smiled at him and looked uncertain for a moment before standing up on her tiptoes to plant a shy kiss on the bottom of Lance's jaw. Giggling softly, Alex looked up at Bran, who was smiling at the sight.

He shook his head and gently guided Alex to Gallagher Hall, where he proceeded to get her upstairs to her room and let her collapse onto her bed. Alex was barely aware of him pulling off her coat and shoes, but sighed happily when he tucked Galahad beneath her chin. Her eyes were drooping closed as he draped the blanket from the living room over her before turning off her bedroom light and leaving her to rest.

33

Surrender of Cathanáil

720 B.C.E. South of Mount Yr Wyddfa

The wind howled across the rolling hills, throwing the icy bite of the late winter weather against Merlin's cheeks. He glared up at the mountains already capped with snow and found himself battling the urge to strike out at something. There was too much in his mind; too many rumors battling against intense guilt that he couldn't suppress.

"Galath was not helpful, I take it?" Morgana asked. She calmly walked up the small hill towards him.

"Of course not: that boy is as stubborn as... as I don't know!" Merlin huffed, rubbing the back of his neck as he turned towards Morgana. "Have you had any luck?"

"There are stories of a magical chalice used to heal the plague," Morgana replied. "But some stories speak of a cauldron instead." She shook her head and chuckled softly. "Strange that there are already so many stories being told."

"Galath may have helped that along," Merlin grumbled. He tightened his cloak and looked towards the small village they'd just departed. "Wouldn't surprise me if he is telling a different story in each village just to confuse us."

"We vanished for almost a year," Morgana reminded him. "When we returned to the isles, both Gofiben and Bran were dead. Need I remind you that I resented you for the loss of my brother for many years? Of course, Galath is angry with us."

"It wasn't pleasant for us; dumped in that horrible heat and chasing after Badb-"

"He doesn't know about that," Morgana cut in with a shake of her head. "Nor does he need to. Besides, it will not bring his brother back to him. Speaking from experience, there is nothing we can say or do that will fix this."

"I should just use my magic-"

"Don't you dare," Morgana growled. She flashed her teeth, and her green eyes turned cold. "You cannot be suggesting attacking, even if only to frighten, Gofiben's brother. We owe the boy more than that. Galath was clear when he told us that Gofiben killed Badb. The boy died fighting her because we were not able to stop her!"

"But then what happened?" Merlin pressed, disliking the helpless feeling in his chest. "What happened then? Galath said that they died, and he hid the Chalice."

"And he says that Bran told him that there was a way to find the Chalice," Morgana said. "Perhaps they had a plan at the end."

"What plan?" Merlin sighed as he looked at the dark gray clouds swirling overhead. "Why hide the Chalice at all? Why hide it from us?"

"We did leave them for Cathanáil. If we hadn't, or one of us had remained, then maybe-"

"It took both of us to get Cathanáil from Badb."

"Still... we chose the Sword over the boys. That may have been the wrong choice, and if we had the Chalice... well, that's one more item that we might choose to protect over the Iron Soul."

"Do you think there will be another life?" Merlin questioned, turning towards Morgana and finding her eyes watery.

She didn't answer him right away, but then he supposed there was no rush. Around them, the wind made the trees sing a deep tune as their branches groaned and carried a faint whistle down from the mountains. The scent of smoke from the nearby village was tempered with the sharp, clean smell of snow.

"Yes," Morgana finally answered. The word was strangely loud. "Sadly, I do. I can feel it."

"You don't usually rely on feelings." Merlin sighed. "Though I am inclined to agree."

They were both silent again, and Merlin did not doubt that Morgana, like him, was wondering when and where they'd find the next Iron Soul. Her talent for scrying could be useful now that they knew what they were looking for, but the Iron Soul might return far away. His knowledge of the southern lands was somewhat limited, and he knew from traders in his youth that the world extended much further. It was a frightening task, and they still had to worry about protecting Cathanáil even if they couldn't find the Chalice.

"Merlin," Morgana whispered, her voice nearly lost on the wind. "Maybe we should give Cathanáil to Cyrridven. She can protect it."

He felt an icy rush of fear and confusion down his spine at the suggestion. It was terrifying that she would say those words. Even as a part of his mind whispered the wisdom of her suggestion, another part of him fiercely railed against it.

"This won't happen again," Merlin protested. He shook his head and looked at Morgana in surprise. "We'll be on our guard."

"It's not that." Morgana toyed with the edges of her cloak with downcast eyes. "Galath isn't wrong, you know. We told Gofiben and Bran that we would help them; that we would guide them, but in the end, we didn't."

"We had to protect Cathanáil. There was no telling what Badb might have been able to do with it. We had an obligation to Arto, to the world, to protect the Sword."

"We also had an obligation to those boys," Morgana reminded him as she looked out across the rolling hills.

It was all he could do to stay still and silent. Morgana's grief had made her frighteningly calm, almost as if she had lost Arto all over again. The whole situation was gnawing at him: there was the sense that the answer was just beyond his reach. Bran's visions remained a mystery; at the end, had the boy realized some hidden truth in them that compelled him to tell Galath where to hide the Chalice, as Gofiben's brother had hinted? His instinct said that yes, Bran had found some sort of solution even as he and Gofiben were dying, but what had it been?

He wondered back on the odd visions that Bran had told them about: strange shining buildings much taller than anything he'd ever seen, people of different skin tones and strange sounds. The boy had certainly been confused, but it didn't even sound like the great cities in the south or to the east. So, what did it mean; what did Bran tell Galath to do? Merlin had the odd desire to tug at his curly hair in frustration. He was already going gray despite being apparently immortal, and this was not helping.

"Merlin," Morgana called to him, pulling him from his musings. "We have to let go of something, and I'd rather it be the Sword."

"We won't always be able to protect the Iron Soul; there are no guarantees."

"No, there aren't; if it is born again, then there is nothing saying it might not be a terrible person, but we still have to try and make things work," Morgana countered calmly. "And someday, that may mean help-ing their rebirth along."

"You..." Merlin shook his head and stepped away from her. "Mor-gana..."

She shook her head at him, and her eyes scanned the horizon. Glancing back at him, Morgana started to walk towards one of the nearby foothills. With a sigh, Merlin followed her in silence as the sun rose higher and higher in the sky. He lost track of time as he focused on the steady sound of their feet crushing the snow. It was calming and distracted him from the tension in his shoulders. He knew that if he wanted to convince Morgana this was a mistake, he needed to speak now, but the words would not come.

Too soon, they had hiked over the crest of one of the sharply sloping hills surrounding the snowcapped mountains. Below them was a small lake with snow up to the edge of the water. It was still and calm, and Merlin felt the urge to run, but Morgana carefully made her way down to the water's edge. He swallowed thickly and reached back to brush his fingers over Cathanáil's sheath. There was a soft hum of magic even though the leather and he felt his heart pounding. For a moment, Merlin felt dizzy and lost. His feet slipped on the loose rocks and snow, and he nearly tumbled down the hill just as the water of the lake surged up with Cyrridven's arrival.

Morgana caught his arm, and Merlin ignored Morgana's concerned look as he studied the flow of the water. He'd always been amazed by Cyrridven's power over water, but his experience in Badb's water tunnel had added a new dimension to his understanding. One that he wasn't sure he had ever wanted. Cyrridven stepped forward, the streams of water weaving together into a humanoid form and a flowing gown. Her features were beautiful with small black and blue lines across her bronze skin, drawing attention to the pair of startling green eyes. Long black hair hung around her shoulders in gentle waves. Small glowing droplets of water on her circlet illuminated her face as she smiled sadly at the pair of them.

"Merlin, Morgana." She nodded to each of them in turn. "My condolences on the passing of the Iron Soul."

"Do you think it will be reborn again?" Morgana asked.

The Old One's eyes took them both in, and Merlin saw Morgana shift uncomfortably. She'd never been completely at ease with Cyrridven, though apparently, Morgana did trust her. Then Cyrridven nodded once again, a sad expression taking over her face. She folded her hands in front of her and looked over at him.

"Indeed: I see no reason to believe that Arto and Gofiben are isolated occurrences. They were merely part of a cycle that is already beginning again."

"Do you mean to say he has been reborn already?" Merlin asked, a hint of terror in his voice.

"No." Cyrridven shook her head and smiled reassuringly. "I only mean to say that with his death, the process of his rebirth has begun. I do not know when or where he will reappear, or if his powers will reemerge. Such things will happen in their own time, and depend on if the Iron Realm needs its champion."

"That is what we feared," Morgana admitted with a soft exhale. "Cyrridven, would you... can you protect Cathanáil?"

A look of honest surprise overtook Cyrridven's face, an expression that Merlin did not believe he'd ever seen on her. She looked between them both, but he felt her eyes linger on him much longer. "You fear that another will try to take the Sword? That is a wise concern. Yes, I could guard the Sword. I am an ally of the Iron Realm, so it should not harm me, and my own power should hide its magic."

There it was then, Merlin conceded. He knew that it was a necessary precaution: they needed to be able to focus on the Iron Soul, and the Sword was a distraction. Looking towards Morgana, Merlin felt a spark of anger, wondering how she could part with Arto's creation. But her eyes were fixed on Cyrridven, and he noted that she was clutching at her robe. This was not easy for her either then. He sighed and nodded softly in understanding.

"Pragmatic as always, Morgana," Merlin whispered to her. "The Queen did you no favors."

Pulling Cathanáil from its sheath, Merlin took a long moment to study the blade. The style of swords had already begun to change slightly, and he knew from his unplanned journey that decoration and size varied, but to him, this was The Sword. It eclipsed all others in every way. Cathanáil was the perfect size and shape and had the ideal balance. Despite being made of iron, the blade was smooth and gleamed in the sunlight. Just over two feet long with its golden hilt, it was beautiful, but he forced his arms to extend and hold it out to Cyrridven.

His mentor smiled softly at him, that all-knowing and gentle look that he'd long come to associate with her. She did not reach for the Sword right away but instead raised one hand to brush over his cheek. An electrical shock sailed through his body before she dropped her hands.

"I will guard it with all my might," Cyrridven promised with a deep nod. "And I trust that you will do the same for the Iron Soul."

"We will," Morgana agreed with a nod. "We will help and guide them to the best of our abilities."

"It will not always be easy," Cyrridven reminded them, looking sadly between the two of them. "The Iron Soul is at its core very human and is capable of good and evil to the greatest extent of any human. You may find the path you walk to be a very trying one."

"Yet it seems to have been decided that it is our path," Merlin muttered as he looked down at the blade in his hands.

Cyrridven gently took the Sword in both of her hands, one on the hilt and the other on the blade. Forcing himself to release his grip, Merlin swallowed and took a shaky step back from the edge of the water. With a smile, Cyrridven drifted away from the shore, sending small waves lapping at the rocks. She shifted the Sword, raising its tip and clutching the golden hilt with both hands. Looking at each of them in turn, she nodded, and the water around her began to churn softly as she began to descend back into the lake.

Cyrridven kept Cathanáil raised towards the sky as she sank into the lake and out of view. The sunlight glistened off of the Sword, and Merlin's breath caught in his throat at the sight of the hand holding the Sword above the waves. Then Cyrridven vanished completely, and Cathanáil slipped out of view into the waters.

"We're done here," Morgana announced wistfully. "Galath will tell us no more."

"You want to give up on finding the Chalice?"

"We have no proof that it is real and no knowledge of where to look," Morgana sighed as she turned her green eyes on him. "Perhaps, for now, we should let it go. Galath's statements seem to hint that we will find it when the time is right."

"You don't sound certain of that."

"I'm not," Morgana admitted with a shake of her head as she began to turn away from the lake. "But then I've been certain of few things in my life. It seems that the magic of the Iron Realm has decided on our purpose." She began to walk away, calling over to him, "It's late, Merlin."

Nodding, Merlin swallowed and turned to follow Morgana. Part of him wanted desperately to turn and look back at the lake, though there was no reason to believe that Cyrridven was still there. No, he told himself; she was already long gone and hiding Cathanáil from any other Old Ones that might seek to abuse it. He put one foot in front of the other and followed Morgana over the crest of the hill, away from the village where Galath was currently living.

He didn't know where they were going, but he supposed that it didn't really matter. There was a wait ahead for them, but at least now they knew what they were supposed to be doing with their immortal lives. It was a sad and bitter purpose, the idea of guiding Iron Souls and losing them to their deaths, but it was a purpose. Inhaling deeply, Merlin straightened up and nodded to himself. He fell into step beside Morgana, intending to allow her to choose their next destination. After all, they had time.

34

Welcome Home

She probably should have waited until the sun was up. Probably should have waited until Bran was awake, but instead, Alex had just written a note and packed up a bag before slipping away from the dorms. Merlin would be really frustrated with her, but Alex couldn't stay in Ravenslake any longer. She'd managed a few hours of sleep before a nervous knot in her stomach woke her up. It was no mystery what she was uneasy about, and Alex couldn't bear just to linger.

The sun came up only a few minutes into her trip, allowing Alex to relax a little. She kept glancing towards her phone, waiting for the inevitable phone call or text from the others. All around her, the curvy roads and tall snow-dusted trees made her feel isolated, and Alex found herself using breathing exercises to stay focused on driving. When she finally hit the interstate near Albany, Alex pulled over just long enough to send a text to the others that she was on her way home, along with a reminder to Nicki to keep her updated on Aiden.

Traffic gradually picked up and gave Alex something else to focus on. Her head began to feel heavy, and she wondered again if she shouldn't have waited to get more sleep, but the knot of nerves in her stomach fluttered once again. The day stretched on, and Alex was finally forced to stop for lunch and sent another series of texts to alert her friends to her progress. None of them were calling, which she was grateful for, and Nicki kept her one text to a simple update on Aiden: he was out of the ICU and in a normal room while they kept trying to find something wrong with him.

The sun was already setting. It was the shortest day of the year, Alex reminded herself, as she navigated her way through the Spokane roads that led to her home. Around her car, Christmas lights were flickering on like runway lights as she passed. Her family's dark gray and blue trim house came into view around the stocky pine trees, and Alex let out a sigh of relief. Matt's car was parked in front of the house, and there were tracks in the snow leading to both doors of the garage. White lights were strung around the lowest roofline and around the porch railing. It wasn't the neatest decorating job in the neighborhood, but Alex couldn't help but smile as she brought her car to a stop.

As she stepped out of the car, almost falling over thanks to her sore muscles, the porch light turned on, and the front door opened. Her mom appeared with a surprised expression that transformed into a wide smile. A flurry of snow blew off the roof, and the porch light highlighted the faint hints of gray in her mother's blonde hair. Alex was frozen in place as she just soaked in the sight of her. Then her mom stepped out of the house towards her with open arms.

"Mom," Alex sighed gratefully as the woman swept her up in a tight hug.

"Oh, sweetie, we were starting to worry that you wouldn't make it home," her mother cheered, rocking her slightly. "You should have called to let us know you were on the road!"

"I'm sorry," Alex whispered as her throat tried to tighten up. "I was just in a hurry to get home. I missed you so much!"

"Okay," her mom said, releasing her and brushing gently at her cheeks. "I'm glad you're home. Your father is out grabbing a few things, I'm afraid. Come inside, and the boys will get your things.

Alex was shuttled into the warm and bright house quickly by her mother. She inhaled deeply the moment she was inside. Her childhood home still had the undefined mixture of scents that something in her bones just recognized, but on top of it was the smell of a cooking roast, the hint of cookies, and the thick aroma of an evergreen tree. Tears sprung to her eyes, and Alex felt her knees tremble, but she kept the tears from falling and moved further into the house. A loud bark of excitement and the sound of claws clicking against the tiled kitchen floor made Alex grin.

Dropping to her knees, Alex ran her fingers through Anne's thick fur as the golden retriever rushed up to her. Anne happily barked at her and shoved her face up into Alex's. She spluttered as the dog licked all over her cheeks and tried to keep from laughing too much. Thankfully, Anne dashed away from her with a happy bark and ran through the kitchen and down the hall before spinning around and running back.

"She'll calm down soon," her mom promised with a laugh, tugging Alex to her feet and pushing her into the living room. "Sit down," she instructed before marching over to the staircase. "Boys! Your sister is home!"

Noisy, almost thunderous, footfalls upstairs moved over her head and to the stairs. Alex shoved her face against Anne's coat and allowed herself another moment to regain some control as her brothers came downstairs. The sound of someone's feet hitting the bottom of the stairs was her cue, and Alex stood up with a smile.

Eddy grinned widely at her, jumping up to stand in front of her and compare their heights. Alex realized with a jolt of horror that he'd finally caught her and could tell the moment he realized it. A horrible grin took over her brother's face, and Alex sighed in defeat. Eddy had caught up to her, and at fifteen, there could be no doubt that he had at least one more growth spurt in him. His blond hair was overdue for a haircut, and their mom's brown eyes were bright with energy. To Alex, he looked wonderful, and she surged forward to wrap her arms around the baby of the family.

"Glad to see you too, Sis," Eddy teased though there was some real surprise in his voice.

Alex released him and turned her attention to her other brother. Matt, on the other hand, was only a little taller than Alex, and he frowned at Eddy, no doubt already figuring out that the baby brother was going to pass him too. He took more after their father with his brown hair and gray eyes. There was the beginning of a mustache under his lip, and Alex nearly laughed at the mental image of what her brother might look like with one. Unlike Eddy, he stepped forward instantly to hug her, wrapping Alex up in a big hug.

"Good to see you," Matt told her gently. "Mom and Dad said that one of your friends got hurt?"

"Yeah, but it's okay now," Alex answered, shoving herself tighter against her brother until he made an awkward little noise. "Good to see you both," Alex told them as she released Matt and stepped back to shrug off her coat.

"Boys, go and get your sister's things," their mom ordered, gesturing to the door. She grinned at Alex. "Your dad should be home soon, but I'm going to call him just to make sure he doesn't try to stop for anything else."

"Okay," Alex answered.

She hung up her coat on the hooks by the door and followed her mom into the kitchen. There were boxes of Christmas sweets stacked on the island, and Alex wondered how much time her mom had managed to get off this year from the hospital. Then again, as a doctor, plenty of her patients sent sweets during the holidays. Alex pulled a glass out of the cabinet and filled it with water, draining it in one long gulp before pouring herself another one.

"Man, Sis, you brought nothing home!" Matt called as he reentered the house carrying her duffle bag while Eddy tried to push past him with her laptop case.

"Yeah, well, I wasn't sure I'd make it home this year," Alex reminded them. Their mom gave them both a look through the kitchen door. "But Aiden's awake and doing fine," Alex said with a wide smile.

"Oh, Alex, that's wonderful news," her mom cheered, reaching over to hug her again. "We understood, of course, that you didn't want to leave, but that is just wonderful!"

"Yeah, Nicki will be keeping us all up to date, but they've already moved him out of ICU."

"So quickly?" Her mom was frowning a little now. "Do they know what caused it?"

"Nothing yet, but Aiden's awake, alert, and everything is coming back normal... well, as normal as can be for Aiden."

"That's good news, at least," her mom agreed though she still looked a little worried. "But go and sit down, Alex. I'm sure you're tired."

Settling on the loveseat, Alex tucked her legs under her and glanced around the living room. A large Christmas tree filled one corner of the room with lights already strung up. An open box of ornaments was sitting on the piano bench next to the tree. Alex's eyes scanned over the fireplace where the family stockings were already hanging, including the one for Anne. She paused as she looked at the set of iron fireplace tools and released a small sigh of relief even as she wondered how likely it would be that her parents would notice the poker missing while she was here. Her iron dagger was still in Lance's truck in Portland.

Matt and Eddy took her things up to her room, judging from the noise overhead, and returned a few minutes later. They crashed onto the couch, and Alex felt the usual twinge of sympathy for the poor thing. It was easy to fall back into the usual habits of light teasing around asking how school was. Matt would be graduating in the spring and heading to law school, so he was just walking on air while Eddy was whining about driver's ed in the spring. Leaning back on the loveseat, Alex just let the sounds of her family wash over her. It didn't change what had to happen during this trip, but a small part of her was beginning to wonder if it had to be tonight or if she could afford to wait until Christmas had at least passed. Maybe one more totally normal family Christmas was in order.

The sound of a car door slamming brought Alex sharply back to reality, and Anne began jumping around by the front door. Matt hoisted himself off the couch and went to let their dad in. Alex turned on the couch and looked over towards the door eagerly. Her dad stepped inside, shaking a bit of snow off his long coat, and handed the bags of groceries over to Matt, who promptly took them into the kitchen.

"I hear my princess is home," her dad called as he looked into the living room at her.

"Hi, Dad!" Alex cried as a warm rush of excitement hit her.

She jumped up and moved over to him. Her father's hair had stopped receding, but the dusting of gray at his temples was spreading through his brown hair. Behind his glasses were gray eyes, much like her own that were bright with excitement as he moved forward and wrapped one strong arm around her.

"Oh, it's so good to have you home!" her dad cheered as he hugged her. "Your mom says Aiden's awake?"

"Yeah, he is," Alex agreed as her dad let her go and began to take off his coat. "Nicki is going to keep me informed, but he's okay, and his family is doing fine." There were happy tears beginning to gather in her eyes.

"A Christmas miracle then." Her dad slung an arm over her shoulder and led her back into the living room. "And we get you home."

As her dad sat down in his armchair and Anne curled up at his feet, whimpering for a cuddle, Alex collapsed back onto the loveseat. Her dad reached down to rub Anne's head, and Alex sighed in relief, rolling her shoulders. She let the warmth of home sink into her bones and smiled. Then her phone began to ring from the pocket of her sweatshirt, earning a small groan from her. Alex reached for her phone automatically and didn't stop to check the caller, assuming it was Nicki or maybe Morgana as she brought it to her ear.

"Hello, lover," Arthur purred, on the other end. "It seems that Aiden's awake."

"Arthur," Alex forced out, her whole chest constricting painfully.

"It's really something, isn't it," Arthur laughed, though it carried a hint of sharpness. "Humans are remarkable, aren't they? Sometimes they accidentally get it right. King Arthur and his, well her, brave knights going on a quest to find the Holy Grail. That is what you used, isn't it? I've been pouring over all the stupid little scraps of mythology to find something worth leaving Ravenslake for while Aiden was dying."

Her dad was looking at Alex with concern and glancing towards her brothers. Alex supposed that she hadn't sounded pleased when she said Arthur's name. Closing her eyes, Alex tried to block them out. She couldn't deal with their worry and Arthur at the same time.

"Cat got your tongue, Alex?" Arthur teased lightly, smugness radiating through the phone.

"Like you said, Aiden is awake and doing just fine," Alex forced out between grit teeth. "And you're still down a Sword."

"But now you have a grail."

"Chalice actually, and no, you can't have it," Alex managed to reply, trying to sound more relaxed than she felt as every muscle in her body seized up. She thought she heard her mom calling her and just waved her hand blindly.

"You gave the Sword to me, darling, you sure you can hold to that promise?"

"Go to Hell, Arthur," Alex growled, squeezing her eyes tight and trying to banish the memory of handing Arthur the Sword; the feeling of honestly believing in him. "And rot there."

"When I go to Hell, Alex, it'll be to become its king." Arthur chuckled smugly. "Enjoy your holiday, dearest; I'm sure we'll be seeing each other again soon enough."

The line went dead, and Alex dropped her phone on the ground in front of her. She brought her hands up and ran her fingers through her hair, trying to calm down and drown out the questions coming from her family. Finally, she looked up to find them all crowded around her with almost identical looks of worry, frustration, and anger.

"Alex?" her dad asked. "What was that about?" He leaned forward and frowned deeply. "What's happened between you and Arthur?"

Her mouth instantly dried up, and Alex's fingers clenched around her water glass. A look of panic must have come over her because her dad shifted back to give her some space. He grabbed Matt's arm and pulled him back too. Raising her glass to her mouth, Alex took a deep gulp of water only to nearly choke on it.

"Alex? What happened?" her mom demanded sharply as she held her shoulders, draping herself over the arm of the loveseat. "Sweetie? Oh god, did he do something-"

"I'm fine," Alex said as she handed the water to Matt. "I'm okay, Mom. Uh..." Alex struggled to breathe as she looked around at her family, who were all crowding around her. Suddenly her mouth was dry again, and her heart was racing far too fast. She closed her eyes and exhaled slowly to calm down even as she knew horrible theories and fears were racing through her family's minds. "Please sit down, guys... I've got something that I have to tell you."

"Alex? If he hurt you-" Matt started to growl, the fierce protectiveness in his voice bringing a soft smile to her face. She wondered if that was how Galath had acted, or was it even worse because she was a girl?

"Just sit down, Matt, it's a long story, and I have to explain a lot of things. Arthur and I aren't a couple anymore because-" Alex shook her head and forced a laugh. "Like I said, I need to explain a lot."

They all looked ready to argue with her, but Alex straightened up on the loveseat and did her best to look calm. When her dad tried to ask her something, Alex shook her head and pointed to his chair. As Matt started to sit down, Alex took her glass of water back from him and took a long greedy drink. She waited until her whole family was seated, though none of them looked at ease. Her parents were glancing between her and each other, and both of her brothers were damn near vibrating on the couch next to each other. Inhaling slowly, Alex reminded herself that this had been the plan all along. All she had to do was start from the beginning and tell them what had happened.

35

Telling the Family

It was simple in concept; just tell her family the truth, but it was infinitely more complicated in reality. The desire to run or try to laugh everything off was overwhelming. Alex hadn't expected to feel more afraid than she had in that tunnel, or worse when lying on the shore dying, but this was horrible. Clenching her fists, Alex licked her lips nervously. She was keenly aware of her father's gray eyes as he studied her with a terrified expression on his face. There must have been dozens of horrible situations running through his head.

How did she even start this conversation— with some stuttered explanation about the Tree of Reality and reincarnation? Feeling lost, Alex shivered slightly and swallowed thickly. Magic it was then: show them what she could do, or at least part of it, and then explain from there. Still, it felt like reality was completely falling away now: this was the last of it, the last little haven she still possessed against the magical war that had taken over the rest of her life.

Breathe, Alex reminded herself and inhaled greedily. She didn't have very flashy magic like the others. Aiden could have simply made a fireball, Nicki, an ice sculpture, and Bran could make items fly around the room. Hesitating, Alex told herself that she didn't have to do anything impressive. Just enough that they could see it and know she wasn't crazy. The connection in her chest fluttered to life, and Alex drew her magic forth, letting the dark gray sparks dance around her arm.

"Alex?" Matt asked in a soft, strained voice. "What the-?"

She focused on making a light and allowed the sparks of magic to swarm together into a condensed dark gray orb that began glowing brightly a moment later. Releasing it gently, Alex guided it up through the air with her eyes until it was hanging amongst the members of her family. They were just staring at it with blank expressions, too shocked to even properly react. Alex swallowed thickly at the stillness and silence. It was Eddy who moved first, standing up from the couch and reaching out to touch the orb.

"Careful," Alex cautioned with an uneasy chuckle. "Uh... my magic tends towards... well, energy, so electrical shocks are pretty common. I, umm, tend to fight with lightning bolts."

"Lightning bolts?" her mother whimpered at the same time that her father gasped, "Fight?"

Staying silent, Alex let the magic disperse into the air, though the glowing orb remained in place. She glanced quickly towards the living room window and sighed gratefully as she realized that the curtains were drawn while fighting back irritation that she hadn't checked that earlier.

"Our world... our universe is one of many," Alex explained slowly, trying not to fidget from her place on the sofa. "It's all pretty complex and a little more physics-based than I'm good at, but the bottom line is that those universes all have slightly different rules and are connected to each other." She paused and licked her lips again, picking absentmindedly at her nail. "When they come into contact with each other, those different physical laws sort of... react oddly, and things go weird." Alex grimaced at the poor explanation and tried to remember how Merlin and Morgana had put it. "Magic is a part of our world, but it's like the defense system of our world. Magic becomes active when a threat to our world enters it, and mages are like white blood cells who fight back against the infection."

They were all staring at her, and she blinked in surprise at seeing that Matt had Eddy in a headlock with a hand firmly across his mouth. The air was electrified with her magic, which wasn't as under control as she hoped it would be. Unable to sit still, Alex jumped off the couch and stepped away, wringing her hands. Her mother slumped into her vacant place, looking lost and stunned.

"So yeah, I use my magic to fight these beings from other universes. That's what it is there for," Alex finished with a wide spread of her arms, trying not to fidget.

"Why you?" her mother asked. She looked pale and worried even as a hint of wonder shined in her eyes. "Why my daughter?"

"It had to be someone," Alex replied with a helpless shrug. "Most of us were born in the northwest. Nicki... I'm not sure where she was born, but Aiden was born in Ravenslake, and Bran is from Oregon." She was stumbling over the words and once again debating with herself. "Besides... I'm sort of..." Alex faltered and shook her head. "I'm a special mage, Mom. I have a soul that was made by the magic of Earth to protect it. It's called the Iron Soul. It gives me stronger powers and connects me to other lives."

"Reincarnation?" Matt repeated. He was so stunned that his hand slipped away from Eddy's mouth.

"Alex, can you do spells?" Eddy asked eagerly. His wide eyes were fixed on her.

"Yeah, spells are basically magical effects that you make happen," she explained, gesturing up at the small light orb. "When we use magic, it takes a raw form that bests suits us, but we can shape it into other forms through our will. I'm learning to do other things now. Nicki's magic first worked like water and ice, but she can also heal, and we can all do little stuff like mending clothes, fixing scorch marks, and that sort of thing."

"Going back to reincarnation," her dad pressed, shaking his head and looking overwhelmed, "Are you serious?"

"I'm afraid so," Alex answered with an apologetic wince. "I don't know much about my other lives, but one of them, the first one was named Arto and he, uh well, he made this Sword and his story got combined and retold with other stories over the years, so he's probably the inspiration for King Arthur."

"King Arthur?" Her mother was stumbling over her words now. She pulled Alex back onto the sofa. "You can't- what?"

"Professor Cornwall is Morgana le Fey, but don't worry, she's on our side and looks after me, and Professor Yates is Merlin. You know, 'Ambrose Yates', immortal gatekeeper, and Morgana was originally from what is known now as Cornwall," she added with a weak, forced laugh. "Not very clever, but it gets the job done."

"But this is dangerous, isn't it?" Her mom asked, clutching at her arm and glancing between Alex's face and the glowing light orb. "That's the cost of your magic; you have to fight things that come into our world."

"Yes," Alex said solemnly. "That is the cost of having the powers I have."

Her mom closed her eyes for a moment and shook her head. Eddy's excitement was fading, and Matt was staring at her like he'd never seen her before. A laugh suddenly escaped her dad that quickly shifted from confusion to hysteria. Matt jumped up from the couch and grabbed their dad's shoulder. Alex flinched at the sound of her dad trying to hyperventilate. This wasn't nearly as simple and easy as she'd hoped it might be. A letter might have been a better idea.

"So is Arthur a mage too?" Matt asked, turning his attention away from their dad. "You seemed angry with him on the phone, did something go wrong?"

"Yeah," Alex answered. "Arthur... well, he tricked us all into thinking that he was the reincarnation of the Iron Soul as part of a plan. He's working with our enemy, the Queen of the Sídhe-"

"Sídhe?" Eddy cut in with a confused look.

"Nasty faeries before the stories made them nicer," Alex supplied quickly. "But Arthur is our enemy." She hesitated and added, "It's because of him betraying us that Aiden was in his coma." Alex tugged at a strand of her blonde hair nervously. "The reason I didn't come home was that I was in Wales with Nicki, Bran, Jenny, and Lance finding... well, this magical chalice that heals people. Another one of my lives made it, and it was our best chance at saving Aiden's life."

"Healing chalice?" her dad repeated as another hysterical laugh threatened to escape him. "Sounds familiar."

"Probably the mythological basis of the Holy Grail," Alex admitted, standing up again shoving her hands into the pockets of her jeans. "But yeah. Anyway, Arthur knows what we did, and he's made it clear that the fight is still on."

"But he was- I mean you two were-" her mom stumbled over the words, looking ill.

"He was just using me," Alex confessed softly. She swallowed down the bile that swelled into her mouth. "Arthur manipulated Jenny and Lance, too; he needed them to create the illusion that he was the Iron Soul. It was all part of the show to fool Merlin and Morgana. He just wanted information and a magical artifact."

"Jenny and Lance..." her dad trailed off. "Oh, good lord, are all the myths true?"

"Not in the sense that they are accurate," Alex offered weakly. She took her hands out of her pockets and toyed with them again, pulling at her nails. "But a lot of the stories have some element of truth. Apparently, another life of mine was the basis for Thor, and I had some connection to the Hindu God Shiva. I don't know the whole story yet. But that doesn't mean that all myths have a magical root. I'm sure plenty of stuff is just made up."

She stopped talking, seeing that she was sharing a bit too much. Everyone, even Eddy, looked ready to fall over. The light shining above their head didn't help matters. To distract herself, Alex gestured towards it and willed it to break apart. It burst into dozens of tiny little lights that danced around just below the ceiling. She watched them and willed her heart rate to normalize.

"Can't you get help from the military?" Eddy asked with wide eyes, his body language changing as the reality of what was happening sunk in.

"No!" Alex snapped before shaking her head. "Look, it's complicated, but the general consensus is that it probably isn't a good idea for the general public to know about magic. Power attracts people, usually the wrong sort, and we don't want them trying to make us weapons." Alex shrugged weakly and continued, "You're my family. I'm not worried about you trying to lock me up in a lab or weaponizing me or trying to make sure that the war never ends so that magic keeps working. Or I suppose they could do what the Sídhe have been doing and try to conquer other worlds for their resources despite the consequences. It's complicated."

"I can see that," her dad agreed weakly. "Is it even safe to tell us? I mean you won't get in trouble with... Merlin and Morgana or cause some sort of magical punishment, right?"

"Why are you telling us?" Her mom asked.

"It's a war," Alex forced out with no small amount of dread and hesitation as she watched her mom's face. "There is a chance that I'll be hurt someday; hurt more than Morgana or even the Chalice could heal, or things may go wrong, and there won't be someone there to help me." She regretted putting it that way as her mom's face went white. "It's not likely. Morgana and Merlin are both very protective, and the other young mages and I are a team. We work really well together and try to keep each other safe. Lance and Jenny don't have magic, but they went with us to save Aiden because they wanted to help. I've got good people with me, but you should know the truth. You should know why I may have to run off sometimes, why I might ask you to do certain things to keep you safe and why someday I might not come back at all." Alex dropped her eyes and made herself keep going. "I don't want you wondering what you didn't know or feeling guilty." Tears were prickling at her eyes, but she forced herself to look around the room at all of them. "I love you, all of you, and I just don't want to do that to you. Maybe it's a bad choice and puts too much on you, but it feels right that you have the truth. This magic thing and the war are so much greater than one mage. I know that. I want you to know that too."

Then Alex dropped her eyes again as the exhaustion of the morning returned with a vengeance. Her knees shook, and Alex considered returning to the couch or just sitting down on the floor. Above her head, the small magical lights flickered out as Alex let the magic dissipate, unwilling to keep using it any longer than necessary. Then her mom's arms were suddenly around her. The little girl in her instantly melted into the comforting embrace even as the mage remained all too aware of her mom's muffled crying. Another set of arms wrapped around them both, and she could feel the vibration of her dad shaking.

Closing her eyes, Alex tried to ignore the signs of their distress and couldn't stand the idea of looking over at her brothers. This wasn't the Christmas she'd wanted for them. This wasn't something she had wanted to tell them, not really. But it wasn't like in the television shows where they'd always win and come back. They'd broken even this time, but Arthur was still out there, and he knew about her family. He knew that he could hurt her without ever coming near Ravenslake. He'd used Jenny for years and manipulated her. There was no honor in this fight, no treaties, and no promises.

Holding back her own sobs, Alex gripped the arms of her parents and leaned against her dad. He wasn't shaking so badly now and managed to bring a hand up to cradle her head. This didn't really change anything; she knew that. Winter break would be over after the New Year, and she'd return to Ravenslake. There was still the problem of Arthur, the Queen, and the faeries who were bound to her kill order, but for now, in this moment, things were alright. She had the people she loved most with no secrets between them. They might not understand all of it, but they knew what mattered most. This thing, this grand story that her life had become was overwhelming and terrifying, but she was surviving it for all of them. That was something she could live and fight for.